Chasing Lightning

Chasing Lightning

Rachel York

KENSINGTON BOOKS
http://www.kensingtonbooks.com

KENSINGTON BOOKS are published by

Kensington Publishing Corp.
850 Third Avenue
New York, NY 10022

ISBN 0-7582-0368-3

First Kensington Trade Paperback Printing: March 2003
10 9 8 7 6 5 4 3 2 1

Printed in the United States of America

Chasing Lightning

Though Scarlett Faye Turner was actually born just north of the Mason–Dixon Line, she claimed the South as home. It was going to look good on the blurb of her future novels. After all, everyone knows the South has a long history of illustrious writers. If you couldn't recite them, she would: Tennessee Williams, William Faulkner, Carson McCullers, Truman Capote and Margaret Mitchell, just to name a few.

Scarltett admired the land of these luminaries so much she even learned to talk just like them. The only time she didn't rehearse that charming Southern drawl was when she was asleep or stoned. But that was later, much later. The beginning of our story takes place a long time ago in the dusty river town of Dillinger, Pennsylvania.

Chapter

1

"Momma, I'm gonna be rich and famous."

Ollie Mae Turner looked down at her only child, the precocious Scarlett Faye, and said nothing. Ever since the little girl could talk, she had proclaimed these mighty intentions upon the world. Ollie set a bowl of hot oatmeal on the table and sneaked a peek at the clock. If she didn't hurry, she would miss the early-bird bargains at the church bazaar.

"When I'm big," Scarlett Faye continued as her mother tidied up the kitchen, "I ain't eatin' this crappy stuff no more!" she exclaimed and slammed her spoon down on the table, imitating her father. Like him, her discontent ran wide and deep.

"I'll have none of that talk, Scarlett Faye. Ain't ladylike." Ollie sighed and hung her apron on the big nail above the kitchen stove. "If only your father were still . . ."

"That bum!" interrupted Scarlett. "I'm glad he ain't here. He was a big meany and he smelt terrible."

A look of hurt and disappointment flashed across Ollie Mae's face. It was true her husband did like to drink and the bottle had put him in an early grave. One day while Scarlett was playing hopscotch, he'd had a stroke right in front of her. To the child's dismay, he fell smack on her marker. When old Joe didn't get up, Scarlett ran down to the five-and-dime where Mrs. Turner worked.

"Whatcha doin' here?" Ollie wanted to know.

Scarlett caught her breath and then made her terse announcement. "I think Daddy's dead."

Ollie Mae's face turned bright red. Her little girl's tendency to tell tales frequently tested her patience. "Scarlett Faye, I told you I don't like no fibbin' and little white lies."

"This ain't no fib and it ain't no lie," declared Scarlett Faye, and she went on. "He moved kinda funny." The child imitated what she had seen, staggering around the aisle of the five-and-dime holding her throat. "Then he felled down and now his tongue's a-hangin' outta his mouth." Scarlett pinched her nose, "And he smells awfuller than ever. Phewy!"

Ollie quickly made excuses to her boss and grabbed the child's hand. They scurried down Main Street toward home. Scarlett Faye's short little legs could barely keep up as they rounded the corner to the old house where, sure enough, Mr. Turner was belly-up on the front lawn for all the world to see. Grief-stricken, Ollie fell down beside him and tried to shake her husband back to sobriety. It didn't work. This time he really was dead.

The next few days were miserable ones for Scarlett. She was forced into mourning. She wasn't allowed to play kick-the-can or hopscotch with her best friend, Billy Ray. Instead, her mother told her, she was supposed to act sorrowful. Scarlett Faye didn't much like this idea, but she went along with it to make her mother happy.

Sorrow and remorse were alien feelings to Scarlett and, to some extent, they were to remain so. Who knows? Perhaps it was congenital. Some swore the girl was born with a giant callous on her heart.

Properly respectful of her mother's wishes, Scarlett and Billy Ray sat on the front steps of the house and talked in low voices about death and stuff.

"God! He sure looked bad when they taked him away."

"Yeah?" inquired Billy Ray, doodling in the dirt walkway.

"He was real pale. White! You know, just like a toad's belly."

"That's white," agreed Billy, finishing his doodle. He had drawn five or six crosses in the dirt.

Scarlett Faye stood up and dusted off her dress and poked one foot at the little dirt Christ crosses. "Nobody's gonna stare at me when I'm dead. I wanna get all burned up good. You know, like after a big bonfire. All that black stuff with gray snowflakes."

Billy Ray looked horrified. "You can't do that, Scarlett. How's God gonna let you in heaven if He can't see you?"

Scarlett smiled smugly. "He'll knows who's me, Billy Ray. Ashes or not. Everybody's gonna know who's me."

Billy automatically nodded his head in agreement. "I know, Scarlett. Someday you gonna be rich. A famous writer. I heared it before." And he had, many times.

Just then Mr. Phepps, the grocer, and his horsey-faced wife came strolling up the walkway looking just the right amount of sad. Scarlett and Billy Ray moved aside so the two could climb the stairs and pay their respects to Mrs. Turner.

Jody Barton and her sorry old husband, Moonie, showed up next. He was his usual drunken mess. At least Scarlett's daddy had shaved once in a while and combed his hair and didn't have a bunch of big, rotten brown teeth.

"Move over, Billy!" yelled Scarlett, elbowing Billy in the side. "He'll spit that stuff right on you. He hates kids."

Billy looked up at the large, ominous pouch sticking out of Moonie's right jaw and scrambled to get out of the way. Sure enough, Moonie Barton let loose a stream of chewing tobacco that traveled some five feet before it landed on Scarlett's pretty flowered dress. She shrieked her disgust and was about to pronounce a bunch of naughty "devil words" on Moonie when her mother appeared on the front porch looking pained.

Scarlett quickly calmed down and went back to acting sorrowful. Only Billy Ray knew how mad she really was. She rubbed her dress hem on the grass, trying to trade a green stain for the ugly brown one.

"Moonie is a pig," fumed Scarlett. "I'm gonna get him."

"How?"

"Don't know yet. But he ain't spittin' on me again!"

By the time five or six other people had come and gone that morning, Scarlett got cranky and restless. She asked her mother if she could go down to the river with Billy Ray and watch the old men fish. Scarlett said her sorrow muscles were beginning to ache. They were tired and needed a rest.

After that, Scarlett didn't think much about death again until Thursday. That was funeral day. The day they put her poor, dead daddy's soul to rest in a small church on Ashbury Street. All of Mr. Turner's drinking buddies and growing-up friends were there. The lack of air in the church made Scarlett think she was going to faint. The humidity and smell of Southern Comfort were more than she could rightfully bear.

The preacher rambled on about forgiveness and human weakness and brotherhood. He was obviously trying to get this sinner a pardon for living such a rotten life. Scarlett didn't remember no such pleading and carrying on when Aunt Fannie died. One might have thought that poor soul was a leper or something. Hardly anybody showed up for the funeral—just her mom and her and a few painted ladies from Fannie's past. For the life of her, Scarlett Faye couldn't figure out how being a "loose woman" (that was what everyone always whispered about Aunt Fannie) was worse than being a drunk who beat his wife.

As her mother sobbed into an embroidered handkerchief scented with the essence of lilac, Scarlett stood up in her seat and tried to get a better look at her daddy. He was up front in a long pine box all decked out in his Sunday best. He didn't look so bad anymore, just a bit stiff with rosy cheeks.

Scarlett's black patent leather shoes made a loud scraping sound as she balanced herself against the back of the seat. Ollie Mae looked over at her little girl and pinched the back of her leg. She wasn't supposed to stand up in church, not on the pew anyway. The pinch sent Scarlett into loud, whimpering shrieks. She rubbed the back of her leg and sat down, furious at her mother, tears streaming down her cheeks.

A neighbor lady poked her husband and said, "Poor little Scarlett Faye. She's taking this whole thing real hard."

Chapter

2

Joe Turner's death was a blessing in disguise. Comparatively speaking, it made Scarlett Faye and her mother rich. Joe's insurance policy paid out ten thousand dollars. That was a small fortune back in the early fifties. It was a big fortune if you were poor white trash—an epithet which, in later years, Scarlett came to sorely resent.

Ollie bought an old boarding house with the money. She figured if she rented out the three extra rooms she could quit her job down at the five-and-dime. For Ollie Mae it was a dream come true. She wouldn't have to take any more guff off her late husband or the weaselly Woolworth's manager anymore.

The two-story boarding house was located at the end of Allegheny Street. Though the passage of one too many years had scarred its original beauty, a certain elegance remained. Ollie saw it through the layers of white paint that blistered and cracked open under the hot Pennsylvania sun. In her mind's eye she painted the house with a fresh, new coat and righted the shutters that hung partially unhinged to one side.

Scarlett cringed as she stared at her new home, frightened out of her wits. Everybody knew this place was haunted. Mrs. Turner nudged Scarlett through the gate onto the brick walkway up to the house. Patches of dandelions choked the yellowing grass that crept

up to Scarlett's ankles and extended out to a collapsed picket fence.
The only sign of life was a sparrow perched on an ancient birdbath
decorated with polished stones from the Monongahela River.

"This place's full of dirt and spooks and stinky old spider poop!"
screamed Scarlett as her mother dragged her up the front steps of
the house.

Still holding tightly onto Scarlett's hand, Ollie repositioned herself on the front porch and appraised her property. The land had a
nice lay to it, sloping gently down to the fence and from there on to
the river.

"Why, Scarlett Faye, stop your frettin' for just one minute and
look at what your eyes will see every day." Ollie sighed and settled
back on one leg, her hand on her hip. "It's beautiful. Like in a picture or somethin'. All those cottonwoods and that green, green ever-
rollin' river.

Scarlett did not see anything but a bunch of locust trees and that
awful brown fish water the local boys used for swimming and unspeakable bathroom acts.

"I don't care about no trees. This place gives me the ickies. I
don't want no headless thing a-choppin' me to bits!" Scarlett looked
around, searching out an escape route in case it became necessary.

Ollie ignored her daughter's superstitious fretting. While Scarlett's imagination was definitely her worst enemy, it was also her
best asset. Right now, it was annoying Ollie Mae. Mrs. Turner
pushed open the front door of the house and led a petrified Scarlett
inside.

Scarlett's hands grew clammy. She was sure some perfectly hid-
eous thing was going to pop up from the cellar or come screeching
out at her from the attic. The more she tried to pull her hand out of
her mother's, the more Ollie tightened her grip. Scarlett was going
to see their new home whether she liked it or not.

The musty smell of the house's undisturbed years made Scarlett's
nose itch. She sneezed three times in rapid-fire succession and instantly stirred up some history. Dusty filaments of light revealed a
hollow, empty place, as quiet as a dead mouse.

"Now see, Scarlett. There's nothing to be scared of. If you just stand still, you can feel it. This house has a gentle soul."

Ollie always maintained that houses, like people, had souls. It was something you could feel the minute you crossed the threshold. If a house had the right kind of feeling, a good soul so to speak, its inhabitants would live happily ever after.

Scarlett didn't put much stock in what her mother said but decided that maybe the house wasn't so bad after all. She didn't see one single ghost or spook or smell any spider poop. In fact, she was secretly delighted to be getting out of that small clapboard house where she had spent the first tender years of her life. She would finally have a room of her own.

Chapter

3

It took time to get the place all properly fancied up. But once it was just right, "pretty as a color postcard," as Mrs. Turner happily observed, she started taking in boarders. She was very careful about not letting the wrong kind of influence into the house. After all, Scarlett Faye would be growing up there.

The first person Ollie Turner accepted was a pretty young woman called Wanda Fargo. In her early twenties, Mrs. Fargo was all alone in the world. Scarlett heard her husband got killed in the Korean War. Somebody put a hand grenade in his foxhole and that was that. He was dead and Wanda was a widow. Apparently, that's why she had to take a job down at the local feed store and move into the boarding house. Nobody was going to take care of Wanda anymore.

In time Mrs. Turner picked up two more boarders, both men. One was a veteran of World War I known as Cecil McMurty. The other was a religious wares salesman named Olan Spinney, a strange little man with blue, beady eyes.

God, sin, and the end of the world were Olan's favorite subjects. His room at the end of the hall was filled with Bibles and brightly painted Jesus statues. There were crosses too, large ones and small ones, according to how religious you were. At least, that's what Olan told Scarlett.

"The bigger the cross, the better the Christian. It never fails," observed Olan as he fingered his best seller, an oversized plywood cross varnished to a high spiritual sheen.

The large crosses, of course, were the most expensive. Olan said it was a matter of pious economics. Five dollars really let the Heavenly Father know how you felt about Him.

"So why don't people just tell God how they feel and save their money?" suggested Scarlett.

Olan patiently explained, "Now, Scarlett Faye, use your head. Suppose Billy Ray moved to Mississippi and you wanted to talk to him. How do you think you'd do it?"

"By telephone! What else?" piped up Scarlett.

"That's right," chuckled Olan. "It's the same principle here. My crosses and statues are like magic telephones to God. Direct lines."

Scarlett was momentarily at a loss for words. She picked up one of the statues and looked for some hidden wiring, something to explain the power Olan was giving it. She didn't find anything. The more time went by, the more Scarlett disliked this traveling salesman and his holy wares. She decided he was what her old dead daddy used to call a word-weasel. But who would have known? This brand of weasel came disguised as your friendly, forgiving, everyday Christian.

"It was hard to get a bead on Olan. He talked such great God," Scarlett would later point out.

It was true. Olan's slick-talking sermonizing even convinced Mrs. Turner to send Scarlett away to a special camp for Christian girls the first summer he was at the boarding house. "It'll be good for her," assured Olan. "They'll teach her how to be a lady, a real Christian little lady."

"Well," added Ollie Mae, "I suppose one can't learn too much about right behavin'. Can they, Scarlett Faye?"

Scarlett said nothing. Instead she glowered at Olan until her eyes narrowed into tiny little slits. When it came to matters of God, she didn't stand a chance with these two. She had to come up with something fast. Some plan. Something that would get her out of Bible Camp so she could stay home that summer and do what she really wanted to do. Find a way to get rid of Olan Spinney!

Chapter

4

Scarlett got sick the morning she was supposed to leave for Bible Camp. She hung her head out the window until her face was hot from the sun. Then she went into the bathroom and made loud, retching sounds. For added measure, she pinched her cheeks until they were beet red and asked her mother if she had scarlet fever.

It worked. Ollie Mae unpacked Scarlett's suitcase and sent her to bed. Needless to say, Scarlett made a quick recovery and joined everyone at supper that evening. She announced that her fever was gone and smiled over at Olan. "God works in mysterious ways His wonders to behold."

If Scarlett couldn't stand Olan Spinney before, she loathed him now. The way he sat at the dinner table and talked holy made her want to puke. But worse than the way he talked was the way he looked at Wanda. The word-weasel used every opportunity he could to engage Wanda in conversation about Jesus so he could watch her breasts rise and fall with the heavy sighs that punctuated her words.

Poor Wanda sighed a lot too. It was guilt that did it. It had her languishing out loud right through the meat and potatoes. Wanda said she knew she should go to church more often. She as much as admitted she was a lousy Christian.

Wanda's confession presented a double opportunity for Olan.

First, he made a sale. He got Wanda to buy another Bible off him. Second, he also got a date. Wanda agreed to accompany him to church the following Sunday. Olan was delighted. He put down the leg of fried chicken and licked his fingers. "I knew you'd see the light, Wanda. For being such a good girl maybe we'll even go on a little picnic afterwards."

That was it. Scarlett couldn't take it anymore. She slammed her glass of milk down on the table and didn't even wipe her mouth before she tore into Olan. "You pig! You awful pig!"

Mrs. Turner bolted upright in her chair and turned to Scarlett, stunned. Wanda put down her fork and steeled herself for one of Scarlett's outbursts.

"The man is a pig. Just look at him!" yelled Scarlett, referring to the grease and food droppings on the front of his shirt. "He grunts when he eats too."

Ollie Mae was horrified. She stammered once or twice before she could get started. "Oh, Mr. Spinney . . . I . . . I . . ."

Olan's face had taken on the high color of the Irish, or perhaps a stroke victim. A rivulet of grease made its way down one corner of his mouth.

"Scarlett Faye, what's the matter with you? Do you have a fever or something?" asked Ollie, feeling the child's forehead in a desperate attempt to find an excuse for her behavior.

"I ain't got no fever," said Scarlett defiantly, pushing her mother's hand away. "He's the sicky. Sittin' there all the time a-starin' at Wanda's bumps and splashin' food all over the place."

At this point Mrs. Turner gasped, Wanda turned beet red and Olan shrank into a little ball. Then, before anyone could react further, Scarlett Faye got up and ran from the table. Seconds later, she slammed the front door of the house so hard it shook the windows clear back in the dining room. It was a wicked tantrum all right, a real hissy fit.

Those remaining at the table quietly finished their dinner and then dismissed themselves from the table. The room had become so uncomfortable one might have sworn the very oxygen had disappeared from the air. Only Cecil McMurty stayed and attempted to comfort Mrs. Turner. As usual, Scarlett's directness had amused him. He swore the girl could give the lie to anyone.

"Don't worry, Mrs. Turner. She'll calm down eventually."

Tears streamed down Ollie's face. "Oh, you don't know, Mr. McMurty. I've tried so hard to make her respect her elders. She's an impossible child."

"Now, now," said Cecil. "Give her time. She's a high-spirited girl. Children like that always get into more mischief."

Try as he may, however, Cecil couldn't dissuade Mrs. Turner from the course of action she would take later that evening. Ollie Mae was plumb out of patience. Accordingly, Scarlett got spanked at eight o'clock sharp and everyone in the boarding house heard it. In a futile attempt to make her mother stop, Scarlett screamed bloody murder and accused Ollie of brutalities beyond mention.

"Stop it! Stop it, or you'll kill me just like you did your other babies."

As the belt cracked louder, Scarlett tried another tactic. She started whimpering and shrieking and then bellowing like a wounded buffalo. If they didn't know better, Mrs. Turner's boarders might have thought she was axing poor little Scarlett to death. But they knew better.

"Now you stop being so ornery to Mr. Spinney. You hear me, Scarlett Faye?" To make her point Ollie picked the belt up once more and brandished it menacingly at Scarlett.

Fearing her mother might start all over again, Scarlett quickly schemed her escape. "You mean old thing! You're breakin' my poor little bones." Scarlett hunched over and fell to the floor. "See!" screamed the child. "You already busted my leg once."

In exasperation, Ollie threw the belt down on the floor and exited the bathroom.

Chapter

5

By the following morning Scarlett had hatched a plan to deal with Olan. She promptly apologized to Ollie for accusing her of murdering her other kids (children she never had, of course) and then asked permission to go over to Billy Ray's. More in desperation than in agreement, Ollie Mae decided to let her go.

As Scarlett left the house, she spotted Olan walking down Allegheny Street. She pretended she was a spy and tailed him at a safe distance. From the bag Olan was carrying and the direction he was taking, Scarlett figured he must be going to peddle his Bibles and crosses. He went past the Yallops' chicken ranch and turned right at the fork in the road, going south to Burning Meadows, an area of old rundown farmhouses filled with tenant farmers.

Scarlett ran up to Billy's house and pounded on the door so hard it hurt her hand. Mrs. Yallop finally answered the door and looked down at Scarlett Faye over the rim of her glasses. She didn't much care for Scarlett. Billy Ray always seemed to get into trouble around her. If it wasn't one thing, it was another.

Scarlett smiled and greeted Billy's mother. "Hello, Mrs. Yallop. Nice day, huh?"

Mrs. Yallop mumbled some inaudible response and then yelled for Billy Ray to come downstairs. "She's here!"

Billy Ray came running down from his room and the two quickly disappeared behind one of the chicken coops. Above all the squawks and cackles, Scarlett explained to Billy Ray about her thrashing of the night before and how Olan Spinney had caused it. She told him that as her best friend he had to help her get something on Olan. A secret maybe. Hopefully, something really awful.

Billy agreed to help. He had never played spy before and Scarlett made it sound very exciting. Before they left, she even gave him an assignment. He was to sneak into his mother's kitchen and get them some food. If he got caught, he mustn't snitch on her. She told him a good spy had to learn to cover up for everybody else.

Billy returned uncaught five minutes later. He had managed two pieces of white bread and a couple of green apples with large brown spots on them. It wasn't much. But it would have to do, rotten or not.

The two spies came to a fork in the road and just like Olan, they took the left side. It was a hot, dusty day, dry as a bone. Mighty corn stalks shimmered, row after row, under the boiling sun. Since Scarlett and Billy hadn't brought any water, they kept stopping to ask for a drink. Each time they did, Scarlett got information on Olan's whereabouts.

They walked across a recently plowed field up to the Seagers' house. Scarlett took a long, cold drink of water from a tin cup and handed it back to Mrs. Seager. She had just bought a Bible from Olan half an hour before.

"Thank you kindly, ma'am," said Scarlett, handing back the cup.

When Mrs. Seager wanted to know what they were doing so far away from town, Scarlett told her they were looking for a runaway puppy. At that point all of Mrs. Seager's kids got excited and wanted to join in the hunt too. Scarlett had to talk fast.

"You can't," warned Scarlett. "He's got them rabies."

Mrs. Seager was horrified but Scarlett assured her everything was all right. "Don't worry. He's Billy's dog and he won't do nothing to people he knows."

Mrs. Seager clutched at her kids and watched the two walk off in the supposed direction of the lost mad dog. It was now midmorning and Scarlett and Billy ate the bread he had purloined. By noon the apples were gone. It took a lot of energy to snoop on Olan and Billy was getting tired. He began to fret and whine about wanting to go home when they finally tracked Olan to a large shack at the far side of the meadow. The place was a real eyesore. The eaves had caved in against its sides and pieces of rusting tin covered holes gnawed there by rats and time.

"Yes, indeed. That was a wonderful lunch, Mrs. Farley. Just for being so nice I'll let you have your Bible for a whole two bits cheaper."

Mrs. Farley protested that she really couldn't afford the good book at any price but by now Olan knew he had her. Accordingly, he went in for the kill.

"Anyone can afford God, my dear lady. He takes care of those who take care of His Word." Olan paused to pick his teeth, barely missing a beat. "And you know as well as I do where that is." The God peddler flashed his merchandise in Mrs. Farley's face. "Right here in this beautiful, one-of-a-kind, gold-embossed Bible." Before Mrs. Farley could raise any further objections, Olan shoved the Bible into her hands and said with great assurance, "It'll help you get your husband back, Edna."

That did the trick. Tears streaming down her cheeks, Mrs. Farley ran into the other room and tore apart the mattress. She produced just enough money to buy the Bible.

"What a rat!" said Scarlett Faye, poking Billy in the side.

By now they were huddled beneath the kitchen window. The smell of hot apple pie was driving Billy Ray crazy. Sure, he felt sorry for Mrs. Farley, but he felt sorrier for his stomach. "I gotta eat, Scarlett. I feel weak and knocky in the knees."

"Sssh, Billy! Stop jabberin'. I can't hear nothin'."

Billy shut up and Scarlett heard Olan polish off his sale by inviting himself to a second piece of pie.

"You're a true Christian woman, Mrs. Farley, and a wonderful cook," testified Olan, smacking his lips and leaning back in his chair. He patted his belly with great satisfaction and burped. "Now, there's just one more thing. I was wondering if I could use your barn for a little shut-eye. I'm sure you understand. It's the heat of the day."

Mrs. Farley said she reckoned it would be okay. Olan thanked her and burped again.

"Come on, Billy. Let's get outta here."

The two scrambled across an open field and ran into the barn. They climbed a ladder and tucked themselves secretly away in the hayloft. It wasn't long before Olan came into the barn and happily counted out the day's money. He had sold two Bibles plus three of God's telephones. A full pocket and a full stomach made him a rich man. Pleased as punch, he lay down in the grain bin and almost immediately began snoring.

Billy Ray became impatient again. "This ain't no fun. He's just takin' a nap and I'm hungry," complained the new spy.

Scarlett whispered for him to be quiet, that sometimes this kind of work took longer than you might expect to produce results. But Billy was restless. No matter how he tried or what Scarlett said, he fidgeted mercilessly. By now his stomach was growling louder than a tiger's and his allergies were acting up. Billy's sniffling annoyed Scarlett too, almost as much as his gastric rumbles. For the life of her she couldn't understand how one body could make so much noise.

She figured she had to do something fast because except for an old cow rubbing her head up against a post, the barn was quiet as a tomb. Scarlett made Billy Ray roll over on his stomach and bury his face in his arms. It worked. She couldn't hear him sneeze or sniffle or complain and it muffled his belly noise.

Olan finally woke up on his own account. He yawned and stretched himself, then made some attempt at unwrinkling his clothes. It didn't work very well. He always looked like he had just had a run-in with a windmill. Olan collected his things and was ready to leave the barn when something caught his eye.

Scarlett leaned forward to see what it was. Olan put everything back down and walked over to the cow. Wasting no time, he took out his pencil, as Scarlett called it, and began humping the cow. Scarlett made Billy Ray get up and look. "Do you see what he's doing?"

Billy Ray wasn't too sure. "He's peein' on the cow?"

"No," corrected Scarlett. "He's pokin' her with his pencil."

Billy let out a sharp gasp and his eyes blew up big as balloons. Scarlett shoved her hand over his mouth and then looked back down at Olan. Sure enough, seeing was believing. Scarlett instantly decided this was where the term "cowpoke" came from and she never liked cowboys again.

Billy pried Scarlett's hand loose and whispered, "I think I'm gonna be sick."

And he was, very loudly. The sound of his retching startled Olan, who suddenly whipped around and looked up. To his total amazement, two sets of bugged little eyes were trained right on him and the cow.

"What the hell!" screamed Olan.

"You better be careful," reproached Scarlett, "or God will hear you," making pointed reference to his black bag full of Bibles and crosses. "He most certainly saw you!"

With that Scarlett and Billy Ray slid down the hayloft and scooted out the barn door as fast as their legs could carry them. Olan zipped his pants and kicked the cow. The jig was up and he knew it, at least in Burton County.

Olan, of course, was absent from the dinner table that night. Several days later, he wrote and asked Mrs. Turner to send his things on, saying an unexpected family illness had taken him back to Florida. Ollie read the letter out loud, ". . . and I hope everyone back in the boarding house is in good health and going to church every Sunday. Affectionately, Olan Spinney."

"Well, I see you're none too sad. Mr. Spinney knew you didn't like him. Even if his granny hadn't taken ill, sooner or later you would have driven him out of here. Isn't that right, young lady?"

Scarlett said nothing. After all, it's difficult to eat and smile at the same time.

Chapter

6

As much as Scarlett despised Olan Spinney, she adored Cecil McMurty. He made a lot of sense, something which most grown-ups didn't. Over the next several years the captain became her best friend, her buddy, her secret-keeper.

Cecil had been dragged from one end of life to the other and wasn't bitter about it. After the end of the First World War, he met and fell in love with someone called Lorraine. Lorraine was everything to Cecil. Right up until the day he caught her exchanging valentines with his best friend. When that happened, the captain took off for Africa and joined the Foreign Legion. Scarlett thought that was a little extreme. After all, it was just a valentine. Even though the subtlety of Cecil's metaphor eluded her at the time, Scarlett sensed something in life had made him very sad.

"Is that Lorraine?" asked Scarlett, pointing to a little picture Cecil kept on a shelf.

"That's her. The lady herself."

"She was pretty," observed Scarlett.

"Yep. I know."

That was about as much conversation as Scarlett could get out of Cecil about his lady. Later, he would share more about Lorraine. But right now he couldn't. He seemed agreeable to just sitting on the front porch of the boarding house playing solitaire. He played it every day, days that ultimately turned into years.

"Come on, Captain, let's play a game I can do too."

Cecil looked up and smiled. He liked Scarlett a lot. He liked her eagerness and sense of adventure, her brightness and her laughter. Her laughter could fill a room. Perhaps Cecil remembered his youth in her. The plans, the dreams, all the loves yet to be. A whole life at the beginning of itself ready to unwind.

"Okay, Scarlett Faye. Sit down and I'll teach you all about gin rummy."

The child hesitated and thumbed evasively through her book on the Civil War, one of many Cecil had loaned her. Strangely enough, it was hard for Scarlett to be altogether direct with Cecil sometimes. He was the one person in the world she didn't want to cause any grief. Her affection was that deep.

"Er . . . I don't know, Captain. I . . ."

"What is it, Scarlett? You look like I just asked you to skin a cat."

Scarlett spent a little more time beating around the bush and then, finally, she told Cecil the truth. "I don't know about no drinkin' games, Captain. I hate the smell of the stuff and I am a little young."

Cecil exploded into laughter and his breath blew some of the cards off the table. Scarlett bent down to pick them up.

"Scarlett, honey. Gin rummy is just a card game. It's one two people can play."

Scarlett got a real sheepish look on her face and smiled sort of silly. She guessed maybe she didn't know everything yet.

"Come on, sit down. You need a break from all that reading."

"Yeah," said Scarlett. "I'm getting tired of war." She put the huge volume down and then sat at the table with Cecil.

Cecil promptly dealt out ten cards apiece, turning the eleventh one faceup. That was the one he called the "knock card." The one you had to peg your hand off of to win. Scarlett was a fast study. By the end of the summer she was knocking and ginning and winning all over the place. She barely even noticed her eighth birthday come and go because every time she won, Cecil gave her a nickel. She had a whole jarful by September and was beginning on her second one. This time she used a huge pickle jar twice as big as the first.

"I just can't seem to get a decent hand anymore, Scarlett. You're beating the blazes out of me."

"I know." Scarlett grinned. "I'm the best."

"Well, now. Let's not get too big-headed about it."

"Why not? The biggest head taught me."

Cecil laughed and winked at Scarlett Faye. She could charm him too, even if she cheated from time to time. He had seen the extra cards sticking out of her back pocket. "What are all those tail feathers you're growing, Scarlett?" he finally asked her one day.

Scarlett turned a rainbow of crimson. She'd never been caught red-tailed, so to speak. She felt behind her and sure enough, there the cards were. She immediately went into survival mode. She didn't want to give back those nickels. "Oh! My butt was aching me real bad, Captain, so I thought I'd pad myself."

"You mean you thought you'd pad your hand and cheat."

Scarlett looked like she might cry. Cecil had caught her in two big ones, and all at the same time.

"Shame on you, Scarlett Faye. Tricking me out of all my nickels."

"Oh, Captain. No, I didn't. I won most of them, really I did." She hesitated and then added in a desperate attempt to build a case in her favor. "You're a lousy gin player, sir."

Cecil looked sternly across the table at Scarlett Faye. She had to realize that cheating and lying were no good. He almost taught her a good lesson that day. Almost.

"I'm sorry, Cecil. I won't never do it again. It's just that I gotta get money. How else am I gonna make it to college?" asked Scarlett Faye, looking longingly at the pickle jars.

"Well, you're not going to get it lying and cheating at cards. From now on, no more nickel bets, Scarlett Faye. I'm afraid I may have taught you a bad thing."

"Oh, no, you didn't, Captain! It's this or what Aunt Fanny did," Scarlett threatened in mock desperation.

Cecil had heard about Aunt Fanny before, Ollie Mae's sister,

Dillinger's late, great trollop. "Now, Scarlett, don't go kidding around. Just how do you think your aunt made money?"

"She rented herself. You know, sort of like my mother rents rooms here. Only Aunt Fanny's room was her body."

Cecil was amazed at Scarlett's dead-on-center perception of Fanny and instantly veered away from the subject. "Haven't you learned anything at Sunday school?"

"Sure enough," said Scarlett, shuffling the cards. "I learned about baby Jesus and his papa."

"What did you learn?"

"That nobody understands nothing they ever said so they scare you with the devil instead. At least Aunt Fanny didn't do no pretending."

"Are you saying that people are hypocrites?"

"I guess so. I didn't know there was a fancy word for it."

Cecil shook his head again. Scarlett had a distinct talent for derailing the conversation when she didn't like where it was going. He put it back on track.

"You cheated, Scarlett Faye. All summer."

"So why didn't you catch me before?"

"Because I wanted to see if you would stop, maybe get a guilty conscience." Cecil paused. "Did you?"

Scarlett shook her head. "No, Captain, I need the money. I got to get out of here. I wanna go to school and learn something. I want to be rich and famous, not poor and stupid."

"Well, you listen here, Scarlett Faye. Cheating and lying are no good. They're sins. Do you hear?"

"You mean like daddy pokin' Aunt Fanny or Olan pokin' a cow?"

Cecil was momentarily stunned into a vast silence.

Scarlett continued, "Sometimes, Cecil, I think the only sin is gettin' caught."

Perhaps it was true. In any event, Scarlett didn't plan to leave a trail.

Chapter

7

"Where ya' going now?" Ollie asked.

Scarlett didn't bother to answer her mother. She had just graduated from grammar school and arrived at that time in life when parents became nuisances, best ignored whenever possible. She waved a book up in the air and continued walking toward the front door.

"That's just plain foolishness, child. Wasting your time on all them books that ain't got no pictures."

"I'm reading them, not looking at them," sassed Scarlett. "They make you smart."

Ollie Mae objected, "The smart thing is gettin' married one day so you have some security."

"I told you already, Momma. I'm gonna be a writer!"

Ollie Mae objected a second time. "Them people don't make no money."

"They do if they're clever," said Scarlett, pushing herself through the screen door out onto the front porch.

"Now, you wait just a jiffy, Scarlett Faye. I'm not finished." Ollie went over to the screen door and peered out at her daughter through the fly spatters. "You'd do just fine marryin' Billy Ray when you grow up and gettin' a piece of that fine chicken farm his parents own."

"I don't want to raise no shitty chickens," Scarlett declared emphatically.

"Now, you watch your mouth, young lady. There's no call to talk like that."

Scarlett didn't answer. Instead she shuffled in place trying to wait out her mother. It didn't work. Scarlett grudgingly broke their silence. "Can I go now?"

Ollie rubbed her hands on the back of her apron and emitted one of those dense maternal sighs. "Be back for dinner."

With that Scarlett raced off to the river and plopped herself down beneath an old cottonwood tree. It was quiet and the water was cool. She turned to a dog-eared page in a thin volume called *The Ballad of the Sad Cafe* and began reading. A confounding tale of love and woe, the book was about a woman saloonkeeper who fell in love with a mean-spirited dwarf, an alcoholic. The story confirmed Scarlett's worst suspicions—love was not only blind, it was a disease. A sickness that made people mad with desire and then promptly destroyed their lives. She had seen it happen more times than she could count in Dillinger.

Scarlett put the book down on her lap. An afternoon breeze was whipping up, blowing across the river and forming gentle ripples on the surface of the water. It was a refreshing breeze filled with the scent of clean things. Scarlett yawned and leaned back against the tree. She didn't have a care in the world right now except for maybe her body changing so fast. She closed her eyes and dreamt of an almost perfect time, one before all the dreadful compromises of puberty, before all the boys in Dillinger got horny and completely on her nerves.

Chapter

8

A loud boom soon jolted Scarlett awake from her nap. It seemed to come from Twila Wabash's house down the river. Then came another awful explosion. Fearing the worst, she jumped up and ran in the direction of the noise. As Scarlett rounded a bend in the river, she saw great puffs of smoke rise from Twila's house. A fiery explosion blew out the last remaining window and fragments of glass sliced through the air, embedding themselves in a giant oak tree at the edge of the yard.

Scarlett glanced nervously about for some sign of Twila. She ran through the front gate and yelled into the burning house. She got as close as she could, but the heat of the fire was too intense. "Twila!" she screamed. "Where are you?"

There was no answer. All Scarlett could do was stand helplessly by and watch Twila's junk palace go up in flames. Strewn about the yard were ancient ice boxes, stoves, tires, milk cans, flower pots, bits and pieces off old cars, couches, chairs, rusting pots and pans, and venetian blinds. In fact, just about anything you might imagine could be found somewhere on Twila's property.

Some people in Dillinger thought Twila was daft, others just plumb crazy. The kinder ones said she was eccentric. But whatever she was, she had been Scarlett and Billy Ray's friend. When they were growing up, Twila's junky old home had been the best playground around. Now the fire was burning it up and taking part of their childhood with it. Just like that and it would all be gone. Smoke and ashes. The physical evidence that connected them with that time would disappear forever. Scarlett's anxiety suddenly spiraled. Maybe the fire was taking Twila too.

"Twila! Twila! Where are you?"

"Calm down, child," answered a voice as rough as sandpaper. "I'm over here."

Sure enough, there Twila was in her favorite place down by the river. She was sitting at the picnic table Scarlett and Billy Ray helped her borrow from Juniper Park one summer night a long time ago. Scarlett sprinted down to her old friend and checked her over. "Twila, you gave me such a scare. Are you okay?"

Twila nodded her head in the affirmative and calmly puffed on a cigarette butt as she watched her house burn down. She finished the butt, then lighted another one of the many she kept in an old snuff can. "Sit down and cool your blood," directed Twila, motioning to a place beside her on the picnic bench. "The fire truck will be here soon."

"Oh, jeepers, Twila. I'm so sorry."

"Hush, child. Don't go gettin' yourself all worked up because of the fire." Twila exhaled a long column of smoke. Then she turned and looked at Scarlett. "I wanted to move anyway."

"But your art, Twila. What about your art?"

Scarlett was referring to Twila's abundant junk inside and outside the house. Twila had always said that what other people saw as trash, she saw as treasure, as art. The eye of the beholder, that sort of thing. It justified her compulsion to collect it.

"Don't ever own nothing, Scarlett. Owning ties your life down."

Scarlett stared at the smoldering junk. She didn't have the heart to tell Twila she wasn't interested in owning the likes of such things, art or not. She was planning a first-class trip through life and she wasn't going to clutter it up with junk.

"Who knows, child. Maybe I finally just got lonely."

Scarlett was caught off guard. She had never heard Twila talk like this. In fact, she never talked about herself at all. For the first time

Scarlett wondered about the woman beside her and what failed hope or dream had abandoned her to this junk pile.

Though Twila was old to Scarlett, she really wasn't that old. Maybe fifty. Perhaps even forty-five. It was difficult to know for sure, but in her day, Twila might have been pretty. Scarlett wondered if too much sadness or grief had worked its mischief on her face and aged her early. It was hard to tell. Twila was plainly a mystery. There was that way she kidded around with language and even deliberately misspoke it. Somewhere, beneath it all, was the cadence and diction of an educated woman.

"I'm leaving here, Scarlett. I'm going to where everything's clean. To where you can see and touch the earth's bare bones."

Scarlett had trouble processing Twila's plans. Too much was changing too fast. As part of her childhood was turning to cinders, she was hearing about her friend moving away, to a destination she couldn't even remotely imagine—a place where you could feel the earth's bones. Where in heavens, wondered Scarlett, was that?

Twila saw the look of bewilderment on Scarlett's face and divined its source. She quickly clarified. "Scarlett, honey. I'm speaking in what you call metaphor. I'm talking about the desert. When I say bones, I mean the outline of the land. How it looks, all naked and plain without no vegetation or confusion growing on it."

"I sort of figured that," bluffed Scarlett. "When you gonna go?"

Twila flicked what was left of the Camel butt to the ground and mashed it out with her shoe. "As soon as the insurance company pays up. That's when." Twila winked at Scarlett and then they both smiled conspiratorially.

"I'll miss you, Twila."

"Me too," said Scarlett's friend, hugging her. "You'll have to come and visit me."

"I will, Twila. Just as soon as I get done educating myself and get famous."

Twila smiled. In the distance a lone fire siren wailed. As it got louder, the two friends fell silent and watched the fire finish its work.

Chapter

9

Twila's insurance money came one month to the day after she moved into Ollie Mae's boarding house and two days before Wanda Fargo got married.

"Don't go frettin' yourself to death, Scarlett Faye Turner. You'll make a right pretty bridesmaid."

Scarlett handed Twila a single battered suitcase as she boarded the train. "You know I hate getting all prissied up. It ain't my nature," declared Scarlett flatly.

Twila smiled and shook her head. "Dear child, one's nature is rarely defined by the way they dress. Besides, yours probably has more parts to it than Carter has little white pills." With that Twila hugged Scarlett one last time. "I love you, Scarlett. You've been a good friend."

The whistle blew twice and the old Southern Express pulled away from the platform. "Like it or not, you do look beautiful in that dress," Twila yelled back.

Scarlett ran down the platform after the train, waving and yelling too. "I'm coming to visit you, you know." Her voice trailed off. "Someday."

Twila smiled and kept waving. It was unlikely she heard anything above the accelerating chug-chug of the train. A gentle rain began to fall and the train soon disappeared into the distance with Twila Jeanette Wabash, carrying her away to New Mexico, to the desert, to the earth's bare bones.

Chapter

10

The storm clouds cleared and, as planned, Wanda got married at high noon. For some inscrutable reason she had chosen that particular time for marrying. Wanda said it had poetry in it. Perhaps it did. High noon was beautiful that Sunday.

Scarlett Faye fidgeted impatiently at the back of the crowd, waiting for the bride and groom to come out of the church. She wanted to go home. She was uncomfortable about more than just the silly dress she was wearing. She had a feeling she couldn't quite place.

"Quit your jittering around, Scarlett. You're makin' me nervous," said Ollie. "You sick or got your period or somethin'?"

"Yes! Yes, I'm sick!" answered Scarlett defiantly. "I'm sick of all this carrying on over a stupid wedding."

Just then Wanda and her husband appeared on the front steps of the church. She was radiant. In fact, Scarlett had never seen her look so beautiful. Chuck took Wanda in his arms and showed her off to the crowd, kissing her long and hard. All the men clapped and whistled, yelling that they wanted to kiss the bride too.

"Okay, then get up here," yelled back Chuck.

Wanda finally pulled away from Chuck and tossed her bouquet over everyone's head right at Scarlett. Scarlett had no recourse but to catch the dumb thing. Now she really felt foolish.

"That, Scarlett," rejoiced Ollie Mae as she pointed at the flowers. "That means you'll be gettin' married next."

"I don't think so," sassed Scarlett as she shoved the bouquet into her mother's hands.

"Now you behave, young lady. We still got the reception to do."

"Yeah. I know," said Scarlett and walked away more disgusted than ever.

Up front all the men had queued up to give the bride a kiss. Chuck admonished his buddies not to do no serious business on his wife's lips. That was his spot. Everybody laughed.

For reasons Scarlett would not fathom until later, she walked up the church steps and got behind the last man in line. By the time she got to Wanda, Chuck was joking around with his buddies, boasting how he was going to "saddle his filly real good and ride her till he broke her."

"Thanks for catching my bouquet, Scarlett. I really wanted you to have it."

Wanda reached over and hugged her young friend. As Scarlett pulled back, her mouth found its way to Wanda's lips and lingered there ever so briefly. The bride flinched and stepped back so fast she almost stumbled. She was dumbfounded.

"What's the matter with you?"

"Nothing," answered Scarlett, putting her fingers to her lips, feeling the sweet kiss Wanda's mouth had left there. "It was my turn."

"But you're a girl!" was Wanda's emphatic observation.

"I was just giving you a congratulation kiss like everybody else," said Scarlett, equally emphatic.

Wanda quickly changed the subject. "Where's Billy Ray?"

"I dunno and I don't care," said Scarlett, staring at Wanda's bright red lips. Something powerful had happened there.

Chuck walked over and put his arm around his new wife. "Come on, sugar," he said, brushing his crotch up against her. "Let's go get this reception thing over so we can go have some real fun." Chuck winked at Scarlett. "Just like you'll get to have when you get married."

"I don't think so," said Scarlett and she winked back at Chuck. "Maybe that's not my idea of fun."

Chuck couldn't quite latch on to what Scarlett meant. In fact, she wasn't even sure. There was an uncomfortable shuffling of feet while everyone tried to figure out whether to go or stay or say something. Scarlett came to the rescue.

"Congratulations, Wanda. I'm glad you finally got to quit your job down at the feed store."

Chapter

11

Scarlett became obsessed with the memory of the magical Wanda kiss and why it had felt so different from kissing Billy Ray. When her sixteenth birthday rolled around several years later, she found herself still thinking about that kiss. She finally decided that Wanda's lips felt the way they did because they were full of experience. Wanda had been to bed with men. She had done "it."

Scarlett decided it was time for her to do "it" too! That way when she kissed a guy it would feel more like what she had experienced at Wanda's lips. This Byzantine logic drove her to the last row of the drive-in theater one Saturday night in Skeeter Boyd's 1952 Ford sedan. She figured that one of the most popular guys in school could do the trick.

Skeeter parked his jalopy and ran to the snack bar before the movie began. Being a football star for the Dillinger Vikings, he had to keep his weight up. Playing tackle was hard work and so was keeping up his reputation as "the destroyer."

As Skeeter loaded up on popcorn, cheeseboats, soda pop and candy bars, Scarlett wondered if she could really let Skeeter do it to her. Billy Ray might be a better choice. After all, he was smaller. But she ultimately decided that Billy Ray would never do. It was like they say, you can take the boy out of the chicken ranch but you can't take the smell of chicken shit out of his clothes. Doing it with Billy Ray would just be far too unpleasant.

Skeeter got back to the car with an armful of goodies. He handed Scarlett a big Coke and popcorn and slid in next to her. The previews were just starting. Skeeter adjusted the speaker and began wolfing down his food as the previews began and the screen filled up with a passionate, Technicolor embrace. A man and a woman promised each other a thousand silly things and then kissed each other hungrily.

"Man, is she hot stuff!" announced an enthusiastic Skeeter, adjusting the crotch part of his pants.

Scarlett silently agreed. Victor Mature was nowhere near as exciting as the blond woman he was kissing. But that was certain to change just as soon as Skeeter and she "did it." She would finally learn the secret of that desperate, primal urge which had driven women into men's arms since the beginning of time.

When the main feature came on, Skeeter had finished enough food for a small army and was sucking on his second large Dr. Pepper. He burped, turned up the volume and settled back into the car seat for the main feature. Scarlett finished her popcorn and ate a box of jelly "Dots." Skeeter's eyes were glued to the screen so he didn't see her picking the sticky, colored stuff out of her teeth. She wouldn't care if he did.

The movie was boring and dumb. There was no plot as far as Scarlett could tell. Just a bunch of cowboys chasing a bunch of bandidos across the desert trying to get their cattle back. No way those cowpokes wanted to lose those cows, thought Scarlett. No, siree, not out there in that big, lonely, womanless desert.

Scarlett decided she would have to make the first move. Skeeter was just too involved with those damn cowboys right now. She put her hand on his leg and ran it up to the bulge in his pants. She hesitated, then suddenly grabbed his crotch.

"Ouch! What are you doing, Scarlett?"

"Doing?" she said, surprised. "Don't you know? I'm going to pound your flounder."

At least that's what Billy Ray called it the day she caught him behind the chicken coop yanking away at it like he was jerking taffy. "Go away. Can't you see? I'm pounding my . . . my flounder?" proclaimed a breathless Billy Ray.

"I see," said Scarlett, transfixed. She couldn't move. Apparently Scarlett's prying eyes made Billy Ray even more excited because all of a sudden he was moaning louder and pounding more enthusiastically than ever.

Skeeter howled and tossed the rest of his popcorn out the window. "What a stupid name for a dick! For a tally-whacker!" He pulled Scarlett into his arms and kissed her way too hard and way too long. With great effort, she managed to break his lip lock. His kisses still felt the same, pretty awful.

"Want to see it?" asked Skeeter.

Scarlett wasn't sure. The lump in his pants seemed to be getting bigger. Skeeter didn't wait for an answer. He unbuttoned his pants and whipped out his prize. Scarlett couldn't believe her eyes. Skeeter's thing was big. Billy Ray's was a Vienna sausage comparatively speaking. She gasped.

"Like him, Scarlett?"

Scarlett was speechless. Maybe she had made a mistake. Skeeter didn't wait for an answer.

"You'll like him. All the girls do," bragged Skeeter and stroked himself. With his other hand, he found his way in between Scarlett's legs. In spite of herself, Scarlett was getting wet. Maybe this would work out after all, she thought.

"Come on now. Just pull down your panties and let me show you what 'Big Boy' can do."

In the blessed name of experience Scarlett lay back and let Skeeter "do it" to her. She waited for the fireworks, but they didn't come and the earth didn't move. There was nothing except a lot of grunting and the noise of a cattle stampede on the drive-in speaker. It was over almost as fast as it began.

Skeeter was exhilarated. "Hot damn, Scarlett! It felt like a jolt of lightning hit me right between the eyes. How'd it feel to you?"

"I didn't feel nothing except for it hurting," said Scarlett resentfully, sensing something was amiss. "Are you sure you're doing it right?"

"Yep!" assured Skeeter. "You're just nervous, first time and all. You've got to relax and let it happen."

After imparting the recycled advice of the ages, Skeeter persuaded Scarlett to try once more. Seconds later, Skeeter was wailing again and soon after that, he was finished. He was getting quicker. Scarlett told Skeeter to get off. She intuited the problem.

"You get there too fast, Skeeter. Can't you take your time?"

Skeeter looked dumbfounded. Obviously, this had never occurred to him. Scarlett tried "it" several more times with him in the months to come. But "it" never got better and neither did Skeeter.

Chapter

12

Scarlett decided she had to talk to Wanda. There was surely an explanation for why a boy's kisses felt the way they did and Wanda could tell her what that was. After all, she had been married twice and had plenty of experience with those kinds of kisses.

"What's your big hurry?" asked Ollie Mae as she watched Scarlett rush through dinner. "The way you're eatin' that corn, shoveling it down so fast, you're just askin' for a bellyache."

"I have to visit Wanda. Chuck's working graveyard so I thought I'd give her some company."

Ollie looked at her daughter quizzically. "Yeah?"

"Girl talk, Momma."

"So talk."

Cecil had already left the table so it was just Scarlett and her Momma. "Well, go ahead. Everyone else is in their room."

Scarlett stuck a spoonful of food in her mouth so she wouldn't have to answer right away.

"What's so high-minded you can't talk to your own mother about? There's nothin' in Wanda's advice pantry I don't got in mine."

As Scarlett grew older, Ollie Mae felt increasingly ignored and left out of her daughter's life. It seemed Scarlett talked to everyone but her, and she was getting a big resentment about it. All of a sudden, Ollie's face pinched up real severe. Scarlett could tell her patience was running thin.

"Well, let's hear it," said Ollie.

If Scarlett didn't think of something quick to avert her mother's displeasure, she'd never get out of the house this evening. She came up with an escape plan. "It's a secret, Momma."

Ollie's face flushed. "It's a what? Now don't you go gettin' my back up, Scarlett Faye. You know that secret stuff don't sit well with me."

"Oh, Momma, please. Don't go spoiling things. It's supposed to be a surprise. I was gonna have Wanda teach me that fancy crotchet stitch so I could make something real pretty for you." Scarlett smiled and, with a final flourish, rested her case, "Remember? It's your birthday next month."

Ollie Turner's eyes lit up, genuinely touched. "Oh, Scarlett, how dear of you. Excuse me for being so nosey. I'll just pretend I didn't hear. Okay?"

"Okay," replied Scarlett, getting up from the dinner table. "I'll be home after the lesson. Can you excuse me from doing the dishes tonight? It's a tough stitch to learn."

Ollie smiled and pushed her hair back from her face. "Of course."

With that Scarlett grabbed her jacket and headed for the door. She had one foot on the front porch when she heard her mother call after her.

"Aren't you forgettin' something, young lady?"

"Oh, I'm sorry," remembered Scarlett and she ran back and gave her mother a peck on the cheek.

"No. I don't mean that."

Scarlett was perplexed. "What then?"

"Your sewing kit, Scarlett. How are you going to learn that new stitch with no needles?"

Scarlett smiled sheepishly. "My enthusiasm does outrun me. Doesn't it, Momma?" She flashed another smile at Mrs. Turner, fetched her sewing kit and flew out the front door.

It was early evening and a breeze was picking up off the river, blowing a coolness over Dillinger. A lone dog howled somewhere in the distance and the night creatures came alive. Crickets chirped, frogs croaked and a bird Scarlett was never able to identify began to sing its plaintive, melancholic song from somewhere deep within the woods.

Scarlett broke into a light sprint toward Wanda's house. That bird was getting on her nerves tonight. She reached Allegheny Street and was surprised to see there were no lights on at Wanda's house. Scarlett decided she must be at the movies but then, just as quickly, decided not. Wanda never went by herself. In fact, she never went at all anymore. Not since her best friend, Thelma, moved away. They had both loved movies and had gone together every Saturday night.

After Wanda's husband died in the Korean War, Thelma's friendship helped Wanda out of a deep depression. For a while, they did everything together. They apparently understood each other so well because they shared a mutual sorrow. Thelma's husband was killed during the war too, the last day of the last big war. That was World War II.

When Wanda met Chuck, she and Thelma drifted apart. It wasn't much later that Thelma went to Texas to do something. Scarlett never found out exactly what. But it must have been important because she never came back.

Scarlett opened the gate to Wanda's house and went up to the front door. She listened for a minute and then knocked. No one answered. Scarlett picked up the evening paper at the side of the door and knocked again. "Wanda, are you there? Did you fall asleep or something?" She waited and again there was only silence.

Scarlett was about to leave when she heard a stirring inside. She put her ear up against the door and heard very soft music playing on the radio. "Wanda, it's Scarlett. What's the matter? How come you don't have any lights on?" She walked around to a window and peeked in. There was Wanda sitting in a rocking chair next to an ancient radio. Its circular dial gave off just enough light to illuminate one side of Wanda's face. She had been crying. Scarlett rapped on the window. "Please, Wanda. Open the door."

"I can't," she answered.

"Why not?" Scarlett asked gently. "I'm your friend. If you're sad about something, you can tell me."

Wanda turned the radio up and rocked back and forth, sobbing. Scarlett went down the side of the house trying windows until she found one that was unlocked. She pushed it up and climbed inside. She walked down the hall and stopped in the doorway of the room where Wanda sat rocking. The other side of Wanda's face, the side she hadn't seen before, was covered with bruises and cuts. She looked like she'd hit the windshield in a car accident.

"What happened, Wanda?"

Wanda covered her face and told Scarlett to go away. "I don't want anyone to see me right now."

"Who hurt you, Wanda?"

She suddenly broke down and cried a deep, anguished sorrow. Her pride and dignity were hurt as much as her face and body. She had no words to express her sense of pain and failure.

"It was Chuck. Wasn't it?"

Wanda nodded. "He didn't mean to. He was drunk. He got out of control and didn't know what he was doing."

Scarlett's face flushed with anger. Wanda was buying the same story her mother had always bought. Her husband's unhappiness, his temper, his frustrations, his miserable life, everything, all of it, was his wife's fault.

"Can I make you a cup of tea?" asked Scarlett. "Maybe it'll help."

Wanda nodded and Scarlett left for the kitchen. As she waited for the water to boil, she heard Patsy Cline on the radio singing "Back in Baby's Arms," and she knew Chuck would wiggle his way back into Wanda's soon enough.

Scarlett had seen it before. Her father had worked his alcoholic charms on her mother a thousand times and she always believed his lies and took him back. He would never drink again. He would never hit her again. He would never chase another skirt again. He would never ever do anything rotten again. Not ever. It was a promise. The litany went on and on and it never changed and it was never true. A marriage with the likes of a Chuck Fowler or Joe Turner was a train ride through pure hell, and it was one Scarlett never intended to take. This much she knew. She didn't want a life with the devil for a conductor.

Scarlett poured Wanda a cup of tea and took it to her. The poor soul was powdering her face in the dark, trying to hide her shame.

"Thanks, Scarlett," said Wanda, taking the cup of tea and stirring in some sugar. She sipped at it and then set it on the table. As she did, the teaspoon fell to the floor.

When Scarlett retrieved it, she noticed a picture frame and some broken glass. She picked up the spoon and the broken picture. It was Thelma.

Wanda took the picture of her friend and spoke her grief in staccato. "Chuck smashed it. Thelma sent me a ticket. Wanted me to visit her in Texas. She knows Chuck loses his temper sometimes."

"Then why don't you go, Wanda, and get away from Chuck before he really hurts you?" urged Scarlett, remembering what happens when drunks get out of control. "My daddy broke my mother's arm once, and another time he got so nuts, he fired a rifle at her. He missed. But sometimes they don't, you know."

"I can't leave. Chuck needs me."

"Maybe you need Thelma," said Scarlett.

For some reason Wanda got the strangest look on her face, shifted uncomfortably in her chair and went back to sipping her tea. "I can't visit Thelma. Chuck doesn't like her."

All of a sudden, a few things from the past began to make sense to Scarlett. Like the time she went to Thelma's with some freshly baked bread her mother made. It was evening going on night as Scarlett made her way to Thelma's small home down by the river. Several towering willow trees hid the house from view with long, draping boughs that rustled gently in the wind. Thelma's shades were drawn down, but Scarlett knew she was home. The lights were on.

Scarlett was about to knock when two silhouettes came together behind one of the shades. The silhouettes embraced and then started dancing. When the music stopped, they kissed on and on for what seemed forever. When they finally pulled apart, Scarlett could have sworn the two silhouettes had long hair. But she couldn't be sure, and it didn't matter then anyway. She wasn't curious about such things yet. However, as the years passed, Scarlett found herself wondering who Thelma's friend was that night because she had never seen her with anyone in Dillinger. That is to say, no one except Wanda.

"Did you love Thelma?" asked Scarlett, the audacity of her question surprising even herself.

Wanda went as white as a sheet and fiddled with the wrinkles in her skirt, trying to smooth them out. She finally answered, "Yes. She's the best friend I've ever had."

Scarlett got more daring. "I mean did you love her like you did your first husband?" By now, Scarlett despised Chuck so much she left him out of the equation altogether.

Wanda looked as if she were going to faint. If what Scarlett suspected were true, it was a rotten time to bring it up. Scarlett quickly tried to ease things over with another question.

"I mean does all love feel the same in here?" asked Scarlett, pointing to her heart.

Wanda sipped her tea, grateful for this new, more general query into the nature of love.

"Yes, Scarlett. It does."

At this point Scarlett decided to tell Wanda about her night at the drive-in theater with Skeeter. Scarlett was hoping her older and wiser friend might enlighten her as to why "doing it" with Skeeter hadn't worked. But Wanda went off on a weird tangent.

"You shouldn't have done that, Scarlett. Not until you got married. What are you going to do now that you've lost your virginity?"

"I don't know and I don't care. It's no big deal."

"Of course it is," defended Wanda. "It's supposed to be a gift for your husband."

"And what about him?" argued Scarlett. "What's his gift to me? Something he's poked into every woman he could and then bragged about to every man who would listen?"

Wanda fell silent. Scarlett knew she had overstepped with her mouth again and she apologized.

"I'm sorry, Wanda. It's just that women seem to have gotten a rotten deal."

Wanda picked up her big, fat cat, Laredo, and sat back in her rocking chair, gently stroking him. "Maybe we have. But there's nothing we can do," she said in that same tone of resignation Scarlett had heard so many times in her own mother's voice.

"There's something I have to know."

"Yes?" Wanda waited.

"Why didn't Skeeter's mouth and body feel good to me? Nothing about it felt right."

"It never feels right, Scarlett, unless you're in love."

"Oh!" reacted Scarlett in total surprise. "So that's the missing part?" She had simply made the mistake of doing it with the wrong person. No one ever told her love was the magic ingredient. For a second she was relieved; then she became sad.

"What's the matter, Scarlett?"

"Then I'll never feel it."

"Yes, you will."

"No, I won't. I promised myself I'd never fall in love. All I see is how miserable it makes people. Like an awful suffering sickness had sprung on them. I don't ever want to go through that."

"Oh, Scarlett. It doesn't have to be like that," said Wanda. "Not if you have the courage to love who you really love." All of a sudden, Wanda started sobbing again, apparently ambushed by her very own words.

"I'm sorry you feel so bad," Scarlett told Wanda, and she meant it. It reaffirmed her intention of never getting suckered in by love. Poor Wanda. Love got her good. Real good. It had undone her.

Chapter

13

Scarlett's walk home that night was filled with troubled thoughts about drunks and the general orneriness of people, especially men beating up on women. She remembered the time when her father came within a cat's whisker of killing her mother. She was barely five years old, but she would never forget the horror of that night.

Ollie was in the kitchen trying to keep dinner warm for her husband who, as usual, was late. Scarlett was at the kitchen table reading since they couldn't afford to put on any other lights in the house except the room where they were. With Joe Turner not working, Ollie's pay at the five-and-dime was barely enough to buy food. Lights and water were luxuries, and Ollie used them sparingly.

"Scarlett, why are you readin' like that again?" asked Ollie, referring to how Scarlett always started a book on its last page and then read backwards.

"The front part's too easy."

Ollie protested, "But that's the way you're supposed to learn, Scarlett. The front part first." She came over and opened the book. "See Spot run . . ." she read aloud. "You start with the simple words first, then go on to the more difficult ones at the end. It's the sensible thing."

"It don't make no sense to me. Why should I do it sensible if I already learned them words in the front? Besides, Dick and Jane are stupid. All they do is watch Spot run."

Ollie sighed and stirred the soup. Scarlett had her own logic and that was that. She checked the apple pie. Almost done; its aroma filled the house.

"Can I have some?" asked Scarlett. The pie was smelling so good she could almost taste it.

"When it cools off," said Ollie, taking the pie out of the oven. Tributaries of piping hot apple juice bubbled up from inside the pie and meandered across its golden-brown crust.

"Okay," said Scarlett. She picked up another book and turned to the back page. As she began reading, Joe Turner's pickup truck could be heard coming down the street.

"There's your daddy now," informed Ollie, brushing the hair back from her face. She quickly checked the fried chicken and gravy she was warming up on the stove. "Why don't you go outside and make room in here for your daddy?"

"Because there ain't no light out there and I ain't no bat. I ain't sittin' in no dark night not readin' or nothin' with mosquitoes suckin' on me. No. I'm stayin' in here with you, Momma."

Scarlett's newly acquired habit of disagreeing with her on just about everything annoyed Mrs. Turner, but there was nothing she could do about it now. Joe was home. The front door opened and slammed shut.

"Chicken again, Ollie. Shitfire, woman! I told you I wanted meatloaf!" he yelled and staggered into the kitchen. "Move over!" he ordered Scarlett, heading for the table.

Scarlett got down off the chair and went over to another one by the window, taking her books with her. She looked back at her daddy, whose bloodshot eyes scared her tonight. They were mean-looking, and he smelled of whiskey and vomit.

"What the hell are you lookin' at?" sneered Joe Turner.

"At your eyes," said Scarlett.

"Yeah. What about them?"

"Now, Joe, let the girl be," intoned Ollie May in a soft, conciliatory voice. "She's studying."

"Yeah?" sneered Mr. Turner, and he belched so hard Scarlett swore she could smell his insides rotting. "Well, I want to know why she's starin' at me like I'm something from outer space. What's your problem, girl?"

Ollie Mae set a plate of fried chicken, biscuits and gravy down on the table for Joe. He ignored the food.

"Bring me a beer! How am I supposed to wash this crap down, woman?"

Ollie retrieved a bottle of beer from the icebox, opened it and poured it into a glass for her husband. As she gave it to him, her hand was shaking. But Joe was so drunk he didn't notice. He was too fixated on Scarlett tonight.

"Well, are you gonna answer me, you little piece of shit?"

"Please, Joe, don't talk to your daughter that way."

"Then, goddammit! Answer me, Scarlett. What's so interestin' that's got you looking at me all bug-eyed?"

Scarlett swallowed hard. She knew she was in an impossible place. If she said something, just about anything at all, her daddy would smack her. And if she didn't say anything, he might smack her too. Joe Turner was in that kind of mood.

"Answer your father, Scarlett," encouraged Ollie Mae.

"Well?" Joe Turner's voice boomed.

Scarlett looked back and forth between her parents, then suddenly slid off her chair and made a desperate try for the back kitchen door. Joe lunged and managed to grab her by the arm.

"You misbehavin' little sonovabitch! Come here!"

Scarlett started screaming bloody murder and blubbering between shrieks, "Don't hit me, Daddy. I didn't do nothin' but look at you."

"You didn't answer me, you shithead!"

With that endearing epithet, Joe Turner smacked his daughter so hard she flew across the room and banged her head up against the stove. Blood shot out of her nose and dribbled down on her tee shirt. "Now, you'll answer me!" said Joe, getting up out of his chair. He yanked Scarlett up off the floor, and just as he was about to punch her again, Ollie Mae interceded.

"Leave her alone!" she screamed and she banged sorry old Joe Turner on top of the head with a frying pan.

Joe let go of Scarlett and reeled around the kitchen, tottering first this way, then that. When he finally got his balance, he swung around to Ollie. "You crazed old coot. Now you're going to get it and get it good." He shoved her out his way and disappeared into the living room. "You've done made my life miserable way too long," he yelled back.

Ollie heard Joe go into the closet and pull out his rifle. She pushed Scarlett toward the back door. "Go outside. Now!" But before she could get her little girl out the door, Joe was back pointing the rifle at them.

"You ugly piece of nothin'. I'm gonna send you to the boneyard where you belong." Joe Turner took aim and fired. The kitchen clock took the bullet and fell crashing to the floor. Glass scattered everywhere. "Goddammit, hold still!" Joe yelled at his wife.

"You're going to kill your daughter," screamed Ollie.

Joe steadied the rifle as much as he could and pulled the trigger. The only sound in the room was a deafening CLICK. Then another click and another as Joe frantically squeezed the trigger on an empty barrel. His futile efforts were finally interrupted by a knock at the front door. Ollie sighed with relief and thanked God. Someone had heard the shot and was coming to rescue them from this drunken madman.

Joe Turner made an about-face and staggered out of the kitchen toward the front door. En route he tripped over the coffee table. "Goddamnit!" he yelled, kicking at the table. "Stay out of my way!"

Ollie Mae and Scarlett edged their way gingerly over to the kitchen doorway and peered into the living room hoping to catch a glimpse of their hero. Joe flicked on the porch light and opened the front door.

"Criminy Jesus!" whispered Scarlett to her mother. "It's Moonie Barton!"

"Hey there, Joe. I thought I heard a gunshot. Got yourself a prowler or something?" Moonie inquired, swaying unsteadily in the circle of light on the front porch.

"Sorta. I caught a cockroach a-runnin' off with that crap my wife feeds me."

"Did ya get him?" asked Moonie, smiling insipidly. He turned and spit a long stream of chewing tobacco off the side of the porch.

"No. I figured he was doing me a favor so I shot the goddamn clock instead. You know, the one on the wall that always says I'm late."

Moonie Barton chortled and then leaned over and whispered in Joe's ear, "The girls are back. Down at the dock."

Joe smiled and tucked his shirt in. "Well, what the hell are we waitin' for, buddy? Let's go."

Joe Turner put his rifle up against the wall and disappeared out the front door with Moonie Barton. The painted ladies down at Molly Disharoon's floating whorehouse were waiting for them.

The following day Joe Turner didn't remember a thing about his drunken, murderous rage of the night before. He looked curiously at his rifle and asked, "What's my rifle doing out, Ollie? You spring cleaning or something?"

Chapter

14

"Hey, Sleepin' Beauty, don't you think it's about time to be gettin' up?" yelled Ollie Mae up the stairs. "It's nine o'clock!"

"Oh, Momma. Come on. It's Saturday."

"You promised you'd go shoppin' with me, young lady."

"I know," answered Scarlett, and she raised her voice to its sweetest pitch. "I just thought I'd finish crocheting your birthday surprise instead."

"Oh!" sputtered Ollie Mae, her face lighting up.

"It's looking real pretty," said Scarlett, turning over in bed so the sun wouldn't hit her face.

"Well, if you need a little more time, I guess that's all right."

"I knew you'd understand."

"I'll see you when I get home," added Ollie Mae, putting on her hat with all the bright, dangly fruit. "Don't forget to eat your breakfast," she reminded Scarlett and with that was out the front door to do the Saturday grocery shopping.

Scarlett Faye covered her shameless, lying face with a pillow. She felt terrible, at least momentarily. Ollie Mae's birthday was in two days and she hadn't even started that silly gift she had promised her mother. In fact, she hadn't even learned how to stitch yet, and she probably never would now that Wanda was avoiding her. She had been on the dodge since that night earlier in the week when her husband beat her up. Scarlett figured it wasn't just the awful beating that had Wanda sidestepping her. It undoubtedly had a lot to do with Thelma and the pain behind all those almost revelations.

Scarlett pulled the pillow off her face and slowly stretched her body out. She knew she should get out of bed. If she just put her mind to it, she would come up with something for her mother's birthday. But she was having trouble concentrating. Instead of thinking about presents, thoughts of Wanda and Thelma kept popping into her head. The notion that they might have once held and kissed each other threw Scarlett's imagination into overdrive. She couldn't get rid of the pictures in her head. They just kept coming.

Unable to control the feverish procession of images any longer, Scarlett jumped out of bed and shot over to several large stacks of books in the corner. She began frantically tossing them down on the floor in a desperate search for one in particular. She found it on the bottom of the last pile, safely tucked away from her mother's prying eyes where she had once taken such great pains to hide it.

When she bought the book at an old thrift shop some years before, Scarlett thought it was about girls studying and getting smart like she wanted to do. It was a logical assumption. The book was called *The Adventures of Two Girls at College.* Its front cover had an innocent picture of two girls on campus, all loaded up with books, looking very studious. Since the blurb had been torn away, there was no way for Scarlett to know what the book was really about until she read it. But she soon found out. She had finished it in a single afternoon down by the river.

Scarlett recalled that the two girls in the title were sorority sisters at a college in California. Somewhere around eighteen and nineteen at the time, they were pretty with lots of smarts and plenty of boyfriends. As the two became better and better friends, an inexplicable tension developed between them and they started arguing. Neither one could figure out what upset them so much or why they fought. Then one night, at a walk-in theater near campus, they found out.

As they watched the movie, their arms and legs began brushing involuntarily up against each other's. Then it wasn't so involuntary and they moved closer together. They didn't dare look at each other because it was then that they realized the unthinkable: they wanted each other. The more bold of the two put her hand on the other's leg and hid the daring beneath a coat. Her hand sat there until the other girl finally had the courage to place hers on top of it. The connection was instant and electric.

The college girls were so positive everyone around them could feel what they had just felt that they quickly pulled their hands away and sat there bewildered, watching each other's breasts rise and fall, aching for each other's touch. But they were scared, petrified. Girls weren't supposed to have feelings like these, not for each other anyway.

Scarlett hurriedly leafed through the book looking for the "dirty part." That's how people referred to "doing it" when she was growing up. Back then all loving, when it got physical, somehow got dirty. Such were the fifties and early sixties.

Norma and June, as the two college girls were called, left the theater way before the movie was over. Norma's roommate was away for the weekend and they went to her room. Once inside they locked the door and dissolved in an embrace so powerful it felt like their hearts might collapse. But they didn't and then the passion came full on. Their mouths found each other and they hungrily devoured each other's kisses. But it wasn't enough. Nothing was enough and somehow they had to feed the hunger. They quickly began undressing each other, and when they were both naked to the waist, June looked at Norma and said—

"I need help. I got a ton of groceries down here," announced Ollie Mae. "You still up there in your room?"

"Oh, Momma!" yelled a profoundly irritated Scarlett. "Of course I am! What do you think?"

"What I think is that you better get that tone out of your voice and get down here and help your poor mother unpack all this food. Right now, young lady! Get down here!"

Scarlett dog-eared the page and threw the book on the floor. June and Norma's fireworks would have to wait. Her mother had just frustrated another delicate moment in literature and along with it her daughter's precarious well-being. Scarlett pulled on a pair of jeans and a tee shirt and marched downstairs to the kitchen. Without a word, she started unpacking the groceries.

"Scarlett, that's no way to handle them eggs. You'll break 'em."

"Okay! Okay! Jesus!" said Scarlett, and she put three cartons of large Grade-A eggs into the icebox.

"There you go profanin' again! I told you not to be usin' Jesus' name like that!"

"Like how?" a very frustrated Scarlett asked testily as she shoved a big sack of flour into the cupboard.

"Don't be sassin' me, young lady. What's the matter with you? Got your period again or something?" asked Ollie, checking out her daughter. "You do look a little pekid."

Scarlett didn't answer. She started organizing the canned goods. Ollie liked them a certain way. Peas here. Baby onions there. The apple sauce in between.

Ollie went over and felt Scarlett's forehead. "My, my. You are a little warm. All that crochetin', I bet," grinned Mrs. Turner as she picked up two sacks of potatoes and handed them to Scarlett. "I betcha it's real pretty, whatever it is, being that my daughter's own two hands is makin' it. Right, honey?"

Scarlett didn't answer. She wanted to go and just puke her guts out. First, because she felt guilty about there being no present. Second, because she was frustrated beyond belief and third, because her mother was jangling her nerves into little, bitty, unbearable bits. "What do you want me to do with this?" asked Scarlett, holding up a new toilet brush. There was just enough sassiness still in her voice to irritate Ollie.

"Put it where it belongs, Scarlett. In the bathroom. And while you're in there, scrub the commode down good and clean."

That was it! Shit duty in the boarders' bathroom. It was almost more than Scarlett could bear. "Sonovabitch!" she whispered under her breath and scowled at her mother.

The look wasn't lost on Ollie, and she issued a stern directive. "In fact, young lady, clean the whole bathroom while you're in there, tub and all."

Scarlett struggled to keep her lip buttoned. If she objected in any way, she knew she'd end up having to mop the damn thing too. It was Ollie's way of taking the uppityness out of Scarlett when her attitude took a bad turn. Today was no exception. The downstairs bathroom was Ollie's humiliation chamber. After Scarlett finished cleaning it, she'd be manageable, at least for a while.

Scarlett completed shit duty as soon as possible and made a beeline back upstairs. She grabbed *The Adventures of Two Girls in College*, opened it to the down-turned page and quickly found the place where she had left off. June looked at Laura and said, *"I want to put my mouth ..."*

"Scarlett Faye! What are you doin' back up there?" screeched Ollie. "I need you down here."

That was it! Scarlett was so frustrated, her libido so hot and crazed, she was on the verge of spontaneous self-combustion. If her mother didn't shut up and let her finish June and Norma's little adventure, she was going to explode into flames and burn up, leaving no visible trace of herself except for maybe a foot or two.

When the sheriff came he would know it was Scarlett Faye Turner because it was her room and the foot or feet would be wearing brown-and-white saddle shoes, her size of course, and he'd arrest Mrs. Turner for burning up her one and only daughter. It would serve her mother right for frustrating her so.

Scarlett stuck the book in her back pocket and went downstairs to face off with her mother. She had to come up with something to get out of the house. "I'm sorry, Momma. But if you really must know, I was breaking into my savings jar so I could buy you a birthday card. You know, one of those big ones with all the silly ... I mean, the flowery words you like so much."

"Yeah?" said Ollie Mae, studying her daughter carefully. This sudden generosity made her suspicious. Scarlett never broke into her savings jar for anyone. It was her college money.

"I have to buy it today because tomorrow's Sunday and Monday's your birthday. I know just the one I want to get for you." She smiled at her mother. "The bathroom's done, all clean and shiny."

In spite of herself, Ollie Mae began relenting and Scarlett moved in for the coup de grace.

"In fact, when I get back, I'll even mop it for you, being that your birthday's so near and all. You shouldn't have to work so hard."

Ollie Mae was touched. She hugged her daughter and told her, "Sometimes you can be such a dear. Go ahead and go get the card."

Scarlett broke the hug and smiled at her mother. "See you later," she said and added, "Do you need anything?"

"No. I got everything when I did the shopping."

Which, of course, Scarlett knew. "Okay, then. I'll see you at supper."

With that Scarlett bounded out the door and ran down to the river, wild with fantasy. She wanted to open the book but resisted. She struggled with herself and all those thoughts about Norma and June, wondering just how kissing a girl would feel.

"No!" Scarlett exclaimed out loud and then looked around self-consciously. A fish leaped out of the water and kerplunked back in again, the sole witness to her torment and confusion. She simply could not allow such "girl thoughts" to mess her head up.

The humidity over the Monongahela rose in shimmering sheets toward the sky. The trees on the other side of the river seemed to jiggle and twitch, even sway, when refracted through the wetness in the air. Scarlett watched them awhile and then, with all the force of will she could muster, threw *The Adventures of Two Girls in College* into the water. It would take Norma and June far, far away, and mercifully dispose of their passion as it would of her obsession, somewhere, deep down, on the bottom of the Monongahela River.

Chapter

15

Ollie Mae's birthday party was a roaring success. Scarlett invited Cecil and the new boarder, Jasper Stubbs, plus several of Ollie's old friends. Wanda was invited too, but she didn't come. Scarlett even asked Billy Ray to the party. She didn't see him much anymore. After they went through puberty, they grew apart. It was as if they were suddenly from two different countries.

When Billy crossed the line into growing up, he left all his boyish charm behind. While his obtuseness might have been cute earlier in life, now it was just annoying. Gangly and pimple-faced, Billy still smelled of chicken shit. Scarlett decided the stench must have somehow gotten locked in his pores. If she hadn't thought it might kill him, she would have talked him into bathing in lye. There had to be a treatment for that smell. A vaccine, something. In any event, she told Billy Ray to make sure he bathed before the party, several times at least, and to put a little bleach in the water.

"Don't forget to make a wish, Momma," prodded Scarlett as her mother was about to blow out the forty-four candles.

Scarlett had talked Etta Paine, Ollie's best friend, into making the cake. It said *HAPPY BIRTHDAY, MOTHER* in big yellow letters and was round, three layers tall, fluffy white on the inside with a lemon filling in between and thick chocolate frosting on the outside. It wasn't Ollie's favorite, but it was Scarlett's.

Ollie thought about her wish and then blew out the candles. She succeeded after two attempts. "Does that count?" she wanted to know.

"Of course, Momma. Everyone over forty gets two tries," Scarlett announced and smiled. "Here read this." She passed her mother a big card.

Ollie Mae smiled from ear to ear as she pulled the card out of its envelope. On the front of the card was a tall birthday cake with bluebirds circling around it and the words: *To My Mother From Her Loving Daughter.* Ollie opened up the card and read its printed, syrupy sentiments out loud:

Dearest Mother, May the bluebirds of happiness sing your birthday song today and for all the other birthdays of your life. You are the sweetest, most loving, most kind and giving mother a daughter could have. It was signed: *Love, Scarlett.*

Ollie was beaming as she looked up at her guests and added redundantly, "It's from my dear daughter, Scarlett." She passed the card down the table for all to see.

"Open this, Momma." Scarlett handed her a birthday present.

Ollie smiled and unwrapped the present. "Oh, Scarlett. What a beautiful, lovely thing," said Ollie Mae, holding up a large pink doily. "Thanks so much, honey. And to think you made it with you own two hands."

"Well, let me see it," said Etta Paine, taking it out of Ollie's hand. She inspected it and smiled at her friend. "Oh, Ollie. Just imagine how this'll look under all them little knickknacks you have in the living room," said Etta and, she passed the doily on to Billy Ray.

Much to Scarlett's displeasure, he accidentally got yellow frosting on it. When Billy Ray tried to wipe the doily off, he got another big glob on it. "Forget it!" scolded Scarlett. "Before you frost the whole damn doily."

"Scarlett!"

"Sorry, Momma."

Billy quickly handed the pink doily with yellow highlights to Wilma Bell, a friend of Ollie's since childhood. Wilma fingered and studied it closely. "Why, Scarlett, I didn't know you were such a good crotcheter? You musta' spent the whole summer doing this."

Scarlett smiled and took a sip of punch as Wilma handed the doily on to Jasper. She was feeling inordinately grateful for thrift shops right now. That pink thing had only cost her two bits.

"You got dollies down pat," said Cecil. There was just enough skepticism in his voice to let Scarlett know he knew better. "When are you going to learn quilting?"

"Right after I learn the presidents," said Scarlett a bit sheepishly. "I'm taking a course next year that teaches you everything there is to know—from George Washington right on up to our own dear Lyndon Johnson."

Chapter

16

Thank heavens for the President's Course. Scarlett didn't have time to think about girls her junior year and had straight A's to prove it. She learned the presidents backwards and forwards, including their successes and their scandals. She even memorized the names of their wives, except for James Buchannan, of course. He never had one. He reportedly got along pretty well with "Miss Nancy" though (something the course didn't teach). "Miss Nancy" was the nickname for William Rufus Devane King, the vice president in the administration before Buchannan.

For good measure, Scarlett also learned the capitals of all the states, as well as their state birds and flowers. She read most of Shakespeare's plays and mastered the soliloquy from *Hamlet*, committing it to heart. Scarlett also went to a lot of movies her junior year. It was what she did for fun between all the studying and learning. Since she didn't have any money except her college fund, she got Skeeter to take her.

Scarlett had started seeing him again on the condition he drive her home after school every day, take her to the movies at least once a week, and not try and feel her up. If he did, she would tell the other girls in school about his "pecker disease." If he were really good, she might let him give her a three-second kiss once in a while. But that was it. She didn't want anything to do with that other stuff.

Skeeter agreed to the deal. It gave a guy status at Dillinger High to date a pretty girl, and Scarlett was one of the prettiest. Even if he couldn't "do it" to her anymore, all the guys would think he was. Sometimes when they went to the drive-in, Scarlett would let Skeeter play with himself. There were two strict conditions on this, however. Number one, he had to give her five bucks and number two, he had to put a towel on top of his pecker. She didn't want to see it, and she didn't want any stray squirt hitting her in the face while she was watching the movie.

Scarlett's college fund grew by leaps and bounds that year. Some people, had they known, might have accused her of being a bit like her Aunt Fannie. But Scarlett would have never admitted the comparison. Unlike Aunt Fannie, who used her body, she had only used her cunning and charm.

Chapter

17

Scarlett tried out for the school play her senior year and got the lead. The play was just one more distraction from all those Norma–June thoughts that sneaked up on her every now and then and got her thinking about girls. One week before the play was to open, the girl playing Mary Queen of Scots got sick. It looked like the production might have to be cancelled when a new girl at school said she would take the part. A girl called Gina Jamison.

Now Gina Jamison was what they called an army brat. Her dad had just been reassigned to the military base near Tullis City a few miles away. It must have been hard on her leaving wherever she was before, thought Scarlett, and coming to a new school just before graduation. But if she were sad or upset about the change, Gina never showed it.

The new girl learned her lines right away. Not that she had that many, mind you. Most of the time she was locked up in the Tower of London, wasting away, accused of treason. Since there was no money in the school budget to actually build a set for the Tower, the director improvised and had Gina speak her lines on a dark stage with a spot on her. It was effective. It showed off every curve Gina had.

As Scarlett sat in the auditorium watching Gina rehearse as Mary Queen of Scots, it dawned on her how attractive the new girl was.

She was tall but not too tall, with large blue eyes and long dark hair. Gina's pedal pushers fit her just a tad too tight, as did her white cotton blouse. She dressed like many of the other girls did at Dillinger High these days, the tighter the clothes the better. It guaranteed the boys' attention.

It finally occurred to Scarlett that was why all the boys were showing up at rehearsal. They were coming to look at Gina's body, every square inch of it they could ogle. Scarlett presently caught herself staring at Gina too. She could not believe the way the new girl's nipples stuck right through her thin cotton blouse, plain as day for the whole world to see. Gina wasn't the least self-conscious about her body. If anything, she was proud of it.

Over the next several days, Scarlett tried to keep her eyes off Gina but couldn't. The girl was an eye magnet. Then, much to Scarlett's delight, the two ended up in the same dressing room the play's opening night.

"Can you help me with this dress?" Gina asked. "The zipper's acting up."

"Sure," said Scarlett, swallowing hard. She went over to Gina and studied the zipper. "A little material's stuck in it." Scarlett nervously picked it out and zipped up her dress.

"That was fast," remarked Gina. "You're good with your hands."

"Not really," said Scarlett. "You should see the way I tie bows."

Gina laughed. "You probably don't care about tying bows."

"Well, I . . . I . . ." stammered Scarlett and then she stopped talking. For some reason her tongue wouldn't mind. She glanced at Gina and finally managed to finish her sentence. "I . . . I guess I never thought about it that way." Scarlett must have blushed because she felt her cheeks get warm. She quickly changed the subject. "What's that smell you have on?"

"Scent," Gina gently corrected. "White Shoulders. Do you like it?"

"Yes," said Scarlett. Anytime Gina had been near her the past week, that scent announced it. "I like it a lot."

"Then you can have some," said Gina. She took a small perfume bottle out of her purse and walked over to Scarlett.

"The secret," instructed Gina, "is to apply it right. Not on the clothes, where it picks up other odors, but directly on the skin."

Gina opened the bottle and put the perfume on her fingers. She rubbed some behind Scarlett's ears and then glazed her neck with a little more. Her touch was so soft, it gave Scarlett goose bumps. Gina felt the reaction beneath her fingertips and smiled.

"It makes you feel good, doesn't it?" she said, putting the cap back on the bottle.

Scarlett nodded. She didn't know what she was feeling, but she suspected it might not have a whole lot to do with perfume.

"What are you doing after the play?" asked Gina.

"I've got a date with Skeeter Boyd."

"The football player?"

"Yeah," answered Scarlett.

"Too bad," said Gina. "I thought it might be nice to take a drive. I've got my older sister's car tonight."

Scarlett liked this idea just fine. "Why don't I bring Skeeter?"

"No," said Gina. "Why don't you just tell him it's girls' night out? He'll understand."

Scarlett was momentarily at a loss for words. She finally managed, "Jeez. I don't know. What about the cast party?"

"We are the cast," said Gina, meeting her eyes. "Aren't we?"

"Yes," said Scarlett, shifting nervously from one leg to the other. She was on the verge of blushing again. "I'll tell Skeeter."

"Terrific," said Gina. "We girls have to stick together."

A knock came at the door and a voice said, "Okay, Scarlett, it's time. Get out here. You're on."

"Good luck," Gina told her.

Scarlett acted her heart out. Only once during the whole play did she falter and almost flub a line. It was when Mary Queen of Scots was supposed to give her cousin a farewell embrace before being locked up in the Tower of London. In truth, the two cousins never actually met. It was an artistic license thing. The playwright wanted to ratchet up the dramatic tension, so he put the two queens in the same room.

For some reason Gina decided to add a little tension of her own.

As she pulled back from Elizabeth's embrace, she brushed her lips up against her royal cousin's cheek. Being that the kiss wasn't in the play, it caught Scarlett off guard and she stepped away from Gina so fast she almost tripped. She felt that kiss like you were not supposed to feel one from a girl, and this one was only on the cheek.

A smile appeared on Gina's face, and she cued Scarlett with her next line. The audience had not noticed a thing. It just looked like it was all part of the play. Elizabeth, Queen of England, flinching in reaction to a kiss from her treasonous cousin, Mary, Queen of Scots. Both actresses got plenty of applause at the end of the play. Gina left the stage and let Scarlett take the final bows. When Scarlett got back to the dressing room, Gina was already in her street clothes.

"I'll go get the car and meet you in back."

Scarlett got undressed so fast, she practically shredded her costume. She broke the zipper and undid the pearl brocade on the front of the gown. "Shit!" exclaimed Scarlett as the pearls snapped loose and scattered like buckshot.

"Scarlett?" came a voice and a tap at the door.

"Yes?" answered a feverish Scarlett.

"It's your Momma, honey. Open the door."

"It's open," said Scarlett, pulling on her blue jeans.

The door opened and a proud and smiling Ollie Mae poked her head in.

"Be careful of the pearls," warned Scarlett, pointing down at the floor. "They popped off the gown."

Ollie Mae gingerly made her way toward Scarlett. "My goodness, Scarlett Faye. You was just beautiful as that there queen." Ollie came closer and inspected her daughter. "That makeup looks real good on you, honey. Everyone was sayin' what a beautiful girl you done turned into. You made me proud."

"Good, Momma."

"What's your hurry, honey? You're working up a real sweat," said Ollie, wiping her daughter's neck with a towel.

"Somebody's waiting for me."

"I know. That Skeeter Boyd's ravin' on about how beautiful you looked up there on that stage. He just can't wait to take you out for a vanilla Coke and show you off."

Scarlett had to think fast. "Look, Momma. Could you take Skeeter back to the house? Tell him I'll be there in a minute."

"But Scarlett, he wants to be with you, not with no old lady."

"Why, Momma. You're getting younger looking every day," Scarlett assured Ollie Mae as she took her hair down and brushed it out.

Ollie beamed. Scarlett had sure enough struck a positive chord with her. "Why, thank you, honey. I don't think you ever said that to me before."

"I know. Sometimes you'd swear I needed glasses," said Scarlett sweetly, smiling at her momma. "Now, please. Run along and get Skeeter. Tell him I've got a big surprise for him and I don't want him to open it in front of other people. That it's kind of a pre-graduation gift."

Ollie was very surprised at her daughter's sudden generosity. Half the time she couldn't stand the sight of Skeeter.

"I'll be home soon," said Scarlett, opening the door and showing her mother out into the hall. Actually, she sort of shoved her out. "Now go on, Momma. Get going."

Scarlett ran back and checked herself out in the mirror. For the first time in her life, she cared about the way she looked.

Chapter

18

G ina was waiting for Scarlett behind the high school auditorium in her sister's red Mustang convertible. Shiny new with white leather seats, it was the prettiest car Scarlett had ever seen.

"Well, come on. What are you waiting for? Let's go," said Gina. "Get in."

Scarlett got in and ran her hand over the leather seats. "Jeez. I've never been in a convertible before. It's beautiful."

"Yeah, I know. I wish it were mine."

"How come your sister's letting you use it?"

"She doesn't know. She's away for the weekend so I just borrowed it. I know where she keeps the extra keys. It's brand new, you know?"

"Yeah. I can tell," said Scarlett, still admiring everything about it, including the shiny chrome on the gearshift and steering wheel.

"Well, where should we go?" asked Gina, driving off down Main Street. "Before the boys spot us in this hot new car."

Just about the second that pronouncement left Gina's lips, Scarlett spotted Skeeter and his buddies in Buford Sales's 1955 Chevy Belair turning off Allegheny Street onto Main. Apparently, her mother either hadn't found him or hadn't talked him into going back to the house with her.

"Shit!" exclaimed Scarlett. "That's Skeeter Boyd in that Chevy."

"So?" said Gina.

"I didn't get a chance to call off our date."

"No problem," said Gina and floorboarded the Mustang, burning rubber all the way down Main Street.

Buford Sales's souped-up Chevy took off after them, but Gina managed to ditch Buford and the boys by driving down an alley. She pulled over and turned off the engine until the Chevy's lights flew past.

"Looks like the pussy posse's going in the wrong direction," said Gina.

They both laughed. It was sure enough true. That posse was headed for the city dump faster than the speed of light. If they didn't find the girls, at least they'd have a place to dump all those hormones.

"Maybe we should go down by the river," suggested Scarlett. "I know Buford doesn't like to get his car dirty."

"Neither does my sister. But we can always wash it afterwards. Right?"

"Right," said Scarlett. "I'll help you."

Gina started up the car and drove toward the river. It was a beautiful night. A breeze kicked up from the south, blowing a coolness across the countryside. It was the absolute perfect moment for a convertible ride down by the river. Magic rode the road and Gina was driving.

"Turn off at the next left," said Scarlett. "It'll take us down to a spot I know."

Gina slowed down and made the turn. The road was a little bumpy but not enough to discourage them from going to their decided destination.

"Remember this song?" asked Gina, reaching for the radio knob.

"Yeah. I remember," said Scarlett loudly. "Dream Lover."

Gina turned down the radio. "When it was popular, I had a big crush on Hans Van Prittwitz. Silly name, huh?" She paused and explained. "My dad was stationed in Germany then."

Scarlett and Gina got quiet and listened to the rest of the song. The grass was getting tall from its spring spurt and swayed gently in the wind on either side of the road.

"Over there," said Scarlett, pointing. "It's the old boathouse."

Gina pulled the car up behind the building and turned off the engine. "Okay. Now what?"

"Let's go out on the wharf," said Scarlett, sensing Gina's eyes on her. "You can feel the river breeze there."

The two new friends got out of the car and made their way to the wharf with the help of a small flashlight that was in the Mustang. They sat down and hung their legs over the edge. The breeze was blowing pretty good now and picking up more coolness off the river.

"Thanks for asking me along," said Scarlett. "I didn't really want to spend the evening with Skeeter."

"I know," said Gina, sliding out of her shoes and sticking her toes in the water. "Have you fucked him yet?"

Gina's abruptness stunned Scarlett. She was suddenly uncomfortable and didn't know what to do but look up at the moon. "Well?" prodded Gina.

"Well," stalled Scarlett. She wondered if she dared tell her new friend the truth. After a few more seconds of edgy silence, she decided she would. "Yes," she said. "A couple of times."

"Did you like it?"

"Not really. But a friend of mine told me that was because he wasn't the right one," said Scarlett. "What about you? Have you done it?"

"In Germany. Spain. Greece," said Gina with a twinkle in her eye. "Just about everywhere my dad was stationed the last four years."

"You started young," observed an amazed Scarlett.

"Yeah," mused Gina. "I guess I did."

With that they both fell silent and felt the night. Scarlett couldn't believe how comfortable she was with Gina. She barely knew her yet they were already sharing secrets.

"A friend of mine drowned in a river like this one," said Gina. "In Greece."

"Yeah?" said Scarlett. "I lost a couple of my friends that way too.

Right here, Norma and June. A freak current. They never found them. It was terrible."

"I'm sorry," commiserated Gina and patted Scarlett on the back.

The big old fib had just sort of tumbled out of Scarlett's mouth and now she didn't know how to tell Gina it wasn't so. She decided she'd better keep her mouth shut. If she told the truth now, it might sound like she had been poking fun at Gina's poor friend over there in Greece. To try and feel better about what she had said, Scarlett rationalized her behavior. After all, June and Norma were at the bottom of the Monongahela. There was no doubt about that. They were down there trapped between the pages of a thrift shop book. So what if she had left out a detail or two.

"No more drowning talk. Okay?" said Gina. "It'll just make us sad."

"Okay," said Scarlett, wondering who'd died in that faraway river. There had been pain in Gina's voice.

"How about a little pot?"

"A little what!" exclaimed Scarlett.

"You know, marijuana. I've got a joint in my purse." Gina took out a square, compact mirror and flicked it open. Inside was a row of hand-rolled marijuana cigarettes.

"I don't know," said Scarlett. "I hear that stuff makes you crazy. That it's just like smoking loco weed."

"Not true," Gina said softly, reassuringly, and lit one of the marijuana cigarettes with her lighter. She took a long, breathy drag on it and handed it to Scarlett.

"I don't smoke," said Scarlett.

"This is different. Just inhale it and hold it as long as you can."

Not wanting to displease her new friend, Scarlett took the joint and drew in the smoke. She immediately started coughing.

"No. Not like that," said Gina and took the cigarette back from Scarlett. She inhaled on the joint and leaned over to Scarlett who reflexively leaned back, away from her. "Well, come here. How am I going to blow smoke down your throat if you're way over there?"

Scarlett hesitated again and then obeyed. She leaned forward as Gina inhaled again.

"Open your mouth," said Gina, and she moved as close to Scarlett as one human being can come to another without kissing them and slowly blew the smoke into her mouth. "Hold it," she directed, "as long as you can."

Scarlett counted to ten and then she just had to exhale. The smoke tickled the back of her throat.

"Good," smiled Gina approvingly. "You'll feel that real soon."

It was true. In no time at all Scarlett felt herself relax and the world around her change. The river sounds became louder and richer, the rustle of reeds along the shore more rhythmic and musical. Even her skin felt different. She felt every pore open as a breeze blew across her body.

"How do you feel?" asked Gina.

"Good, I think," answered Scarlett.

"Well, let's see if we can take the doubt completely out of it."

Gina inhaled once again and blew her breath into Scarlett's mouth, brushing her lips ever so slightly up against Scarlett's as she did. Scarlett recoiled and felt herself begin to burn inside. Unsure of what to do, she turned away from Gina and looked up at the sky where the little sliver of a moon grew incandescent and the stars brilliant beyond bearing.

"How about another hit?" said Gina, holding up the joint. That twinkle was back in her eyes.

"Cool," said Scarlett, trying to calm down and control the fire.

Gina leaned over to Scarlett and then suddenly pulled back. "Whoops!" she giggled. "I almost forgot what I was going there for." She put the joint to her red lips and drew in the smoke.

"Maybe you were going to kiss me," said Scarlett with a boldness that surprised them both.

Gina smiled. "Maybe I was."

As she turned back toward Scarlett, the mood was suddenly broken by the insistent backfiring of a 1955 Chevrolet Belair. "Shit!" exclaimed Scarlett. "They're here. The boys found us."

Buford's Chevy bounced across the road and came to a stop alongside Gina's sister's red Mustang convertible. All the guys jumped out and admired the car and started commenting, like boys do, on such things as horsepower and all that cam stuff. Skeeter got to Gina and Scarlett first.

"What happened to you?" Skeeter asked Scarlett. "We had a date."

"Didn't Boonie tell you to meet us here?" Scarlett replied, making up a name to buy time. "He was supposed to."

"Who's Boonie?"

"You know, that sort of silly-looking new guy. The one who transferred to Dillinger High the same time Gina did."

Skeeter looked confused, trying as he was to remember somebody who didn't exist. Gina winked at Scarlett.

"Come on, big guy. Sit down and have a hit. There's one here just for you." Gina took a brand new cigarette out of her compact and handed it to Skeeter. He looked somewhere between dazed and delighted.

"I didn't know you smoked grass, Scarlett?"

"I bet you there's a few other things you don't know either," Gina laughed as she lit Skeeter a joint.

The rest of the boys finally came out on the wharf and saw the party in progress. "Hot damn!" yelled Buford. "I smell heaven."

Chapter
19

The last month at school was pure torture for Scarlett. She wasn't being very successful at getting Gina or that night at the boathouse off her mind. She could still feel Gina's lips brushing up against hers. In fact, she had begun fixating on Gina's mouth, wondering how a whole kiss would feel. But being sensible, as Scarlett most surely was, she knew she had to bring this new obsession to heel. There was too much at stake. Her straight-A grade average automatically made her the valedictorian speaker on graduation night. She hadn't even thought of a topic, much less written a speech and memorized it.

On top of all that she had been invited down to Charleston, West Virginia, for an interview at Claremont, the girl's college where she was in the running for a scholarship. She had to stop thinking about Gina. She was in the final lap of her race out of Dillinger and nothing must get in her way. Not even those wonderful red lips.

Every time Gina asked Scarlett to do something, even having a Coke, Scarlett said she couldn't. Scarlett finally explained that having to be valedictorian and say just the right thing to inspire people for a whole lifetime was a lot of pressure. She had to be alone and get her thoughts together. Gina acquiesed only after making Scarlett promise they would get together on graduation night, after Scarlett's big speech.

"We're not finished," Gina said, pressing up against Scarlett in the school hallway and whispering in her ear. "I still want that kiss."

Gina's words sent a shiver through Scarlett. As she pulled away from her, she saw a look in Gina's big blue eyes that she would never forget. It was a look she would later see in a lot of girls' eyes, a kind of a secret code between those who shared another language. A language Scarlett was about to learn.

Wanda volunteered to drive Scarlett down to Charleston for her interview with the scholarship committee. They could go and come back in a day. The principal of Dillinger High, Mr. Wainscot, let Scarlett take that Friday afternoon off because he knew how important receiving a scholarship was for her. It was the only way she could go to college. Scarlett was glad she had the chance to be with Wanda again. They hadn't been together in a long time.

"What are you going to call the baby?" asked Scarlett, noticing that Wanda was just beginning to show.

"Barbara Ann if it's a girl and Charles William if it's a boy." Wanda elaborated, "After Chuck."

"I bet he's beside himself, huh?" said Scarlett.

"Seems to be," said Wanda, looking at the scenery. "Isn't it just glorious the way the wildflowers bloom this time of year? All those splashes of color against the green."

"It's really pretty," confirmed Scarlett.

The two drove on in silence for a while, admiring the countryside and thinking their separate thoughts. Scarlett finally broke it. "Are you happy, Wanda?"

"Sure. I guess so," she answered. "Chuck's been watching his drinking."

"He still working?"

"Well," Wanda said, straightening up behind the wheel and looking hard at the road ahead. "He was until last week. He got laid off again."

"Over at Woody's Headstone Service?"

"Yeah," said Wanda, nodding.

They were always laying off Chuck Fowler. He couldn't keep a job to save his life. Scarlett was surprised he had kept the one sandblasting headstones as long as he had. Just a month ago she heard Chuck got so drunk he pulverized five or six grave markers to smithereens and Woody had to replace them. Chuck told his boss that "the damn things was so dirty I hadda blast the hell out of them to get the grime off." He said he couldn't help it if the shitty things kept falling apart.

"What are you going to do for money?" asked Scarlett.

"They're giving me my old job back at the feed store," said Wanda. "Until the baby comes."

"He should get another job," said Scarlett, barely able to hide her contempt for Wanda's husband.

"Oh, he will."

Scarlett noticed a big black-and-blue mark on Wanda's arm as she turned the steering wheel to round a bend in the road. "What's that big bruise under your arm, Wanda? He's been hitting you again, hasn't he?"

"Oh, no, Scarlett. That's from an accident. I tripped and fell up against a fence."

Scarlett didn't believe her, and Wanda knew she didn't. Wanda quickly changed the subject. "Now, what about you, young lady? Have you found the right person yet?"

"I dunno. Maybe."

"Really?" said Wanda, sounding surprised, and then she got a big grin on her face. "Have you kissed yet?"

"Almost," smiled Scarlett. "Almost."

"Good," said Wanda approvingly and patted Scarlett on the back. "Well, here we are," she announced, turning off the main street. "Your new home. It's pretty, isn't it?"

Scarlett surveyed the campus as Wanda drove up the cobblestone street to the administration building. "Yes," she answered, then took a deep breath and got out of the car. "I shouldn't be long."

"Good luck. Not that you'll need it."

"Thanks for the confidence."

Scarlett's interview with the scholarship committee went very well. They asked her lots of questions and she could tell they liked her answers. There were several occasions, however, when Scarlett thought it prudent to dress the truth up just a bit. Instead of telling the committee she wanted to be a writer so she could become rich and famous, she told them she planned to major in the classics and teach them at a fine school just like this one. The committee was charmed. Charm was easy for Scarlett. She could turn it on like a faucet and that day, of course, she had it on full blast.

When she was asked what she did in her spare time, Scarlett told them she read Homer, Virgil, Aeschylus and Plato, and in between reading the works of these wonderful classical authors and philosophers, she donated her time to various charities around her hometown. The whole committee smiled in unison, touched by this applicant's discipline, dedication and generosity.

The thing about the charity stuff wasn't exactly a lie. The thrift shop Scarlett liked so much was run by the Salvation Army. That meant all that money she spent on used books and odds and ends went for charitable causes like feeding the forlorn and saving sinners and such.

When Scarlett was finished with her interview, the committee all but assured her she had a place at their school on a full scholarship. They would be getting in touch with her by letter in a few days. Scarlett thanked them in her most gracious way and rode back home to Dillinger on cloud nine. Just before they got to town, Scarlett told Wanda, "I want you to call the sheriff if Chuck ever hits you again."

"Believe it or not, Scarlett, I did call once."

"And?"

"And Chuck told the sheriff I was all hopped up on pills. That I was out of my mind and didn't know which end was up. That it was really me who had hit him."

"You can't tell me Sheriff Pritchett believed him?"

"I don't know. But I guess maybe he did. Because after I went back in the house, Chuck stayed out shooting the breeze with him for a good piece and laughing about God knows what."

"Well, there's a new sheriff now."

"I know. Sheriff Beechum," said Wanda. "He's Chuck's cousin. They grew up together."

Scarlett could see it plainly enough now. Wanda was caught between a rock and a hard place, between a drunken, abusive husband and his cousin, Donny Beechum, the friendly neighborhood sheriff. "Don't let him hurt you again, Wanda," Scarlett begged her. "Don't. Go to Thelma's."

Wanda looked at Scarlett and tears suddenly welled up in her eyes, but she didn't say anything. She just looked back at the road, wiped her eyes and kept driving, driving back to Dillinger, driving back to a life she didn't want but didn't know how to leave.

Chapter

20

Scarlett had butterflies graduation night. She thought it was about the speech but it wasn't. She had that down pat. Her uneasiness was really about after commencement, about seeing Gina and that unnamable thing which drew them to each other.

Scarlett looked in the mirror and fiddled with the folds in her long black robe. She adjusted her mortarboard and decided the tassel looked better on the left side. She pinned it there just in case there was wind. She didn't want a bunch of purple strings flopping around in her face right in the middle of her speech.

"You ready, Momma?"

Ollie Mae scooted out of her bedroom dressed in a large yellow-print dress. Even though she had always been on the plump side, Ollie had an attractive face and beautiful hair. Of course, you'd never know it. Ever since Scarlett could remember, her mother hid her face behind glasses and knotted her hair up in a bun. It was like she was saying, "Please don't look at me. I ain't nothing." Joe Turner had done a real fine job on his wife before he died. It would be difficult for Ollie to ever have a shred of self-esteem again.

"You look real pretty, Momma."

"Do I really, honey?"

"Yes, you do. It's nice to see you without your glasses once in a while."

Ollie went over and gave her daughter a big hug. "I'm so proud of you," said Ollie. "I got me the smartest girl in Dillinger."

"Yeah? Then you forgive me for readin' all them books with no pictures in 'em and for not marrying Billy Ray?" kidded Scarlett.

Ollie laughed. "Oh, Lordy me. Yes!" she declared. "Them's a couple of times I'm glad you didn't pay me no never mind."

A long honk came from outside, once, then again, real insistent-like. "That's Etta now. Come on, Scarlett, it's time we get you graduated."

Etta's old Dodge crept toward Dillinger High, toward the end of a big part of Scarlett's life, toward the end of innocence.

Chapter
21

As Scarlett was finishing her speech, the wind picked up. She was glad she had tacked that purple tassel down. She could see it fluttering out of the corner of her eye right now. She could also see her mother and Etta Paine, their pride beaming like two beacons, lighting up the audience.

"So remember, Class of 1964, time waits for no man," Scarlett hesitated. Out of nowhere the English language's ridiculous he-centeredness suddenly struck her. Time didn't choose up sides. It didn't wait for one sex or the other. Scarlett quickly edited her speech and with her arms defiantly akimbo blurted out, "Or woman!"

A big round of applause accompanied the end of Scarlett's speech. She smiled and sat down. Although she had inspired her classmates, she knew it didn't much matter. Most of them would never leave Dillinger. It would be too hard for most of them to overcome their genes, and being that they were mostly from a long line of breeders, babies and back-breaking jobs would be what was in store for them. Their thoughts didn't travel beyond the county line.

Principal Wainscot took the podium to give out awards. When he announced Scarlett's scholarship to Claremont, she looked over at Gina. Gina smiled and winked. It didn't surprise her. Not one bit. Now all of Dillinger would know too. Scarlett Faye Turner was the smartest girl around and to prove it, she was getting out of town for good. Just like she always said she would.

Diplomas were then handed out to each of Dillinger High's fifty-five graduating seniors. After that, the high school chorus sang, "When the Sun Goes Down." That doleful tune would have made you think the Class of '64 was being executed, not graduated. The orchestra played "Pomp and Circumstance" and Dillinger's ex-seniors solemnly filed offstage. Everyone would have thrown their hats up in celebration, but old sourpuss Mrs. Sneddon with the whiskered cheeks was waiting to check in their hats and gowns. The Class of '65 had to use them next year. The Class of '64 only got to keep their purple tassels. As Scarlett pulled the gown over her head, she heard Gina's voice behind her.

"I've got my sister's car again."

Scarlett gave Mrs. Sneddon her gown and quickly turned around. Gina looked beautiful in her white cotton dress. Though it was the most modest thing Scarlett had ever seen on Gina, it still did not succeed in hiding the extraordinary body beneath.

"This time she let me borrow it," announced Gina, holding up a set of car keys. "Your speech was terrific. I liked it a lot."

"Hey, Scarlett," yelled Billy Ray across the room. "Skeeter's outside waiting for you. There's a big party over at Buford Sales's. Sally Sue and I are going."

"Tell Skeeter we'll meet him there," said Gina and turned to Scarlett. "Are you ready?"

Scarlett told Gina, "I'm not sure I know where Buford lives."

"It doesn't matter," said Gina. "That's not where we're going." She grabbed Scarlett by the hand. "Well, then, come on. We've got a party to go to."

"Whose?" asked Scarlett.

"Ours," said Gina, pulling Scarlett out the back door of Dillinger High, away from the known world.

Chapter

22

Seconds later the graduating girls were headed for the river in Gina's sister's red Mustang convertible. The night was just right. It was filled with a million stars, a big bright moon and the scent of White Shoulders.

"Where are we going?"

"A terrific place," said Gina. "I've already checked it out." She turned to Scarlett and smiled. "No boys."

Gina swung off the main road and drove to a small inlet on the Monongahela where she pulled the Mustang beneath a canopy of trees and switched off the motor. She looked over at Scarlett and smiled. "Well, come on, girl. We've got a party to attend." Gina got out of the car and handed Scarlett a picnic basket from the backseat.

"This is heavy," said Scarlett.

"I know. It's probably enough food for a week. I just wanted to make sure I brought something you liked."

"I'm easy."

"I hope so," said Gina, and she winked at Scarlett.

Scarlett didn't exactly know what to do or say. "It's a beautiful night, isn't it?"

"Yes, very. Come on," said Gina, walking around to the back of the car and opening the trunk. "I've got a surprise for you."

"Champagne!" exclaimed a delighted Scarlett upon seeing the bottle chilling in an ice bucket.

"Of course. We graduated, didn't we?" said Gina. "It's time to celebrate."

Scarlett smiled and tried to act sophisticated, but she figured Gina had already guessed the truth. She had never drunk alcohol before, much less champagne.

"You'll like this," said Gina. "I tried it the first time when I was fifteen, when my dad was stationed in France."

Scarlett and Gina made their way through the trees to the inlet. Gina put the champagne down and took the picnic basket from Scarlett. She took out a blanket and spread it out on the ground.

"Lets get this open," said Gina, picking up the bottle of champagne. "Here, I'll show you how."

Scarlett watched Gina as she unwound some chicken wire-looking stuff from around the top of the bottle. After that, she removed a crown of gold tinfoil and exposed the cork.

"This is the tricky part," explained Gina. "If you pop the cork too fast, the champagne will spew out. You have to do it very slowly." Gina put her hand over the top of the bottle and demonstrated. "Like this. Rotate the cork back and forth, gently, very gently, until you feel it pulsate beneath your hand." She smiled at Scarlett. "Then all you do is wait and let it come."

There was a hollow pop as the cork came out of the bottle. Gina hadn't spilled a drop. She retrieved two champagne glasses from the picnic basket, handed one to Scarlett and then filled each of their glasses. "A toast?" said Gina, touching her glass to Scarlett's. "To success and happiness and feeling good."

Scarlett had never made a toast before. Since she wasn't sure what she was supposed to say, she copied Gina. "Ditto," she agreed. "My thoughts exactly."

Gina smiled and raised the glass to her lips. Scarlett followed suit and quickly discovered how wonderful the taste of champagne was. She drank the whole glass and held it out for a refill.

"No," said Gina. "You're supposed to sip champagne, not guzzle it."

"Oh!" reacted Scarlett, surprised. She didn't know there was such a thing as "sipping etiquette." That certainly wasn't the way her daddy used to drink.

The two girls sat down on the blanket, and Gina turned on the radio to a station with soft music. She poured more champagne into Scarlett's glass. "Remember, now?"

"Yes," said Scarlett. "No guzzling."

They both laughed and fell silent, watching the river, sipping their champagne, feeling each other's joy, happy to be together on their graduation night. It wasn't long before the champagne worked its way to Scarlett's head and she began feeling good, unbelievably good. It was different from the time she had smoked marijuana. She wasn't concentrating so much on what was going on around her, on the river sounds, the wind and such. No. Tonight she was feeling her body, every sinew of it, every stirring, every heartbeat.

"I think I'll go for a swim," said Gina, and she started taking off her dress. "Come on. No one will see us."

In seconds Gina was undressed and in the water. "Scarlett? Don't you know how to swim?"

"Of course. It's just that I've never gotten naked in front of anyone before."

"What about when you did it with Skeeter?"

"We kept our clothes on," said Scarlett.

"Look. I'm not Skeeter, okay? I'm a girl," affirmed Gina, smiling back at Scarlett. "I didn't know you were so modest. I'll turn around."

When she did, Scarlet quickly pulled off her clothes and jumped into the water, bra and panties still on.

"See how nice it is," said Gina, swimming across the inlet. "It's a perfect night for a swim. The water's just right and look at that moon."

Scarlett followed Gina across the cove to a felled tree that had snagged up against the riverbank. "Have you ever noticed there's a rabbit in the moon?" said Scarlett, looking at the heavens. She was flat-out nervous and just couldn't think of anything to talk about except that stupid rabbit. "It was never a man. It was always a rabbit.

See on top of the moon up there," said Scarlett and she pointed, as if Gina could follow her finger direction in the air.

Gina looked up in search of what Scarlett was describing, more amused than curious.

"See? It's a rabbit!" confirmed Scarlett. "Well, actually, it looks more like a big hare, jumping down toward the bottom of the moon," she jabbered on. "See there. The long ears and feet. It's all there, all his body parts!"

"Yeah. I think I see what you mean," said Gina, wanting to laugh, but she knew she didn't dare. "In fact, I don't even have to look up. The moon's right here." She paused. "In your eyes." She moved closer to Scarlett. "Now let's see if that rabbit's where it's supposed to be."

Gina put her hand on Scarlett's shoulder and ran her finger under her bra strap. "I thought you were taking this off too? Here," she said, reaching behind her. "Why don't you let me help you?"

In two or three beats of Scarlett's racing heart, Gina unfastened her bra and slid it off. She was so close now that Scarlett could feel her breasts up against her own, and then she felt her entire body press into hers. At that precise instant every nerve ending in Scarlett's body came alive for the first time. Her skin became pure sensation.

"I'd like that kiss now," whispered Gina.

Gina put her mouth to Scarlett's and waited for her to yield. When she did, Gina kissed her gently at first, then passionately. Sensing the moment, Gina's hand slid down to Scarlett's panties and pulled them away from her body. "Help me," she said softly.

Scarlett hesitated, then slipped out of them. "Darn!" she exclaimed. "There they go. Floating down the river."

Gina smiled and caressed the inside of Scarlett's thigh, then moved up to her breasts. Scarlett trembled and closed her eyes as Gina pulled her to her once again, kissing her. Long, deep kisses. Fevered kisses. Kisses of longing and desire.

"Let's go back," Gina said, suddenly pulling away from Scarlett. "Now."

The two swam quickly back to shore and lay down on the blanket, breathless, their bodies still wet from the river and the sweltering humidity. They looked at each other and felt the energy between them build, then quicken and burn. The rush had begun even before they touched.

Gina teased the curve of Scarlett's breasts with her fingertips, stopping at the nipple, circling it and then taking it into her mouth. As her lips left one breast and went to the other, Gina's hand trailed down Scarlett's waist to the inside of her thigh and rested up against her wetness, at the softness between her legs.

"I love you," Gina said.

Then there were no words anymore, just the eloquence of their bodies expressing themselves as the passion that bound them grew until there was no place left for them to go. Except into each other. And they did, body and soul.

Chapter

23

When Scarlett learned Gina was leaving for Europe three days later, she was devastated. She had been so busy with her own plans, she hadn't stopped to consider the possibility that Gina might have any. While she was writing her valedictorian speech, Gina received the good news but hadn't told Scarlett. She had been accepted at a small but very exclusive fashion school in Paris.

Gina wanted to design "haute couture," high fashion. It was the first time Scarlett had heard that term for fancy dresses. Apparently, Gina wanted to be another Coco Chanel, a woman who made a lot of money dressing the rich and famous.

"How come you have to leave now?"

"Because summer school begins next week," answered Gina.

"Why didn't you tell me last night?"

"We were busy becoming lovers."

Between Gina packing her suitcases and Scarlett lying to her mother about why she was never home, especially that night after graduation, the two had been together every second, making love. The impending separation only intensified their feelings for each other, and they soon found themselves cut off from the rest of the world, sharing an intimate, unrepeatable experience they would never forget, not in a whole lifetime.

Scarlett and Gina spent their last night together at the old boathouse on the river. The radio they brought didn't work, but they didn't care. They danced anyway, for hours, to a musicless waltz. When desire came, and it came often, Scarlett and Gina made love. Each time it was different, with its own rhythm, its own surrender and giving.

"Do you think we'll ever see each other again?" asked Scarlett, feeling an awful anxiety in the pit of her stomach.

"Of course."

"You'll find someone else."

Gina stroked Scarlett's hair, gently pushing it away from her face. "What we had is ours. Nothing can change that. It will always be here and here," said Gina, touching her heart and head. "Forever."

Scarlett became as still as a stone, unable to speak. She didn't dare utter what she was feeling out loud because that might make it real and confirm the unthinkable—that she too had been infected with the dreaded love disease.

"It's okay, Scarlett. You don't have to say anything." Gina paused and looked at her in that unnerving way she had, the one that stripped Scarlett naked. "I know how you feel."

Gina took Scarlett in her arms and kissed her again, and then again. Long, intimate kisses. The kind of kisses that can bond two souls forever.

Chapter

24

Scarlett was depressed after Gina left. The withdrawal from the physical pleasure and the emotional joy of those three days was almost unbearable. If this wasn't pain she was feeling, it was most decidedly its first cousin. She felt terrible.

"What's gotcha moping around here with that long, hangdog face?" asked Ollie. "I never seen you so quiet."

"I miss my friend."

"Which one's that you're talkin' about?"

"Gina. The one who played Mary Queen of Scots. I told you already. She went to France."

"My, my. Lordy me. France!" Ollie had always thought Gina was a little "uppity."

Ollie heard the lid on the mailbox open and close. "That's the postman. Please, honey, go get it. I'm expectin' the Sears catalogue. I wanna buy me a new dress for the summer. Maybe a yeller one like I saw the other day with them big fancy clumps of grapes all over it."

Scarlett went out on the front porch to the mailbox. Sure enough, inside, along with the boarders' mail, was the Sears catalogue. But there were some other things too. A letter from New Mexico and a postcard from Gina with the Empire State Building on the front.

Scarlett's heart started racing. She sat down on the porch swing and read the card:

Dear Scarlett,
I'm writing you from the airport in New York City. The big silver bird will soon take me away, away from everything but the memories. I won't forget a minute of it, or you, ever. I promise.

Love,
Your Special Friend

The postcard had the scent of White Shoulders all over it. Scarlett put it to her nose and then pressed it up against her lips, aching, remembering Gina.

"Whatcha doin' rubbing the mail all over your face?" asked Ollie, peering out the screen door at Scarlett. "You got my catalogue there?"

"Yes, Momma. It's here. The yellow dress is on sale," said Scarlett. That would get Ollie's mind off her mail-smelling. She didn't want her to ask any questions about the postcard.

"Well, bring it here," said Ollie excitedly.

Scarlett went into the house and handed her mother the catalogue and the rest of the mail except, of course, the postcard and the letter from New Mexico. Ollie flipped through the fashion section.

"Where'd ya see it, Scarlett?" asked Ollie anxiously.

"In the middle there."

Ollie sat down and started going through the pages a bit more methodically. At one point she glanced up over her glasses. "What's that letter ya got there?"

"Something from New Mexico," answered Scarlett, tearing it open. "It's got to be from Twila. I don't know anyone else out there."

As Scarlett pulled the letter out of the envelope, a Greyhound bus ticket dropped on the floor. She picked it up and quickly read Twila's short message out loud so her mother could hear. She was going to ask anyway:

Dear Scarlett,
    Congratulations on graduating from high school and getting a scholarship. Billy Ray wrote me all about it and your speech. Inside is a round-trip ticket to visit me in New Mexico. Its your graduation gift for getting so smart. Let me know when you're coming.
                                        Affectionately,
                                        Twila Jeanette Wabash,
                                        Denizen of the Desert

Scarlett looked up at Ollie, and before she could say anything about how whacky Twila was and that going there would not be a good idea, she said, "I'm going, Momma." And then she added with a flourish, remembering how Twila had described the desert, "To see the earth's bare bones."

Ollie stared somberly at her daughter, getting more concerned by the second. "What's goin' on in that head of yours, Scarlett? You're gettin' me worried here. First, you spend three nights out nursin' a sick friend. Then you start rubbin' the mail on your face. And now you're talkin' crazy about visitin' the earth's bones like it was some big museum or somethin'!"

"Oh, Momma. I'm okay," said Scarlett reassuringly. "I'm just speaking metaphorically."

"You're what?" said Ollie, raising her voice, not so reassured. "What's that you're speakin'? You don't know no other language I know of 'cept English. Unlessing, of course, that uppity Gina girl taught you one before she left for France."

Little did Ollie know that not only had she hit the target with that observation, she had hit the bull's-eye.

Chapter

25

The Greyhound bus trip across the South to Texas took several days traveling day and night. The Texas panhandle was a bleak, flat place with ever-blowing wind, dust and tumbleweeds. Scarlett couldn't understand how human beings could live in such utter desolation. But they did. There was a whole bunch of them huddled together in a place called Amarillo.

The bus stopped there, and Scarlett got off for lunch. She ordered a Coke and a grilled cheese sandwich. As she waited for her food, she watched Amarillo. A few people dared the insufferable heat and dust to walk the sidewalk going to God knows where.

One man suddenly ran under the bus terminal's porch, his wild, tufty red hair blowing crazy in the wind. Scarlett craned her neck to see what was after him. A large dust devil was spinning toward the terminal picking up paper and small boxes and pelting any passers-by braving its proximity. Just as it was about to hit the terminal, the dust devil took an abrupt turn and headed back out toward the flatness, toward the edge of the earth, precisely where God had put Amarillo. At the edge of nowhere.

The grilled cheese sandwich was done to perfection. Each side was toasted just the right amount of brown, and it had lots of mayonnaise and American cheese on the inside. Scarlett squeezed one end of the sandwich and licked the cheese that oozed out.

Taking the trip had been a good idea. Scarlett knew she had to get away from the memories for a while. Every time she looked at the Monongahela she thought about Gina and it scared her. She knew that missing someone like that could break your heart in two, and there was plenty of evidence to prove it. All one had to do was look at poor Cecil when Lorraine left, or Wanda when Thelma went to Texas, or the saloon keeper in *The Ballad of The Sad Cafe* when the dwarf dumped her. Then there was her own mother's unending heartbreak when Joe Turner died. The devastation leavers left behind was enormous.

Twila had always said the desert could cure anyone of anything. Scarlett hoped that included the thing she didn't want to name. The thing that had sneaked into her heart and was tearing it apart with a feeling worse than the worst homesickness on earth.

Scarlett finished her Coke and sandwich and reboarded the bus. A crush of new people got on in Amarillo, trying to get away from the edge of the world. A woman, somewhere in her early twenties, asked several people if she could sit next to them and they all told her, "The seat's saved."

Scarlett pointed to the seat beside her, "This one's free."

"Thank you," said the woman, sitting down. "The name's Clotelle. Clotelle Carver."

"Please to meet you. Mine's Scarlett Faye Turner."

The people on the bus all turned around and looked at Scarlett like she was crazy. She knew the look. She had gotten it lots back home, every time she had a black friend. Judgment and disapproval were the two things Dillinger did best.

"I don't mean to be rude," Scarlett told the stranger, "but I'm exhausted." She put her head back and quickly dozed off to sleep.

Clotelle smiled and looked straight ahead at the road going to L.A. She was grateful to be leaving Texas. She was bound for a new life and the beginning of a dream. A small law school had accepted her and given her free tuition based on her grades at Waller College. The future was laid out. She would live with an elderly aunt and stretch out the thousand dollars her mother had left her as long as she could.

There wasn't much left of Clotelle's family now that her mother had died. Her father had disappeared long ago, abandoning his wife and children, and two of Clotelle's brothers had died since. One had been crushed in a tractor accident, and the other got a bullet in the head.

Clotelle and Ella Louise were now all that remained of the Carvers. Clotelle was proud of her older sister. She was the best second-grade teacher around. Clotelle would miss her terribly. Her eyes blurred with tears. She quickly told herself how much better life would be once she started lawyering. Then she would have enough money for her and her sister's dreams and maybe even justice for Augustus, the brother whose brains got spattered all over a back Texas road. Clotelle's thoughts suddenly shifted back to her traveling companion, who had started twitching and talking in her sleep.

"You okay?" Clotelle asked.

Scarlett opened her eyes, a little startled until she looked around and got her bearings.

"You were moving around and talking pretty good there."

Scarlett knew she talked in her sleep. She wondered what she had said this time. "Did I say anything interesting?"

"Could be. You were carrying on about this Gina girl."

"Yeah?" said Scarlett, a little surprised.

"Yeah," confirmed Clotelle.

"Anything understandable?"

"Yep," answered Clotelle. "You said you loved her."

Scarlett suddenly developed a severe case of indigestion. That grilled cheese sandwich felt like it was backing up into her throat. Her face flushed.

"Honey, you feel all right?" inquired Clotelle.

"No. I feel sick to my stomach."

"Here," said Clotelle popping the cap off a bottle of Coca-Cola. "This will settle it."

Scarlett took a big swallow of the Coke and wondered what else this woman had heard.

"Gina sounds like a pretty potent brew," observed Clotelle. "Want to talk about it?"

Scarlett felt her face getting warmer. She turned and looked out the window.

"Well, let me know if you do. My sister, Ella Louise, used to tell me about the Gina in her life. She just about drove poor Ella south sometimes."

Clotelle's disclosure flabbergasted Scarlett. She took another sip of Coke. It sounded like this woman was saying there were others out there besides her and Gina. Real live ones, not just book ones like the two at the bottom of the Monongahela River. Scarlett turned back from the window and looked at Clotelle, unable to conceal her astonishment any longer. "Your sister likes girls?"

"I think she prefers to call them women."

Scarlett felt a little silly about how she had blurted out the question. But the odds were, she would never see this stranger again. She was suddenly emboldened. "Do you mind if I ask you something else?"

"Go ahead," said Clotelle. "Shoot."

"Has your sister ever fallen in love with a girl . . . I mean . . ." Scarlett quickly corrected herself. "A woman?"

"Yes. Several times."

Scarlett looked back out the window. "I'm not going to love anyone," she announced defiantly. "I've seen what it can do to a person."

"Pain's part of the deal," said Clotelle. "No one gets away scot-free. Not from love anyway."

A long silence passed between the two. Clotelle finally broke it. "Sounds like you got a bad case of soul chiggers."

"What's that?" asked Scarlett, a little nervous.

"Mean suckers. The worst. They burrow into your soul until they get you crazy with self-doubt. Then, if you're not careful, you get left with nothing but a big old zero the wind blows through."

Scarlett didn't like this metaphor one bit. "So how do you get rid of them?"

"By paying attention to your heart," said Clotelle. "Because in matters of the heart, your head is not the answer."

Scarlett suddenly felt exposed, defenseless. She wanted to crawl into a hole and "bunker down" (that was what Twila called it) until she felt safe again.

"Enough of this talk. Here," offered Clotelle. "How about a Toll House cookie. Ella made a batch of them for the trip."

Scarlett took one. "Thank you, Clotelle."

"Clo. Call me Clo."

"Okay," said Scarlett and bit into the cookie. The chocolate melted in her mouth and momentarily soothed the soul chiggers as she looked out at an ever-widening landscape of sand and succulents.

The rest of the bus ride to Socorro, New Mexico, was filled with small talk and talk about each other's future plans. Clotelle told Scarlett about her family, her last boyfriend, her dreams, and her ambitions to become a lawyer. That was why she was going to Los Angeles, to study the law.

Scarlett was impressed. She shared a few things about herself too. Nothing too revealing, though; she wasn't about to be as open as Clotelle. She talked mostly about her school plans and how she was going to become a writer. The bus finally pulled into the depot at Socorro, and the two new friends got off.

"Here's where you can reach me this summer," said Scarlett, handing Clotelle a piece of paper. "After that you can write me in Dillinger or Charleston."

"This is my aunt's address in Los Angeles and her telephone number," said Clotelle.

The bus honked, and the other passengers started boarding. Scarlett and Clotelle gave each other a quick hug. Scarlett wondered if it were the sudden intimacy of strangers or the beginning of a real friendship.

"Friends then," said Scarlett.

"Friends," assured Clotelle.

The bus honked one last time and Clotelle got back on. She waved at Scarlett through the window, and Scarlett waved back until the bus disappeared down the lonely highway headed for California.

"Well, I'll be damned," said a gravelly voice. "Ain't you growed up!"

The voice was unmistakable. Scarlett swung around and gave Twila a big hug.

"Here, now. Let me look at ya'," said Twila, pulling back and appraising Scarlett. "I'll be. You done become a woman, Scarlett Faye."

Scarlett smiled. It was the first time anyone had called her a woman, and she liked it.

"Where's your suitcase?" asked Twila.

"Right over there," said Scarlett, nodding in the direction of the bus depot.

"Well, go get it and let's get going. Could be a storm's moving in."

Scarlett looked up. Clouds were gathering sure enough, and she heard distant thunder in the New Mexico sky.

Chapter

26

Twila's old wood-paneled station wagon with green chipped paint bounced up and down pretty good. Could have been the shocks that were doing it. Could have been the hardscrabble road they were on. It didn't much matter. Twila was just grateful the station wagon moved and took her where she wanted to go.

Scarlett looked out at the vast New Mexico desert west of Socorro. Twila was right about being able to see the earth's bare bones out here. She wondered what the spiny ridge off in the distance was called.

"Those are the Magdalenas," said Twila, reading her thoughts.

The afternoon sun broke through the clouds and shined down on the Magdalenas. The filtered light made the mountains look mysterious, even majestic, like a giant, medieval cathedral, suddenly displaced in time and space.

"Darn it!" exclaimed Twila. "Looks like that storm's gonna blow over without so much as a lightning strike."

Scarlett must have looked a little odd because it wasn't long before Twila offered an explanation.

"I chase lightning," she said. "Would you get me one of them Camel butts out of the ashtray, Scarlett? A good one, please."

Scarlett slid the ashtray open and poked around for a decent-sized butt. "Here," she said, handing one to Twila, who examined it and approved, then dragged a wooden match across the blistered wood on the dash. After several attempts the match caught fire and Twila lit her Camel, inhaling on it with great satisfaction.

"I love taking pictures of lightning," said Twila, exhaling a large cloud of smoke.

"Aren't you afraid it might kill you?" asked Scarlett, a little unnerved, remembering her daddy's cousin, Joe Bob, who got struck by lightning and died.

"I don't think about that. Besides, dying in the desert would suit me just fine. Next big storm I'll take you on a chase. Nothing in the world like it. Gets your blood moving."

Scarlett leaned back in her seat and mumbled an unconvincing, "Really."

Twila smiled and puffed on her cigarette stub. "You gotta tell me about your life, Scarlett. About what done made you look so womanly."

"That'll take a bit of talking," said Scarlett. She couldn't imagine telling her about Gina.

"That's fine with me," chirped Twila. "We got plenty of time between lightning strikes." She took one last drag off her cigarette and flicked it out the window.

Both women fell into a comfortable silence and peered off into the desert, lost in thought. The only sound for miles was Twila's old station wagon thumping up and down on a dirt road that seemed to lead nowhere.

"Well, here we are at last," Twila announced as she pulled up to a small adobe house the color of mud. "The old homestead. Welcome."

Scarlett was surprised not to see any junk around the house. In fact, Twila's yard was neat as a pin. Just a few beavertail and cholla cactuses decorated it. As dusk fell, Scarlett surveyed the great emptiness around her. To the west the Magdalenas were turning magenta. It was that time of day, Scarlett would learn, when ever-shifting colors, mostly pastels, swept over the desert and something ineffable visited the spirit.

"You like it?" asked Twila.

"Yes," said Scarlett. "It's just like you said. Bony and bare."

Twila laughed. "And filled with unimaginable magic."

They both watched a lone buzzard ride an air thermal upward and disappear into the clouds.

"Who's your neighbor?" asked Scarlett, pointing to the only other visible house a ways off in the distance.

"Margaret. Maggie. She paints. Does some sculpting too."

As Twila and Scarlett got out of the station wagon several cats came to greet them. Twila bent down and petted each one of them. "This one here's Geronimo. He's a tough puss. Survived a coyote attack." The huge yellow-striped tabby was missing an eye, now sewn shut, and part of an ear.

"Hello, Geronimo," greeted Scarlett, bending down to stroke the giant cat. He immediately took to her and pushed up against one knee so hard, Scarlett almost lost her balance.

"Meet Midnight," said Twila, introducing a feline that matched her name. Only a small white patch on the cat's forehead interrupted her velvety blackness. "This kitty's got a lot of soul. I think maybe she was a medicine woman in her last incarnation," laughed Twila. "I swear she can heal." A haughty tomcat strolled over to Twila and let her stroke him a few times. "And this is Luis."

"Why Luis?" asked Scarlett.

"You'll see. He prisses around here like some macho king of the desert. Had him fixed but he still tries to have at poor Midnight." Twila stood back up. "Well, come on. I'll show you your room and then we'll have us some supper."

Scarlett looked back in the direction of Maggie's house and picked up her suitcase. She had never met a sculptress before. "How old is Maggie?"

"Somewhere in her late twenties, early thirties maybe. Why?"

"Just curious," said Scarlett. "Don't she and her husband get lonely out here?"

"Who said she was married?"

"Oh," replied Scarlett. "Then she must really get lonesome."

Twila looked at Scarlett curiously. "Never said so."

Scarlett was mystified. It didn't make any sense for a young woman to live out in the middle of the desert with no one for company but the buzzards and the coyotes. As the two were about to enter Twila's little adobe, Scarlett noticed a sign above the doorway: *I entertain angels. Welcome.*

"Met any of those?" asked Scarlett with an amused smile.

"Nope," answered Twila. "But you never know. They don't always announce themselves."

Chapter

27

The inside of Twila's adobe was as neat as the outside. An amazing change had taken place in Twila. She had gone from a junk collector, the creator of the biggest eyesore on the Monongahela, to a meticulous housekeeper. Furthermore, her home was decorated in sparse but abiding good taste and captured the feeling of the desert she loved. Bright greens and reds emboldened the Indian patterns on her rugs and couch. Every piece of furniture, pottery vase and picture was exactly where the house invited it to be, in "its spot," as Twila pointed out.

As Scarlett's eye moved through the house, room by room, it was never stopped by an ungraceful line or an unwise choice in color or design. The high-beamed ceilings made the house appear larger than it really was and numerous arches gave it a simple elegance. Large windows were cut into every wall. Right now one of them framed a huge full moon rising over the desert. Scarlett went to the window and looked out at the emptiness. An emptiness which, according to Twila, was filled with magic and infinite possibilities.

"The desert is a place for change," Twila had told Scarlett, driving in from Socorro. "A place where you can find out who you are if you're willing to do the work."

Such notions didn't interest Scarlett. She was on vacation. Right now she just wanted to rest her head and heart, not invite in more confusion.

"I hope you like corn tortillas and refried beans," said Twila in a raised voice from the kitchen.

"Never had them," answered Scarlett, looking at Twila's lightning pictures.

"What about red chili peppers and cilantro?"

"Never had them either," said Scarlett. "Twila, your pictures are terrific. I didn't know you were such a good photographer."

"My last husband taught me. Dear old Gus," Twila reminisced. "As good a man who ever wore a two-bit pair of shoes."

Scarlett almost knocked over the cow's skull on a table in Twila's studio. She had never talked about being married. Scarlett picked up a picture of a beautiful redheaded woman with a big smile and green eyes. "Who's the woman in this picture here, the one next to the cow's skull?"

"That's Maggie Donovan. The one down the road," said Twila as she walked into the dining room with two plates of food. "Come on. Get out here, Scarlett, let's eat this before it gets cold."

Scarlett admired Maggie's picture a little longer before she joined Twila in the dining room. She sat down at the table and watched Twila slather some mashed-up brown beans on a flat round thing called a tortilla. Then she sprinkled shredded lettuce and tomato chunks on top of the beans. Next came the "picante," or hot sauce. Twila explained that it contained liberal doses of red peppers, cilantro and other spices. It could burn the very soul out of you.

"What's this?" asked Scarlett, picking up a bowl of awful-looking green sludge.

"Guacamole. Great stuff."

"What's in it?" It could be mashed up green snakes and toads for all Scarlett knew. She could never tell with Twila.

"Avocado with lemon, some garlic, and a sprinkling of red onions. Plop some on top of your beans and lettuce."

Scarlett did as Twila instructed and built herself a rather tortured-looking creation called a tostada.

"Go on. Try it," encouraged Twila. "I know it ain't much to look at but how it tastes is another matter altogether."

Scarlett screwed up her courage and took a bite.

"Well?" Twila wanted to know.

"It's great!" said Scarlett. She was definitely surprised. It was hard to believe the mess on her plate could taste that good.

"I thought you'd think so. Here," said Twila, handing her a glass of wine. "I know you ain't twenty-one yet, but . . ."

"It doesn't matter," said Scarlett, proudly interrupting Twila. "I've already had champagne."

"My, my! Ain't you the cat's meow," mused Twila as she poured Scarlett a glass of red wine. "You'll have to tell me about that."

Scarlett finished her tostada and made herself another one. Twila refilled her wineglass. It wasn't long before Scarlett was feeling full and content.

"You never told me you were married, Twila."

"Twice. First one very nearly killed me with a crystal candle holder." Twila lifted up the hair on one side of her head and showed Scarlett the physical evidence of that beating. The scar was so long and wide that Scarlett was surprised Twila had survived it.

"Why did he hit you?"

"Said I looked at another man. It wasn't true, but it didn't matter. He was going to teach me a lesson. If I hadn't managed to knock him out with the other candle holder, you and I probably wouldn't be sitting here talking right now."

"How did you get away from him?"

"I almost didn't. When he came to, he had me put in jail on attempted murder charges. Never mind that my own head was gashed and needed stitches. He told the law I whacked myself."

"Jeez!" exclaimed Scarlett. "How terrible!"

"I'd have stayed in jail and rotted if I hadn't threatened to expose his moonshining operation." Twila stopped and took a sip of wine. "He finally dropped the charges and I left town. He rigged a divorce. Never got a penny. Didn't want one. Not from that monster."

"What happened to him?"

"I heard tell somebody tied him up and stuck him in a moonshine vat. Died pickled in his own sin," said Twila with no apparent satisfaction in the deed and no malice. Her life had gone past that.

"What did you ever see in him, Twila?"

"Surfaces, Scarlett. Bright, shiny surfaces. He was good-looking, rich and charming. Exteriors like that can hide a bunch of meanness for a long time. It fooled me." Twila paused and got a far-off look in her eye. "Or maybe it didn't. Sometimes I think I just didn't want to see what was there. Money and appearances were very important to me then," said Twila, getting up. "Want to see a picture of my folly?" She pulled a picture out of a nearby drawer and handed it to Scarlett. "I keep it to remind me of how shallow I can be and how dangerous superficiality is."

Scarlett stared in amazement at the wedding photo of Twila and Desmond. Desmond was handsome, all right, but Twila Jeanette Wabash had been beautiful. "You were some looker, Twila."

"Yeah. I was," said Twila with no emotional investment in the statement. It was simply a fact.

"How does it feel to . . ." Scarlett didn't know how to put it. "To change?"

"To get older, you mean?" chuckled Twila. She lit up another Camel butt and inhaled with great enjoyment. "If exteriors are all that matter, then I imagine it can be rather frightening."

"I don't want to get old," said Scarlett.

Twila leaned back in her chair and took another long drag off her cigarette, then looked over at Scarlett. "Unless you plan to die young, my dear Scarlett, I'm afraid there's no way around it." She smiled and picked up the wine bottle. "Care for more?"

"No, thanks," answered Scarlett, looking disquieted.

Twila poured herself another glass and continued. "We're all headed down the same road. Some of us are just getting there a bit sooner than the others. Not by much, though, because, trust me, life whizzes by." Twila smiled again and mashed out the Camel. "Everyone's does. One day you look up and you realize your whole life is sneaking off on you, way down the road there."

Scarlett suddenly became uncomfortable. She didn't want to talk about wrinkles and old age, no matter what metaphor you used. She changed the subject. "Where'd you go to school, Twila?" During supper she had noticed Twila's speech change several times and stop being so folksy. It was something she'd always suspected, that underneath Twila's easy drawl might be an educated lady. "College, I mean?"

"You've got a good ear, Scarlett," said Twila, grinning. "I went to Sarah Lawrence." She paused and her eyes twinkled. "No doubt about it, I'm a Sadie Lu girl."

Scarlett was visibly stunned. She had heard about Twila's alma mater. It was up there with the best.

"Yep," Twila went on. "Parents had the money then. That was before the Depression."

"Then why do you sometimes talk like you do, especially the way you did back in Dillinger?"

"To put a distance between me and the life I left. I did the same with the way I looked. Wanted to roughen up the exterior so no man would ever be attracted to me again."

"Why?" asked Scarlett, both astonished and horrified. "Why bury your assets?" Hearing how that sounded, Scarlett revised the question. "I mean your gifts?"

"Foolishness. The desert is getting me over that," she said and looked out the window at the rising moon, then back at Scarlett. "Like so many women in my day, instead of forgiving myself when I made a mistake, I beat myself up. After my marriage to Desmond, I felt worthless. I blamed myself for his cruelty and punished myself by trying to destroy who I was." Twila paused and retrieved another Camel butt from a small tin box. She lit up and continued. "I almost did. Then I met Gus."

"The lightning chaser?"

"Right. Gus. Mr. Gus Van Sykes himself," said Twila, her eyes brightening. "He saw right through me. None of my defenses or disguises put him off." Twila fell silent, perhaps lost for a second in some far-off time. "You know what it's like, Scarlett, to have someone know your true worth? Really know it?"

Scarlett had decided years ago she didn't want anyone knowing her that well. She had spent her short lifetime building walls to keep people at a distance. Walls were all she knew. They were safe. She wasn't about to invite people behind them where they could hurt her.

"Gus knew who I was from the moment he met me. I never had to explain myself. He just knew." A loud miaow jarred Twila loose from her chair. "Oh, dear. I better let the cats in before a night prowler gets one of them. You have to be very careful out here in the desert."

Twila opened the front door and all three cats marched in and took over the house. Midnight jumped up on the sofa and started cleaning herself. Geronimo came over and rubbed up against Scarlett's leg. Luis stood at a bowl and demanded food. Twila gave him some tuna.

"Okay," said Twila, sitting back down. "Let's hear about you now, Scarlett."

"Oh, Twila," yawned Scarlett. "The bus ride and wine have knocked me plain senseless."

"Okay," said Twila. "You're off the hook until tomorrow."

"Before I go to bed, though, I have to know what happened to Gus."

"The lightning, honey. The lightning got him."

"I'm sorry," said Scarlett.

"Don't be. He died happy. Doing what he loved. Chasing the great, hypnotic flashes of wonder."

Scarlett thanked Twila for supper and went to her room. As tired as she was, she couldn't resist the magic of the desert moon. She turned off the lights and stared out at the emptiness it illuminated, thinking about Gina and that last full moon down by the Monongahela. The one they shared together. A century ago.

Chapter

28

Scarlett woke to low rumblings of thunder and a big fat cat lying next to her on his back. Geronimo had decided she was his. Scarlett petted him and affectionately tweaked his good ear. He purred with great contentment and stretched out. Scarlett found herself liking this cat and not liking that she did. Something about him reminded her of William.

Billy Cat, as Scarlett had nicknamed him, was a gray kitty with a big heart and bright yellow eyes. It had been a love affair. Nothing in the whole world mattered more than Billy Cat. He was Scarlett's pal, her best friend. He slept with her at night and amused her during the day. He followed her around just like a dog.

Maybe Billy Cat thought Scarlett was his momma. She had found him down by the river, all wet and shivering, no more than three weeks old. Maybe somebody had tried to drown him. Scarlett heard lots of people in Dillinger got rid of extra cats that way. The town was like that. It wasn't too nice to anything it didn't want, including people.

Scarlett fed Billy Cat with a doll's bottle and kept him warm with an old dish towel. They soon bonded and the attachment was fierce. Billy Cat was normally very well behaved, but one day he made the mistake of getting sick on her daddy's favorite faded old blue chair.

Exhausted after a four-day drunken tear, the last thing Joe Turner wanted to do was to plop himself down in the middle of cat puke.

"Sonovabitch! That's it! Where's that dumb piece-of-shit cat?"

Ollie Mae was down at the five-and-dime, and Scarlett didn't know Billy Cat had thrown up on her daddy's favorite chair.

"Billy Cat's in bed. He's sick," informed Scarlett, having no idea what kind of rage her father was working on when he suddenly stormed into her room and grabbed Billy Cat. She started screaming and yelling, "Billy's sick. Let him alone!"

Joe Turner shoved Scarlett out of his way and locked the door to her room. She heard her cat howl several times like he was real scared and then the front door slammed. Scarlett did her best to get the door open but couldn't, and then she tried the windows. They wouldn't open either. They were painted shut. Scarlett knew there was no way out. She finally gave up and sat down on her bed crying. Several seconds later, a single rifle shot rang out from down by the river.

"Come on, Scarlett Faye," yelled Twila. "Get up. Looks like a storm's rolling in. We got us some lightning to chase."

Scarlett rubbed Geronimo's tummy a couple of more times and told him, "Okay, big guy. Time to rise and shine. Miss Twila is hell-bent on taking pictures of the devil's pitchforks."

Geronimo didn't move. Scarlett finally climbed over him and threw on a shirt and a pair of jeans. She ran a brush through her hair and caught up with Twila as she finished loading the station wagon with cameras and a tripod.

"Need any help?" asked Scarlett.

"Nope. We're ready to go," said Twila, and she handed Scarlett a small brown paper bag. "Food. I don't want to hear any hunger complaints while I'm shootin' lightning."

Scarlett reached in the bag and pulled out two chocolate cupcakes with a white squiggly line running down the middle of them. She looked at Twila and smiled, "You didn't forget?"

"Of course not," answered Twila. "Now, come on. Hop in. We've got to get a lot closer to that storm."

Scarlett climbed in the old station wagon and Twila took off, kicking up the desert as she drove toward the storm. Dark, swirling clouds hid the Magdalenas, illuminated with increasing frequency by lightning flashes.

"This could be a humdinger," said Twila. "Lots of energy."

"Looks a little scary," said Scarlett.

"Only if a tornado comes spinning out," laughed Twila.

Scarlett was glad Twila hadn't lost her weird sense of humor. She broke open one of the chocolate cupcakes. She stuck her tongue into its puffy white center and went to heaven for a second.

"Holy Toledo!" exclaimed Twila. "Did you see that lightning strike?"

Scarlett looked up from her cupcake, then over at Twila. "No."

"Don't worry. There'll be plenty more," said Twila, pulling off the dirt road and hopping out of the station wagon. "This here will do just fine," she yelled. "Bring me my tripod, Scarlett. Please.

Scarlett put down the cupcake and got out of the car with the tripod. As Twila set it up, an ominous thunderbolt suddenly ripped open the sky. Scarlett's heart jumped. "Why do you chase lightning?" she asked Twila nervously, staring up at the darkening clouds.

"The same reason you do, Scarlett. Flirting with danger is exciting."

"What do you mean?" insisted Scarlett.

Twila finally looked up from her camera and smiled. "You know what I'm talking about, Scarlett. Your lightning just takes a different form, that's all. Hell, yours might even be more dangerous."

There were more lightning strikes now, followed by immense, reverberating thunderclaps. Scarlett ran and hopped into the station wagon. As she sat there pondering Twila's metaphor, the ferocity of the storm suddenly increased. She looked anxiously over at Twila.

"I need more film, Scarlett," Twila shouted, waving her hand at her. "Come on, bring it here. One more roll should do it."

Scarlett opened the cubbyhole and retrieved the film. "Here, catch," she yelled at Twila, pitching the roll at her friend's outstretched hands.

Twila caught the film and quickly reloaded the camera. The wind was howling and kicking up thick sheets of swirling dust. There was an ominous electricity in the air, and hardly a second went by without a thunderbolt crashing out of the sky.

If Scarlett had been inclined to prayer, she would have prayed. If the lightning didn't get them, one of those flash floods that come roaring out of nowhere might. It was storming up in the Magdalenas, and all the creeks and gullies led right down to them. She had heard people drowned in the desert all the time. Even in the Sahara.

The driver's-side door suddenly flew open, and for the first time today, Twila looked concerned. "Here," she said, shoving the camera and tripod at Scarlett as she jumped in and started up the engine.

As Twila turned the station wagon around, Scarlett saw the problem. A funnel-shaped cloud was tearing across the desert in their direction.

"Don't worry. We'll outrun it," said Twila, pushing the accelerator through the floorboard. "But keep an eye on it."

Scarlett's heart was suddenly up in her throat. The tornado ripped along at hellish speed, tearing up the desert, capriciously changing directions from one instant to the next, lifting up off the ground and coming back down again. And then, as fast as it had appeared, it disappeared.

"It's gone," said Scarlett in amazement.

The tornado had just sucked itself right back up into the clouds. The skies suddenly opened and let loose hailstones as big as golf balls. They thumped the top of the station wagon so hard, Scarlett was sure they were going to find their way inside any minute. But they didn't and the hail stopped as quickly as it had started. Next came the rain. Torrential sheets of rain, so heavy at times, you could barely see the road in front of your face. Twila pulled over.

"I guess we better stop before we run ourselves into a ditch or a wash full of water," said Twila. "When it lets up a bit, I'll introduce you to Maggie and we'll be on our way." She pointed just beyond to the vague outline of a house.

Five minutes later the rain let up and the sun broke through the clouds, dappling the desert with bright, shiny light. Scarlett looked over at the house again and saw a beautiful redheaded woman standing in the doorway.

Chapter
29

"Catch any lightning?" the woman wanted to know, a smile on her face as bright as the emerging sun.

"Five rolls," said Twila, hopping out of the wagon. "Some storm, huh?"

"Expressive," agreed Maggie. "Very expressive. You're lucky you stopped when you did. The wash is still churning."

Twila looked toward her house. A torrent of rainwater cascaded over a low place in the road, depositing bushes, stones and bones at high-water's edge. A roadrunner was suddenly thrown up out of the wash and plopped down on terra firma. As Twila and Maggie watched, the dazed roadrunner flapped his wings, picked a direction and ran off.

Twila chuckled and murmured, "You lucky bird, you."

"How about a cup a tea?" said Maggie. "It'll be a while before you can get across."

"Thanks. That'd suit me fine just now," answered Twila. She turned back to the station wagon and waved at Scarlett. "Well, come on. We've been invited for tea."

Scarlett didn't care much for tea. Coca-Cola was her drink, no matter what the weather, chilled and right out of the bottle. Today, however, she didn't think she'd mind drinking tea. She got out of the wagon and walked toward the two women.

"Maggie, this here is Scarlett Faye," said Twila, introducing Scarlett. "She's out here all the way from Pennsylvania to visit me. Done graduated high school with straight A's."

"Congratulations," said Maggie, extending her hand to Scarlett. "Welcome to the desert."

Maggie kept Scarlett's hand in hers until Scarlett got so nervous, she retrieved it. It was the way Maggie looked at her. Scarlett could have sworn the woman peeked right into her soul.

Maggie smiled. "I'm sorry. I didn't mean to make you uncomfortable. It's just that Twila and I don't have many visitors. It'll be nice to have a new face around here, Scarlett Faye." She paused and then added, "And a very pretty one."

"You can forget the Faye. I'm not using it anymore," said Scarlett, deciding right then and there that her second name had to go. For some reason, it had suddenly sounded too hokey, like she was a peasant or something.

"Of course, as you wish," said Maggie. "Well, ladies. Shall we?" She gestured toward the house.

Maggie's hands were very expressive and wonderfully graced, noticed Scarlett, as if the only friction they had ever known was the air. Scarlett smiled and followed the tall redhead into her house.

"Make yourself at home, Scarlett."

When Maggie and Twila disappeared into the kitchen, Scarlett looked around. Maggie's home was simple and uncluttered and had an immense feeling of peace. There were no hard edges, no ghosts, no grinding sorrows of days past hiding within its walls. It was a sanctuary.

Scarlett ran her hand over one of Maggie's paintings, feeling the colors that had caught the power of the desert and the New Mexico sky. Twila referred to it as the "moment of magenta," that instant just before the sun went down, when a dark rose flush spread over the Magdalenas and made them appear almost magical. It was eerie the way Maggie's brush had captured that light. Scarlett found the sculptures in the room were more down to earth. She ran her fingers over the breasts of a nude woman and wondered which Maggie preferred, the men or the women she sculpted.

Rachel York

Books filled two walls of the room, floor to ceiling. Everything imaginable sat on those shelves. History books, novels, biographies, art books, something on every topic. Those on religion and the soul outnumbered all the others and included exotic titles like *The Bhagavad Gita* and *Shambala*. There were books by Gurdjieff, books on Buddhism, on Sufism, on Hinduism. It went on and on. The Bible was there and books by the desert fathers and Thomas Merton, a monk, and by nuns, including a sixteenth-century one called St. Theresa of Avila.

Scarlett shuddered. She couldn't understand why anyone would want to read this whacky stuff, especially all by themselves way out here in the desert. She wondered if Maggie might not be a little like Kate Brummell, the Bible-banging, salvation hawker back in Dillinger. God was in every sentence Kate spoke and the promise of paradise in every breath.

"Contrition and repentance will take you there," Kate swore. "Just get down on your knees and pray."

Scarlett decided Maggie couldn't be like Kate. All one had to do was look at her bronze nudes. Maggie was a passionate woman. There was no doubt about that. She looked over at a picture of Maggie and several other women on a bleak plateau with a towering mountain range behind them. Next to them were several yaks loaded with bags and supplies. Written at the bottom of the picture was *Tibet, 1958*.

The next thing that caught Scarlett's eye was a painting of the desert sky at sunset shot through with the color of fire. A magnificent, unforgettable fire that burned open the clouds and shone down on the Magdalenas. Light and darkness, stillness and turmoil, all embracing the same space.

"You like it?" asked Maggie as she came in with a tray of cookies and a pot of tea. She set the tray down and walked over to Scarlett. "It's called 'Wild Serenity.'" It's how the sky looked that day or, at least, how it looked to me."

Maggie's nature seemed to be as oxymoronic as the sky in her painting. Somewhere in her there had to be a wildness every bit as passionate as the serenity she emanated. It was the duality equation, the combination of opposites, the juxtaposition of unimaginable contraries.

"What are you thinking, Scarlett? Something about the painting?"

"Yes," Scarlett smiled. "I was wondering what was going on in you when you painted it. It's so, so, I don't know. Untamed. Passionate, perhaps, is the word?" Scarlett paused and met Maggie's gaze. "But I suppose that's not possible, is it? To experience what you felt then? That same passion?"

"Why not?" was Maggie's simple response. "That's why I painted it. To try to communicate just that."

"Well, well. How about some tea, ladies?" announced Twila, pouring herself a cup. She sipped it and glanced back over at Scarlett, wondering what she was up to. "And some biscuits too, before they get cold. How about you, Scarlett? You're looking a little frayed."

Chapter

30

Twila pulled the station wagon up in front of her old adobe and got out. "How about giving me a hand with this stuff?"

"Sure," said Scarlett and the two unpacked Twila's photographic gear and took it into the house, setting it down next to Twila's makeshift darkroom.

"I need a cigarette," said Twila and she went over to a tin can with a bunch of butts in it.

"Aren't you going to develop your pictures?"

"No. Actually, I'm a little tired. I thought I'd sit out on the back porch and watch the mountains change color." Twila looked at her watch. "It's about that time."

"Mind if I join you?" said Scarlett.

"Come on," Twila said and put her arm around Scarlett.

The two went outside and sat in a couple of old red chairs that were not particularly comfortable and whose last coat of paint was blistering open, shedding flecks of vermilion. Twila lit up the cigarette butt.

"Look. It's starting." Twila puffed on her Camel and the two watched the Magdalenas slowly turn magenta in a silence as solemn and deep as a prayer.

"It's beautiful in a strange way," said Scarlett.

"Why strange?"

"I don't know. It's just different from a beautiful meadow or river or . . ."

"Or a beautiful woman?" finished Twila.

Scarlett looked at Twila, bemused and puzzled, wondering why she had finished her sentence like that. "Well, yes. I suppose," she finally answered.

"You can forget about Maggie," said Twila, exhaling a series of concentric smoke rings, each one fitting inside the other. "She's not into girls."

Scarlett emitted an inaudible gasp, amazed at Twila's intuition. She might as well have had a big red "L" stamped on the middle of her forehead.

"But then, she's not into boys either."

For an instant Scarlett felt relieved. Twila wasn't on to her after all. But she was wrong. Twila was just warming up.

"I saw the way you looked at Maggie this afternoon," said Twila. "It's a little like you used to look at Maybelle Lotty. Just with more knowing now, that's all."

Maybelle had been Scarlett's best friend the summer she graduated from eighth grade and just before she bought that thrift-store book about Norma and June's wonderful little adventure. Freckled-faced with long, brown hair and the sweetest smile, Maybelle had come to Dillinger that summer to visit her Aunt Maple Lotty. Since Maple lived right next door to Ollie Turner's boarding house, Scarlett and Maybelle saw a lot of each other. Bright as two pennies, the both of them, they shared a summer filled with books and stories and dreams and long afternoon walks down by the river.

What they talked about and what they did no doubt was innocent enough, but there was that way Scarlett looked at Maybelle, a look usually reserved for boys. Twila had had plenty of time to observe the two girls being that she was living at the boarding house at the time. It was right after her house by the river burned down and the insurance money hadn't come yet. Maybelle had supper at the boarding house almost every night that summer, every night Scarlett didn't eat over at her aunt's house.

"Well, what did you two girls do today?" asked Ollie Mae.

"We read poetry," said Maybelle.

Ollie's back stiffened. "Reading, always reading them books that don't have no pictures in them."

"What did you read?" asked Twila, finishing off a big ear of corn and helping herself to a second.

"Some stuff by Edna St. . . ." said Scarlett.

Before Scarlett could finish her sentence, Ollie jumped in exclaiming, "I didn't know Edna wrote no poetry!"

"Not Edna Ballou," replied Scarlett, exonerating one of Ollie's friends. "Edna St. Vincent Millay."

"Oh," said Ollie, relieved. She didn't know her.

"Which poem?" asked Twila.

"You've read her?" Scarlett was surprised.

"Every poem she ever wrote."

"We read each other lots of different poetry," gushed Maybelle. "Love poems mostly."

Maybelle smiled. Scarlett smiled. Twila smiled. Ollie frowned. "Don't nobody ever read no fairy tales anymore?" she asked. "Them ones with pictures?"

"Maybelle and I are too old for that."

Ollie looked down the table at Scarlett, then over at Maybelle. "Well, I'm guessin' ya are. What about the *Saturday Evening Post* then?" Not really expecting an answer, Ollie got up from her chair and told the dinner table, "We're having peach cobbler tonight. Nice and hot it is. Anyone don't want no ice cream on theirs?" No one declined so Ollie went to get the dessert.

"Oh, Scarlett. Peach cobbler's my favorite. Did you really make it for me?"

By now Ollie had disappeared into the kitchen, and since Cecil and the other boarders were away on vacation, only Twila saw Scarlett lie to Maybelle with several nods of her head and that big, winning smile of hers. Maybelle beamed. She had a crush on Scarlett and didn't even know it. Scarlett probably did, though, decided Twila, and the crush was mutual. You could tell by the way Scarlett looked at Maybelle. There was an intensity in that gaze of hers which, inevitably, would have its say-so. The only question in Twila's mind was when.

"Don't tell me you didn't know, Scarlett. You had Maybelle wrapped around your little finger."

"I knew she liked me. I liked her. Being with her felt good. But I didn't know exactly what that energy meant or what to do with it."

"You've found out since, though, haven't you?" declared Twila.

"Found out what?" countered Scarlett evasively.

"About chasing lightning."

Scarlett felt a big lump in her throat. There was no use trying to kid Twila. She'd get the truth out of her one way or another.

"Yes," answered Scarlett. "Just before I came to New Mexico."

"What's her name?"

"Gina," said Scarlett. Her voice quivered slightly.

"Want to tell me about her?" asked Twila. "I've got a feeling she was pretty special."

Chapter

31

"These are amazing shots," said Scarlett, looking at Twila's lightning pictures. "Even if we had to dodge lightning, a tornado, hail and a flash flood to get them."

Twila laughed. "But no brimstone. I guess we got lucky, huh?"

Scarlett laughed too and looked back down at her favorite photograph of simultaneous lighting strikes, each with multiple flashes radiating out, tree-like, into the stormy sky above the Magdalenas. "I bet Maggie would like to see these."

"You want to take them over?"

Scarlett was surprised and her face showed it. "By myself?"

"Why not? You might as well satisfy that curiosity of yours now so you can settle down and enjoy the rest of the summer."

Twila slid a set of photographs into a large manila envelope and handed it to Scarlett. "Tell Maggie hello and to pick one she likes."

"Okay," said Scarlett, delighted with her mission. "I'll tell her. See you."

Scarlett walked out the front door and down the road toward Maggie's. Twila watched her out of the window as she lit up a Camel. She wondered if Scarlett would ever learn to respect and accept the choices that ordered other people's lives.

Scarlett wiped the perspiration running down her face and started humming, switching from one melody to another, trying to take her mind off the heat. It was hot, unbearably hot, a day barely fit for the devil. As she got near Maggie's, Scarlett thought about what Twila told her the day before when she had asked, "If Maggie's not into boys or girls, what's she into?"

Twila's answer was strange, and Scarlett wasn't sure she even understood it. It was just too bizarre. "The Source," Twila had said. "God, Allah, Jehovah, whatever you want to call it, for Maggie it's all the same. The Source. That's what she's into and from where I sit, it looks like Maggie loves whatever that is as passionately as one human being might love another. Maybe more."

Scarlett, of course, thought this was a bunch of desert malarkey, real baked-brain stuff. It was beyond her comprehension that someone could love the clouds, the air, an unseen source as they might a lover. Since the spiritual side of her nature was still pretty much undeveloped, Scarlett had no idea how those things might have a rush all their own.

"Why, Scarlett," said Maggie, answering the door. "What a nice surprise."

"Hi. Twila sent me over with these." Scarlett handed Maggie the manila envelope. "The pictures she took yesterday. She said you should pick one."

"Wonderful. Please, come in."

The two walked inside Maggie's home and sat down in the living room. As Maggie pulled out the pictures and sifted through them, Scarlett studied her face. It was hard to tell how old Maggie was, in her late twenties, early thirties maybe. She looked the same today as she had in that picture taken in Tibet years before. In Maggie's face time stood still. There was a radiance, something changeless, something beyond physical beauty that never left her face.

"I like them all," Maggie said. "But I like this one especially."

"Me too," beamed Scarlett. "That's the one I picked."

"I guess we think a little alike, huh?" said Maggie, and she smiled at Scarlett, her eyes staying on her.

Scarlett shifted on the sofa. Maggie's look was making her nervous again.

"Forgive me," said Maggie. "I didn't mean to stare. I was just thinking how pretty you are. Maybe you could see your way to letting me sculpt you sometime?"

Scarlett was secretly delighted. "What would I have to do?" asked Scarlett, muting her enthusiasm.

"Pose for me," said Maggie and she told Scarlett as gently as possible, "Without your clothes."

"Well," said Scarlett with a deliberate tentativeness in her voice. She timed her pause to perfection and then said, "Okay. I think I could do that." She paused again. "When?"

"Now. If you feel comfortable enough?"

Scarlett's libido took off as she looked around Maggie's house and laid it on. "I'd love to be a part of your work," smiled Scarlett. "What do you want me to do?"

"Just get undressed. I'll do the rest."

Maggie's words alone gave Scarlett an incredible rush, intimate and direct as they were. Scarlett was convinced that voice of hers, ever so serene, covered up a passion deeper than the deep blue sea.

"There's a robe behind the dressing partition in the studio," said Maggie, standing up. "You can put it on after you undress."

"Okay," said Scarlett casually, careful not to betray her excitement.

"Let me know when you're ready."

Scarlett went into Maggie's studio and began taking her clothes off. As she hung them up, she looked at her nakedness in the mirror and smiled. Gina had taught her to like her body. She slid into the robe, then went over and stood below the tinted skylight in the ceiling. She let the muted light wash over her, knowing how well it would show off her body.

"I'm ready," said Scarlett.

Maggie came into the studio and immediately began loading a camera with film. After fussing with it for a minute, she went over to Scarlett. "You can take the robe off now. I need to get a light reading."

Scarlett took off the robe and put it on a nearby chair. Maggie held some kind of gauge with a flickering needle up next to her and made adjustments on its dial.

"Good," she said, seemingly pleased with the light, and then she told Scarlett, "I'm going to have to move you into place with my hands. Okay?"

"Sure," said Scarlett, waiting, as Maggie looked up at the light coming through the ceiling.

Finally, Maggie touched her. Her hands were so soft, so gently persuasive that goose pimples popped out all over Scarlett's body. "Are you cold?" asked Maggie, surprised at the reaction.

"No," said Scarlett and quickly dissimulated. "It's a family condition. Just happens sometimes." She didn't want Maggie to think she was so uncool.

"You sure you're okay?"

"Yes," answered Scarlett, determined not to blush. "It'll go away. You don't sculpt goose pimples, do you?"

"No." Maggie laughed, turning Scarlett into the light, positioning her to the side so her breasts were in semi-silhouette to the camera. "Hold it there," she said and went back to look in the lens. "Beautiful. The light is perfect," she informed Scarlett. "We should get some terrific shots."

"I thought you were going to do a sculpture of me?" asked Scarlett, a little surprised as Maggie adjusted the aperture and shutter on her camera and began taking pictures.

"I am, Scarlett. But I am going to make it from a photograph. I think you'd get a little tired posing for hours on end as I worked."

"No, I wouldn't."

"That's very sweet of you, but believe me, you would. You see, I like to work from a photograph because the pose is always the same," said Maggie, and she took several more pictures in rapid succession.

Scarlett wasn't too thrilled about Maggie's work technique. If she could get all the pictures she needed right now, she wouldn't get to take her clothes off again. Not much time to work her charm on Maggie.

"Scarlett, do you mind turning just a bit to your left now. I just need a couple of more shots."

Scarlett obeyed. "You really love your work, don't you?"

"Yes," answered Maggie. "I do."

"Twila says you also love the stars and the unseen, something about the source."

"Yes, Scarlett," said Maggie, looking up from her camera. "I love the stars and many things, seen and unseen." Maggie adjusted the aperture and took another picture.

"What are you really doing out here in the middle of the desert?" asked a suddenly emboldened Scarlett.

Maggie looked up from her camera. "This is where I feel rooted, Scarlett, where I'm able to breathe, where meaning happens for me." She paused and briefly glanced out the window. "Where I can be open to the mystery."

"Mystery?" exclaimed Scarlett. "What mystery?"

Maggie laughed. "I guess that sounded a little weird, huh?"

"Well," murmured Scarlett, and she softened her observation. "Maybe." She didn't want to insult Maggie.

"Then let's just say this is where I feel open to the bigger picture," explained Maggie. She smiled and unloaded the camera. "You've got a beautiful body, Scarlett. I'll enjoy sculpting it."

Scarlett had to bite her tongue in order not to smart-mouth Maggie and tell her what else she might enjoy doing with it.

"Okay, that's it. You can get dressed now," said Maggie. "And I'll make us a cup of tea."

"Shit!" Scarlett murmured under her breath. That wasn't exactly what she had in mind.

Chapter

32

"Great tea," said Scarlett, lying. Maggie didn't have any Coca-Cola.

"It's Twila's best work so far," said Maggie, looking down at the lightning photograph she had picked. "I guess you inspire her, Scarlett. Maybe you'll do the same for me."

"I hope so," said Scarlett, trying to drink that tea, looking at Maggie's lips, so full, so sensual, so unused.

"I got some close-ups of your hands," said Maggie, taking Scarlett's free hand, stroking it, studying it. "The light gave them just the definition I needed. It'll be easy to sculpt them later."

Scarlett felt that rush again and this time it was overpowering. She put down her cup and kissed Maggie full on the mouth. Maggie didn't flinch or pull away. She let Scarlett kiss her. Scarlett wanted more, but she pulled herself back. For some reason she instinctively knew this was as far as it would ever go. She looked at Maggie, who didn't seem in the least perturbed by the kiss. She was as calm as ever.

"I think maybe we should talk," she said, still holding Scarlett's hand. "Was there anything I did to make you feel I was available this way?"

"No," said Scarlett, wanting to feel those lips again. Everything she had imagined about Maggie was so. The energy, the serenity, the wildness, the passion, they were all there. She had experienced the boundless Maggie in a single kiss.

"Why did you let me do it? Did you hate it?"

"No, Scarlett. I didn't," said Maggie and smiled.

"Then you're not upset?"

"No," she answered.

"I'm very attracted to you," was Scarlett's declaration.

"Attractions have many different forms and not always this expression," Maggie said softly. She got up and went over to the window, where she looked out at the desert. "Just like love. There are other forms and other expressions."

Scarlett had hoped Maggie wasn't going off into voodoo land with that source stuff. She had heard enough of that talk. She was interested in the here and now, good-feeling stuff.

"You mean you don't do it!? You don't do it with anyone?" blurted out Scarlett, instantly regretting her crudeness.

"My passion has a different form. Believe me, I don't feel denied."

"You're referring to that source thing, aren't you?"

Maggie smiled, and in that smile was her answer. "Looks like we have company and no wonder," she said. "A storm is blowing up."

Just then Twila rapped on the door. "Open up in there," she yelled.

Maggie went over and opened the door.

"Well, let's go, girls," said Twila. There was a sudden flash of light in the sky. "Time to ride the body electric," she announced. "Well, come on, Scarlett. You're not looking too peppy. Got to get that blood moving."

Chapter

33

One monsoon (that was what they called those summer storms in Arizona and New Mexico) after another swept across the Magdalenas that summer, turning loose the surging desert stream and washing the sand and fossils clean. It was Twila's best summer for chasing lightning and a productive one for Maggie's sculpting.

"Do you like it, Scarlett?"

"Yes," said Scarlett, fibbing. She was still unable to see anything that looked like herself in the clay glob.

"It takes time," smiled Maggie. "Even though you might not see much progress right now, the work is going on." Maggie's hands expertly worked the clay, patiently molding Scarlett from the photograph she had taken. "Sometimes it's your last efforts that reveal the hidden form."

Scarlett stared at Maggie's work and wondered why her words always seemed to mean more than she said.

"You'll see what I mean before you go home."

"You promise?"

"Yes, Scarlett."

When Scarlett wasn't talking to Maggie or Twila, she was off reading poetry or writing letters to her mother and Clotelle and, of course, to Gina. She wrote how she was beginning to appreciate different kinds of beauty, like that of the desert, describing the sunset sky and the Magdalenas in endless detail. She told them about Maggie and Twila, what they did with their time and how, at the close of the day, they all came together for dinner and watched the sun go down, sometimes in silence, sometimes in discourse, but always in communion.

Gina wrote back saying it sounded like she had a crush on Maggie. Scarlett replied in a long missive that it was a spiritual connection. Somehow, that struck Gina as odd since this was the same woman who was sculpting Scarlett's naked body.

Clotelle wrote and told Scarlett it seemed like these two women, Twila and Maggie, were good for her. They apparently had a strong sense of themselves, following their hearts like they had out to the middle of the desert. "Now, that takes guts," she wrote. "Living smack-dab in the middle of nowhere."

A late monsoon lashed the desert the day Scarlett's summer vacation ended. As Twila stood at the window waiting for it to stop, she used both humor and metaphor to wax poetic. "The gods must be sad you're leaving, Scarlett. They're bawling their eyes out."

"Whole gullies, I'm sure," said Scarlett, laughing as she picked up Geronimo. "Trying to wash out the roads so they can keep me here and bake my brains a little more. Maybe they want me to suffer. What do you think, Geronimo?" She petted her one-eyed, earless tiger and kissed him on top of the head.

"I don't think so," said Twila after a long bit. "And I doubt Geronimo does either, no matter how tattered-looking the desert has left him." The mood in the room suddenly shifted. "Suffering out here is optional," she went on. "Inflicted not by the gods, but by ourselves when we ignore the language of the heart."

"What language? I don't know what you mean."

"Feelings, Scarlett. The words of the heart."

Scarlett didn't respond. It sounded like Twila had just issued a challenge. One she didn't even remotely want to contemplate.

"It's the language you need to learn if you're ever going to write," continued Twila. "Really write, I mean."

A steamroller might as well have rolled over Scarlett. In an instant, she felt flattened, her self-confidence shaken. She thought

Twila realized it was the words in her head that had gotten her out of Dillinger, not the ones in her heart. Words she would someday use to write her books. Scarlett shot Twila a defiant glance but kept quiet.

"The desert and the sky have been talking to you, that's for sure," said Twila. "I hope you listened." She paused and softened. "Just a little maybe?"

Talk interspersed with salt and sugar. Sugar and salt. It was Twila's way. She invariably made her point. Scarlett didn't say a word. She couldn't. She felt paralyzed, powerless against the anxiety washing over her. Huge, seismic waves of it. She put Geronimo down and, after a lull that seemed longer than life, she walked over to the window next to Twila and looked out at the desert. The rain had stopped.

"I'm going to miss you bunches," said Twila, putting her arm around Scarlett.

"Me too," replied Scarlett, her throat so constricted she could hardly talk. It was all those unsaid feelings stuck in there like a lump of oatmeal.

Maggie went with Twila to the bus station to see Scarlett off. The Greyhound was pulling up just as they arrived so they all rushed into the station to check Scarlett's bag and buy her ticket. When the good-bye moment finally came, Scarlett felt tears well up inside in spite of herself. Twila hugged her and said she could count on another trip to the desert when she graduated from college. Maggie hugged her as well and told her very softly, "I love you."

"I love you too," whispered Scarlett, disbelieving she had actually uttered those words the instant they left her mouth. But they had been uttered and they had been meant, meant in a way she did not quite understand yet.

"Take care and enjoy the journey," said Maggie. "Write us and try to remember, love is grace. It lightens the way."

Scarlett had no idea what Maggie was talking about. It sounded like that ethereal stuff again. Rather than respond, she just smiled at her and Twila and got on the bus. It soon pulled away from the depot, and she watched her two friends disappear out the window.

Twila, her eccentric, surrogate mother, and Maggie, in whose arms she would always feel safe. After a while, Scarlett sat back in her seat and composed a letter to Gina:

Dear Gina,

I'm on the bus leaving New Mexico. It's been a strange, awful, wonderful summer. I think I finally sort of like the desert but I'm not sure. It has a perverse way of making you open your eyes and teaching you what you don't want to learn. Maybe that's why Twila and Maggie call it beautiful, this vast stretch of sand and cactus, because of what it does to your heart. As we said good-bye at the bus station, Maggie said the oddest thing. She said love is grace. I'm not sure what she meant.

I don't know, Gina. I want to embrace this experience but somehow I feel wounded by it. Like it got too close to the quick of me. I wish life was as simple as Twila and Maggie say it can be. Perhaps it is, if you live in the desert. But I need the edge of life, the wildness of it to be creative. Like I told you, I'm going to become a writer and be rich and famous so nobody can push me around. Twila says what I want may not make me happy but I have to find out, don't I? Just like you do, Gina. We have to find out. We must move on toward the life in front of us.

The bus just made a detour onto a dirt road and I'm bumping up and down pretty good. I hope you can read the rest of this letter.

I guess what I'm trying to say is I feel like I'm hovering in a split between the worlds. Other times I feel like I'm on a hell-bound train and can't get off. Maybe it's that duel, the split—"the dark and light side of one's being," as Maggie calls it. I don't know. It's hard to explain. Maybe it has to do with having to live a secret life and hiding an essential part of yourself like it was dirt or something.

Maggie finished the sculpture of me. It looks like me, just like she said it would. It's a little odd though, living in bronze like that. "Forever young and beautiful," as Twila says. I don't know whether that's comforting or scary.

What a ramble this letter is, so uneven and confusing. I guess all I do know right now is the desert outside my window is powerful and even beautiful in its own way and that I start college next week. I think of you more than you can imagine. I miss you and dream of being in your arms once again, dancing on the edge of paradise.

Hopefully, destiny will someday oblige the dreamer and our lips will meet in something other than a dream.

Affectionately,
Scarlett

Scarlett simply could not use the word love yet, even after the lessons of the desert, not in the context of Gina. It was just too threatening. If she let her defenses down, those bogeymen might come and get her.

Chapter

34

Ollie Mae didn't look so good when she met Scarlett at the bus stop. Her face was drawn and tired looking. She might have been crying. At least that's what it looked like to Scarlett.

"Welcome back, honey," Ollie said, hugging her daughter. "I've missed you so much."

"How much, Momma?"

It was a game Scarlett and her mother had played for as long as either one of them could remember.

"A feeling the size of Texas," said Ollie. She pulled back and looked at Scarlett, then stretched her arms out to show the magnitude of her sentiment. She tried to smile but couldn't. She was holding back too many tears.

"What's wrong, Momma?"

"Please, baby. Can we sit down?"

"Sure," said Scarlett.

She took her mother's arm and guided her over to a bench. They sat down and Ollie's tears began to flow. She pulled a handkerchief from her purse and wiped at her face. Scarlett put her arm around her mother and tried to comfort her, dreading whatever it was that was causing all this pain.

"What is it, Momma?"

"It's Wanda," sobbed Ollie. "She's dead."

Scarlett's head suddenly tightened and she felt sick to her stomach. Nausea. The nausea of loss had come again. Like it always did, out of nowhere, when the heart could least make room for it.

"They found her last night down at the river," Ollie Mae went on, her voice breaking. "Drowned. Maybe killed. There's a lot of talk. Sheriff Beechum thinks it was suicide."

Donny Beechum was Chuck Fowler's cousin. What else was he going to say? Out in these parts blood was thicker than murder.

Everybody in Dillinger was shocked, of course. Speculation centered around the river transients who showed up every summer. Others thought it might be someone from shantytown. Remembering bad stuff lasted a long time in Dillinger. It hung on to the collective memory like stick fleas did on a dog.

Scarlett could barely make out her mother's words now, as punctuated by grief as they were. But even though Ollie couldn't piece together all the disparate information, Scarlett could. A slow rage began to build in her.

Wanda's body was found floating in the river around midnight, badly beaten and bruised, her wrists sliced open. As far as Sheriff Beechum was concerned, the cut wrists made it an open and closed case of suicide. He didn't care about any other theories. There were no other suspects.

Tears fell from Scarlett's eyes. Tears of sorrow. Tears of fury. She knew Wanda hadn't shredded her own wrists. Even if she had wanted to, she wouldn't have. Wanda loved that baby she was carrying too much. Becoming a mother meant everything to her. All Dillinger knew that.

"What about the baby?" asked Scarlett.

"Died with her." Ollie sobbed bitterly.

"Come on, Momma," said Scarlett, standing up. "Let's go home."

Chapter

35

Scarlett knew Chuck had killed Wanda. There was no doubt in her mind he had done it in a fit of rage. He had beaten her to death and then cut open her wrists to make it look like suicide. Only a fool could think she had done that to herself. But then, as Twila always said, the world was full of fools who want to believe lies and in Dillinger, there were a bunch of them.

Chuck would get away with it. Sheriff Beechum would see to that. Any trail leading to the real perpetrator, his cousin, would be covered up. It was an easy fix. The murder victim was a woman and it was small-town America on the early side of the sixties.

The coroner's inquest was a joke. Malcolm Dooley was verging on senility and he was a distant relative of Sheriff Beechum. His ruling was death by suicide. Lots of pictures of Wanda's wrists were produced showing the cuts on them. One wrist had been so vigorously slashed that it hung only by a thread of tissue to the rest of her arm. As anyone could see, the victim had died of massive blood loss.

There weren't too many pictures of how the rest of Wanda looked. Maybe one or two of the blackened eye, the swollen face, the busted lip, the bruises around her neck and the gash in her forehead. Even the funeral makeup couldn't cover all that up. The mortician did the best job he could, and though Wanda might not have looked as pretty as life had made her, she finally looked at peace. Death had resolved for her what living could not.

Scarlett and Ollie Mae sat near the rear of the church and waited for the ceremony to begin. Chuck Fowler was sitting up front. He turned and checked out the church. Bleary-eyed and tired, he looked like shit. He had been drinking and numbing himself out real good.

Right now Scarlett despised Chuck Fowler more than any human being on earth. She hoped the "hounds of hell," as her mother called them, would chase him into eternity or better yet, catch up with him in this lifetime and do what mad dogs do when they corner prey.

As Chuck was about to turn around and face the front of the church again, someone caught his eye. Scarlett craned her neck to see who it was. From what she could determine it was either the balding man on the aisle several rows back from Chuck or it was the woman sitting next to him. At the moment she couldn't see either of their faces.

The choir in the loft started singing one of those songs they sing when people die. This time it was "When the Roll Is Called Up Yonder." It was good the dead couldn't hear. When the hymn finished, Pastor Mabus came out and began eulogizing Wanda. The normal stuff. He said how terrible this tragedy was, taking Wanda like it did in her prime. Then he deplored the violence that claimed her and her baby's life. He exhorted her husband, Chuck Fowler, to be strong. That he must accept this as God's will.

Scarlett swore under her breath and looked around the church. She knew Wanda's death had nothing to do with God's will unless, of course, one considered Chuck's violent temper and murderous hands an expression of divine sentiment.

Scarlett couldn't cry. She was too mad. Now she knew for sure why God had given people assholes. That's how most of them behaved. For the time being her anger helped blot out all the sadness. It kept the past and its legacy of ungrieved losses safely at bay, behind that great wall she had erected.

The congregation of mourners stood up as Pastor Mabus gave the final benediction. When he finished, everyone started filing past Wanda to say their final good-byes. Scarlett watched the baldheaded man and the woman approach the casket. The man touched Wanda's forehead and left the church. Scarlett didn't know him. Then the woman suddenly leaned down. It looked like she might be kissing Wanda good-bye. When she turned to leave, Scarlett gasped. It was Thelma James.

Chapter
36

Nobody knew exactly how it happened, but the night of the same day Wanda was buried, Chuck Fowler lost both his hands. It was pretty bizarre, all right, severed clean off at the wrists. Those same two hands he used to beat his wife to death. It must have occurred right after the reception, after everyone went home. Chuck, of course, couldn't remember much except that the bald-headed man had been one of the last to leave. But who knew who left last? Chuck was so drunk, he almost died from alcohol poisoning and not from losing his hands.

No one had seen Thelma go into Chuck Fowler's house as it was getting on toward midnight. It was just about the time Chuck would have been hopelessly drunk and passed out on the couch. There weren't too many clues about what went on at that late hour. Just some dry ice near Chuck's dismembered hands and a blindfold over his eyes. Then there was that strange paralysis in Chuck's body that lasted for a better part of the following day. He couldn't even talk. The reaction was something like you see in people injected with curare, a drug used to induce temporary paralysis.

Since no tests were performed, the doctor put Chuck's condition down to shock. No one even thought to check his blood, which, of course, was good for Thelma. It might have pointed a finger in her direction. She had learned all about curare when she was a nurse in World War II.

In spite of everything, Chuck was lucky. The dry ice stanched the bleeding and help had been called in time. They said a woman with an unidentified voice telephoned the doctor that night and saved Chuck's life. An invisible Samaritan. How do you like that?

You might say Chuck was also lucky in another respect. Unlike Wanda, who must have felt her pain until the moment she expired, Chuck couldn't remember the pain of losing his hands. But hopefully, there was something Chuck Fowler would remember. He would look down at those stubs and remember the hands he used to have, the hands he used to murder Wanda, the hands he would never use to hurt anyone again.

Chapter
37

"I may not be as smart as you, Scarlett, but I do know hurtin' must be talked about," said Ollie, taking off her hat and setting it down. They were just home from the funeral.

"Oh, Momma, please. I can't. It hurts too much."

"That's right," said Ollie, taking Scarlett by the hand and leading her to the couch. "It hurts too much. So much so it can get in the way of feelin' other things. Like the memory of your father that got between me and my life, aggrievin' me so bad I never did get my heart back for no other man."

Scarlett was glad they sat down. She suddenly felt nauseated. In her eighteen years she had never heard her mother talk the way she had just now.

"Here," said Ollie Mae, picking a picture album up off the coffee table.

"I've seen that."

"Yeah," agreed Ollie. "We both seen it. Sorta. This time, though, we're really gonna look at it."

Ollie opened to a picture of Scarlett's father, that old drunken cuss, Joe Turner. "He wasn't so bad at one time, Scarlett. We was kids together, and he did real good by me as we growed up. Used to come help my momma with the crops after daddy died. Then I dunno, a bunch a misery got in his way and Joe begun a-changin'."

Ollie's voice quivered. "Then the bank took his family's farm away durin' the Depression and then his big brother, your Uncle Willy, was killed in the Pacific. His momma didn't do too good with losin' so much. Stuff she never talked about because she believed ya' kept a stiff upper lip about such things. Then after your Aunt Ethel got dragged to death by that horse, foot caught in the stirrup, she just went to pieces. Day came when they had to put her in a place for people with them head jim-jams."

"You mean an insane asylum?" asked Scarlett, astounded at this new piece of family history.

"Yeah. Only then they called them nuthouses and loony bins. Your daddy couldn't bear seeing his momma like that, shockin' her even more senseless with all them electric volts to the head."

"How come you never told me this?"

"Joe made me promise I wouldn't tell nobody, and he began sayin' his momma was dead. He was ashamed and I guess I got that way too. Silly, huh?"

Scarlett understood. Mental illness back then was unspeakable, still was, actually. It was something that didn't happen but if it did, the family covered it up as best they could. They didn't want the stigma attaching itself to anyone else in the family. People were afraid it might run in the blood.

"Anyhow," continued Ollie, "that's when your daddy began drinkin' and pretendin' your granny was dead, not just sick in the head which is what she was."

"What happened to her?" asked Scarlett, pursuing the skeleton.

"Died in that place, alone and who knows with what part of her mind left. I don't know, but I think they cut her brain so she wouldn't think no more. Last five years Joe never did visit her. Couldn't bear it."

"What couldn't he bear? The shame? The shame he made it."

Ollie didn't rise to Scarlett's challenge. She didn't have the energy. Besides, as far as Ollie was concerned, it was more than the shame of it that had kept Joe away. "No, Scarlett," she finally answered her. "I think it was the pain of it. Seeing his momma all mindless like that. He never did handle pain none too good." She paused. "A little like you."

Scarlett's body stiffened and her face flushed. "I'm nothing like him," said Scarlett, with a coldness that could have frozen water. "Nothing!"

Ollie began crying. "Oh, Scarlett, I did love your daddy. I did because I can still remember how Joe Turner once was, all them years ago." She blew her nose and the tears flowed. "Don't hate your daddy, Scarlett."

Scarlett choked up for a while and couldn't say anything. When she did, she lied, "I don't, Momma."

As far as Scarlett was concerned, Joe Turner belonged to that mean-minded, mean-spirited batch of people, daddy or not, that took up hurtful space in this world and the sooner gone, the better. She put her arm around her mother and together they wept. All that pain bottled up inside them demanded grieving so all those bad memories could be put to rest. The dead needed to die so the living could live again.

Chapter
38

"Somethin' came in the mail for you this morning," said Ollie, handing Scarlett a letter. "Must be from that Paris city 'cause the Eiffel Tower is right on this here postage stamp."

Scarlett's heart raced as she took the letter from her mother and put it in her purse. The last one she received from Gina was in New Mexico over a month ago.

"Aren't you goin' to read it?"

"Yes," said Scarlett. "On the way to Charleston."

"Then I guess we'd better go catch that bus," said Ollie Mae, and she looked at Scarlett with tears in her eyes. "See. I'm already gettin' heartsick knowing you'll be gone all the way to Christmas."

Scarlett hugged her mother. "I promise, I'll write every week. I'll be home again before you know it."

"Then let's get goin'. You know how I hate good-byes."

Scarlett picked up her suitcases. Etta was already honking outside, ready to drive them to the Greyhound bus station.

"Who's the letter from?" asked Ollie, opening the front door for Scarlett.

"A friend."

"Yeah?" intoned Ollie quizzically. "From that uppity Gina girl?"

"Good guess," said Scarlett, grinning at her mother's perpetual curiosity. Even though Ollie didn't know what it was yet, she instinctively divined there was something very different about this friend of Scarlett's.

Etta honked again.

"Hold your horses. We're comin'," said Ollie, closing the door.

As the Greyhound bus left Dillinger, Scarlett pulled out Gina's letter and hungrily read each word:

Dear Scarlett,

The summer term is over, thank God. It was rough. We had a week's vacation so several of us went to the Mediterranean and laid on the beaches without our tops just like Bridgette Bardot. The women here are exquisite and natural, so sensual. You would enjoy looking at them and feeling the wind and sun on your bare breasts. I do.

My French has gotten very good. If you were here, I'd show it off for you. Oh, Scarlett, I do wish you could come to Paris. All the bodies of all the women in the world don't mean as much as yours does to me because I know there's something special in yours, something I need and want.

Yes, I would love "to dance on the edge of paradise" with you. I dream too. Of everything. Of all that was. I desperately want to breathe you in again until we dissolve. We did, you know, that last night down at the river. We dissolved and went somewhere I had never been before and I know you went there too. It was a rare journey and I've got a feeling we won't be going there often, Scarlett, at least not with anyone but each other.

There must be a way for one of us to cross the ocean and hold each other. Maybe next summer? Excuse how this letter rambled but you're the writer, I'm not. Write me when you get to Charleston.

I love you,
Gina

There was a part of Scarlett that felt jealous about Gina looking at other women's breasts. It surprised Scarlett. Jealousy had been an alien feeling until Gina. The idea that she might sleep with one of those French women drove Scarlett crazy. She couldn't stand the thought of Gina being in someone else's arms. Scarlett used the jealousy to cover up her other feelings, the real ones, the ones she didn't want to think about, much less feel. The ones that Gina spoke so eloquently of, not in English or French, but with her heart.

Chapter
39

There was no way you could call Charleston, West Virginia, beautiful. Located in a dirty little fold in the Alleghenies, Charleston's petrochemical industry spewed out a stubborn brown haze that hung over the city much of the time. It was the price of doing business, and no one seemed to mind. Not in the mid-sixties anyway.

Ollie had given Scarlett money to take a taxi from the bus station to Claremont College, a small campus of eight or nine brick buildings at the edge of the city. As colleges go, it was pretty typical with just enough serious ivy climbing its buildings and strategically placed bronze plaques to look academic.

Brick walkways divided large areas of manicured grass bordered by rows of colored flowers and pigeon-spattered statues of Civil War heroes. The taxi slowed down, and Scarlett noticed several girls reading and sunning themselves on random benches around the campus. Claremont looked promising.

The taxi pulled up in front of the administration building and let Scarlett off. She paid the driver, tipping him the extra dollar her mother had provided for that purpose. He thanked Scarlett and wished her good luck.

"I hope to read a book of yours one day, Miss Turner."

"You will," answered Scarlett and smiled at him. "Sooner than you think."

Mrs. Buckley, a taciturn woman with a bun and a tired life some-where in its forties, matriculated Scarlett. She showed her a map of the campus, pointing to a small square on it. "Here's your dorm." Just as Scarlett took that in, Mrs. Buckley folded the map in half and handed it to her along with a schedule of classes. "You got all the classes you wanted, Miss Turner. Welcome to Claremont."

"Thank you," said Scarlett. Orientation was apparently over.

"I hope you enjoy all the wonderful young ladies here. They're your new sisters."

"I'm sure I will." Scarlett couldn't help but smile, tickled as she was at the idea of being around so many girls and by Mrs. Buckley's portrayal of them as sisters.

"What seems to be amusing you so, Miss Turner?"

"Oh!" said Scarlett, wiping the smile off her face. "It's not that I'm amused, Mrs. Buckley. I'm pleased. In fact, I'm just delighted to be in the company of so many young ladies. Sisters, as you call them. You see, I never had one."

It was a great save. Mrs. Buckley looked levelly at Scarlett and emitted a laconic, "I see."

Scarlett thanked Mrs. Buckley again and said, "I'm so happy to be here. I've got a great feeling about Claremont."

Scarlett picked up her bags and left the administration building, checking out the girls walking around campus as she glanced at her class schedule for the Fall Term. It was ambitious, all right. There was English Literature, Psychology 1A, Philosophy, Homer & Virgil: A Literary Analysis and Geology. Other than Homer & Virgil, all the other classes were mandatory, required for graduation.

Scarlett was glad she had arrived at school early. Since classes didn't begin for a couple of days, she would have a chance to get settled in before her roommate arrived. She walked to a dorm called Marsh Hall and up a short flight of stairs to Room 22. When she opened the door, she was surprised. Her roommate was already there.

"Hi, I'm Sissy Langtree," said a girl with long blond hair as she got up to greet Scarlett. "I'm early too. My parents dropped me off en route to Europe."

Scarlett smiled. Charleston might not be much to look at, but

Sissy Langtree sure was. Tall and pretty, she had a body that moved with extraordinary grace. Scarlett wondered who had taught her to walk—correction, glide—like that across the floor. Scarlett put down her suitcases and gave Sissy her hand. "I'm Scarlett Turner."

"Pleased to meet you, Scarlett. I already picked the bed I want. I hope that's not a problem with you."

"You were here first," said Scarlett, noticing an attitude in Sissy's voice. "You get first dibs."

"Good. I knew you would understand," said Sissy with just enough snootiness in her voice to irk Scarlett. "It would be terrible for us to have a problem right off. Wouldn't it?"

Scarlett decided she had to do something immediately, before this Southern belle-of-a-pain-in-the-ass's attitude got even more out of hand. "If you'll excuse me," announced Scarlett. "It was a long trip. I need to take a crap."

The well-timed irreverence worked. Sissy was horrified. Her jaw dropped. In less than a toilet flush, her pretentious sensibilities were mortally nicked. "It's over there," she said, the words stumbling out of her mouth in disbelief.

Scarlett went into the bathroom and closed the door. Several seconds later she yelled out, "What the hell's this cello doing in the bathtub?"

Chapter

40

Sissy was a music student and the only logical place for her cello, she later explained, was where it was because their dorm room was so small. They could trip over it and damage it and that would be unthinkable. Her cello was not only very expensive, it was irreplaceable.

"It's the counterpart of a Stradivarius," exaggerated Sissy in her most snippy fashion.

Scarlett agreed to the bathtub arrangement. Not because Sissy's cello was the questionable cousin of a fancy violin but because Scarlett did not want to fall over it and hurt herself. Thus it was, when Sissy wasn't practicing or one of them wasn't bathing, the cello was in the bathtub.

"Just make sure you air the bathroom out and get it real dry before you put the cello back in the bathtub," instructed Sissy. "I don't want my instrument getting warped. It would ruin it. Do you understand, Scarlett? Do I have your word on that?"

Sissy's sudden rushes of speech annoyed her. For the time being, however, it was easier to agree with her. But Scarlett swore the day would come when she would wrap Sissy Langtree around her little finger. It would just take a little strategy and a lot of patience.

"Yes, ma'am," said Scarlett, nodding her head. "My word, your highness. My sweetest word. I won't warp your cello."

Sissy, her hand on her hip, stared petulantly at Scarlett. She didn't like her sarcasm. "Where'd you get that mouth? Can't you be nice."

"Yes, and maybe someday I'll show you how nice I can be."

"You're impossible," said Sissy. In a huff she went and got the cello out of the bathtub and started practicing. Her irritation with Scarlett was growing.

An only child, Sissy was spoiled rotten, and on top of that, she suffered from a whole flock of affectations, the upper-class kind. At one point she told Scarlett fine rearing was "bred in the bone," pure and simple. Generations of money and Southern gentrification had made her special, and though Sissy didn't say it, she was sure her Southern breeding put her notches above everybody else, certainly above any Yankee.

"What's the name of that place where you were born again, Scarlett Faye?" asked Sissy. "You know, just north of the Mason-Dixon there?" She refused to remember "that trashy little Yankee river town" by name.

Sissy knew Scarlett wanted to pass for a Southerner more than anything in the world except for, perhaps, becoming a writer. In Scarlett's mind being identified as Southern would place her among a long list of elite authors from that part of the country—as if geography alone could infuse her with talent and give her literary credibility.

"Dillinger, and I told you not to call me Scarlett Faye."

Sissy's condescensions were getting to Scarlett. She decided she had to take this snooty piece of southernness down a peg or two. She started with guilt. "With all your airs, Sissy, you'd think you'd have a little more noblesse oblige. It's the duty of the rich, you know?"

"What is?" she asked.

"To take care of the poor. Where's your conscience, or did that get left out of the bone?"

Sissy suddenly looked flustered. She wondered if Scarlett was calling her fine Southern breeding into question. "It's my understanding noblesse oblige is European."

"Who told you that?" challenged Scarlett.

"My parents. They said here in the United States welfare takes care of that. It's the American version of noblesse oblige."

Scarlett howled. "I see. It's the government's duty to behave nobly toward others."

"Well, yes," said Sissy, a little thrown. "Why not?"

"Because there's the rub, my dear Sissy. The government is us, you and I. And since you've got the bucks, it's your blue-blooded duty to behave kindly and generously toward the less fortunate."

"And I suppose you know just how I should do that, Miss Smarty Pants?"

"You could spring for a dinner once in a while. That'd be a good start. After all, I couldn't count the times you've told me how unfortunate I am." Scarlett imitated Sissy to perfection. "'Oh, poor Scarlett, it's just amazing. What's the name of that trashy little town you're from again? How ever did you get out of there? On a mule?'"

Sissy winced. Scarlett had mocked her right down to her self-righteous core. Sissy got up and walked out of the room. After that, Miss Langtree was somewhat more pleasant and a little more down to earth. She even bought Scarlett dinner once in a while at little restaurants off campus.

Being that guilt had worked so well on Miss Langtree, Scarlett implemented the second part of her plan, switching on the charm. She stopped playing "I Can't Get No Satisfaction" at full volume because she knew Sissy hated the Rolling Stones and its rubber-lipped crooner, Mick Jagger. "I know it bothers you, so I just decided not to play it anymore," Scarlett explained.

Sissy was dumbfounded. She had asked Scarlett a hundred times to do what she had just voluntarily done, and done with a smile. But that wasn't the only surprise in store. While Sissy may have hated the Stones, Scarlett knew she adored the Beatles, "those sexy boys with the mops on their heads." Since "Yesterday" was her favorite song, Scarlett bought Sissy the single. She left the 45 record on her desk along with some flowers.

"Scarlett, did you leave these flowers here?"

Scarlett had purchased two vases at Charleston's thrift shop, one for Sissy's desk and one for hers (she didn't want to look too obvious) and filled them with flowers she had picked from all over campus. "Yes. Pretty, aren't they? There's nothing like them to brighten one's day and heart."

"Why, thank you," said Sissy haltingly, still not quite believing Scarlett had it in her to be so nice. "And my favorite Beatles song." She clutched the 45 to her bosom and swooned.

"Enjoy," said Scarlett, flashing her most winning smile.

A week later Sissy found a poem from Scarlett on top of her cello in the bathtub. It described how Sissy's music had inspired her to write poetry. Next to the poem was a thank-you note in which Scarlett offered her most saccharine gratitude.

"Why, Scarlett. I didn't know you wrote poems. This is just wonderful."

"I told you I was going to be a writer."

"Yes. But I didn't know it included poetry," said Sissy, and she read the poem and the thank-you note again. "This is just so unimaginably sweet of you."

Scarlett smiled. Deep down, she had actually begun to develop a certain affection for Sissy. She admired her passion for music and for making that cello sing. Other than her musical talent, Sissy was blessed with other gifts too. She had brains, beauty and bucks, and flawless, straight white teeth, qualities decidedly hard to ignore.

Scarlett even found herself able to overlook some of Sissy's more galling affectations after she met her parents at a school function. It was then Scarlett finally realized why her roommate was the way she was. Mr. and Mrs. Langtree were the embodiment of effete Southern snobbery. If they could have lengthened their noses to have more to look down when they met Scarlett, they would have. At that moment Scarlett wished her mother was there too. The Langtrees would have gotten whiplash after meeting Ollie Mae Turner, their attitude being what it was toward folks not of their kith or kin.

"Pleased to meet you," said Scarlett. She tried hard to ignore the Langtree airs, the studied indifference, their high-horsiness, but she couldn't. They were barely acknowledging her presence, and it was pissing her off.

"I see Mr. Neeps over there," said Mrs. Langtree, a stiff octave above her normal register. "Come, Sissy. I must say hello and get a report."

With a haughty toss of her head and with no good-bye to Scarlett, Mrs. Langtree grabbed her daughter's hand and walked off. They were headed in the direction of Bertrand Neeps, the world-renowned cello player, Sissy's teacher.

While they were gone, Scarlett took the opportunity to size up Mr. Langtree. In his late forties, he was in good shape, tanned, with a certain physical attractiveness about him. He might have even been a little sexy if he weren't so uptight about being short. Since he apparently didn't want to make conversation with her, Scarlett decided to make it with him.

"I understand you doubled your family's already sizeable fortune in oil and munitions, Mr. Langtree." Scarlett took a bite of her cookie and continued, not caring whether she had crumbs stuck in her teeth or not. Sissy's father was an asshole. "Your daughter brags on you a lot."

Mr. Langtree gave Scarlett a what-the-hell-do-you-know look. He didn't answer and instead glanced around the room. It looked as if he might be checking out the girls. His wife and daughter were now clear on the other side of the student union talking to Mr. Neeps.

"It takes a smart man to do that."

Now Mr. Langtree gave Scarlett his what-the-hell-business-is-it-of-yours-anyway look. This time, however, he deigned a response. "It certainly does."

He sipped at his punch and once more looked away from Scarlett, galled that Claremont had roomed his precious daughter with poor white trash. He would speak to the dean about this. Not that it would help. Claremont had a long tradition of independence. Funded years before by a wealthy suffragette, the college was immune to money and power plays. Roommate assignments were rigorously planned.

Lanie Lockmoor, the suffragette who founded Claremont, believed girls should be exposed to others of different interests and social backgrounds so they could learn to get along. Women must learn not to put each other down, but to bond. Ergo, Sissy and Scarlett as roommates. By the lights of the college founder, there were things they could learn from each other.

Scarlett went on. "Owning most of the oil refineries in Charleston. Now that's something, Mr. Langtree."

"It's also something that's none of your business, Miss Turner," he let her know, and looked away for a third time.

Scarlett ignored his grandiosity. "I know it isn't, and neither is your munitions business and all those guns you run to Cuba."

All of a sudden Mr. Langtree looked apoplectic, as if he might stroke out. He glared at Scarlett and demanded in a very low voice, "Who told you that?"

It must have been something Sissy had said at one time that suddenly inspired Scarlett to put two and two together and infer what she just did about Mr. Langtree's business empire. The gun actions he secretly ran out of Spain into Cuba.

"No one," said Scarlett. "But it looks like it was a very good guess."

Astounded, Mr. Langtree's face flushed and he put his punch down. A smart-aleck eighteen-year old had just cat-and-moused him into a tacit admission of his darkest business secret.

"Don't worry. I won't tell anyone. Sissy is my best friend. I wouldn't want anyone to know her daddy's a crook."

Now speechless, Mr. Langtree stared at Scarlett, his eyes narrowing by the second.

"Besides," Scarlett continued. "Who would believe me anyway? I'm just a kid and I'm not even a business major. So I would say you really don't have anything to worry about."

"Oh, you would, would you?"

"Yes, I would," said Scarlett and she defiantly met his gaze. "Try and be nice, Mr. Langtree, and stop your better-than-thou crap because it's irking me to the very marrow of my little white-trashy bones." She paused and added, "It could give me a nasty resentment."

Mr. Langtree's mouth twitched. He felt as if he had just been broadsided by a 16-wheeler disguised as a Nash Rambler.

"Looks like you and Daddy got acquainted," said Sissy, walking up and putting her arm through Mr. Langtree's. "I could see you two just jabbering away from across the room over there."

"You've got a great daddy," said Scarlett, smiling. "He's so smart. Now I know where you got your brains, Sissy." She smiled again, this time at Mr. Langtree, with just a lingering touch of that defiance.

"Excuse me, girls," said Mr. Langtree and patted Sissy on the shoulder. "I think I'll join your mother and say hello to Mr. Neeps."

"A pleasure meeting you, Mr. Langtree," said Scarlett.

Mr. Langtree hesitated and then forced the words out of his mouth. "A pleasure it is."

Scarlett grinned from ear to ear as Sissy's daddy walked away from his little girl, away from trouble he couldn't even imagine yet.

Chapter

41

Sissy Langtree was at Claremont instead of Julliard or the music conservatory in Paris because of Bertrand Neeps, reputedly one of the best cello teachers in the world. Why Mr. Neeps was at Claremont and not elsewhere, at some prestigious music academy or such, had to do with one of those quirks of fate that gets played on people from time to time, plopping them down in places like Amarillo, Texas; Wedowee, Alabama; Pocatello, Idaho; or Charleston, West Virginia. Sometimes for a week, sometimes for a lifetime.

In Bertrand's case it had to do with Lawrence Evermore, who once taught theater at Claremont. Being that their friendship was rather intense at one time, Bertrand joined the faculty and they continued to relate, intensely, for many years. But then Lawrence, or Larry, turned out to be not so "evermore" and he left Bertrand for a math teacher in Iowa. Bertrand stayed on at Claremont because of loyalty to his students and in hopes Larry would tire of Iowa and come back. He never did.

By now, pupils where coming from all over the world to study with Bertrand Neeps in Charleston. To help repair his heart and soul Bertrand started giving concerts again. When his fingers were on those cello strings, all memories of the faithless Lawrence Evermore went away. Music grounded his being. Bertrand's concerts became famous and began drawing devotees from everywhere. After his appearance at the White House, Pablo Consuelo even came to Charleston for one of Bertrand Neeps's concerts and they ended up playing a duet together. It put the little city on the map.

Now in his early fifties, Bertrand was endearing. Apart from being a brilliant teacher and cello player, he was a caring and sensitive man. His only fault, if one might be so hard-hearted as to call it one, was that he cried a lot. In fact, he cried at just about everything.

The evening he played the duet with Pablo Consuelo, tears ran down his face the whole time. It had simply overwhelmed Bertrand that the world's greatest cello player would honor him in such a way. People talked about that duet for years afterward. The two had made beautiful music together, and though no one would ever forget Pablo Consuelo playing his cello in Charleston, neither would anyone forget the tears of joy rolling down Bertrand Neeps's face. Apparently, most of the audience ended up bawling too. That's how much emotion those two sets of cello strings produced that magic night in Charleston, West Virginia.

Many times when Sissy played for Bertrand, he would start crying. She would stop and he would inevitably rehearse the same sentiments. Music was sacred, he always told her. It was the voice of the muses, how we knew other dimensions existed. It was just like Leonardo da Vinci once said, "Music is the shape and the form of the invisible."

"Music can save your soul," Bertrand said to Sissy over and over again, perhaps reassuring himself that it could.

Mr. Neeps's sudden soliloquies puzzled Sissy, but she always listened with great attention, waiting for him to finish and return to the lesson.

"Now, Sissy. Sustain that last note you played until you're breathing with it," instructed Bertrand, as if the digression had never happened. "Be one with it. A single vital force."

Sissy drew her bow across the strings and played the note, sustaining it, becoming one with it.

"Oh, yes," swooned Mr. Neeps. "That's it, Sissy. That's perfect."

Sissy was Bertrand Neeps's most promising student ever. He

wanted to pass his gifts on to her. If that could happen by osmosis and desire alone, he would infuse his musical soul into her. And perhaps he did. Years later when she played Europe's top concert halls, you could hear Bertrand in Sissy's cello.

Bertrand never said what he was crying about, but Scarlett imagined it had a lot to do with Larry. If Sissy had realized her dear Bertrand was homosexual early on, she might have been scandalized. By the time she found out, however, scandal was no longer an issue. She had just been in one of her own.

Inspired by the story of Bertrand's duet with Pablo Consuelo, Sissy practiced harder than ever. Her unselfconscious devotion to her music was as attractive to Scarlett as her passion for it. Then there was the way Sissy straddled her cello that Scarlett couldn't help noticing. Since the weather was still warm, Sissy wore a light robe when she practiced, a decidedly sheer one. Silhouetted against the sunlight, her naked body moved in perfect rhythm to the music she was playing.

Scarlett didn't bother to leave the room anymore when Sissy practiced. Listening to her and looking at her made the study of geology a whole lot easier. It softened her resistance to learning the names of all those rocks and how time and the earth had made them. One day, as Sissy was playing her favorite cello sonata, Scarlett recognized something in her geology book she had seen in New Mexico. "Jesus! There's a hoodoo in here!"

"A what-do?" said Sissy, putting down her bow.

"A hoodoo," answered Scarlett, and she took the book over to Sissy. "I can't believe it." She showed her the picture. "See."

Sissy looked at the strange-looking rock formation. It was tall and skinny, pointing straight up at the sky, a pinnacle of sculptured stone.

"The water shapes it," explained Scarlett. "Moisture gets between the cracks in the rocks and freezes, contracting then expanding endlessly over millions of years." Scarlett paused in amazement. "I saw lots of hoodoos in New Mexico last summer, but I never knew how they were made or that they even had a name. Aren't they fantastic?"

"I guess so," said Sissy softly, and she rubbed her neck, not quite sharing Scarlett's enthusiasm for hoodoos.

"Of course they are," declared Scarlett. "Nature sculpted those rocks. Here, just look at this one, Sissy. It could be the profile of a human being. George Washington maybe. The pigtail and the nose, the forehead. And this one." Scarlett studied the hoodoo more closely. "Why, this one looks like a cello!"

Sissy glanced down at the picture and smiled. "You're right. I guess it does." She rubbed her neck again and then turned it from side to side.

"Your neck's sore, huh?" asked Scarlett.

"Yeah, and my shoulders too."

"It's all the practicing. Maybe you should rest a minute and let me give you a massage."

"Oh, how sweet of you, Scarlett. You'd do that for me?"

"Yes," said Scarlett. "I think I can put aside geology for a minute to help my roommate feel better. Besides, there's only so much you can learn about hoodoos."

Sissy laughed and pulled her robe back from her shoulders, exposing the outline of her breasts. It was remarkable, Sissy's geology.

"What are you waiting for?"

"I'm warming up my hands," bluffed Scarlett and she rubbed them together. "Just for you."

"Well, hurry up," ordered Sissy. "I need to finish practicing."

Scarlett began massaging Sissy's neck and shoulders with soft, gentle, circular motions, just like Gina had taught her. Sissy closed her eyes and began to relax.

"You're so good at this, Scarlett. Who taught you?"

"Instinct," said Scarlett. She wasn't about to tell Sissy about the real teacher. "I just do to you what I think would feel good to me."

All of a sudden Sissy got goose bumps. Scarlett grinned. Her roommate had just taken the first unconscious step toward pleasure of another kind.

Chapter

42

Scarlett's poem writing became prolific those first few months at Claremont. Many were for Gina, some were for Sissy, a few were interchangeable. After all, neither of them would ever know a certain poem hadn't been written just for her and it would make them both happy to think it had. There was one poem, however, written for Gina alone. It had come unbidden, from somewhere deep within Scarlett. She didn't know what to call it and assumed its source must be geology, teasing her imagination as that subject did with all those vast, imponderable spans of time.

Though the poem's real meaning eluded Scarlett for many years, it didn't Gina. She knew its source wasn't geology. It was love. She kept it in her wallet and read it every day until there were no days left.

> *Arching across time*
> *A dream that keeps repeating.*
> *How long does this feeling endure?*
> *A minute*
> *Or*
> *A million light years?*
> *Or, perhaps,*

Eternity . . . ?
Does the soul keep time?

After Gina received Scarlett's poem, she immediately wrote her back:

Dear Scarlett,
    I love your poem. It's true. Real feelings don't erase. It's like you say, they go on like a constantly repeating dream. Maybe forever. At least I think so, and somewhere you do too or you couldn't have made up those words. I ache for you. I need your touch. I want to feel it everywhere on me while I tell you how much I love you. What about you, Scarlett? Will you ever tell me?
    I'm in the middle of exams again. I have to cut patterns for the dresses I've designed and talk about fabrics in my orals. I hope I do okay. I've been a little distracted by my new roommate, Henri. I decided to move off campus so I'd have more freedom. Henri is studying fashion too. He's lots of fun and helps pay the rent. Please keep writing poems for me.

I love you, the forever kind,
Gina

"Who's the letter from, Scarlett? You look a little upset."

Scarlett's face was flushed. She didn't understand why Gina was living with a man. On second thought, she guessed that was better than her living with a woman.

"Oh, someone I was in a play with my senior year. A friend of hers drowned in Greece." Scarlett didn't want to talk to Sissy about Gina.

"She lives in Greece? She's Greek then?"

"No. Her friend was. She lives in Paris."

"She's French?"

"No," said Scarlett, irritation coming into her voice.

"What is she then?"

"She's American," answered Scarlett, a tad testier.

"What's the matter with you? It was her friend who drowned. Not yours."

Scarlett apologized but shied away from talking about Gina or her feelings. "I'm sorry, Sissy. It must be the pressure of my midterms. They're all bunched up together next week." She paused, still upset. "Maybe I've been writing too much poetry. I'm getting a stomachache."

"Now, now," said Sissy. "No tummyaches." She got up and went into the bathroom to put her cello away. "I'll tell you what. How about a movie? My treat. It'll relax you," she said, coming out of the bathroom.

Scarlett looked at the books piled on her bed and then down at the letter. "Maybe you're right. I need to get out."

"Good. *A Summer Place* is playing. It's an old movie but who cares? I never saw it. Did you?"

"No."

"It's with Troy Donahue. You know, the real cute, sexy blond guy? Wouldn't you just love to squeeze him?"

Chapter

43

Troy Donahue was cute and so was Sandra Dee, but Scarlett wouldn't want to squeeze either one of them. Bee-stung lips or not, Sandra was about as sexy as a loaf of white bread and Donahue wasn't much better. In the movie they get marooned in a lighthouse with nothing but their desire to keep them warm. It worked. They smothered each other with kisses and quivered and moaned until they reached that most coveted of all paradises, the forbidden, carnal one.

Though the movie didn't do anything for Scarlett, it did a lot for Sissy. She was wriggling around in her seat so much, she made it squeak. Donahue was steaming her up. Scarlett suddenly remembered the old movie house gambit she had read about in that thrift shop book years before and decided to put it to use. She began inching her way toward Sissy. At first, Sissy and she shared an armrest, then they shared the sides of each other's legs.

Sissy was so engrossed in Troy and Sandra that she didn't notice how close Scarlett was to her. When she finally realized it, she almost flew out of her chair. Then, as if to compensate, Sissy leaned her body in the opposite direction, as far away from Scarlett as she could get.

Scarlett pretended she hadn't noticed Sissy's sudden erotic epiphany. Several minutes passed and Sissy settled back down. When she did, Scarlett could feel Sissy's body heat radiating out hotter than a fired pistol. Her ardor for Troy, it seemed, had shifted to her. How conscious that was, Scarlett didn't know. But she intended to find out. The screen went black and the lights came on.

"Well, how did you like the movie?" asked Scarlett.

"I . . . I did," Sissy stammered. She looked confused. Something was out of kilter, and she couldn't seem to put words to it. Not yet anyway.

Sissy's nervous tension was still palpable when they got back to the room. She immediately took out her cello and started playing Dvorak's "Cello Concerto in B Minor." She played it with a passion Scarlett had never heard. She was surprised the cello didn't start smoking. After several minutes, Sissy stopped as unexpectedly as she had begun.

"That was terrific," said Scarlett, applauding. "It's the best you've ever played it. Why don't you finish?"

Sissy put the bow down. "I can't. My neck hurts." She rubbed it and looked over at Scarlett. "Would you? Please?"

"Of course," said Scarlett, inwardly delighted. "For my talented roommate, anything. You have to keep those shoulders and neck in good condition." Scarlett went over and began massaging her. She could feel Sissy begin to yield to her touch. "I can do this a lot better if you stretch out on the floor." Scarlett wanted to say bed but she decided she'd better not. Not at this point anyway.

"The floor?"

"Yes. I'll put a blanket and towel down. That way I can massage you with oil. It'll take the soreness right out."

Scarlett quickly put down a blanket and got a large towel from the bathroom. She spread it out on the blanket and motioned for Sissy to lie down.

"Try and relax," she told Sissy as she retrieved a bottle of perfumed oil from a nearby drawer. She had bought it at a local thrift shop in hopes of just such an occasion. It had never been opened, not until now. Scarlett warmed the oil in her hands and smoothed it over Sissy's neck.

"Where'd you get that, Scarlett? It smells delicious."

Scarlett fibbed. "I can't remember. I've had it awhile. It's wonderful, isn't it?"

"Yes," said Sissy, sighing.

Scarlett gently worked the oil up and down her roommate's neck, but instead of relaxing, Sissy seemed to get tenser. Her body was talking, speaking volumes, and though Sissy didn't know what it was saying yet, Scarlett did.

"Perhaps I should massage your whole back, Sissy. All that practicing's got you knotted up real good." She paused and then calmly told her, "Why don't you take your blouse off?"

"Okay," said Sissy, sitting up and taking off not only her blouse but her bra as well.

Scarlett was determined to remain calm. "Please lie back down," she instructed as cooly as she could. "Let's get to work."

Sissy turned around and lay down. Scarlett poured the oil into her hands and let it sit for a while, warming it, then slowly, with artful technique and deliberation, she began massaging Sissy's back.

"I don't understand. Practicing has never made me so tense before."

"You've never had Bertrand Neeps as an instructor before."

"You think that's it?"

"Part of it."

"Your hands are wonderful, Scarlett."

"Thank you. They're self-taught."

Sissy laughed and finally thawed a little.

"Hang on just a minute," said Scarlett. "I know something else that will help you relax."

She got up and turned on Sissy's radio. The station was tuned into classical but right now that was fine with Scarlett. It would help set the mood. She sat back down and continued working on Sissy. Her touch was lighter now, more of a caressing motion than a massaging one. "How do you feel?" asked Scarlett after several minutes.

"Much better," answered Sissy.

Scarlett noticed her goose bumps were back and took it as a signal that she could be a little more daring. She began massaging the sides of Sissy's back, down toward her breasts. Scarlett's hands registered all the subtle shifts in Sissy's muscles. Her body was responding.

"Why don't you turn over?" said Scarlett, trying to sound professional, like she imagined a masseuse might sound. "We've got to work on those knots on the front." She quickly clarified, "Around your throat I mean."

Sissy hesitated, then turned over. When she did, the room suddenly pulsated with sexual energy. Scarlett knew Sissy felt it. It was powerful.

"I need to put some oil on your neck," she told Sissy with remarkable reserve. "Around your throat. You okay?"

"Yes," answered Sissy. "Why?" she said, straining to compose herself.

"I don't know. Maybe it's all the stress you're releasing. You looked a little edgy there for a second," said Scarlett. "But now you look fine."

Scarlett rubbed the oil along the side of her neck and then moved downward. Sissy took in a deep, nervous breath as Scarlett's hand stopped just above her breasts. She didn't know what to do. She was suddenly caught in the crossfire of confusion and desire.

The tension in the small room grew unbearable. Scarlett could now see in Sissy's face what she knew was in her body, the passion, the curiosity, the desperate need to connect despite the forbidden nature of her wanting. Unable to endure the unendurable a second longer, Sissy took Scarlett's hand and pressed it to her breast. What felt like an electric current rushed between their bodies, connecting them in an arc of pure energy. There was no backing off now. They were bound to each other.

Scarlett unbuttoned her blouse and let it slide down her arms; then she unfastened her bra. Though they didn't speak, Scarlett could see the anticipation in Sissy's eyes. The waiting had become intolerable. Scarlett put her mouth to Sissy's and felt her lips tremble. The journey had begun.

Chapter

44

Scarlett and Sissy made love until morning. There was no resistance in either one of their bodies to the total unfolding of their mutual pleasure. Their lovemaking had been wonderful and effortless. At the time it surprised Scarlett how easily Sissy participated in all that night held.

Scarlett didn't know it then, but many women were like Sissy. They were natural lovers, taking their pleasure where they could find it, often without the burden of guilt or social censure or even gender consideration. Pleasuring was pleasuring for such women, pure and simple. In Sissy's case it also had a lot to do with the carte blanche attitude of the rich. Since she didn't run with the herd, she was not going to be judged by its standards, sexual or otherwise.

"You're pure, bottled lightning," Scarlett told Sissy as the early morning light found its way into their room. "No. You're more exciting," she declared. "You're the whole damn storm in this one, incredible body." Scarlett's fingertips traced a lingering path down Sissy's neck to her breasts and stomach. "Lightning can be dangerous, huh?" mused Scarlett.

Sissy laughed and agreed, "Most decidedly."

Scarlett buried her face in Sissy's hair. Her scent was delicious, so full of secrets, and now they were hers. As her head lay nestled in Sissy's neck, Scarlett mused about the correlation between a woman's passion for something in life and her ability to give and receive pleasure in bed. Scarlett imagined that passion could be for just about anything, even planting tulips. It didn't much matter. If it was there, it fired up a woman's soul. You could see it in her eyes, hear it in her voice, feel it in her touch, like with Sissy. Her passion for playing that cello was the same passion she brought to bed.

"Let me up," whispered Sissy. "I want you to hear something."

Scarlett moved off her, and Sissy threw her long legs over the edge of the bed.

"It's six-thirty in the morning," protested Scarlett.

"I know," said Sissy. She went and got her cello out of the bathtub and began playing. After a few bars, she stopped and looked over at Scarlett. "I composed it for you. For all the poems you wrote me."

Transfixed, Scarlett watched Sissy play as the sunlight filtered through the window and bathed her naked body in a golden glow. It was as sensual as anything Scarlett would ever see, the dance of light that fall morning on Sissy and her cello, making the most exquisite music.

"Well? Do you like it?" asked Sissy when she finished.

"Yes," answered Scarlett, stunned at what she had just heard. "You're a composer."

"Oh, no," she demurred, loving the compliment.

"Have you played it for Bertrand yet?"

Sissy shook her head.

"Then play it for him," directed Scarlett. "Let him tell you. You have a remarkable gift." Scarlett paused and looked at Sissy's other gifts. She couldn't help herself. They were equally remarkable. "Please come here."

Sissy stood up, shimmering in the sunlight as she walked away from the window. Scarlett slid down the edge of the bed and waited for her.

"Please," whispered Scarlett placing her hands on Sissy's thighs, parting them. "Stay just like this."

Scarlett kissed her stomach and slowly, ever so slowly, moved down to her wetness. She felt Sissy's body tense and her breath quicken, growing louder, heavier with each exhalation. She loved Sissy's sounds, all of them. Every sigh, every moan, every breath excited her almost as much as her mouth being where it was. She held Sissy at the waist and when she came, Scarlett felt her own body release too. Without even being touched, she had gone there with Sissy. They had gone there together.

Sissy ran her fingers through Scarlett's hair and pulled her up to her, holding her, kissing her, tasting the taste of her own pleasure on her roommate's mouth.

Chapter

45

"Oh, Sissy. Your fingering in that section is superlative." Bertrand Neeps raised his voice above Sissy's playing, then sat back and admired his student, loving every exquisite note those hands executed. She was his best student yet. Concert material. And, now, maybe even a composer. Her "Forbidden Sonata" had all the elements of a great composition.

"Magnificent! Magnificent!" exclaimed Bertrand, transported. When she finished, he stood up and circled Sissy's chair. "There's just one thing I might change. Now, it's not a criticism, mind you. Just a suggestion."

"What is it, Mr. Neeps?"

"The title of that wonderful piece you composed," he hesitated. He did not want to offend Sissy. He knew how high-strung she was. "Perhaps the word, 'forbidden,' could be changed to something . . ." Bertrand paused and searched for the right words. "A little less negative. The word detracts and it's such . . ."

"But," objected Sissy, interrupting Mr. Neeps for the first time ever. "The title is perfect. The forbidden was its inspiration."

Bertrand glanced at Sissy curiously. "I see," he said, struggling for some nuance of understanding.

"I would rather not elaborate, Mr. Neeps."

Sissy looked up at the clock. The lesson was over. She got up and put her cello in its case. "Thank you, sir. See you tomorrow."

Bertrand went over and stood at the window as Sissy left the building. She walked over to a bench and sat down next to a very pretty girl who was reading a book. The two smiled at each other and started talking. At one point the other girl discreetly touched Sissy's hand. They stopped talking and looked at each other. That gaze was unmistakable. It was the one shared exclusively by lovers.

Bertrand smiled. He just hoped their forbidden sonata would never interfere with Sissy's gifts. He knew how fierce such attachments could be and how wrong that kind of passion could go.

Chapter

46

Scarlett and Sissy pleasured themselves right through their second set of midterms. It must have agreed with them. They both made straight A's. However, as soon as exams were finished, Christmas was upon them and so was a lot of anxiety. Sissy had to spend the holidays in Madrid with her parents. Scarlett guessed Mr. Langtree was still there because of all the gun actions Cuba needed. According to the newspapers, Fidel's army was getting bigger by the day.

"Jeez!" said Scarlett. "Two weeks is a long time."

"I know," whined Sissy, but then she brightened. She snapped her suitcase shut and walked over to Scarlett. "Take heart. Just imagine how this will feel then?" She kissed Scarlett on the mouth and ran her hand over one of her breasts.

"You're wicked."

"Yes." She smiled. "And just barely enough for you."

Scarlett laughed and kissed Sissy back, soft at first, and then hard, with an almost passionate ferocity. She felt like she wanted to devour Sissy and leave her so ravaged by the encounter that she wouldn't be able to leave her and go to Madrid. Scarlett suddenly pulled back. She didn't like what she was feeling or what she had just done to Sissy. "I'm sorry," she said, astonished at her behavior. "I hope I didn't hurt you."

"No," said Sissy, wiping a small amount of blood from her mouth and rubbing it on Scarlett's lips. "You didn't." She smiled teasingly. "Welcome to the edge."

Scarlett couldn't believe her ears. The same reckless energy that startled her had aroused Sissy, and now she wanted more. Sissy pulled off her clothes and went and lay down.

"Well, Scarlett? What are you waiting for?"

Sissy was playing to that wildness in Scarlett and, unbidden, it came rushing back. Sissy wanted that energy to possess her, to transport her to new sexual dimensions. Dimensions she knew must exist. She could sense them in Scarlett.

"Please come here."

Scarlett hesitated, then went over and sat down on the bed. "I can't."

"Yes, you can," urged Sissy.

"I don't know if I like feeling like this. I . . ."

"It's just a different kind of passion," interrupted Sissy, pressing Scarlett's hand to her mouth, wetting her fingers with her tongue. "A wilder kind."

"What do you mean?"

"Oh, Scarlett!" exclaimed a frustrated Sissy, her exasperation suddenly careening out of control, overwhelming any remaining shred of Southern decorum. "For heaven's sake! Please just shut up and fuck me!"

Chapter

47

Sissy looked a mess. Her hair was tousled, her makeup smeared, her body weak from all those excursions into indescribable bliss. "That energy of yours."

"Yes?" said Scarlett.

"It's intoxicating. It makes me high." Sissy ran her hand across Scarlett's naked breasts. "How come you don't let it out more often?"

"I didn't know it was there."

"Well, believe me," said Sissy, rolling over on top of Scarlett. "It's there." She paused and kissed Scarlett lightly on the mouth. "And it makes you irresistible."

Scarlett smiled and buried her face in Sissy's neck, drifting into sleep, away from the confusion, away from what Sissy had unwittingly just taught her. That sex could be used as a drug. That it could induce forgetfulness and drive away pain.

Sissy felt Scarlett's body relax beneath her. She knew she was sleeping. Little wonder. Who would believe anyone had that much capacity for pleasuring? Sissy sat on the edge of the bed and stared down at Scarlett, wanting more, not understanding the nature of her own hunger. She finally pulled a blanket over Scarlett and got up and showered. Tomorrow she would be in Madrid.

"What's this?" asked a bleary-eyed Scarlett, finally waking up from her nap. Next to her on the bed was a present not much larger than a pack of cigarettes.

"Something for your Christmas tree," said Sissy. "But you can't open it until I call you from Madrid. Promise?"

"Okay," agreed Scarlett, shaking the box. She finally got up and pulled on a robe. "I've got something for you too." Scarlett opened a drawer and took out a badly wrapped gift. "Here," she said, handing it to Sissy. "It's not done yet, but I wanted you to see what I had."

"Can I open it now?" said Sissy, staring at the mangled gift, tickled at Scarlett's total lack of bow-tying talent.

"That's probably a good idea," said Scarlett and smiled. "Somehow I don't think your parents would appreciate it."

As Sissy unwrapped the present, Scarlett explained, "It's only half done."

It took Sissy a while to undo the bow and remove the paper. "A diary?" she said, holding up a dime-store journal.

"Actually, it's a manuscript," explained Scarlett. "What they call a work in progress."

Sissy opened the book to the first page and read aloud, "Dedicated, with all affection, to Sissy Langtree."

"I'm calling it *Poems to My Cello-Playing Southern Muse.* It was your music that did it, Sissy. It inspired me." Scarlett paused. "What do you think of the title?"

"Catchy," said Sissy, turning another page. "Oh, Scarlett. This is just the sweetest. A book inspired by little old me. I can't wait to show it to my parents. Mother loves poetry."

"I don't know if that's a good idea."

"Why not? They're my poems."

"Read the first one, Sissy."

Sissy began reading out loud:

flowing
moving
bending
wanting to touch

touch and know
the incredible form
of you
matching mine
from head to toe
how quickly
I throw off my clothes
to feel you fit,
lock into my soul

"So?" said Sissy.

"So," said Scarlett. "Since when does a guy's parts match yours from head to toe?"

"You have a point. I suppose it could give them the wrong idea," said Sissy and she read the poem again to herself. "Oh, Scarlett!" she swooned and then clutched the unfinished book to her bosom. "Just for me, really?" Sissy's ego was leaving the airstrip.

"Just for you," confirmed Scarlett and grinned. "Most of them are real sexy."

"Where?" said Sissy, flipping through the pages. "Oh, this one looks good!"

Scarlett took the book out of her hands. "You can read it on the plane. I wanted to make sure you didn't forget me while you're gone."

"How could I?" said Sissy, opening her robe. "When you're in every pore of my body." She let her robe fall to the floor. "What do you say we make another poem? A real hot one," teased Sissy. "Before I leave for Madrid."

Scarlett looked at Sissy and felt the craving again. She was the perfect antidote. In Sissy's arms she forgot, forgot it all, everyone and everything that caused her pain.

Chapter
48

The bus ride to Dillinger was a long, lonely trip. Scarlett thought about Sissy, but mostly she thought about the one who was always there, hovering, never quite going away. The one stuck in her heart. The one called Gina.

Dear Gina,

Merry Christmas. I'm on the bus headed to Dillinger to spend the holiday with my mother. I would rather be with you but since neither one of us is rich yet, letters will have to do. I try not to think of you but I can't help it. You are always there, lingering somewhere in my thoughts. My skin, my hands, my mouth, my senses, all retain a memory of you. I wish I didn't remember you so often because, if I can't be with you, what's the point? Life's pleasures weren't meant to be postponed. They were meant to be lived. You never know how much time is left.

What did you do to me, Gina? What part of me did you sneak into and steal those few short days we spent together? You persist in my thoughts and dreams like a tenacious ghost. I guess I should be grateful for what we shared. But how can I be thankful for what I do not have now? You're in Paris trotting around with Henri and I'm headed for a sinkhole called Dillinger?

Life's disarrangements are positively wicked. Why should we be given this longing and then given no way to fulfill it? It was a shitty trick. Fuck fate or whatever or whomever played it on us.

Being a lesbian is difficult. I don't want to hide my essential self but most of the time I do, Gina. If I didn't, I'd be shunned and labeled a pervert or some such thing of that irregular nature. I know I never speak about these things but I think about them. I think about them all the time. These thoughts come to me when I'm alone or scared. Sometimes I don't know who I am. But enough of this.

I'm writing a book of erotic poetry. It's probably what caused the neurotic detour you just read because, you see, its about women with women. Maybe someday I'll have the nerve to take it to a publisher. But I don't know. I'm so confused. When I think of Momma and how upset she would be if she found out I'm this way, my daring fades. Excuse the rambling but I feel lost. It must be the holidays. Merry Christmas.

Affectionately,
Scarlett

P.S. Enclosed is a poem I wrote just for you. I wish it weren't so despairing but it's what my pen wrote when I thought of you, of us, of this ridiculous disarrangement.

I would that I could
Forget I knew you
But impossibles
Exceed my strength
For like the echoes of a whisper
Or the shadows of a dream
You are impossibly a part
Of what I cannot quite forget
And may never ever retrieve

Gina wept when she read the poem. She wondered if Scarlett would ever overcome her fear of loving and admit she loved her.

Chapter

49

As the bus pulled up to the depot in Dillinger, Scarlett felt her heart sink. Just coming back here made her anxious because somewhere, down deep, she was still afraid she might get stuck here. The same nightmare would recur many nights across many years. She was back in Dillinger, married, with three kids and a husband in tow.

The marriage erased any suspicion of the big "L" from Scarlett's forehead and made Skeeter Boyd happy, at least for a while. Ollie Mae, of course, was as pleased as punch. It made her a grandmother. But as time passed, life for Scarlett got smaller. She found herself peering through the curtained windows of her mock-up home trying to catch a glimpse of happiness. Sadly, it was years before she realized it had skipped out of town the day she said "I do" to a lie.

Scarlett spotted her mother and Etta Paine on the waiting platform, their breath frosted by the bitter, wintry cold outside. Scarlett pulled on her jacket and reached under her seat searching for the bag of Christmas presents. In a couple of hours Ollie would ask her about the boys she had been dating, and Scarlett would make up names and looks, IQ's and talents, family histories that never existed, dates that never happened.

"My, my. Don't you look the student," said Etta Paine as Scarlett stepped down off the bus. "Here, honey. Let me help you with those."

"Thank you," said Scarlett, and she gave Etta an armful of books.

Ollie smiled and hugged her daughter. "You know how much I missed you, honey?"

"I dunno," said Scarlett, pulling back. "Let me guess." She put down the paper sack with the Christmas gifts she had bought at Charleston's thrift shop and stretched out her arms. "A feeling the size of Texas?" said Scarlett and then she spread her arms out even wider. "And Oklahoma together!"

Ollie laughed. "Yep!" she said, the tears starting to roll down her cheeks. "How'd you know?"

"A good guess," said Scarlett and hugged her mother again.

"Let's get to the car," advised Etta Paine. "You two can do your geography there. My blood's too thin for this nippy weather. I feel like I'm making ice cubes for Dracula."

Scarlett laughed. She loved Etta Paine's sense of humor, droll as it was.

Chapter

50

In the days before Christmas Scarlett wrote up a storm, producing as many as two or three poems a day. She kept several "tame ones" on hand to show Ollie, since her mother got real curious about why she was staying up so late every night. Scarlett showed her mother a poem she said she'd composed just for her. After that, Ollie Mae liked her daughter's writing a lot better.

It was pure magic, poetry was. Women loved it, especially if they thought they had been the inspiration. It meant they were being immortalized, sort of like Dante's Beatrice or Petrarch's Laura or Shakespeare's Dark Lady. Of course, most of them didn't know who those other women were and they didn't much care. The fact of the matter was they were worth a whole poem too.

"Momma, where's the divinity?" asked Scarlett, referring to the lush white Christmas fudge her mother made every year.

"I'm makin' it after Baby Jesus Day this time," said Ollie. "Just so you don't go stuffin' yourself silly and gettin' sick like you do every Christmas."

"But, Mom."

"No buttin' me, Scarlett Faye. Go suck on those cute little red-and-white canes in the living room."

Scarlett went and grabbed a handful of canes, then ran back upstairs to write some late Christmas cards. She had been so busy with studying, poetry writing and Sissy, she had gotten out of touch with her friends.

Downstairs the radio played Christmas songs as she made cards out to Twila and Clotelle and, of course, Maggie. Bing Crosby crooned "White Christmas," Rosemary Clooney sang something else and Nat King Cole caroled "Winter Wonderland" the way only he could. She finished Gina's card just before the news came on. She hoped Gina liked the new poem she had written for her.

"Come and see what I've done with the lights," yelled Ollie upstairs to Scarlett.

As always, Ollie had decorated the boarding house in true Christmas spirit. Over the years she had scrimped and saved so she could buy a new decoration every year. Her latest acquisition was for the front yard. It was Santa and his sleigh pulled by a herd of lighted reindeer. Ollie actually saved three years for this extravagance. She knew that Jasper Stubbs, her boarder who worked down at Dillinger's power plant, could make Santa and his reindeer twinkle like they should.

"It's real pretty, Momma," said Scarlett, peering out the window. "You outdid yourself this time. Why just look at all those cars."

It was some sight all right, the way those reindeer blinked off and on, especially Rudolph's nose, beckoning cars to slow down in front of the boarding house and admire Ollie's decorations. She loved to stand at the window and watch the cars go by, as proud as she could be. Some of those cars were from the other side of the tracks and they had come all the way over here just to see her lights.

Besides Santa and his reindeer, Jasper had strung lights in the two elm trees, others along the picket fence and some on the front of the house. Most prominent was the star of Bethlehem, which Jasper had strategically placed in the center of the boarding house's second story, flashing on and off, proving to everyone in Dillinger how much Ollie Mae Turner loved Baby Jesus.

Scarlett wished Cecil were there for the holidays. She would have talked to him about some of her worries. But he had gone to spend

Christmas with his sister in Pittsburgh. So when Christmas Day rolled around, it was just Scarlett and her Momma, Jasper Stubbs and a new boarder, Mitzi Polk, Dillinger's new librarian.

Mitzi was pleasant enough and very smart but her huge, Coke-bottle glasses were distracting. They made her eyes look the size of two full moons, blue ones. Scarlett figured the poor woman might be close to being legally blind. The irony touched Scarlett: a librarian who couldn't see her books. On a few occasions Scarlett saw Jasper reading to Mitzi. Apparently, the little guy who made electricity for Dillinger was courting her. What Dillinger's terminals and wires and lamps couldn't light up for Mitzi, Jasper could, using his own two eyes.

"Please read that section again," asked Mitzi. "That Jane Austen certainly had a way with innuendo, didn't she, Jasper?"

Chapter

51

"Well, dessert time, it is," said Ollie, getting up from her Christmas Day table. "Mince meat or pecan? Your choice."

Mitzi and Jasper wanted mince. Scarlett decided on pecan. As Ollie walked into the kitchen, the phone rang.

"I'll get it, Momma. I'm expecting a call." She ran and grabbed the phone. "Hello," said Scarlett and smiled. "No. I haven't opened it yet." There was a pause. "Okay. I'll go get it."

Scarlett ran into the living room and got Sissy's present. When she returned, she put the phone under her chin and tore the wrapping paper off a gold box with a velvety blue case inside. She opened the case and gasped, "Oh, Sissy! It's beautiful. You bought me a Rolex?"

Scarlett couldn't believe it. She had always admired Sissy's watch and knew how expensive it was, hundreds and hundreds of dollars, maybe thousands. After all, her roommate had repeatedly told her so.

"I don't know what to say," said Scarlett. There was a long pause as she listened to Sissy talking to someone on the other end of the line. "What!" exclaimed Scarlett. "Jesus! What snoop hounds! Tell them it's Fidel Castro. That's who!"

Sissy's parents wanted to know who was on the phone with their daughter. Sissy told them what they wanted to hear, that it was

Bertrand Neeps praising her latest composition. Yes, she would tell him Merry Christmas.

"You have to go now? This very minute!" Scarlett sounded exasperated. "Okay. Okay! Then I'll thank you when I see you." She lowered her voice and quickly removed the irritation from it. "In bed. Doing what you like to do best."

Sissy giggled. "I can't wait."

Scarlett said good-bye and hung up. She fastened the Rolex to her wrist and held it out, admiring the watch. She finally went back and sat down at her mother's Christmas table with a big smile on her face.

"Who was that?" asked Ollie, passing her a piece of hot pecan pie.

"Steven."

"Steven?" mused Ollie. "Who's that? I've never heard you talk about him before."

"He's the one who gave me this," said Scarlett, proudly showing her mother the watch.

"Nice. What kinda brand is it?"

"A Rolex!" answered Scarlett, forgetting whom she was talking to.

"Is that anything like a Timex, honey? Them's real good watches."

Chapter

52

The day didn't start out so good, and it only got worse. First, a couple of stray dogs got into a dog fight on Ollie's front lawn and mauled Santa and a couple of his reindeer into pathetic little bits. The next thing was a telephone call. The kind that causes a huge, vast silence on this end of the receiver as someone listens to what they don't want to hear. Ollie Mae finally hung up and turned around, as pale as a sheet. It was all she could do to blurt out the information before she dissolved into tears.

"It was Mrs. Yallop," she told Scarlett. "Billy Ray's dead. Killed in that Vietnam."

Scarlett felt herself numbing up inside. God was throwing more people down into deep, dark holes. She looked at her mother, tried to speak but couldn't, then ran out of the house. She walked around in the rain for hours, almost ending up with pneumonia, coughing her guts out, barely able to talk the following day.

It was an old trick. When Scarlett didn't want to feel, she would either escape into her head or get sick. That is, until she found another way, the antidote way. But since Sissy wasn't around and her mind was brimming with more confusion than she could handle, Scarlett had no choice but to use her body. All the aches and pains racking it right now were the perfect decoy for all that emotional pain she didn't want to feel.

Billy Ray died a hero in that "green jungle hell" some called Vietnam. He took a large-caliber bullet to the head as he dragged a wounded buddy to safety. That's why it was a closed-casket funeral. This time the mortician's makeup wouldn't help.

Billy Ray's buddy wired Mr. and Mrs. Yallop about their son's bravery, and Pastor Mabus read the letter at the funeral: "Billy Ray Yallop saved my life. If he hadn't pulled me out of a rice paddy in Vietnam, I'd have bled to death. He's a real hero. Last count there were at least half a dozen other men who are still alive because of your son."

Pastor Mabus pulled off his spectacles and rubbed his eyes. Being that his would-have-been son-in-law was now a hero of some repute, the charitable pastor finally forgave him for fathering his daughter's bastard baby, Dusty Jay. It seemed that some people in Dillinger just knew how to forgive.

The following week Scarlett packed her bags and headed back to Charleston. She got to sit by herself on the bus, since there were only a handful of passengers, and she took advantage of the moment to write Gina:

> *Dear Gina,*
>
> *Billy Ray just died in Vietnam. We buried him here in Dillinger last week. Remember him from high school? Billy was a big part of my childhood, the part of it that was fun and silly and adventurous. I never did but now I wish I had thanked him for our crazy, wonderful friendship.*
>
> *How do you thank the dead, Gina? How do they hear your heart when theirs has stopped? The tether that attaches us to life seems so impossibly fragile right now. I miss you. I wish I were in your arms.*
> > *Thinking of you,*
> > *Scarlett*

Scarlett didn't know it then, but Gina knew all about the dead and the walking wounded they left behind. She was one of those who had gotten left.

Chapter

53

Sissy's first concert recital was a smashing success. Bertrand was overjoyed. He took great pride in being the architect of all that talent. Sissy had been perfect that evening. Those long, slender fingers played with a passion and precision far beyond her years. There was now no doubt in Bertrand's mind—Sissy would have a luminous career. The reviews raved about Charleston's prodigy, its magical music maker.

"Not only is Sissy Langtree a gifted cello player and composer," wrote the music critic for the *Charleston Sentinel,* "she is a beautiful girl with the face of an angel. Even the most tin-eared among us cannot help but hear the music of the spheres in her playing."

Scarlett smiled and put down the paper Sissy had carried with her for the last two weeks, all the way to Key West. "You certainly wowed Charleston. They've made you into an angel," said Scarlett. "I wonder if they would use as much hyperbole to sanctify your other talents?"

Sissy looked over at Scarlett, lost somewhere in time and the heat of the sun, not quite following her.

"I would," said Scarlett.

"Would what?" asked Sissy.

"Praise your talents in all things including the less lauded ones." Scarlett paused and smiled mischievously. "Your erotic ones."

"Yes, darling, but not in print. Remember, they think I'm an angel."

"With just enough devil in her to make her interesting," said Scarlett. "Do you know how provocative that is?"

"I've got a glimmering of an idea," said Sissy and she wet her lips with her tongue, dry from the heat and wind. "But I think I need you to jar my memory a little. It was a long plane ride."

Scarlett laughed and jumped on top of the chaise lounge with Sissy. Beyond, the sun blazed down on Key West, fading the once brilliant primary colors of its shotgun houses into ghostly pastels.

"Out here in broad daylight, Scarlett?"

"Why not? We're practically undressed already."

Scarlett snapped off her bikini top and quickly undid Sissy's. They embraced and felt their suntanned bodies dissolve into each other as the sun sweltered down. Exchanging slow, languid kisses, they let the fever build.

"What are you waiting for?" whispered Sissy. "You're driving me crazy."

As Scarlett slid down Sissy's well-oiled body, she noticed a reflection in the sliding glass door behind them leading to their hotel room. The shiny spot darted about like a frantic bird.

"What the hell's that?"

"What!" exclaimed Sissy anxiously. "Is there something wrong with my body?"

Scarlett didn't answer. She turned around and looked across the street. There, ensconced in another balcony were three guys passing a pair of binoculars back and forth.

"Shit!"

"What?" said Sissy, turning to look.

"They're spying on us," said Scarlett, putting a towel around her and handing one to Sissy.

"Who?"

The catcalls began.

"The jerks over there," said Scarlett, indicating the balcony across the way.

"Save some for us," one of the guys yelled.

"Yeah," hollered another. "We'd sure like to dip our wicks in that."

The third added his two bits. "What do you say we come over and show you how to really fuck? Don't you know you haven't got the right equipment?"

"And you think you do, needle dick?" yelled Scarlett.

"Aw, come on, you pretty little thing. You're just jealous you can't bang her the real way."

"And I suppose you think you can?"

"In the wink of an eye."

"Go fuck yourself then, because I bet you come even faster than that."

"Hey, sweetie, cool out and let me tell you something," said the second guy. "If you can guess what I'm holding in my hand, I'll let you kiss it."

"Don't say anything," said Sissy, grabbing Scarlett's arm. "You're just riling them up."

"Hey, asshole," yelled Scarlett, ignoring Sissy's advice. "If you can hold it in one hand, it's not worth a damn to anyone."

As Sissy cringed, the other two guys howled at Scarlett's put-down.

"You bitch," yelled the tall guy. "Dyke! How would you know?"

"Don't answer!" insisted Sissy. "That mouth of yours is going to get us into trouble. Let's just get dressed and leave before they come over here."

"Sonovabitches!" mumbled Scarlett as she stood up and started to go inside.

"Well, come on," said Sissy, already in their room.

Scarlett suddenly turned around to the boys and yanked off her towel, flashing her naked body at them. Now the catcalls began in earnest. In the background Scarlett heard Sissy say, "Oh, Jesus! Sweet Jesus," over and over again.

Chapter

54

Sissy decided it would be prudent to change hotels. This time she made sure there was no window or balcony higher than theirs across the way. She was still upset about Scarlett's outrageous behavior.

"Why did you tease them like that?"

"Because they deserved it. Guys always think they have a right to interfere, to force themselves on you just because they're guys."

"What do you expect? Catching us like that?" she said in their defense. "It excited them."

Scarlett looked at Sissy with growing curiosity, wondering if her instincts might be right. "Do you like boys?" she asked her. "That way, I mean?"

"I suppose," answered Sissy. "I like kissing them."

"Would you do it with them?"

"Why not? I'd like to know how it feels," said Sissy. "You've done it."

"And what did I tell you about it?"

"That it wasn't for you."

Scarlett looked at her lover, taking in the whole erotic package that was Sissy Langtree: the sultry innocence, the coquettish turn of the head, the tilt of the eyes, the graceful movements that veiled her explosive, delicious sexuality. Could it be that what she always suspected was true? That Sissy might be a crossover? That she could enjoy either sex in bed? She had to find out.

"Come on," said Scarlett. "Put on a dress."

"Why?"

"We're going to a discotheque. I want to see how you like it when they start bumping against you and feeling you up."

"Why, Scarlett. I think you're jealous I might like guys."

"You must be kidding," was Scarlett's crisp retort as she pulled on a pair of shorts and slid into a halter top. "I'm only jealous of real competition."

"That ego, Miss Turner, is going to get you."

"Really," said Scarlett, smiling. "Like it got you?"

Exasperated, Sissy shook her head and put on a white backless dress. The contrast was stunning against her bronzed skin. She looked sexy and inviting, ready to make trouble.

"Terrific," said Scarlett, running a brush through her hair. "You've just turned yourself into a human lure." She walked over and opened the door. "Well, come on. Let's go fishing."

Chapter
55

Beautiful wall-to-wall bodies filled the disco, suntanned and young, on spring break from the mainland. The music was so loud, Scarlett and Sissy could barely hear themselves talk. A waitress came over and, shouting, asked what they wanted to drink.

"A Cuba Libre," yelled back Sissy, producing a fake driver's license. She thought it was stupid having to lie about her age. She never did it in Europe. Drinking was no big deal there. It was a natural part of life.

"What about you?" the waitress asked Scarlett.

"I'd actually like two Cuba Libres," said Sissy, taking charge. "For myself," she quickly added and smiled at the waitress. She knew Scarlett didn't have any ID.

Before the waitress got back with the drinks, a veritable pussy posse had circled their table. A real cute guy wanted to know if he could sit down next to Sissy. She told him he could. He waved the rest of the guys off and went to get a chair.

"You be nice," Sissy told Scarlett. "After all, you brought me here."

"Okay."

"Do I have your word?"

"Yes," pledged Scarlett.

Mark reappeared shortly with a friend of his and introduced him to Sissy and Scarlett. Bud smiled and pushed his chair up to the table next to Scarlett. "Hi, good-looking."

"Don't you have anything more original than that?" challenged Scarlett.

"Well, well . . ." stuttered Bud. "I . . . I . . ."

"It's okay." Now Scarlett felt sorry for him. This good-looking hunk had a speech impediment. "Thanks for the compliment," she said contritely.

Across the table Sissy and Mark were already deep in lust. Sissy finished her Cuba Libre and Bud ordered another one for her.

"Would you ca . . . ca . . . care for another drink?" Bud asked Scarlett.

"No, thank you," she answered. "I'm not a big drinker."

"Me either," said Bud, and he ordered himself a soda. "It makes people act stupid." He smiled and offered Scarlett a stick of gum. Scarlett accepted and slowly unwrapped it as she watched Sissy and Mark. He was moving in fast. He was practically on top of her and Sissy wasn't objecting.

Bud told Scarlett he was studying paleontology at the University of Miami. When he saw he had an audience, Bud talked and talked, almost without stuttering, about how fossils were the key that could unlock man's distant past. Scarlett liked Bud's enthusiasm for fossils. However, something much more interesting than old bones suddenly caught her attention. It was the attractive brunette sitting at the bar. She was staring at Scarlett, and she had that look in her eye. Scarlett smiled and went back to her conversation with Bud, teasing her.

Sissy and Mark were now out on the dance floor. Scarlett could see him grinding into her, and the look on Sissy's face was hardly one of displeasure. Then he kissed her and she kissed him back. It was just as Scarlett suspected. Sissy liked guys too. It was only a matter of time before one took her to bed.

When Bud excused himself from the table to go to the rest room, the sexy brunette came over. What legs she had, noticed Scarlett, long, shapely and deeply tanned.

"Do we know each other?"

"I don't think so," said Scarlett.

"Would you like to?"

"I think so," smiled Scarlett.

"May I sit down then?"

"Please."

Scarlett liked this woman's style. She had self-confidence and the broad shoulders to match it. As she pulled out a chair and sat down, Bud returned to the table. "Oh, Bud. If you don't mind, I need a few minutes with a sorority sister of mine," said Scarlett. There was no way she could introduce the woman to him. She didn't know her name yet.

"Sure," said Bud. "I'll wait over at the bar."

When Bud left, the brunette stuck her hand out and said, "I'm Tracy. Sigma Chi."

Scarlett took her hand. "My name is Scarlett, and I don't belong to a sorority."

"It's not required." Tracy smiled. "Mind if I pull my chair a little closer? It's very noisy in here."

"Come ahead," flirted Scarlett.

Tracy positioned her chair next to Scarlett just as the music stopped. While the band took a break, Sissy and Mark returned to the table. Sissy eyed the brunette suspiciously and wondered why she was sitting so close to Scarlett.

"Who are you?" asked Sissy.

"Tracy Hanson."

Sissy almost missed her chair as she sat down. She was feeling those Cuba Libres and they were setting her free in a way Scarlett had never seen before.

"Would you like another drink?" Mark asked Sissy.

"Yes," answered Sissy, her eyes still on Tracy.

"Okay," said Mark, getting up. "Order it. I have to hit the head."

"What can I get for you?" Tracy asked Scarlett.

"A Coke would be fine."

Tracy ran her hand over the top of Scarlett's. "Is that all?"

"You're damned right that's all," said Sissy, standing up. When Tracy started to object, Sissy cut her off. "The lady's spoken for."

She grabbed Scarlett's hand and pulled her up from the chair. "It's time to go, Miss Turner."

Scarlett couldn't believe it. Sissy was jealous. She looked sheepishly at Tracy. "Nice knowing you."

As Tracy watched the two disappear out the door, more amused than disappointed, Mark returned to the table. "Where'd Sissy go?" he asked.

"That way," Tracy said, pointing to the door. "With pussy in tow."

No matter how he tried, Mark just couldn't make sense of Tracy's remark. He finally decided it was one of those new, hip sorority girl expressions. "Do you mind if I sit with you?" he asked, putting down his beer, disappointed at the loss of Sissy but right back in the saddle. "My name's Mark."

"The name's Tracy," said the beautiful brunette as she got up and walked away.

Chapter

56

The nights in Key West continued hot and humid. As Scarlett and Sissy made love, their bodies perspired, getting hotter and wetter. Sissy took an ice cube out of a glass and rubbed it on Scarlett's lips, then slid it into her mouth.

"Show me that cool-down trick again," teased Sissy. "You know, igloolingus, or whatever tacky thing it was you called it."

"You liked that," said Scarlett, moving the ice to the side of her mouth. "Didn't you?"

"Yes. Lots. Who taught you?"

"My devoted muses," informed Scarlett, sucking on the ice. "The amorous ones."

Sissy laughed. "Well, please thank them for me." Sissy leaned over and kissed Scarlett lightly on the lips.

"Here, take the rest," said Scarlett, and she pushed the ice into Sissy's mouth. "It's your turn."

Sissy let it roll around on her tongue, then swallowed it. "In a second, okay? I want to say something first." Sissy paused and seemed to struggle for the words.

"Well? I'm waiting."

"I love the way you love me, Scarlett. All the different ways." Sissy paused again. "I guess what I'm trying to say is I think maybe I kind of love you."

"What!" exclaimed Scarlett.

"What's the matter with you? You heard me."

Scarlett's stomach knotted up. "You never said that before."

"So what? I'm saying it now."

Scarlett looked at Sissy and then pulled the wet sheet over her body, as if to protect herself from the feelings Sissy had just professed. She was definitely confused. First Sissy had been jealous of Tracy and now she was making threatening declarations. She seemed to be changing before Scarlett's very eyes, going sappy on her.

"Aren't you going to say anything?"

Scarlett finally managed a few words. "What am I supposed to say?"

"How you feel about me," said Sissy. "I told you."

"I care," said Scarlett tentatively. She was moving into dangerous territory. "Didn't I write all that poetry for you? Doesn't that tell you?"

"Yes and no. I'd like to hear you say it over dinner once in a while or have you whisper it in my ear when we're hot."

Sissy was making Scarlett nervous. As far as she was concerned, it didn't make any difference how or when it was said. In fact, she didn't want to say it at all.

Sissy got up and walked over to the window, where she looked out at Key West. "Don't you find it odd we've never told each other what we feel?"

"No," was Scarlett's succinct response. "If it was so important to you, why didn't you say something before now?"

"I guess I thought this was all just a big sexual adventure. I never connected the word love with women. The only kind of love that existed in the novels I grew up reading was reserved for men." Sissy rolled her neck from side to side, perhaps trying to relieve the anxiety of this surprising confession. "But I guess I realized this evening I've been fooling myself. It's natural for feelings like this to happen. You're the first person I've ever been to bed with."

Scarlett didn't answer. She had always figured love would never be part of the equation with Sissy. It was the perfect arrangement by

Scarlett's lights, a good time unfettered by emotional complications, by "those kind of feelings." She couldn't figure out what had gone wrong.

"I learned something tonight."

"Yes?" Scarlett said, not sure she really wanted to know.

"When I saw you sitting next to that woman, I realized I couldn't bear you doing to her what you do to me."

"Well, that doesn't mean you love me. It just means you're jealous."

Sissy started crying. Now Scarlett was even more confused. Tears and Sissy Langtree didn't mix. She didn't know what to do. She finally got up and went over to Sissy. She wiped the tears from her cheeks and said, "I love you." The words didn't get stuck in her throat the way she thought they would. They only got stuck when it came to Gina; then they would barely come out at all.

"Oh, Scarlett," said Sissy, smothering her in kisses. "Tell me again."

Scarlett did. It was easier that second time and even easier after that. In addition, it produced remarkable results, those words did. Sissy slid an eighteen-carat gold bracelet onto Scarlett's wrist, the wrist without the Rolex.

Chapter
57

The magic of Key West quickly disappeared. Back in Charleston, Mr. and Mrs. Langtree were waiting for the errant lovers to return. Apparently, a poem Scarlett sent to an underground newspaper in New York City had been published the week before. Filled with erotica of all description, its title left little doubt as to the source of the poem, "Sissy, Your Cello Turns Me On."

Lovers and parents (sans Ollie Turner) convened for their summit in Mrs. Buckley's office. Everybody looked pretty grim and the day was dark. Clouds covered the sky, making the dreary meeting even drearier.

"Did you write this, Miss Turner?" asked Mrs. Buckley.

Scarlett glanced at Mrs. Buckley and then at *The Village Crier*. Sure enough, it was her poem. She marveled at how good it looked in print. Her elation, however, soon turned to regret when she saw Sissy's face. She was mortified.

"Well?" Mrs. Buckley waited, tapping her pencil on top of the desk.

Scarlett looked at the poem again. She would have never thought something published in a small newspaper in New York, under a nom de plume, could surface in Charleston and point a finger at them. But it had. Here it was, right before her eyes. Apparently, pimply-face Rebecca Armistad put two and two together when she visited her parents in New York City during spring break and read the paper.

Rebecca, who had lived in the same dorm as Scarlett and Sissy, never forgave them for scaring her with that Alaskan bug story. She had cowered in her room for more than a week convinced that if such a thing bit her, her nose would gangrene and fall off from frost-bite. Scarlett and Sissy figured it served Rebecca right for snooping around their door trying to divine the source of all those interesting noises coming from inside.

"Where did you get it?" asked Scarlett.

"That's beside the point, Miss Turner," growled Mrs. Buckley. "Did you write it?"

"No," said Scarlett.

"Don't lie to me, Miss Turner. How many deviant poets do you think just happen to know a cello player named Sissy?"

Scarlett got defensive and surly, like she always got when she was scared. "I don't know. You tell me. How many?"

"There's only one," spat out Mrs. Langtree, sounding venomous. "And you're looking at her, Mrs. Buckley."

"There are coincidences, Mrs. Langtree. We've got to be sure."

"That piece of rubbish," hissed Mrs. Langtree, pointing to the paper, "has a line in it that refers to a small birthmark, a port-wine stain, on the back of the cello player's neck. My daughter has one there."

Sissy involuntarily rubbed the back of her neck and slumped down in her chair, closing her eyes.

"That certainly ups the odds," said Scarlett, trying to buy time and think of something. But this time, there was no time to buy. There was a knock at the door.

"I'm busy," said Mrs. Buckley. "What is it?"

"A book of poems Rebecca Armistad found," informed a woman's voice. "It is called *Poems to My Cello-Playing Southern Muse.*"

Scarlett almost came out of her chair. It was obvious the little creep had been snooping around in their room and found it. She silently fumed and swore she would leave a hornet's nest between Rebecca's sheets when this torture session was over.

"Bring it in," said Mrs. Buckley, shooting a damning glance in Scarlett's direction.

When Mrs. Buckley's capable assistant came in the room and produced the book, it looked as if Mrs. Langtree might faint. Sissy did. Scarlett went to help her, and Mrs. Buckley waved her off.

"Sit down, Scarlett."

"Don't touch my daughter," ordered Mr. Langtree.

As Mrs. Buckley revived Sissy, the Langtrees skimmed through the book. Mrs. Langtree's eyes grew larger with the turning of each page. In another second, Scarlett was sure they would leave their sockets.

"Oh, my God! My God!" exclaimed Mrs. Langtree.

"Which one was that?" Scarlett wanted to know.

Chapter

58

It was a quiet deal and quite a deal for Scarlett Faye Turner. The Langtrees paid her handsomely not to refer to their daughter again in print and to delete from her present collection of erotica any reference to Sissy, no matter how veiled it might be. This stipulation included omitting the use of the word cello in the book's proposed title and in one of its poems. These precautions were taken because Mrs. Langtree felt some "sapphic rag" might actually publish the filthy little manuscript. In light of such she had to make sure that nothing associated with Scarlett's writing would ever be able to point a finger at their daughter and taint her good name.

On the advice of Clotelle, Scarlett signed the agreement with the Langtrees. She would never, ever write about Sissy again. "In perpetuity" was the fancy legal term for it. Scarlett rechristened her book, *Poems for Lovers of a Different Kind*, and was delighted she had already started making money off writing.

Mr. Langtree gladly paid Scarlett the money. He wanted her signature on that agreement. He saw it as a kind of insurance policy against possible future damages since the "agreement" also prohibited her from making written reference to "any other member of the Langtree family in any context whatsoever." He didn't want his business skeletons dancing out of the closet anytime soon.

The final part of the deal was Scarlett's. She insisted Claremont recommend her to Townsend, a fancy girls' school in Savannah, Georgia, and that she be sent there on a full scholarship with something for extras, for entertainment and such. Scarlett told Mrs. Buckley when and if her "request" were granted, she would leave quietly. If not, the whole world might find out Claremont's deep, dark secret. That it was just brimming with sapphos and lesbos.

"They might even get the idea you're one," Scarlett told Mrs. Buckley. "Married or not. It doesn't matter. You know how vicious people are. Once their tongues start wagging, you can't unwag them." She paused and added archly, "I mean, look what happened to me?"

The veiled threat wasn't lost on Mrs. Buckley. She knew Scarlett could cause trouble. She had been very unhappy that last month at Claremont, especially after Sissy was spirited off to Switzerland. Then there was Rebecca Armistad's mouth. It had not stopped yapping except for those few days when she ended up in the infirmary with hundreds of bug bites of unknown origin.

Mr. Langtree encouraged Mrs. Buckley to recommend Scarlett for a scholarship and even used his influence with Townsend to get her accepted, anything to get her away from Charleston and hush the breath of scandal. Townsend took her and awarded Scarlett a full scholarship with extras. After all, she did have a straight-A average and that small endowment from the Langtrees didn't hurt.

The Langtrees could never quite accept the fact that their daughter had slept with a lesbian. So before they shipped poor Sissy off to Switzerland, they subjected her to a whole battery of medical tests. When the electroencephalogram revealed no brain tumor and the spinal tap no pathology, her parents almost appeared disappointed. Sissy's conduct had no physical explanation, at least not the medical kind.

Accordingly, the Langtrees made arrangements for Sissy to see the best psychiatrist in Lausanne. Her aberrant behavior had to be nipped in the bud so it could never surface again and interfere with her studies, her cello or her bank account. Sissy's deviation had been expensive. A Rolex watch, gold bracelets, clothes, expensive vacations and a Vespa scooter were just a few of the gifts that scoundrel,

Scarlett Faye Turner, had managed to con out of their daughter while simultaneously committing unspeakable acts on her person.

When Sissy was packed up and sent off to school in Switzerland, Bertrand Neeps wept bitterly at the loss of his prize student and recommended a teacher at the Royal Music Academy in Lausanne with whom Sissy could continue her studies. It was a difficult time for Bertrand. He glowered at Scarlett every time he saw her.

"I didn't send her to Switzerland, Mr. Neeps," Scarlett called after him one day on campus, trying just one more time to get him to listen.

"No," he said without turning around. "You just packed her bags."

"You haven't lost her, Professor Neeps. Remember, you taught her to play like an angel. You opened her soul to the universe."

Bertrand Neeps stopped and turned around. He looked like he might start crying.

"No one can undo what you've done. Your gifts are hers now."

Bertrand stood there, tears streaming down his face. "You think so, Miss Turner?"

"Yes. And I'm sure we'll both hear them in the next few years from every concert stage in the world."

Bertrand was now sobbing. "Thank you, Miss Turner," he said and walked off, grateful Scarlett had helped ease his heartache.

Scarlett missed Sissy terribly, but in a way she was relieved. Sissy had gotten far too serious at the end there. It was best this way, and she was sure Sissy would realize it in time. Love had no permanence. It was an emotional mirage, a trick of the heart.

Chapter

59

Even Dillinger looked good after that last month at Claremont. Rebecca Armistad had made Scarlett's life miserable. She started telling tales on Sissy and her that weren't even true, saying they had given each other the pox "bumping nasties." Scarlett decided the twit was dangerously short of firing neurons and that something had to be done about it once and for all. She escalated her bug warfare.

This time Scarlett stuck a Wallapie Tiger between Rebecca's sheets. Commonly known as the kissing bug, the Wallapie Tiger packs a mean bite. The nasty little sucker "kissed" Rebecca so many times and left so many red, puffy welts on her body that it wasn't hard for Scarlett to start a rumor of her own—one about Rebecca. It took off like wildfire and was all over school in a matter of hours.

Rebecca Armistad had all those puss-filled, oozing sores because she had done it with the calculus teacher's syphilitic son, Mortimer Brambles. Morty had gotten infected in New Orleans where he attended military school. Sex was easy in the Big Easy. Everyone knew that. It was especially easy with hookers and, as everyone knows, hookers had lots of those sexy, wiggly spirochetes to pass around.

Deny as Rebecca might that she didn't know Mortimer Brambles and that she was still a virgin, the rest of the girls at Claremont began to shun her. A sexually transmitted disease or not, nobody was taking any chances. Rebecca Armistad was a fright. It looked like that suppurating mess on her face might explode any second.

"If you don't get better soon, they'll have to hang a bell around your neck."

"What do you mean?" asked Rebecca, glaring at Scarlett.

"To let people know you're coming so they can get out of the way. It's what they did to the lepers back in Bible days."

Rebecca's eyes filled with pure venom. She had just divined who started that terrible rumor about her.

"Ding-a-ling," said Scarlett, smiling. "You ever say another word about Sissy or me, and next time I'll put a Brazilian Tongayonker in your bed."

"What's that?" exclaimed Rebecca with great alarm. She was now sure Scarlett was capable of anything.

"An ugly old arachnid. A big bugger," explained Scarlett. "One that waits until you're asleep and then crawls inside your mouth and does the most unbelievable thing."

Rebecca's eyes were getting bigger by the second. "What?"

"It bites your tongue and in seconds it swells up so much you can end up choking on it. Imagine that, Rebecca? Getting throttled by your own wagger."

Scarlett walked off, leaving Rebecca immobilized, speechless, in abject horror. Brazilian what? But it didn't matter that she couldn't remember the name of that bug. It didn't exist. The important thing was Rebecca never wagged her tongue again, not about Sissy and Scarlett anyway. But by then the damage had been done and lives had been parted, scattered hither and yon. Gossip was like that. It had the power to alter destinies forever.

Chapter

60

"It's suppertime, Scarlett," Ollie yelled to her daughter out on the front porch. "Get in here and wash your hands."

"Okay, Momma," said Scarlett, putting down a copy of *Modern Screen* with Delores Sheridan on the cover.

Lately, Scarlett seemed unable to concentrate on anything except magazines "with all them nice pictures," and Delores did the trick. A big box office star, she was easy on the eyes, beautiful in fact, and she had a delicious sensuality about her. Scarlett remembered how Delores steamed the boys up back in high school. When she was up there on the drive-in theater screen, Skeeter never missed a beat. Scarlett smiled and ran her fingers over Delores's face. Half her college fund had been inspired by this actress. Just ask Skeeter. No one else could make him pound his flounder like Delores did or, and thank God, finish faster.

"Scarlett," yelled Ollie again. "Your supper's gonna get cold."

Scarlett finally went inside and sat down at the dinner table. She quickly served herself some meatloaf, okra and mashed potatoes.

"Don't you want no gravy on your mashed potatoes, Scarlett Faye?"

"No, Momma. I'm watching my weight."

"But you ain't fat."

"I will be if I keep eating meatloaf and potatoes every other night."

"So what? A little meat on a woman's bones is a fine thing. Gives a man somethin' to hang on to." She turned to Mitzi and chuckled. "Ain't that right, Miss Polk?"

Mitzi blushed and looked down at her plate through those big Coke-bottle glasses of hers. Scarlett wondered how she was able to see her string beans well enough to spear them.

"I've gained five pounds eating your mother's cooking," said Mitzi proudly.

"You're looking just fine," Jasper reassured her, ignoring the fact that she was still as skinny as a rail.

"Bein' a skinny minny ain't no way to attract a man, is it, Mr. Stubbs? Has to be the real reason why Scarlett ain't got no boyfriends 'ceptin' the one who gave her that there Timex watch."

"Rolex," said Scarlett. "I'm not interested in any man who needs 'somethin' to hang on to' because he's probably a big old pig himself with pants sliding so far down his behind his butt crack shows."

"Scarlett Faye! How dare you go talkin' like that at the dinner table." Ollie thought about her reprimand and extended it. "Or anywhere else."

Jasper and Mitzi twitched in their seats and pretended not to hear the exchange going on between Ollie Mae and her daughter.

"I'm the perfect weight for my height, Mother."

She was but Ollie decided to give the whole issue a little more consideration. "It's them fancy clothes you been stickin' yourself into, ain't it? That's why you're turnin' to bones justin' so you can look like one of them mankins."

"Mannequins," said Scarlett. It was one of the few times she had ever corrected her mother.

"Where'd you get all them outfits anyway?"

"I told you, Bettelheim's. Charleston's most exclusive thrift shop."

It was actually Charleston's most exclusive and expensive department store, Sissy's favorite. Scarlett quickly changed the subject. She didn't want to talk about her clothes, her weight or her boyfriends. The first was her obsession. The second two were her mother's.

"Where's Cecil? He hasn't had supper with us since I've been home."

"Out with a lady friend," said Ollie crisply.

"A woman?" Scarlett was surprised. "Who?"

"Phyllis Wolverton."

"I've never heard of her," said Scarlett.

"She's new in these parts. Come over from Tullis to work at the feed store."

"Is it serious?"

"Imagine so," said Ollie. "They been seein' each other goin' on several months now."

"Cecil looks real happy," volunteered Jasper.

"I wonder why he hasn't told me anything," said Scarlett, disappointed Cecil hadn't yet taken her into his confidence.

"Give him time, honey. You know how shy he is."

Scarlett could hardly believe it. Cecil had met someone at last. She wondered if Phyllis had been as good an antidote for not thinking about Lorraine as Sissy had been for Gina. In reality, Scarlett wished she could forget all about antidotes and simply tell Gina how much she loved her. But she couldn't. She was too afraid. Gina had the power to hurt her. Scarlett wondered how many others there were like her, unable for whatever reason to reveal their true feelings, to honestly show their heart.

Thankfully, Scarlett didn't have to think about her heart much that summer. She buried her face in movie magazines and saw every film she could. It was a great escape and time passed quickly. All of a sudden she found herself leaving for school again. This time, for Georgia.

Chapter

61

Everything about Savannah charmed Scarlett. Its people, its beauty, its high-riding clouds, its sunsets, its shady squares with fountains and huge magnolia trees, its ubiquitous Spanish moss, its cobblestone streets, its southernness, its passion. Everything.

Located just inland from the Atlantic Ocean on a river of the same name, Savannah would, in time, become Scarlett's adopted home. It fit her fantasy about the South and her need to be part of it, a part of the mystique she felt compelled to create about herself. Savannah, Georgia, would look good on the dust covers of her future books. She certainly wouldn't use Dillinger. First off, it wasn't even in the South and second off, it sounded ridiculous. Dillinger? People would probably think they made pickles there.

By the end of her second year of college and her first at Townsend, Scarlett had developed a true Southern accent. It would become a studied part of her charm. That seductive drawl would eventually talk more women into bed than even Scarlett would care to remember.

Except for one small affair with skater Heidi Dusseldorf, a Teutonic ice queen of considerable talent both on and off the ice, Scarlett behaved herself that year at Townsend. She wrote lots of letters to Twila and Maggie in New Mexico, Clotelle out in Los Angeles, and Gina over in Paris. It was a good thing she didn't know

Sissy's address in Switzerland. It was best to let that alone for a while.

Predictably, Scarlett made straight A's that year at Townsend. In addition, she worked hard at polishing *Poems for Lovers of a Different Kind*. In the spring she submitted the manuscript to an offbeat New York publishing house. Much to her surprise and delight, it was accepted.

Being that Ollie Mae was still very much alive, Scarlett opted for using a pseudonym. She didn't want to cause her mother any more grief than Dillinger or Joe Turner already had. Or maybe that was Scarlett's excuse. She was still nervous about coming out of the closet. It was 1966 and girls who looked like her just didn't do it with other girls or, at least, that was what the world wanted to believe.

Scarlett returned to Dillinger that summer thinking about her buried life. The lie she was living was beginning to dog her, but she didn't know what to do about it yet. The truth had too many consequences.

Chapter

62

Scarlett had been back in Dillinger only a few weeks when a letter arrived from Switzerland. Inside there was a plane ticket and a short note from Sissy saying she just had to see her, that she missed her desperately. Something she had read by Colette reminded her of them. Scarlett smiled. It sounded like Sissy was horny.

Sissy went on to tell Scarlett she didn't care about "the deal" she had struck with her parents the year before; that was between them. After all, they were the ones who offered her the money. She had just taken it. Scarlett was delirious. Sissy wasn't mad at her after all and their long separation was to be remedied by nothing less than a European vacation. Such sweet medicine it was, and it wasn't going to cost her one red cent.

Sissy's parents, of course, had no idea about their daughter's trysting plans and even if they found out, it wouldn't have affected Scarlett's deal with them one way or the other. The agreement she signed prohibited her only from writing about Sissy, not from seeing her. The Langtrees had mistakenly figured time and the Atlantic Ocean were enough to keep their daughter and Scarlett apart.

"Who's that letter from?" Ollie wanted to know as she stood shelling black-eyed peas into a metal bowl.

"Oh!" said Scarlett. She would have to come up with something fast if she wanted to get her mother's blessing for this trip. Ollie Mae distrusted rich people and all the more so after "they done gone and stoled" her late husband's family farm. Why would one of them send her daughter a free plane ticket anywhere? Their two worlds didn't mix.

"It's from the Royal Poetry Academy of Europe," Scarlett explained. "They've invited me to a special workshop to read some of my poems—and imagine this, Momma." Scarlett held up the plane ticket. "They're even paying my way to Switzerland. That's where they're meeting this year." She smiled at Ollie and then sprinkled on the garnish. "They especially liked the poem I wrote about you."

"Oh," said Ollie, flattered, grinning from ear to ear.

"It's a real honor to be asked, Momma."

"Then you'll just have to go and do your family name good."

Scarlett got up and hugged Ollie. "It must have been your poem that did it. I really put a lot into that one."

Ollie was beaming. Maybe it was true what her daughter had been saying all these years. That she was going to be a writer and become rich and famous. Well, she was writing. That was certainly so. And now she was maybe even getting a little famous. Hadn't they heard about her all the way over there in Switzerland?

"I promise I'll write you every day, Momma. You'll hardly miss me."

Scarlett was delighted. Providence was again proving bountiful. She was traveling to Europe to see Sissy and she was going first class. On top of that, there was something else equally providential. Switzerland was right next to France. When she got to Lausanne, she would only be a stone's throw from Gina.

Chapter

63

As the plane banked over Lake Geneva and made its final approach into Lausanne's airport, Scarlett quickly ran a comb through her hair and put on some lipstick. She dabbed a little perfume on her neck and took a deep breath. The moment had arrived. She would soon be in Sissy's arms and, before the afternoon was out, in her bed.

The second Scarlett walked into the terminal, however, she knew something was wrong. There was that strange look on Sissy's face, and the glide in her walk was gone. Even her normal Southern hauteur was absent. As they hugged, Scarlett felt Sissy's body tense.

"What's wrong?" Scarlett asked.

Sissy pulled back and forced a nervous smile. "Is it that obvious?"

"Yes," said Scarlett. "You look like someone just stole your puppy."

"We'll talk about it later," said Sissy and suddenly affected a gaiety Scarlett knew she didn't feel. "Welcome to Lausanne. It's beautiful, isn't it?"

Scarlett ignored the question. "Let's get my luggage and get the hell out of here. I want to know what's going on."

Scarlett noticed a new maturity in Sissy's face. It wasn't just the makeup and heavy Mary Quant eyeliner showing off her eyes, now gray, now hazel, now indefinable. No, it was more than that. It was

Sissy's body. In the year since they had seen each other, a certain womanliness had emerged, which only made her that much more exciting.

The taxi driver deposited Scarlett's luggage in the trunk as his two passengers slid into the backseat. Scarlett could still feel Sissy's anxiety. She wasn't even responding to her touch. When Scarlett let go of her hand, Sissy hardly noticed. She began chattering nervously about the sights and told Scarlett how much she liked living in Lausanne.

"That's the Theatre Municipal," said Sissy, pointing. "They stage some great opera there. I just saw *Rigoletto*. You would have liked it."

Scarlett didn't respond. Sissy knew she hated that opera and the hunchbacked court jester whose stupid antics got his own daughter raped, then murdered. For Scarlett that shit was too close to what went on in Dillinger. In any event, the opera wasn't worth sitting through just to hear one or two good arias.

The cab finally pulled up in front of the old but very elegant Hotel d'Vichy overlooking Lake Geneva. Sissy paid the driver as a uniformed valet whisked Scarlett's bags inside the hotel. The lobby's high, vaulted ceilings and marble columns were impressive, its scale so immense, the decor so grand, it could have been something out of a fairy tale. Expensive paintings and tapestries decorated the walls while crystal chandeliers, too many to count, caught the sunshine in a prismatic dance of light.

Around the lobby wealthy guests sat taking their afternoon tea. They looked to be from everywhere on the globe. Scarlett felt a little intimidated. The place was opulent, ritzy beyond her wildest dreams. Sissy directed the valet up to Room 810. As he disappeared into the service elevator, they got on the passenger one.

"It's a beautiful hotel, Sissy."

"I knew you'd like it," said Sissy, forcing yet another smile.

"This place must cost a fortune. Why are we staying in such an expensive hotel?"

"Because you deserve it. Coming all the way from Pennsylvania to see me like you did."

Scarlett thought that was an odd answer. Sissy could spend money all right, but Scarlett knew she didn't throw it away. She wondered how Sissy was going to hide this little indulgence from her parents. There was another thing Scarlett wondered about as well. It was that guilt she had just heard in Sissy's voice. Scarlett was burning to talk, but it would have to wait. An American couple had just walked into the elevator chatting about some Gothic cathedral they wanted to see later in the day.

"Are you sure it's the one with the rose window?" the man asked his wife.

"Yes, yes," she said, consulting her travel guide. "I told you it's right here."

Sissy and Scarlett got off at the eighth floor and walked down the hall in an increasingly tense silence. A hundred thoughts ran through Scarlett's head. Whatever it was that was going on, she was sure it would prove quite interesting.

The valet was waiting for them in their room with Scarlett's bags and a bottle of champagne, compliments of the hotel. Sissy tipped him and he quickly disappeared. Scarlett uncorked the bottle and poured Sissy and her a glass.

"It's nice to see you again, Sissy. I've missed us."

Tears began streaming down Sissy's face. Scarlett put her glass down and went over and held her. "You want to tell me about it?"

Sissy was anguished. She pulled away from Scarlett and sat down in a chair next to the window. "I've met someone," she finally said, taking a deep breath.

Scarlett was incredulous. "What are you talking about?"

"Right after I mailed you the plane ticket, I met Michel."

"Yes?" said Scarlett, secretly relieved, positive that a teeny little affair of less than ten days couldn't be that serious. "So who is she?"

"He," said Sissy.

"I thought you said Michelle?"

"I did. It's a guy's name too."

"Oh," mumbled Scarlett, once again relieved. If it had been another woman, she might not have been so obliging. Her ego could not have withstood it. "And it's this heavy already?"

"Yes," said Sissy. "He plays the cello."

"Of course," said Scarlett, a touch of mirthful skepticism in her voice. She was beginning to understand. "Have you been to bed with him yet?"

"Yes," answered Sissy.

"And?"

"I liked it. I liked it a lot." Nervous as a cat, Sissy got up from the chair and looked out the window at Lake Geneva.

"So? You were bound to try it sooner or later."

"I just don't want you to be mad at me. Coming all the way here only to find out I've met someone else." Sissy hesitated and then turned to Scarlett. "Who I'd like to spend the summer with."

"I see," said Scarlett, her face showing her surprise.

"Please don't be mad at me."

Scarlett wasn't. She realized that Sissy's fledgling affair might actually be a blessing in disguise. It was the perfect excuse for her to bail out and go to Paris, to Gina. On top of that, Sissy felt so guilty about Michel that she would no doubt offer her the money for the vacation they wouldn't be spending together at this posh hotel. Scarlett figured that had to be a lot of francs, probably enough for a whole summer in Paris.

"Are you hurt, Scarlett?"

"Surprised is more like it," said Scarlett. When she saw the bewilderment on Sissy's face, Scarlett quickly amended her answer. "Certainly I'm hurt." She went over to Sissy and put her arm around her waist. "But happy for you."

"Oh, Scarlett," said Sissy, throwing her arms around her. "How understanding."

Scarlett couldn't resist Sissy's touch. Scarlett brushed her lips up against her neck and felt her yield. "Do you think Michel would mind if we had a little friendly parting of the ways?"

"I can't," said Sissy, pulling back. But she relented the instant Scarlett's mouth found hers.

Chapter

64

The large marble bathtub was as good a place as any to say goodbye. As they luxuriated in the warm, bubbly, perfume-scented water, they sipped at champagne and laughed and talked about old times. They also talked about the present. As Scarlett guessed she might do, Sissy told her to take the money it would cost to stay at the Hotel d'Vichy and do whatever she wanted, to go anywhere she wanted.

"Thanks, Sissy. Now I can go to Paris. You know how I've always wanted to visit the Louvre and see that loft where Oscar Wilde died. Then there's the boat ride I'd like to take on the Seine, climb the Eiffel tower and . . ."

Scarlett quickly muted her enthusiasm when she saw the look on Sissy's face. She was sounding far too excited about Paris. "I guess what I'm trying to say is, I hope Paris can somehow soften the disappointment of losing you."

Sissy looked a little dubious. "You don't act very disappointed."

"It must be the shock," said Scarlett, suddenly looking distraught. It was what Sissy wanted to see. "It's been a big blow."

Sissy took pity. Scarlett did love her after all. "I guess while you're there you'll see your friend whose friend died in that Greek river?" she said. "What's her name?"

"Gina," said Scarlett casually. "If she's in town. She travels a lot."

Scarlett veered out of this territory as fast as she could. Even though Sissy was now with Michel, Scarlett wasn't sure what she would do if she found out about the real nature of her relationship with Gina. She remembered what happened in Key West when that woman tried to pick her up in the bar. The less said, the better. Besides, Scarlett was sure Sissy's generosity would never allow her money to be used on another woman. Sissy's guilt over Michel didn't extend that far. Scarlett blew a handful of bubbles at Sissy and quickly changed the subject.

"I'd love to meet Michel before I leave."

"You would?" Sissy was surprised.

"Sure." Scarlett smiled, and she poured some champagne into her glass and toasted Sissy. "To you and Michel."

"Oh, Scarlett. I just love you to itty-bitty pieces," said Sissy, moving closer to her. "I can't believe how well you're taking this." She was high and she was hot.

Scarlett took a sip of champagne and kissed Sissy, offering what she had in her mouth to her, then taking part of it back and swallowing it. "Now it tastes like you," said Scarlett. She brushed the bubbles off Sissy's breasts and poured the rest of the bottle down the front of her, kissing her, tonguing off the champagne as her hand slid between Sissy's legs.

"Scarlett!" exclaimed Sissy in mock surprise. "Here?"

"Why not?" Scarlett caressed Sissy's ear with the tip of her tongue and whispered something Sissy didn't quite hear.

"What did you say?"

"Not to forget this was mine first."

Sissy smiled and then moaned. How could she forget any of it, especially Scarlett's ego?

Chapter

65

Michel was likeable and good-looking. He wasn't big but he had a well-muscled body and a head of thick dark hair. No more than twenty-three or twenty-four, his horn-rimmed glasses made him look sexy, not bookish. His finely chiseled profile was a definite plus. It was almost feminine.

Sissy arranged for the three of them to have dinner down at the wharf, al fresco, so they could feel the night air and see the harbor lights. Michel lit a cigarette and relaxed back into his chair. Sissy was almost giddy, being with her two lovers like this. She, of course, hadn't told Michel about Scarlett. He thought she was a virgin and she had been, as far as men were concerned.

"I understand you're a writer," said Michel in elegant but clipped English. You could hear just the trace of a Swiss accent.

"Yes," said Scarlett. "Right now it's mostly poetry."

"Do you know T.S. Eliot wrote his poem, 'The Wasteland,' here in Lausanne?"

Scarlett was surprised that this beautiful place had produced that extraordinary but, for her, depressing work. "No," Scarlett replied. "I didn't know that."

Sissy beamed. Michel was so smart. He knew something Scarlett didn't know.

"Actually," continued Michel without a bit of pretense in his voice, "this city has been a temporary home to quite a few thinkers and writers. Voltaire, Dickens and Byron were here as well and now, of course, you."

Scarlett could see what had attracted Sissy to Michel. He was a charmer. Plus he was bright, handsome and played the cello to boot. She just hoped Michel was as nice as he seemed. "I'm afraid it won't be home for long," acknowledged Scarlett. "I'm leaving for Paris tomorrow."

"Oh," said Michel, genuinely disappointed, turning to Sissy. "Can't you talk her out of it? At least for a day or two."

Sissy was surprised. She had never expected these two to get along so well. "Well, Scarlett, what do you say, a little while longer? For Michel and me? For Byron and Voltaire?"

Scarlett smiled, delighted by their mutual attention.

"Come on, Scarlett. Say yes," intoned Michel. "You've got to see Lausanne's Gothic cathedral and its famous rose window. And we can go for a drive in the country and maybe even take a boat ride on Lake Geneva. Anything you'd like." He smiled. "We do have a few civilized amusements in this country."

Scarlett was ecstatic. Everything was working out better than if she had planned it. When she had called Paris earlier that morning, she found out Gina was in Morocco. In broken English, Gina's roommate let Scarlett know she was expected back late the following day. She thanked Henri and wondered what in the world Gina could be doing in Morocco.

Scarlett held up her glass of Schweppes lemon water to Sissy and Michel. "To the both of you and another two days in Lausanne."

"Good," said Michel. He clapped his hands and a waiter brought a menu over. "Well, ladies. Shall we eat?"

Chapter

66

Just as Scarlett glanced at her watch, there was a knock at the door. It was barely seven o'clock. If she had any doubts before, she didn't now. The Swiss were precise. She opened the door, and a big smile came on her face. Standing there in the hallway was Michel dressed in a tuxedo and Sissy in an elegant, long black gown, with their cello cases in their hands.

"So formal?" observed Scarlett.

"You wanted a concert, didn't you?" smiled Michel. "We have to do it right, you know."

Sissy and Michel snapped open their cases and pulled out their cellos. They tuned them and rosined their bows. Michel grabbed two chairs from a nearby table. They were ready to begin. Michel announced they would play several "Caprices and Etudes" composed for the cello by Auguste Joseph Franchomme. Michel counted out the beat and they began playing, he with just as much passion as Sissy.

Scarlett couldn't help but wonder how they must be in bed together. All that fire. All that emotion. All that music that moved within them. "Encore!" she clapped when they finished and insisted, "Play something else. Please."

"What about the Beethoven sonata?" suggested Sissy.

"For your lady's pleasure," said Michel, turning to Scarlett. "Beethoven's 'Cello Sonata in E Minor,' without the piano accompaniment." He smiled and gestured to a piano in the corner of the suite. "Unless you care to join us?"

"I don't think so," laughed Scarlett. "'Chopsticks' is my complete repertoire."

This time Sissy counted and they began the sonata. Scarlett felt transported as she listened and watched their bodies sway in rhythm with the music they were playing. When they finished, Scarlett applauded and rewarded them with a glass of champagne she had ordered for the occasion.

"To the beauty that is music," said Scarlett, raising her glass. "And the talent that makes it so."

"There she goes again," said Sissy. "Trying to charm the birds out of the trees."

"I think maybe she did," grinned Michel. "She got a private concert, didn't she?"

After Sissy and Michel put their cellos away, they sat down on the sofa across from Scarlett. When they finished their champagne, Sissy got up and poured everyone another glass and then another. The three were feeling good and it wasn't just the champagne, it was the energy in the room. It flowed easily between the three of them and gave everything a soft, sensual edge.

"What about someone else making the music?" said Sissy and turned on the intercom. A waltz was playing. "Okay, Strauss. Do your thing. Well?" she said, looking at Michel. "How about it? Shall we dance?"

Scarlett sat back, enjoying the music, watching Sissy and Michel dance together. They glided across the floor as if they had been waltzing together for years. When the music ended, Sissy poured herself and everyone else yet another glass of champagne. They were now on their second bottle. Scarlett knew she shouldn't take another sip but she did. Another waltz began playing, and Sissy took Scarlett by the hand.

"Scarlett and I used to dance together back in Charleston," said Sissy, looking over at Michel. "After all, what are you going to do at a girls' school but dance with your best friend? Do you mind?"

Michel smiled at them both. "Not at all. Please."

Sissy put her arm around Scarlett's waist and they danced. Several bars of music later, Sissy must have forgotten where she was because she suddenly pulled Scarlett closer to her and kissed her on the neck.

"Stop, Sissy. Stop it," whispered Scarlett, looking over at Michel, who just smiled and nodded in their direction.

Sissy moved from Scarlett's neck up to her lips and gave her a long, passionate kiss, tongue and all. When Sissy finally returned to consciousness, she pulled back from Scarlett's mouth so fast, she almost gave herself whiplash.

"I must be drunk!" she protested to Michel. "I could have sworn it was you."

"Then maybe you should sit for a minute and figure it out." He smiled and pulled out a chair for her. "And let me dance with Scarlett."

Sissy sat down, stunned at Michel's nonchalance.

"May I?" Michel asked Scarlett.

"Of course," she said, glancing over at Sissy, every bit as surprised as she was.

Michel was gentle and sure of his movements. Scarlett didn't even mind him leading. It was hard to believe he had not reacted to Sissy kissing her.

"I bet you'd like Sissy to stay here tonight."

Scarlett suddenly stiffened in Michel's arms. She wasn't sure how to answer him. She wanted to protect Sissy, but she also wanted to spend the night with her.

"Well?" he smiled.

"Yes, I would," Scarlett finally answered.

"Would you mind if I stayed too?" asked Michel with a twinkle in his eye.

Chapter

67

Sissy and Michel took her to the airport the following morning. Needless to say, they were all hung over but decidedly content. They had shared an unforgettable night, a night of perfect pleasure. On a certain level it was inconceivable to Scarlett that they ended up in bed together. But they had. More incredible yet was the fact Scarlett had enjoyed Michel making love to her, over and over again. As a lover, he was sensitive and exciting. He took pleasure in pleasing a woman, maybe as much as another woman.

Scarlett was confused, and in a way it was ironic. While Sissy was completely relaxed with the emerging complexity of her sexuality, Scarlett only seemed more uptight with hers. On one level she was sure the night had been an aberration, a momentary erogenous lapse.

As the three waited for Scarlett's flight to be called, Michel gave Scarlett a present. "Open it on the plane," he said. "It's a camera. For Paris. From Sissy and me."

Scarlett hugged them both. "Thank you," she said. "And thank you for . . ." She paused, trying to find a way to say it. "For Lausanne."

They all looked at each other and smiled. When Scarlett's flight was announced, a tearful Sissy told her, "Make sure you write."

"I will," Scarlett assured her, and then she kissed both Michel and her on the cheek. "Give your parents my regards." Then Scarlett told Sissy with a mischievous glint in her eyes, "Tell them I'm terribly sorry I missed them."

Sissy laughed. Mr. and Mrs. Langtree were due in Lausanne tomorrow to meet Michel. From what they had heard, he was perfect for Sissy. He came from a good family with lots of money and he played the cello, almost as well as Sissy. Apparently, all that money the Langtrees had spent on their daughter's therapy was paying off. She had found a man.

It would have been interesting to hear how Sissy explained the bill for the last three days at the D'Vichy as well as that substantial withdrawal from her bank account. But who knows? Maybe they wouldn't even care. Once they met Michel, they would no doubt start hearing wedding bells.

Chapter

68

The plane took flight and Scarlett closed her eyes, remembering the night before. Seeing Michel and Sissy in bed together hadn't upset her the way she thought it might. No. It wasn't that way at all. It had turned her on. Up on his hands and arms, bracing his body just above Sissy's, Michel had penetrated her a little at a time, teasing her, until he was all the way inside. Then he slowly began making love to her, rhythmically increasing his strokes as Sissy's body asked for it. As their breathing became heavier, Sissy reached over and took Scarlett's arm, drawing her near them. Michel leaned down and kissed Scarlett on the cheek. When she gave him her mouth, he gave her his tongue and Scarlett took it. Sissy ran her hand between Scarlett's thighs. When she pulled her hand back, it was glistening with her lover's wetness. Sissy stuck her fingers inside Michel's mouth, then into her own.

"Touch her again," Michel told Sissy, even more aroused, but it was too late. Sissy was almost there.

"Faster," she told Michel. "Please."

Sissy and Michel's energy completely enveloped Scarlett. She put her hand between her legs and watched their rhythmic, driving dance, becoming more and more excited until, finally, she moved in great undulating waves toward the fulfillment of her own pleasure.

Scarlett suddenly opened her eyes as the stewardess was folding her tray down into the eating position.

"What can I get you to drink, mademoiselle?"

"Coffee. With cream, please."

When the hostess left, Scarlett slipped back into the fever of the night before and remembered Michel. Just as with Sissy, he had entered her slowly, until she couldn't wait to have all of him inside her. When he finally acquiesced and slid inside, Scarlett came. Actually, she exploded and held on to Michel as tightly as she could while Sissy buried her face in kisses.

"Cafe au lait," said the stewardess, putting Scarlett's coffee down. "This should wake you up and get that blood moving."

Scarlett looked up at her and grinned. "Oh, it's moving all right. In fact, I think it got a bit overheated."

The stewardess was a bit perplexed. "What about a cool glass of juice then?"

"Okay," said Scarlett. "But I doubt it will help much." She couldn't resist delivering the quip poised on the end of her tongue. "I run hot."

Something must have gotten lost in the translation from English to French or the stewardess simply chose to ignore Scarlett's baudy aside. "Oh, I'm very sorry, mademoiselle. Something for the fever then. An aspirin, maybe?"

"No." Scarlett laughed, shaking her head. No aspirin was going to cool down this fever. It was the fever of living and right now, it was running red-hot. "Just a little breakfast, please."

"*Bon*, right away. *Un petit déjeuner.*"

It was her second breakfast of the day. Scarlett needed the energy. She hadn't been to sleep yet, and she would be in Paris in less than an hour.

Chapter

69

Even though it was the beginning of July, Paris was overcast. Low-lying, wispy clouds hid the city and its charm. You couldn't even see the Eiffel Tower. As the plane descended toward the airport, Scarlett nervously combed her hair and touched up her lipstick. She couldn't wait to see Gina. What she remembered most about her were her eyes. They were eyes you never forgot. Expressive and extraordinarily beautiful, they had a haunting, unforgettable gaze, one that you would swear held secrets.

Scarlett straightened her skirt and pulled down her light green sweater. She knew she looked good in this outfit. That was why she wore it. It showed off her body and set off her eyes. She slid into the light mauve jacket matching her skirt and checked her heels. No scuff marks. Thanks to Sissy, Scarlett now had a wardrobe and a sense of style. With her help, Scarlett had shaken off most of Dillinger's dust.

"Who is it?" Gina had asked in French as she answered Scarlett's telephone call the evening before.

"It's Scarlett. I'm coming to Paris tomorrow."

"What!" exclaimed Gina. "Don't tease me, Scarlett. My heart just fell through the floor."

Apparently Henri either hadn't understood Scarlett or had forgotten to give Gina the message. "Where are you?"

"Switzerland. In Lausanne."

Gina took Scarlett's flight number and said she would meet her at the airport. "Oh, Scarlett," she said excitedly. "This is the best surprise. Tomorrow's my birthday. I'm going to be twenty-one."

"I know," said Scarlett.

All that moving around in Europe when Gina was a kid, going from army base to army base, had put her a year behind in school. That was why, even though they were a year apart, Scarlett and Gina had graduated together.

"You're an old lady already," Scarlett kidded her.

"Sometimes I feel like it," laughed Gina. "I'm so excited. I can't wait to see you."

Chapter

70

Scarlett spotted Gina the instant she entered the terminal. Her long, black hair was tied back from her face, showing off her remarkable blue eyes. She was so much more beautiful than Scarlett remembered. When they reached each other, they embraced without saying a word and held each other for the longest time, oblivious to everyone, honoring the powerful, familiar feeling that swept through them.

"Happy Birthday," said Scarlett, suddenly pulling back, needing to break the intimacy.

"Thank you. Are you okay?" asked Gina.

"A little tired, I guess."

"Well, you look wonderful." Gina sensed the shift in Scarlett. "Heels?" she asked, looking down.

"Yes. I even know how to walk in them."

"And nicely."

"You approve then?" said Scarlett, delighted that how she looked pleased Gina.

"I always did."

Scarlett had been around Sissy so long she had forgotten that the woman standing next to her wasn't just about surfaces. Gina plumbed the depths and that was where she was right now, deep inside a part of Scarlett that Scarlett didn't even know existed.

"Come on. Let's get your bags and get out of here," said Gina.

Chapter

71

Gina's apartment was small but seemed larger because of its high ceilings and polished wooden floors. In the living room several armchairs and a sofa formed a sitting area at the center of a Moroccan rug. Monet and Renoir prints, along with a Degas or two, hung on the walls. Books on fashion and design filled shelves on either side of wide French doors opening onto a balcony overlooking Paris and the Eiffel Tower.

"What a view," raved Scarlett. "Even the rooftops here are beautiful."

Gina laughed. "Wait until you see the city at night. I don't know what it is, but when its lights come on, Paris becomes the most romantic place in the world."

"That's some recommendation."

"It's true," said Gina, slipping her arm around Scarlett.

As soon as they touched, it began. The "magic dissolve," as Gina called it, the soul embrace, the blending of two human beings, one into the other. It was rare and it was scary. Scarlett had only experienced it with Gina. But once again, just as she had done at the airport, Scarlett pulled away.

"I like your apartment."

"Thanks," said Gina, feeling Scarlett's anxiety, intuiting what had happened.

"Where's your roommate?"

"Henri moved out. He knew I needed the privacy. Besides, I can afford the place by myself now. I just sold a few designs."

"Really! Before my first book is even in print?"

"I guess poems take a little longer than dresses," teased Gina.

"Yes," Scarlett teased back. "They take longer because they're made to last longer."

"Touché!" replied Gina. She gently brushed Scarlett's hair away from her face. "You look tired."

"I guess I am. Switzerland was exhausting." Scarlett caught herself. "You know, all that sightseeing."

"Then why don't you rest awhile? A nap might do you good."

"It probably would. Care to join me?"

Gina took Scarlett's hand and led her down the hall to a room where the afternoon sun filtered through half-opened shutters and fell across a large bed. Gina went over and opened an armoire. "Here," she said, handing Scarlett a silk robe. "You can wear this."

"How pretty."

"Only the best for you, madame."

"What are you going to wear?"

"One just like it."

"Good," said Scarlett. "Silk should never be worn alone."

"Never," agreed Gina. "Who would dare?"

They both undressed and slipped into their robes. Scarlett adjusted her sash several different ways, but it still didn't look right.

"It doesn't matter," Gina told her. "I know you're not any good with bows."

They both laughed, recalling their conversation the night of the school play back in Dillinger.

"I bet you don't remember what you told me then," said Scarlett.

"Oh, but I do. I said that you were undoubtedly very good with your hands. That bows just weren't important to you."

"And?" prodded Scarlett playfully.

"And I was right. You tie a lousy bow," kidded Gina. She patted the bed next to her. "Now come here and get some rest."

Scarlett went over and lay down next to her. "I'm glad I'm here for your birthday," she said softly.

"Me too. Birthdays are rough for me."

Scarlett was about to ask why when she felt a sudden, intense need to connect physically. It was overpowering. She ran her hand over Gina's breast.

"I can't," said Gina and took Scarlett's hand. "Not right now."

Scarlett was stunned at the rejection.

"I hope I can explain." Gina paused and took a sip of mineral water. "People sometimes use sex to avoid being truly intimate. I don't want us to do that."

Scarlett's frustration spiraled and she suddenly felt manipulated, trapped in some kind of ridiculous sexual conundrum. She couldn't remember Gina ever talking like this. Maybe she was having a birthday breakdown of some sort. She heard that could happen when you turned twenty-one.

"I guess what I'm trying to say, Scarlett, is that I hope we can share who we really are while you're here and that you won't pull away from me every time you feel we're getting too close."

Not a word left Scarlett's lips. The kind of intimacy Gina was suggesting was unthinkable to her. She had no idea how you did that, how that kind of closeness felt, what kind of surrender it required. Just then Gina's robe fell away from her body, revealing her beautiful breasts and tapering waist, the hollow in her thigh, the slight rise at her belly, the triangle of dark hair. Scarlett took a deep breath. She couldn't imagine wanting anyone more.

"Have you ever shared that part of yourself?" asked Scarlett. "Who you really are?"

"Yes," said Gina, pulling the robe back over her body. "And I'll tell you about it. But not now."

"Did you go to bed with her?"

"No. It wasn't like that." Gina got up and walked over to the window where, without looking back at Scarlett, she asked, "Do you think you could give me that part of you?"

Gina might as well have asked Scarlett to go hang herself. Her request was that scary, its fulfillment that improbable.

"Think about it," said Gina, turning around. "It would mean everything to me."

"I'll try," said Scarlet, scared out of her wits, sensing that a part of her was about to change forever.

Chapter
72

"What happened to the rest of your skirt?"
"This is a mini-skirt," said Gina. "It's the latest style."
"But I can practically see your underwear."
"I don't think so," smiled Gina. "I'm not wearing any. They leave a line. But I do have on pantyhose."

Scarlett was flabbergasted. Paris and Charleston were light years apart.

"Why don't you try one on too?" said Gina, opening her closet. "We're the same size." She took a skirt out and handed it to Scarlett. "Put it on. Believe me, you'll look terrific. You've got the best legs of any girl in Paris."

"How do you know?"

"Remember, I dress them."

"Is that all?"

"If you're asking whether or not I have sex with other women, Scarlett, the answer is yes."

Scarlett was surprised and hurt. Now she really didn't understand why Gina hadn't slept with her this afternoon. When Gina saw the look on Scarlett's face, she went and put her arms around her.

"It's you I love."

"Then why wouldn't you do it with me earlier?" asked Scarlett.

"That's what I've been trying to say, Scarlett. With us it's not just about sex. It never was. Not even that first time down by the river in Dillinger."

Gina could feel Scarlett wanting to break the embrace. She held her closer. "Like it or not, we're stuck here," she said, sliding her hand between them and pressing it up against Scarlett's breast. "In each other's heart."

Chapter

73

The taste of Gina's lipstick was still on Scarlett's mouth as they walked into the Katmandu. A few women stared at them, smiled and then went back to their drinks as a new Tom Jones song blared out of the speakers. It was an exciting, sexy place to be. It was the first time Scarlett had ever been to a lesbian bar.

The club's high-charged atmosphere was heightened even more by its flashing strobe lights, the cigarette smoke hazing the air, the scent of commingled perfumes, the edgy sensuality and, on the dance floor, the syncopated rhythm of the hunt, uninhibited, playful, intense—the collective erotic rush.

Not just French women came to the Katmandu; there were women from everywhere. The club was world famous. Being named after the capital of Nepal, however, might seem a bit odd since the spiritual side of a woman was of no apparent interest here. Sitting off in one corner Scarlett noticed half a dozen men seated at tables surrounded by women.

"What are those men doing here?" Scarlett asked Gina.

"They're Johns."

"Johns?"

"Men who keep women."

"But the women they're with are lesbians. Aren't they?" asked Scarlett incredulously.

"Yes," answered Gina.

"Then why are they with those men?"

"They have an understanding," said Gina. "The women they're with are here with their own girlfriends."

"That's cozy!" observed Scarlett sarcastically. "Now that just doesn't make any sense. Does it?"

"I'll explain later," said Gina, taking Scarlett's hand and leading her to the other side of the club. She wanted to discourage any further questions for the time being. "There they are," said Gina, gesturing toward five gorgeous high-fashion models, all friends of hers, and all lesbians except Britt, a blonde from Sweden, and a redhead called Patrice, the most beautiful of them all. "This is Scarlett," announced Gina, raising her voice above the music.

"So you're the one we've heard so much about?" said Britt.

Scarlett was surprised and embarrassed, even nervous. Beautiful women always did that to her. They appealed to the shallow side of her nature, and at this point in her life, that side was still extensive.

"Sit down, Scarlett. Here, next to me," said Patrice with a French accent, patting a spot on the couch. "I want to hear all about you. This time from you."

Gina smiled. "Go ahead, Scarlett. But be careful. Patrice loves to dish."

Scarlett finally sat down, so nervous not a syllable left her mouth. Patrice was just too gorgeous.

"Gina's description hardly does you justice. You're lovely," said Patrice. "And some legs." She looked over at Gina. "You never said anything about her legs."

Gina smiled again and lit a cigarette. "There are a lot of things I never told you about Scarlett. They're private."

Patrice laughed. "Gina has such a diplomatic way of putting you in your place. Doesn't she?"

Scarlett didn't answer. She just kept trying not to stare at Patrice, but it was impossible. Head to toe, she was flawless. Not one feature could have been improved. Before Scarlett came off as completely rude, a waitress arrived at the table with a magnum of expensive champagne and everybody began singing "Happy Birthday" to Gina.

The cork was popped and the dry sweetness flowed. Britt proposed a toast and everyone at the table raised their glass.

"To Gina Jamison, Paris's future couturier formidable," said Britt. "And we won't mention her birthday again."

As everyone laughed and made more toasts, Scarlett looked around at the other women in the club. Some were dressed like men, looked like men, but not many. Most wanted to look like what they were, women. Scarlett's eyes drifted back over to that other corner, the one with the men and their lesbian dates. For the life of her, she could not understand how gay women could be whores.

A large number of single women stood at the bar cruising the others and keeping an eye on the door, just in case someone new walked in. One woman caught Scarlett's eye. She looked familiar, but Scarlett could not place her. The woman saw Scarlett looking at her and smiled. Scarlett turned away. She did not want to give the stranger the wrong idea. She was with someone.

"Want to dance?" asked Gina.

"Yes," said Scarlett and got up. "I haven't heard this song in a while."

"Me either."

Gina guided Scarlett out onto the floor and pulled her to her. A revolving kaleidoscope on the ceiling bounced colored light around the club in time with the music. Gina pulled Scarlett still closer. Dancing next to them were two tall, extremely attractive women, one dark, one blond, oblivious to everyone else. Gina watched them for a moment and then turned her attention back to Scarlett.

"Are you enjoying yourself?"

"Yes," answered Scarlett. "I like your friends a lot. Especially Patrice. She's a real trip."

"He certainly is."

"What!" exclaimed Scarlett, staring at Gina in total disbelief. "What did you say?"

"He. Patrice is really Patrick."

"You're kidding?" replied Scarlett incredulously.

"No," said Gina with a wry smile. "You're looking at Paris's top model. He's on more Vogue covers than the rest of them put together."

"A transvestite!"

"That's right." Gina laughed. "One who sells a lot of clothes. Women will pay anything to own an original worn by Patrice. They all want that look and they think Patrice can give it to them."

"It's hard to believe," said Scarlett, still staring at the man who looked better in women's clothes than most women did. "What if they found out?"

"They won't," assured Gina. "Just a couple of us know."

"Is he gay?" asked Scarlett.

"You really don't think a straight man could pull that off, do you?"

Scarlett shook her head, unable to keep her eyes off Patrice. He smiled and waved a little feminine wave in her direction. "No. I guess not," said Scarlett, looking around. "This club is something else. I've never seen so many beautiful and exciting women in one place." She glanced over at the same two women Gina had noticed earlier. "Is it always like this?"

"Always." The music ended and Gina brushed her lips up against Scarlett's. "I love you."

"Me too," said Scarlett spontaneously. She looked surprised, obviously caught off guard by her sudden admission and how vulnerable it made her feel. She pulled away from Gina.

"Where does a girl freshen up around here?"

Gina smiled and nodded toward a darkened hallway on the other side of the club. "Over there."

"I'll be right back."

"Don't flirt with anyone," kidded Gina.

"Moi? Never."

As Scarlett made her way to the bathroom, a lot of ladies looked in her direction. More confident now, Scarlett smiled at them and wondered where that face was she had seen earlier, the one that was so familiar. When Scarlett opened the bathroom door, she quickly found out. Standing there was Delores Sheridan, the face Skeeter Boyd loved to jerk off to back in high school, the actress whose face had adorned more movie magazines than Scarlett could count.

"Hello," said the sultry voice.

"Hi," answered Scarlett.

"I'm Delores. Delores Sheridan," she announced, giving Scarlett her hand.

"Scarlett Turner. Nice to meet you."

"First time at the Katmandu?"

"Yes," said Scarlett. "First time in Paris."

"Ever been to Greece?"

"No," said Scarlett.

"Would you like to?" asked Delores.

"Sure. Someday. Who wouldn't?"

"I'm going tomorrow," said Delores, and she pushed a piece of paper into Scarlett's pocket. "Here's my telephone number. You can make that someday any day you want."

"I'm with someone," objected Scarlett but she was nonetheless flattered.

"My number is for when you're not. Nothing is forever." With that Delores smiled and walked out of the bathroom.

Chapter

74

Gina and Scarlett left the Katmandu a little after midnight and walked along Paris's Left Bank in the direction of Gina's apartment. The rush of the night air felt good on their skin.

"There's a nice view from here," said Gina.

"Want to sit for a minute?"

The two sat on a bench next to the Seine and watched a few barges drift down the river stringed with flickering lights. Now and then a stranger strolled by behind them.

"How did you like the Katmandu?"

"It's a trip," said Scarlett. "All those hot women in one place. But what about those men?" she asked, suddenly remembering Gina hadn't answered her question yet. "How come they let them in the club?"

"Why not?"

"It's a club for women," insisted Scarlett.

"And whoever they want to bring," said Gina. "Did you see anyone getting uptight?"

"No."

"People don't get into other people's business in Paris. That's what I like about it."

"What was it you called them again? Those men, I mean."

"Johns," said Gina. "Men who keep women in return for sexual favors."

Scarlett shook her head. "I don't understand how a gay women can let her body be used like that."

"Many of them are students or putting careers together. It's an arrangement that benefits both sides."

"But they're fucking men to do it," said Scarlett, derision in her voice.

"And loving women," said Gina. "It works out for everyone. After all, what safer mistress can a man have than a lesbian? She's not going to ask him to leave his wife and marry her."

"I think it's ridiculous," declared Scarlett with uncharacteristic vehemence.

"You surprise me," said Gina, lighting a cigarette. "I didn't realize you were so judgmental."

The observation caught Scarlett off guard. She had never thought of herself as judgmental. "Maybe I'm still upset about Aunt Fannie."

Gina looked at her questioningly and inhaled her cigarette.

"My mother's dead sister. She used to work down at the river, at Molly Disharoon's floating whorehouse." Scarlett leaned back on the bench and stared out at the Seine, trying to deal with the meaning of these sudden memories. "What I remember most about Fanny is her laughter and the way she hugged me. Her arms felt so safe. Isn't that odd, Gina? The same arms that held all those men."

"What happened to her?" asked a stunned Gina.

"She killed herself with rat poison. She was twenty-seven. I think, but I'm not sure," informed Scarlett in a monotone, trying to control her emotions. "It took her two days to die."

"Jesus," murmured Gina. "I'm sorry."

"When we got to the hospital, I could hear her pain clear at the other end of the corridor." Scarlett's voice faltered. "It's those screams I can't forget. It sounded like the devil himself was torturing her."

"Go ahead and cry," said Gina, putting her arm around Scarlett. "It's okay. It's a sad thing."

Still the tears did not come, and Scarlett went on. "Fannie told my mother not to be sad because she was already dead. That Momma was looking at nothing. 'A soulless body,' is how she put it. Then," said Scarlett, snapping her fingers, "just like that Aunt Fannie was gone." Scarlett took in a deep breath. "My momma didn't know it then, but my father used to fuck her sister down at Molly Disharoon's. He even took me there once."

Gina winced at this revelation. "To a whorehouse?"

"Yes," said Scarlett, wiping away the tears that had finally come. "To Molly's. My mother was at work and he probably figured that since I couldn't talk yet, I wouldn't remember. Or maybe he was just too drunk to care."

Gina lit another cigarette.

"You smoke too much."

"Yes," replied Gina. "I guess I do." She inhaled and blew the smoke away from Scarlett's face.

"Come on," said Scarlett, standing up. "Please, let's go."

They walked for an hour or so, walking off the sadness. Gina was silent but she touched Scarlett's waist now and then to let her know she was there.

"Thanks for listening," Scarlett finally said. "I feel better. How about you?"

"I'm okay." A quick smile came to her face. "My birthday's over and you're in Paris." She tossed her cigarette away. "Ready to go back to the apartment?"

Scarlett's heart raced. "Yes. But I'd like a kiss first, while no one's around." The wanting had suddenly returned.

"I taste like smoke."

"I know how you taste," said Scarlett and nudged Gina into the shadows of a building, where they kissed. Only the echo of footsteps finally forced them apart and they walked on.

"Some people believe you share souls when you kiss," said Gina. "That you leave a piece of yourself with them."

"Poetic notion," answered Scarlett, not meaning to sound as sarcastic as she had.

"Yes, I suppose it is."

"That's what you want, isn't it?" said Scarlett, stopping and turning to Gina. "The part of me I've never shared?"

Gina looked at Scarlett and said nothing for a while; then she kissed her briefly on the lips and whispered, "Let's go home."

Chapter

75

Scarlett and Gina made love all night. The earth itself seemed to disappear, swept away by a lovemaking so passionate that neither Gina nor Scarlett could imagine a time when what they felt for each other had not existed or a time when it might not exist. When day finally broke, they watched the sun rise over Paris without a word between them. For the moment words had become unnecessary, almost superfluous, a bruise to their closeness.

The intimacy that Scarlett so feared had finally been embraced. Now no matter how much she might want to, she would never be able to take back what she had given that night or give back what she had taken. The exchange was forever. It was a pact, not between bodies, but between souls.

"You look beautiful this morning," said Gina, cradling Scarlett's head in her lap. She gently stroked her hair as the bright sunlight fell across their bodies. What she saw in Scarlett's face was the peace true surrender brings. The panic and fear in it were gone and, at least for the moment, so was the civil war that always seemed to rage within her.

"I love you," said Scarlett. She rolled over on her side and pulled Gina down to her. "It's just like Maggie said," she whispered. "Love is grace."

"Then let's hope ours is forever," whispered back Gina, cherishing the moment, overjoyed that Scarlett had actually dared to share her feelings.

It was Scarlett who finally broke the powerful silence. "What about some breakfast?"

"What about sleep?"

"We can always do that," answered Scarlett. "Right now, I just want to look at you."

"And eat," said Gina, getting up from bed. "I know your appetite." She went over to the closet and took out a sheer white dressing gown. When she put it on, Scarlett could see the outline of her breasts.

"Nice choice," said Scarlett. "Very sexy."

"I have others. Try one on while I fix breakfast. It's slit up the sides so it'll show off your legs."

When Gina left the room, Scarlett looked at all the beautiful clothes in her closet and wondered how she could afford them. They didn't look homemade. Scarlett put on the blue gown Gina had suggested and instantly loved the way it felt on her skin. It was soft and the scent of Gina lingered in every fold.

"Where'd you get these?" asked Scarlett from the bedroom.

"Morocco. It's called a jellaba. Someday I'd like to design a line of clothing around it. I just love the way it falls over the body. That's why I have so many of them. I need their inspiration."

The comforting aroma of coffee and toasting bread filled the air as Scarlett came into the kitchen. Gina put down the orange she was cutting and looked at her.

"There you go staring at me again," said Scarlett.

"I can't get over the way you look." Gina put a bowl of sliced fruit on the table. "So soft. Here," she said, taking a small mirror off the wall and handing it to Scarlett. "See for yourself. It's your eyes," Gina explained, pouring steaming milk into two large coffee cups as Scarlett searched in the mirror.

Scarlett sat down and blew her breath on the glass, then polished it with her napkin. She finally saw what Gina was talking about.

"Jesus! What's the matter, Gina?" she asked, looking up from the mirror.

Gina's face was contorted in pain. She slumped down into a chair and tried to speak. When she found she couldn't, Gina buried her face in her hands and wept.

"What's wrong?" Scarlett pushed her chair near Gina's and took her hand. "Please. What is it?"

"When you blew on the mirror right now, Scarlett, it brought back terrible memories. Memories of Greece and the day she drowned."

Gina pulled her hand out of Scarlett's and lit a cigarette. "When they dragged her body from the river, an old woman dressed in black suddenly appeared out of nowhere and put a mirror in front of Abby's face. She wanted to catch her breath. You know? See it on the mirror. But the mirror never clouded over. Not like the one that you just blew on." Gina exhaled the smoke from her lungs. "Because there was no breath left to catch."

"I'm sorry," were the only words Scarlett could manage, and she instantly realized how dumb they sounded, how utterly comfortless they must be at this moment.

"It was Abby's birthday. She turned nine that day," said Gina, and she looked at Scarlett. "And so did I. She was my sister. My twin."

Gina's revelation stunned Scarlett. "How come you never told me?"

"I almost did. Back in Dillinger that first night out at the river. But I choked up and couldn't."

Scarlett could see the Eiffel Tower from where they sat. It seemed almost surreal at this moment, all that steel presiding over so much pain. Now she understood why Gina hated her birthday. It brought it all back.

"Do you know what it's like to go to your own funeral? To bury yourself?"

Scarlett felt a chill move up her spine. She had no idea.

"From that day on it felt like a piece of me was missing," said Gina. "All of a sudden I was a "twinless twin.""

Gina talked and talked before her sorrow ran out. "I'm still learning Abby's way of loving." Gina picked up another cigarette and lit it. "It wasn't given to me at birth like it was to her. I was closed and guarded. She was open and trusting."

Scarlett was surprised at Gina's perception of herself. "But that is the way you love, just like Abby. That's the part of your sister that didn't die that day. The part that lives in you."

Scarlett couldn't account for the source of her words or the power they would have on Gina. But that day she affirmed a life in the most extraordinary way. In a way Gina would never forget. Then, just as Gina had reached deep within and revealed herself, so did Scarlett. She finally talked about all the loss in her life, about all those people besides Aunt Fannie that God had thrown down into deep, dark holes. Among others, Gina heard about Billy Ray Yallop, Wanda Fargo, and "good ol' Joe," Scarlett's own drunken daddy.

Later that day Scarlett and Gina dozed off in each other's arms and shared the sweet sleep of dreams. All those disclosures had exhausted them and precipitated an emotional quickening of sorts, an unveiling of souls, the kind that joins two people in a way their bodies never can. The afternoon soon faded away and half the night crawled by before the lovers opened their eyes again. Then, without a word between them, they made love, celebrating their deepening intimacy.

Years later when Scarlett tried to write about that summer in Paris she discovered just how powerless words were to describe affairs of the soul. Seven weeks. One summer. Paris, 1966. But who can say when such affairs really begin? There are people who believe some souls have been in love forever.

Chapter

76

The day was so hot, you could almost smell the sunshine. Scarlett moved closer to Gina and the partial shade of the cafe's umbrella. From there she looked back out at the street and Montmartre, the artists' quarter of an earlier Paris.

At one time or another all the great ones had passed through here and through Gertrude Stein's Paris salon, huge talents, the writers and artists of a generation: Hemingway, Juan Gris, Matisse, F. Scott and Zelda Fitzgerald, Picasso, Apollinaire, Cezanne, and so many more, famous and not so famous. The list was endless. Stein and her lifelong companion, Alice B. Toklas, had entertained them all with good food and drink and enviable conversation. For decades the charmed circle at Gertrude's house was the only place to be.

Scarlett took a sip of coffee and then examined the blue decorations at the top of her cup. They were wearing away. She wondered about all the people who might have drunk from it at one time or another. The painters. The poets. The writers. What inspirations had been born out of this simple white cup?

"What are you thinking, Scarlett?"

"About a love story. I've got the opening," said Scarlett excitedly.

"Want to tell me?"

Scarlett composed her thoughts. "I think I'd tell it in the third person. It would begin like this. 'I want to tell you a story about two friends of mine, two women, who loved each other.' "

Gina smiled and took Scarlett's hand beneath the table. "Just make sure you tell them how much."

Chapter

77

"It looks just like a big stink bug."

Gina laughed as Scarlett continued to stare at the strange-looking car the French called a Deux Chevaux and foreigners, a Citroen. Scarlett pushed on its front fender. The car quivered, then bobbed up and down as if it were sitting on a giant bowl of Jell-O.

"Is this thing safe?" she asked.

"Yes," assured Gina, putting her suitcase in the rear seat.

"Then why is it so shaky?"

"It's the suspension system. That's the reason why it's comfortable on the road."

"Yeah? American cars are comfortable and they don't jiggle like this." Scarlett pushed on the car and it shuddered again.

"American cars use springs for suspension. This one uses rubber bands."

"No way!" exclaimed Scarlett.

"Oh, yes," said Gina. "I'm sure there's a couple of extra ones on the car somewhere." She smiled at Scarlett. "In case one breaks."

"You're kidding me, Gina Jamison."

"No," she answered, sliding into the driver's seat. "I've already replaced one or two."

Scarlett was incredulous.

"Well, come on. Get in. It's time we put this Deux Chevaux on the road."

Scarlett slid into the passenger seat. "You're putting me on, aren't you?"

"No," answered Gina, pulling away from the curb. "I'm not."

After a couple of hours Scarlett grudgingly conceded that the Deux Chevaux was comfortable enough. That it was great on gas was not in dispute. The two-cylinder oddity almost never needed filling because it was as light as a feather. Maybe too light. The wind knocked it around pretty good.

"Don't worry," said Gina. "I've never seen one blow over."

"Somehow that's not reassuring," observed Scarlett just as a strong gust suddenly leaned the car off center.

"How about some music? It'll help you forget the wind." Gina turned on the radio and guided the needle across the dial. "Do you mind?" she asked, selecting a station with opera music. "I'm crazy about this stuff."

"Me too," said Scarlett.

Gina was surprised. "Really?"

Scarlett turned up the volume and hummed along with *La Traviata*. "Yeah. In fact, this is the first opera I ever heard."

"Where?"

"On the radio. I must have been about twelve at the time."

Scarlett conveniently left out how many times Sissy had taken her to the Opera in Charleston. Instead she explained how, as a child, while fiddling with the radio looking for Elvis, she discovered this powerful music. Even though she didn't understand a word they were singing, she got goose bumps. There was just something about it she couldn't resist. "Isn't it ironic that misery makes such beautiful music?" observed Scarlett.

"I really hadn't thought much about it. But I guess that's opera. It's almost always about dying, sickness or suicide," said Gina, glancing over at Scarlett. "What are you smiling about? Violetta just died of consumption."

"No," said Scarlett. "It was love. Alfredo left her."

Chapter

78

Gina pulled off the highway and drove toward an arcade of tall sycamores. The sun, now high in the sky, pierced the trees with intermittent rushes of light and shadow, making the road seem like the passage into another world.

"Where are we going?" asked Scarlett, admiring the tall, wild grass that rolled up to the horizon, bending beneath the wind.

"Why not let the road decide," said Gina. "How's your mood for adventure?"

"High," answered Scarlett. "Very high."

"Okay. Then which side do we take?" Gina pointed to a fork in the road up ahead.

"The left."

"You sure?"

"Yes," said Scarlett. "That's where the adventure is."

Gina smiled and turned down the left fork. Before long they encountered a series of small farms, their grassy pastures rolling ever onward into the distant horizon.

"When do I get to drive?"

"When you learn how," said Gina.

"How difficult can it be? You turn the wheel a little this way, then you turn it a little that way, push down on the pedal and press on the brake. It's no big deal. Where's that mood for adventure?" Scarlett prodded teasingly.

Gina smiled and pulled off the road. "Okay. The wheel is yours. Just don't kill us."

"I promise. I wouldn't want to cheat the fashion world out of its rising star."

Gina laughed and met Scarlett at the back of the car where they spritzed each other with bottled water. It was hot and getting hotter. Scarlett poured some water in her hand and rubbed the back of Gina's neck with it.

"I love you, Miss Jamison."

"That's only because I let you have your way."

"No," said Scarlett, grinning. "But it's good strategy. Keep it up."

Scarlett gave Gina a light kiss on the mouth and headed for the driver's side of the car. She slid into the seat and fitted her hands to the wheel. She turned on the ignition as Gina got in and the Deux Chevaux sputtered. A couple of more attempts and it finally started.

"Make sure you keep the clutch pressed in as you give it gas."

"I'm not a complete novice," said Scarlett. "Skeeter used to let me drive his old Ford once in a while."

"That guy back in Dillinger? The one you did with your clothes on?"

"Yeah, Skeeter Boyd, the moose himself. He had the biggest thing I ever saw."

"I wasn't aware you had seen that many."

"His was enough," replied Scarlett, giving the Citroen some gas, pointedly avoiding any mention of Michel.

The Deux Chevaux sputtered again and lurched forward, almost hitting a tree before Scarlett managed to get it back on the road. Gina was going to complain when Scarlett quickly pointed out, "This clutch takes a little getting used to, doesn't it?"

"Please, Scarlett, be careful. I don't want to have to buy this car. I can hardly afford to rent it."

"I said I had money."

Gina looked at Scarlett curiously. "That must have been some advance. I still don't understand how you could afford the ticket to Paris."

"It was enough," said Scarlett, quickly sidestepping Gina's sudden inquisitiveness.

"Jesus!" exclaimed Gina. "Please keep your eyes on the road. You almost hit that cow."

"There you go exaggerating again. I missed her by a mile. Why don't you relax?"

Gina sat back in her seat and lit a cigarette. As it turned out, Scarlett was a pretty good driver. It was just that she was easily distracted. Her eyes were everywhere but on the road.

"Just look at the way those clouds ride the sky, Gina, so high up there, and the light. It's extraordinary, like in one of Maggie's paintings."

"You mean the woman in New Mexico?"

"Yes," replied Scarlett, "Maggie Donovan. She said certain kinds of light were the reflection of angel wings unfurled in flight to God."

"Then there must be lots of them out today," said Gina, looking up at the sky.

"Yeah," agreed Scarlett. "Lots."

Gina put out her cigarette and rested her hand on the back of Scarlett's neck. "You loved Maggie, didn't you?" The observation came as a simple statement of fact.

"I still do," answered Scarlett. "But it has nothing to do with desire."

"I understand," said Gina. "When are you going to see her again?"

"I'm not sure. Twila's last letter said she was headed off into another desert, the Sahara. How the hell do you find anyone in that place?"

Gina thought about the part of the Sahara she had visited in Morocco. She couldn't remember its name right now but it was at the foot of the Atlas Mountains, a place where civilization itself seemed to end.

"I don't know," Gina finally answered. "Maybe you don't."

The road went in a straight line, on and on forever, deeper into the countryside. Neither Scarlett nor Gina said anything for a while, lost in their separate thoughts, past and future.

"I'm hungry," Scarlett suddenly announced. "My stomach's growling."

"Then I'll look for a spot to eat. Just keep your eyes on the road."

"I haven't hit a cow yet," teased Scarlett.

They both laughed.

"While you look, let's play a game," suggested Scarlett.

"Okay. What?"

"Guess What's Around The Bend," said Scarlett, pointing to the first curve in the road in a long time. "You go first."

Gina looked down the road, thinking about her answer.

"Hurry," urged Scarlett. "You gotta go fast. Before we get there."

"You could drive slower."

Scarlett smiled and eased off the accelerator. "Come on, for heaven's sake. Hurry up and guess."

"Okay," said Gina. "I see a farmhouse. A red one. With horses and dogs. Cows, chickens, a cat with a litter of kittens. Freshly washed clothes drying in the wind. Inside that farmhouse I see two women in love making a life for themselves." Gina paused and squeezed Scarlett's hand. "What's your guess?"

"Paradise," answered Scarlett. "A place where clocks stop and feelings blossom like flowers. Where lovers find the courage to reveal to one another who they really are and what they really feel."

Gina smiled to herself. She was always surprised when Scarlett connected with her feelings and spoke this other language, the one that came from her heart.

"But that's where we've been the last few weeks, isn't it, Scarlett?"

Chapter

79

"This looks like a good spot. Pull off here," said Gina. "No." She changed her mind. "Up ahead, where that wooded area is."

As Scarlett looked up the road where Gina had pointed, a cow suddenly ran out in front of them. "Damn!" exclaimed Scarlett, swerving just in time. She flew off the road and crashed through a split-rail fence. The Citroen ended up in a cornfield with one of its headlights dangling from a fender.

"*Merde!*" said Gina under her breath.

"What could I do? I couldn't kill that cow. Besides, in this tin can the cow would have probably killed us."

Gina got out of the car to survey the damage. Without its elevated headlight, the Citroen looked like a mutant stinkbug. The rest of the car was fine. She looked at Scarlett. "You all right?"

"Yeah," said Scarlett.

Gina went over and held her. "Then that's all that counts."

Scarlett was relieved Gina wasn't mad. "Where's the extra headlight?" she joked.

"What do you mean?"

"Isn't this the car with all the spare parts?"

Gina laughed. "Come on. Get in the car."

They drove over to the nearby farmhouse and Gina explained to its owners what had happened. She asked if they could pay for the fence. The farmer said no, that it was okay and thanked them for not killing his cow.

"You're welcome to spend the night," offered the farmer's wife. "It's getting late."

"No," said Gina and she graciously thanked them in French.

The woman insisted. She told Gina they could stay in the guest cottage down by the lake. If they didn't want to eat dinner with them, she would send them some food. She pointed to a narrow dirt road, explaining it would take them down to the cottage. Gina finally accepted the invitation.

"*Bon,*" said the woman. "Then go and enjoy yourselves."

Gina and Scarlett waved good-bye and took off in the direction the woman had pointed. The road was full of ruts and bumps, but the Citroen smoothed them out. Even Scarlett was impressed and finally gained some respect for this mutant stinkbug as it delivered them to their destination.

"It's beautiful here," said Scarlett, getting out of the car. "A divining rod couldn't have guided us to a better spot."

Gina came up behind Scarlett and slid her arms around her waist. They stared at the farmer's guest cottage a short distance away. "Think it's enchanted?" asked Gina.

"Don't know," answered Scarlett, looking at its chinked, white-plastered walls. "But it's sure old. I bet it's as old as France."

Gina laughed. "Old can be charming."

And it was. The cottage's wood-shingled roof, blue shutters and window flower boxes made it look like something out of a fairy tale. It even had a bricked path leading up to the front door.

"Maybe we got to paradise after all," said Gina.

Scarlett shook her head. "You're an incurable romantic."

"It's not a terminal disease, you know," defended Gina, a slight smile coming to her lips. "Just a slight weakness of the heart."

Scarlett was about to make a crack when a sound intruded, a lilting, almost mournful one. She recognized it immediately. It was the haunting birdsong of her youth, the call of the whippoorwill.

"I didn't know those were here too?"

"They're everywhere," said Gina. "I love how they sound. They sing from their heart."

Scarlett didn't tell Gina how much that sound haunted her. Instead she looked straight ahead at the woods. The sun was now low on the horizon and the few clouds in the sky took on a reddish glow.

"I love you, Gina. Don't ever leave me."

Gina tightened her embrace. "Where'd that come from?"

"I don't know. Just don't."

"I won't. I told you a long time ago. This is for keeps."

"You promise?"

"I promise. In fact, why don't we drink to it? I'll open that bottle of wine I brought." Gina spread out a blanket and the two sat down. She quickly uncorked the bottle and handed a glass to Scarlett. "Go ahead, taste it."

Scarlett took a sip. "This is wonderful," said Scarlett, raising her glass to Gina. "To night picnics and adventure."

"To love," enjoined Gina. "The biggest adventure of all."

Scarlett smiled. Gina was right. The discovery of another human heart was the biggest adventure of all, and the most dangerous.

"With a full moon and all those fireflies, we won't need candles," said Gina. "It looks like a jillion stars just fell to earth."

Scarlett looked over at the woods and the flickering lights of the fireflies. It was an extraordinary sight; their luminescence lit the night.

"I wonder how they make themselves glow? Love?" mused Gina.

Scarlett laughed. "Nothing quite so romantic. Someone at school told me it's just a biochemical reaction. Each species apparently has its own unique blinking pattern. That's how fireflies attract a mate."

"Just like we do," asserted Gina.

"What do you mean?" said Scarlett, giving Gina a curious look.

"Don't lesbians have their own 'unique blinking pattern' too?"

Scarlett howled. "Maybe you're right. I've always heard you can recognize another lesbian by the look in her eye. But I never realized it had anything to do with blinking. Not until now anyway." Scarlett continued laughing as Gina rolled over next to her.

"Look at me," she told Scarlett. "At my eyes."

"Okay," said Scarlett.

"What do you see?"

"My mate. According to the blinks anyway," grinned Scarlett. "We do it the same way."

"We sure do," said Gina, running her hand over Scarlett's body, feeling its warmth rise. She pulled Scarlett to her and smothered her neck in kisses. Scarlett was ready. She was waiting, wet, so wet, aching for the one touch that could take her to paradise.

Sometime early in the morning Scarlett awoke in Gina's arms. She looked up at the full moon and stared at the rabbit. She was feeling a happiness she couldn't put into words. Perhaps time had stopped. She felt strangely free of the past.

Still asleep, Gina stirred and pulled Scarlett closer. Scarlett looked down at Gina's hands and felt a sudden shiver. Hands were very important. They taught you about your lovers, Gina once told her, about their capacity for intimacy, about how much they really cared. Scarlett closed her eyes and smiled. Her lover's hands had always spoken eloquently.

Chapter

80

"What are they doing?" asked Scarlett as Gina parked the car. "They're playing boules."

Fascinated, Scarlett watched as one man after another took turns throwing a ball at a cochonnet, or target ball, some distance away. An old man in what must have been his eighties heaved the ball toward the cochonnet, then snatched the red beret off his head and slapped his thigh with it in obvious jubilation.

"Trying to hit each other's balls, so to speak," explained Gina with a slight giggle. "It's one of the favorite pastimes out here in the country. That and drinking pastis." She smiled and took Scarlett by the hand. "Come on. Let's have breakfast in that cafe over there."

As they crossed the street, Scarlett checked out the square and the village around it. It was old, Gina said, built slowly across the centuries from rock blasted out of a nearby quarry. Without exception, every house and shop was cut from the same gray stone. Only the shutters and doors of the town, painted in bold blues and greens, interrupted the collective monotony.

Scarlett and Gina sat down at a small table in front of the cafe. Scarlett quickly studied the menu. She was delighted she was starting to recognize a few words. "Is this strawberry?" asked Scarlett pointing to *fraise*.

"Yes," said Gina. "They're in season. It says they serve them with fresh cream."

"That's what I want then. And coffee. Au lait, of course."

"Of course," said Gina.

As Gina ordered, Scarlett looked back over at the park and the game of boules. It seemed to be a game for old men, at least today anyway. All the players were way over sixty with stubbly gray beards and berets cocked at different angles on their heads. When they weren't tossing balls, they were busy drinking and exchanging money.

"They're betting," said Gina. "I've never seen a game where they don't all get mad at each other by noon. Between the betting and the pastis, it usually ends up getting pretty heated."

The same old man from before picked up a ball, adjusted his beret and took aim. He threw it within inches of the target ball. A couple of the other men instantly started yelling and pointing down at the ground.

"They've accused him of stepping over the line," said Gina. "Of cheating."

"Is he?"

"Probably," said Gina. "It sounds like the pastis is beginning to take its toll."

"What kind of drink is that?"

"A potent cordial flavored with licorice and aniseed."

"Aniseed?"

"That's what gives it the kick."

Breakfast arrived and Scarlett speared a big, juicy strawberry and plopped it in her mouth. She licked her lips trying to catch the escaping cream. "This is delicious."

"I can tell," said Gina, buttering her toast.

"You know what I'd like to do with the rest of these?" announced Scarlett with a mischievous glint in her eye. "Other than eat them myself, I mean?"

"No. But I'm sure you're going to tell me."

"Yes," said Scarlett. "I am." She leaned over and whispered in Gina's ear.

"Have you ever done that?" asked Gina, scooping some marmalade into a spoon and giving it to Scarlett.

"Only with champagne," smiled Scarlett. She briefly savored the marmalade's tangy sweetness, then picked up a strawberry and slowly slid it into Gina's mouth.

Chapter
81

"These sheets are beginning to smell a little ripe," said Scarlett.

"That's what you get for eating in bed."

"Do I hear a complaint?"

"From moi? Never. I love fruit salad."

Scarlett looked over at the table still piled high with strawberries and grapes. "Maybe champagne is a better idea in the summertime."

A knock came at the door and Madame Petra, the owner of the inn, asked them if they would be joining her and the other guests for dinner. Gina looked over at Scarlett and translated for her.

"Sure. It might be fun," said Scarlett and quickly added, "Ask her for clean sheets."

Gina did and Mme. Petra asked if there was anything wrong with the ones presently on the bed. Gina said no, nothing at all, that they just needed fresh sheets. Not one to be contrary with her guests, Mme. Petra said, *"Bon,"* that she would have them changed while they had dinner.

"I wonder what she'll think about all those grape and strawberry stains?"

"That she has two guests who like to eat in bed. What else?" replied Gina with a twinkle in her eye. "What about a shower?"

"Good idea," said Scarlett, looking down at her body. "I'm going to need help getting rid of all these red and purple stains."

Scarlett and Gina shampooed each other's hair and then lathered each other with lavender-scented soap, gently scrubbing away the physical evidence of their lusty afternoon together. Afterward, they playfully smoothed lotion on each other's bodies.

"Gina?" whispered Scarlett, standing naked before the bathroom mirror.

"Yes?"

"Please. Don't go yet."

When Gina heard the desire in Scarlett's voice, she turned around and a flush of heat passed over her skin as she looked at her lover. The fever was suddenly back and with it the need to be consumed in a single, rapturous moment—in *la mort douce* as the French called it, love's "sweet death."

"We'll be late for dinner."

Scarlett made no reply. In fact, she barely heard the words at all. Her eyes had drifted down and fixed on the contours of Gina's body beneath the white silk robe. "Come here," she said.

"No. You come here," teased Gina, letting the moment build.

Scarlett went to Gina and quickly untied the sash at her waist, letting it fall away. She kissed her hungrily on the mouth, then opened her robe and threw it back from her shoulders, exposing the nakedness beneath, the body she wanted to possess in every possible way. As she kissed Gina's neck, she pushed her up against the wall and held her there while her mouth traveled slowly downward. She lingered at her breasts long enough for a nipple to harden in her mouth and then, sliding to her knees, savored what she ached for.

As Scarlett made love to her, all boundaries collapsed and she found herself feeling what Gina felt, almost as if they were one person. She felt her quickening heart, her tensing muscles, her immense pleasure in being touched. She also felt Gina's love, intense and passionate, now yielding, obliterating all but itself as she climaxed against Scarlett's lips.

"I was with you," whispered Scarlett, looking up at Gina.

"I know," said Gina, kneeling down. She pushed Scarlett back on the towels and covered her body with her own, pressing into her, kissing her over and over again. "Tell me when."

"Now," came the whispered reply.

Gina went inside her and slowly began moving her hand back and forth, quickening her rhythm as Scarlett's breathing increased. A fine film of perspiration covered both their bodies, glistening against the light of a dozen candles. Sensing the moment, Gina bent down and put her mouth against Scarlett's sex, her tongue caressing her, conferring love's "sweet death." Scarlett came, letting out a sharp cry.

"Are you girls okay in there?" intruded Madame Petra's voice in French.

"*Oui*," answered Gina, pulling back from Scarlett.

"*Bon*. The other guests and I are having a glass of wine on the patio waiting for you."

Scarlett quickly turned around and looked up at the open window. She had understood the untranslated French perfectly. "Jeez, Louise! Everyone heard us."

"You, *mon cherie*," laughed Gina. "You made the noise."

"Well, hurry up and tell them we're coming."

"I think they already know that."

Scarlett's face was flushed, and not just from the lovemaking. "I can't believe it. They all heard us."

"I doubt they'll mind," said Gina. "They're French."

Chapter
82

"How do I look?" asked Scarlett as they made their way downstairs toward the dining room, her hair still slightly wet from their second shower.

"Tousled."

"Jeez," said Scarlett, straightening her dress.

"Just be cool. Believe me, the French love romance."

"No matter who's doing the romancing?"

"No matter."

"Okay," said Scarlet, taking in a deep breath as they entered the dining room.

"Good evening, girls," smiled Madame Petra.

Everyone at the table turned in unison and smiled at Scarlett and Gina. *"Bon soir,"* one of them said and asked, *"Ça va?"*

"Very well," answered Gina.

"Please sit down. We're just about to begin," said Madame Petra. "You two must be very hungry."

Everyone tried not to smile after that remark, but everyone in the dining room did. Scarlett and Gina smiled back and sat down at Madame Petra's table. It looked set for royalty with delicately rosed china and brightly polished silverware. A profusion of summer blooms, including dragonsnaps and colorful zinnias, were at its center. On either side of the table were lighted candles in crystal holders.

"I wonder what the occasion is," Scarlett whispered to Gina, running her finger over the lace tablecloth. "Doesn't this seem a bit much?"

The feast before them was extravagant for a little country inn. Of that there was no doubt. There were exquisite oysters that slid effortlessly over the tongue and a mouth-watering entree that included wild duck and cranberries served with greens tossed in a lemony vinaigrette. Everything on Madame Petra's table was designed to impart pure pleasure to the palate. Wine, a delicious sauterne, was served between courses and later, a vintage port.

Dessert came in the form of strawberry mousse, a luscious pink creamy mound surrounded by strawberry puree, deep red in color, topped with a single plump strawberry, its cowl of green leaves still attached. Scarlett finished her serving and turned to Gina.

"This is unbelievable," she said and then added not too loudly, "I think the strawberries are almost as delicious this way."

"Almost," agreed Gina.

"Ladies and gentlemen," Mme. Petra suddenly announced, and she raised her glass. "To my late lover, Andre, who blessed my life with this inn, Mimi, his wonderful cook and the money to enjoy food like this."

Though Gina had translated, Scarlett actually caught most of what Mme. Petra said. The reason Mme. Petra ran the inn was to have people with whom to share her table. Half the enjoyment was in watching other people discover what she already knew, the pleasure of good food.

Everyone thanked Mme. Petra effusively and she graciously accepted. In fact, no one seemed to be able to thank her enough. They didn't know it then but everyone at Mme. Petra's table, including Scarlett, would remember that evening and everything they ate, how it tasted, how it smelled, the people who were there, the conversations they had, everything, all of it, for years to come. Good food makes good memories.

Scarlett and Gina were the last to leave the table. They thanked their hostess again and promised to return. Mme. Petra was delighted.

"Would you girls care for some more fruit?" she asked and then added with a playful look on in her eye, "For later, I mean? The strawberries are especially wonderful, are they not?"

Gina smiled at Madame Petra and graciously declined the offer. Then all three women smiled at each other. They exchanged a few parting amenities and quickly retired in different directions, content with life.

"This has been the most perfect summer of my life," said Scarlett as she and Gina climbed the stairs to their room. "It almost seems like a dream. One I don't want to leave."

"Then don't," said Gina.

Chapter

83

They had only been back in Paris a few days when Scarlett went to the Louvre again, this time by herself. Gina was meeting with an investor who was interested in putting up some money for a small boutique where Gina could sell the clothes she designed.

Before becoming a museum in 1793, the Louvre was the palace home to the French kings of the sixteenth and seventeenth centuries. Within its walls were hundreds of thousands of works of art, including paintings, tapestries, sculptures, vases from Egypt and Greece, the French crown jewels, rare manuscripts, on and on, priceless masterpieces of every description.

The Venus de Milo and the Mona Lisa were two of the Louvre's most famous pieces. As Scarlett looked at the painting of the Mona Lisa for the umpteenth time, she didn't understand the big deal about her smile. It hardly looked enigmatic. It seemed more like a smirk.

Scarlett ate lunch down the street from the Louvre, planning to go back for the rest of the afternoon when she started her period. She got such terrible cramps that she decided to go back to Gina's early and hailed a taxi. As it pulled up in font of Gina's small apartment building, she rifled through her purse searching for some loose francs.

"Nice," she heard the driver say in French. *"Tres jolie."*

Scarlett looked up to see what he was talking about. It was Gina. She was on her balcony smoking a cigarette, looking out at Paris. The way the sunlight caught her hair and fell across her body gave Gina the look of an angel.

It was the first time Scarlett had seen her in that black lace peignoir. No wonder the taxi driver got excited. It was so sheer you could see her breasts. Scarlett smiled. She found some change and handed it to the driver. Just as she was about to get out of the cab, a handsome man in a white suit walked through the arcade in front of the apartment building. He held up his hand and signaled the driver to wait.

"Mademoiselle," the gentleman said as he opened the cab door for Scarlett.

Scarlett thanked him and slid out. As she did, the man turned his face up toward the balcony where Gina was standing. He smiled and nodded his head to her, then got into the taxi and closed the door. Scarlett looked up at the balcony too and when she saw Gina's face, her heart sank and so did Gina's.

Chapter
84

"How could you?"

Gina was crying. "I didn't tell you because of the way you behaved at the Katmandu." Her hands trembled as she picked up a cigarette and lit it. "My parents don't have any money. This is the only way I can stay in Paris and become a designer."

Scarlett was devastated, sick to her stomach. "So you're whoring for your dreams? Is that it?" Scarlett snapped angrily.

Gina began sobbing. The words stung. "Please, Scarlett. I don't give myself to him."

"Jesus! What kind of crap is that?" screamed Scarlett. "What about your body? What do you do with that when you're in bed with him?"

Gina was defenseless against Scarlett's anger. She sat down and looked away from those accusing eyes.

"How could you let him be where I was? Have you any idea how that makes me feel? Knowing he was touching everything I've loved?"

"Scarlett, please," said Gina, looking up. "I'm sorry I didn't tell you. I didn't know how after the way I saw you react at the Katmandu. Then when you told me about your Aunt Fannie, I . . . I guess there's no excuse really. Please forgive me."

"What a fool I've been," declared Scarlett, her face flushed. "All those secrets we shared and you didn't tell me the most important one of all. That you fuck for money." Scarlett walked directly in front of Gina, where she delivered the lowest blow of all. "How do you think Abby would feel about what you're doing?"

"Please, Scarlett, you mustn't. You can't say these things."

"Like hell I can't!" said Scarlett.

"I have an arrangement with one man," Gina protested feebly.

"Now there's a clever turn of phrase," Scarlett shot back. "What's that supposed to mean? That it's no big deal because it only involves one dick instead of ten?"

Scarlett went on until she was exhausted, until she had nothing left to say, until she felt nothing except a gnawing, empty feeling in her stomach. She told herself she should have known better. She had seen it too many times back home in Dillinger. Love never worked. It always betrayed. It always devastated. It had no permanence. It was breath on a mirror.

"What can I do, Scarlett?"

"Nothing. You cut me too deep."

The wounded lovers finally fell silent. There was nothing left to say. Though they slept in the same bed that night, Scarlett and Gina might as well have been on different continents. The emotional *abattoir*, or slaughterhouse, as Gina described it, left them both bleeding and nothing, it seemed, could stanch the flow.

Scarlett left Paris the following evening. Delores Sheridan, the actress she met at the Katmandu, wired her money for a plane ticket to Greece after Scarlett called her and said, "You're right. Nothing lasts forever."

Gina insisted on accompanying Scarlett to the airport. Scarlett didn't object because, by this time, she was so shut down she hardly knew where she was. She just looked at Gina with a blank expression on her face as remote as the Sahara Desert.

"Do you want your ring back?" asked Gina, referring to the simple gold band Scarlett had purchased several weeks before. There was a moment of chilly silence as Gina twisted the ring nervously about on her finger, waiting for an answer.

"Yes," said Scarlett. "I'd like to have it."

"You can take the ring back, Scarlett, but you can't take back the words." Gina slid the ring off and read the inscription etched inside, *Love is grace and ours is forever.* "That's what you said here, and that's what I will believe forever." With tears filling her eyes, she handed back the ring. "You're the one I love, Scarlett. The one I want to keep."

Scarlett felt herself relenting. For an instant she felt the power of Gina's love drawing her back. But her will was strong and she resisted. "Good-bye, Gina. I have nothing left to say." With that Scarlett turned and walked off, away from all that pain in Paris.

Chapter

85

Businesses in Mykonos had a reputation for catering to gays. Even the small island population learned to appreciate the seasonal influx of same-sex lovers. They had a lot of motivation to do so. Gay tourism was profitable, extremely profitable, and besides, this way of loving wasn't new. Hadn't it been Greek to begin with?

During the summer gay men and women came from the four corners of the earth to soak up the sunshine beaming down on Mykonos. It was as close to paradise on earth as homosexuals could get. A place, where in the full light of day, they could openly be who they were. Plunked down in the middle of the Aegean Sea, Mykonos was on a rocky island where Poseidon once slew giants. Thatched houses and windmills with flagged, gossamer arms now replaced those mythical forms. Beyond was the endless sea. The sea of Poseidon and Odysseus.

Scarlett was the only one in the cafe. Seated at a small table by the window, she gazed without expression at the hot sand and the view beyond. The sun burnt everything with its white heat, the sea, the breakwater, the small fishing boats, and the whitewashed houses arching in a semicircle around the bay.

"May I have another Coke?" Scarlett asked the bartender and looked back out the window.

A few birds waded in the water, waiting for the ebb before digging their long beaks into the browning foam. By accident Scarlett had opened her address book to Gina's name. She suddenly felt heartsick as she stared at those four letters that held title to a life she cared about more than anything in the world. The memories came flooding back, thoughts and images and pieces of dreams. Even the walls Scarlett had thrown up could not hold them back.

She remembered Provence and the way the light caught Gina's hair as she looked over her shoulder, smiled and then walked into that lake with her clothes still on. It all came back. The night picnic. The fireflies. That silly, bouncy stinkbug of a Deux Chevaux. Mme. Petra's feast. The sunflowers. The red farmhouse. Paris. The Katmandu and the Eiffel Tower. All the unforgotten nights of love and shared sleep. Gina's touch. The astonishing beauty of her eyes. The deep, endless craving. Their passionate pledge to love each other forever.

Scarlett quickly composed a letter in her head. She would tell Gina how sorry she was, to please forgive her, that she missed her beyond imagining, that without her, her heart had turned into a hollow, lonely place. Finally, she would tell Gina she agreed with what she said that July evening as they walked down the Champs Elysées.

"The big love sometimes happens on this end of life," Gina had told her. "If you're lucky enough to realize it, you get to spend the rest of your life with that person. Imagine, Scarlett. Sharing a whole lifetime with the one you truly love."

Scarlett had said nothing in reply. It was too scary then to think like that, committing to one single human being, watching her grow old, loving her with your whole heart until life itself left. As Scarlett stared at the page, tears came to her eyes. It was painful to see Gina's name there, scrawled letters dispossessed of her presence. She took a deep breath and tore out the page. She crumpled it up and tossed it across the table. Deep down she knew it was a foolish gesture. True love resisted such canceling.

"Twenty-five cents, please," said the waiter, putting the Coke down on the table.

Scarlett gave him fifty. "Keep the change." She looked at her watch and wondered where Delores was.

Delores Sheridan, America's almost sweetheart, first runner-up in a Miss America contest back in the early fifties. No one would ever guess Delores Sheridan was a lesbian. Real dykes didn't look like her. She didn't fit the stereotype and her public relations firm, Hawker & Lowe, wanted to make sure it stayed that way. They sent out lots of pictures showing her with lots of men, just in case anyone became the wiser. At the present moment, though, Delores wasn't making their job easy. Hawker & Lowe complained to her daily about her running around the Greek Isles with a woman. What if *Photoplay* or one of the other magazines had them followed?

"Fuck *Photoplay!*" Delores told them. "So what if I'm vacationing with a friend who happens to be a woman? Unless they see me going down on her, what the hell do they know?"

Delores could be a little blunt, especially if she had been smoking her favorite tobacco. For some reason that brand didn't mellow her out, it just made her more contentious than she already was. When Delores's press agent told her about the rumors, that she had been seen dancing with another woman in Greece, Delores got really testy.

"So?" she said. "Float a story. Tell them I sneaked off and got married in Mexico." There was a pause. "You figure out to whom! That's why I pay you, you asshole." Delores hung up the phone. "Sonovabitches. Do I have to teach them their job too?"

That was Delores. She thought she knew it all and most of the time she did. She was smarter than most of the people she worked with in Hollywood and that made them nervous, especially the men. A good-looking woman with brains was a big threat. They liked bimbos. They were controllable and they were fuckable. Delores was neither.

Scarlett sipped at her Coke and waited for her new lover to return from the small house she had rented up the beach. Delores had been on the phone all morning negotiating her next film, the one to be shot on location the following year in Brazil.

Scarlett looked back out at the beach and saw Delores striding toward the bar, her long blond hair tossed wildly about by the wind, her violet eyes drinking in the vast erotic landscape. Several people, both men end women, stared as she passed, seduced as much by her beauty as by her charisma. When Delores Sheridan was around, you knew it, and when she was on screen, well, it came alive. She was bigger than life, radiant, magnificent, quite simply beautiful. That she was also intelligent delighted Scarlett. They could talk about anything and often did, for hours on end.

It was easy for Scarlett to be with Delores. Miss Sheridan didn't allow her emotions to run that deep. All she wanted was company, pretty, smart company, and good sex. Delores used sex the way Scarlett did, as a drug, to avoid what she didn't want to feel.

Delores smiled as she came into the bar. "Retzina," she told the bartender and sat down at the table with Scarlett. "A done deal," she announced. "How about a celebration dinner at our favorite restaurant?"

"I'd like that," said Scarlett. "Congratulations. I assume you got everything you wanted."

"And more. If you want to join me on location, you can. I cleared the decks and had them include you and all your expenses in the deal."

"What about your neurotic press agent?"

"He's arranging a boyfriend for you."

"Oh, Jesus."

"It's the way the game is played. Fabrication is the secret of good publicity." Delores leaned over to Scarlett. "I need a kiss."

Scarlett gave her one.

"You've got the best kisser," said Delores, pulling back. "Who taught you to smooch like that?"

"I told you. I learned on an angel's mouth."

Delores laughed. "A fallen one, I'm sure. That mouth knows how to sin." Delores leaned back in her chair. "There's an expression for girls like you."

"Yeah?" said Scarlett.

"*Ingenue libertine.* Innocent libertine. It's part of what makes you so appealing."

Scarlett wasn't quite sure she liked the idea of being likened to a libertine, no matter how innocent.

"They used to say the same about me. What was it? 'Her face is that of a fallen angel. She has the mouth of a woman about to be. She lives untouched, detached, yet at the same time, infinitely experienced.' "

"That sounds familiar."

"I think Colette wrote it, but I'm not sure." Delores spotted the wadded page from Scarlett's telephone book. "Paris?" she asked, picking it up.

Scarlett nodded. Delores took out her gold lighter and set the page on fire. Scarlett's heart sank. If she had any thought about changing her mind, it was too late. Gina's telephone number and address were going up in smoke.

"Believe me, it's best with these things," said Delores knowingly. "They have to be slashed and burned, X'ed out of existence."

The waiter brought over Delores's retzina and she knocked it back. "How about a quick fix?" she said. "Before dinner."

It sounded good to Scarlett. When she was in bed with Delores, the world went away. Sex had become a narcotic and Delores was the best drug around. In her arms came pleasure, forgetfulness and the cessation of pain.

Chapter

86

The Athena was a small cafe hugging the bay in Mykonos. Scarlett and Delores sat in a private niche off in the corner. Cozy with a large window over the bay, it was the most romantic spot in the cafe, especially tonight. A full moon lighted the water with a shimmering, silvery glow.

Delores leaned back into the pillow seat and puffed on her favorite brand of oblivion. It wasn't so much the romance she liked about this table as its privacy. She could see everyone from here and no one could see her, plus she could get stoned out of her mind. "You sure you don't want some?" Delores asked, taking another toke and pushing the joint in Scarlett's direction.

"No, thank you."

Scarlett marveled at the impunity with which Delores broke all the rules and got away with it, living life unfettered by the taboos and values controlling the rest of society. That was the way the Big Three worked. Power, fame and money bestowed carte blanche upon its recipients, seemingly sanctifying their right to do as they pleased, giving them a unique sense of entitlement, undetermined by God or man.

Both Delores and Sissy lived by their own rules, not the herd's. Society's standards, Sissy said, were for breeders, not thinkers. Most of their rules were stifling and hypocritical. After being raised in

Dillinger, Scarlett agreed. Power, fame and money not only conferred privilege, they provided a margin of safety. Women who had them didn't get stepped on as much. Not like the women she had seen growing up, women without hope, women like Wanda Fargo and Aunt Fannie and, to a lesser extent, her mother. All were victims of a life they seemed powerless to change. Being a victim was soul-killing and Scarlett vowed never to be one. She held her glass up and toasted Delores, her passport to the Big Three.

"To the best dealmaker in the world."

Delores smiled and finished off her wine. "Thanks," she said, reaching under the table and sliding her hand up Scarlett's leg. "And thanks for not wearing any underwear." Delores scooted closer. "You know how crazy I am about you?" she whispered in Scarlett's ear.

"I've a faint notion."

"Good," said Delores. She briefly caressed the inside of Scarlett's thigh again and then disappeared under the table.

"Jesus, Delores! What the hell are you doing?"

"One guess," said Delores. "And somehow I just know you'll be right." She pushed Scarlett's skirt up and spread her legs.

"You can't do this," protested Scarlett, as excited as she was nervous. "Not here."

"Relax. I'm doing it," were Delores's last words.

Scarlett pulled the tablecloth down on the side facing the interior of the cafe and held on to the edge of the table. It would be difficult not making any noise. Delores was eloquent tonight.

"Madam," said a waiter, suddenly appearing at the table with a phone attached to a long extension cord. "There's a phone call for Miss Sheridan."

"As you can see, she's not here," said Scarlett. "They'll have to call back."

"Who is it?" demanded an unseen voice.

The waiter's eyes darted about the small enclosure and informed the voice, "Her agent."

Delores's hand reached out from beneath the tablecloth and gestured for the phone. "Gimme the phone."

"I guess she'll take the call," said Scarlett sheepishly.

The waiter slid the phone beneath the table and tried to look casual, his eyes scanning the ceiling.

"Sonovabitch! I don't care," yelled Delores. "Get me the fucking part. That's what I pay you for, getting me work, not making excuses." Delores slammed the phone down and shoved it out from beneath the table. "Cocksucker!"

"I think she's finished," said Scarlett.

The waiter reached down and picked up the phone.

"Scarlett, honey," said Delores. "Tell that nice waiter we'll order in a few minutes. Just as soon as I find my diamond earring."

"Did you hear her?" asked Scarlett.

The waiter nodded. "Does she need help?" He started to pick up the tablecloth.

Scarlett quickly brushed it out of his hands. "No."

"Let me know when you're ready, Miss Sheridan," said the waiter. He smiled at Scarlett, then turned and left.

"If that asshole agent calls again," instructed Delores, "tell him I'm busy."

"Okay," said Scarlett.

"Scoot closer. You don't want me to break my neck, do you?"

"No," answered Scarlett. "Not that bit of perfection." She moved to the edge of her seat and grabbed hold of the table again.

"Good answer," laughed Delores and then she fell silent.

Chapter

87

"Incredible," said Delores, finishing the last bite of her apple tart. "How was yours?"

"Delicious. I could eat another piece."

"You know too much sugar makes you sick."

"Maybe some coffee then. I am a little tired."

"Not for long," said Delores. "You just need a little pick-me-up." She reached in her pocket and pulled out a small metal box. "Voile. Fairy dust."

"What's that?" asked Scarlett, staring at the fine white powder.

"Cocaine. After a hit off this stuff, you won't be tired anymore."

"It's illegal," protested Scarlett.

"So is marijuana. So is homosexuality. So what?"

"I don't know," said Scarlett lamely.

"Let me give you a little history lesson. You know all those Cokes you drink?"

"Yeah?"

"They used to make them with cocaine, with coke."

"No way."

"It's true," said Delores. "America's favorite drink was originally bottled with the big buzz. No wonder it became so popular," she added, dipping one of her nails into the powder. "Look," she showed

Scarlett. "Close off one nostril and sniff it up the other." The coke disappeared from under Delores's nail. She repeated the procedure and sniffed the fairy dust up her other nostril. "Here, go ahead and try it," said Delores, scooping up some more powder. "You won't be disappointed."

Scarlett inhaled first into one side of her nose, and then into the other. The rush was immediate. She soon felt exuberant, excited, aware. The buzz was big all right.

"Like it?"

"Yeah," said Scarlett, smiling. "I'm not tired anymore."

"Good, because I've got big plans for that energy."

Scarlett smiled again and so did Delores.

"Let's get out of here."

Delores threw some cash down on the table and grabbed Scarlett's hand. As they walked toward the front door, Delores flashed that movie-star smile at the waiter. "I found my earring."

"Good. Come back and see us soon, Miss Sheridan."

"Do you really think he believed that story?" asked Scarlett.

"Darling, I tip him not to believe anything he sees or hears."

"Delores. Delores Sheridan. How are you?" said a husky voice as Delores and Scarlett emerged from the restaurant. A tall, good-looking man got up from an outdoor table and held out his arms. "I can't believe it. You're more beautiful than ever."

"Jonathan!" exclaimed Delores, hugging him. "What the hell are you doing in Mykonos?"

"I've got a little time between assignments."

"But here?" Delores asked again.

"Why not? Sun is sun and there are a few straight ladies on the island."

"And I bet you found both of them," joked Delores as she turned to Scarlett. "I'd like you to meet Jonathan Lucas. The best photojournalist in the world. Jonathan, Scarlett Turner."

Jonathan extended his hand to Scarlett. "Nice meeting you."

"Likewise," said Scarlett, noticing Jonathan's eyes. They were a pretty blue with thick, curly lashes.

"I see your taste is as good as ever," said Jonathan, speaking to Delores and looking at Scarlett, his hand still holding hers.

"It is," confirmed Delores, removing Scarlett's hand from Jonathan's. "And I see your hormones are as annoying as ever."

They both laughed.

"How about a drink?" said Jonathan, nodding in the direction of his table.

"Okay," said Delores. "But just one. We can visit tomorrow. Scarlett's tired."

"Really," said Jonathan, looking at Scarlett. "She looks on top of it to me."

"Youth," quipped Delores. "It never shows."

Jonathan walked the two over to his table. "Allow me," he said, pulling out a chair for each of them. He signaled to a waiter and then sat down. "What'll it be, ladies?"

"Retzina," said Delores.

"A Coke," intoned Scarlett.

Jonathan ordered everyone's drinks and turned to Delores. "It must be at least four years."

"Ever since you started chasing wars." Delores looked at Scarlett. "At one time Jonathan was the best still photographer in Hollywood. The only one I'd let shoot me. But that wasn't dangerous enough. He had to go off to Vietnam and shoot the war."

"You do that?" asked Scarlett, remembering Billy Ray. "Take pictures of dead soldiers?"

Jonathan was a little surprised by the question. "Living and dead. Why?" he asked.

"I don't know. It seems a little ghoulish."

"Scarlett!" said Delores.

"No. It's okay," said Jonathan. "Perhaps in a way it is."

"Why do you do it?"

"The excitement's part of it, being on the edge. But mostly it's about making a record of the horror so man stops doing it. War, I mean."

"But we've got records," said Scarlett. "Way back to the Civil

War. Pictures of brothers killing each other." The cocaine was making Scarlett's mind race a mile a minute. "Even that didn't stop anyone. Neither did the pictures they took of all the other wars. Snapshots don't edify or change anyone."

"Umm-hum," mumbled Delores, hoping to derail the conversation on to a more pleasant subject. When Scarlett got feisty, you never knew what she might say or do, which, of course, was a lot of what Delores liked about her. In some ways she was a younger version of herself.

"You're awfully young to be so cynical," observed Jonathan.

"And you're awfully mature to be so idealistic," fenced Scarlett. "Does old age make one's perception of the world any clearer?"

Delores smiled. Scarlett, as usual, was on point.

Jonathan chuckled. "I guess I deserved that." He paused and reappraised Scarlett. He liked her. Delores had always picked intelligent women, and it sounded like Scarlett might just be the brightest of the lot. "What do you say we call a truce?"

"I wasn't aware we were engaging in hostilities," said Scarlett.

They all laughed and toasted their chance meeting; then, with just a few trips to the bathroom for fairy dust, they reminisced until dawn, promising they'd all see each other in L.A.

Chapter

88

Scarlett and Delores left Mykonos with just enough time to catch their plane from Athens to New York. Vacation was over and Delores was already back in the work mode, reading her new script as they flew over the Atlantic.

"What a piece of crap!" said Delores, slamming the script down in her lap. "It's a complete rip-off of *The African Queen,* right down to the leeches. The only difference is that it takes place in South America instead of Africa. Stupid sonovabitches!"

Scarlett sipped her Coca-Cola. "You want a soda?"

"No!" Delores was still fuming. "I don't know how you drink that sweet crap, one after another."

When Delores was getting ready to do a film, she mustered up Spartan-like discipline. No hard liquor, no nose candy, no grass, no cigarettes, nothing. Delores had to get her face and her body ready for the camera. Needless to say, the effort made her very cranky. Scarlett understood. She knew how hard it would be to give up Cokes.

"How's the writing?"

"Lousy," said Delores, picking the script back up. "Here they have my character falling into the Amazon River just so they can show my tits off." She was getting pissed. "It has nothing to do with the story. Do you ever see a man's penis gratuitously poking up through his pants?"

"No."

"Of course not. It's the women who are degraded."

"Refuse to do the scene."

"I can't," said Delores bitterly. "If I didn't let them sell my body up there on screen, I wouldn't work. Not in Hollywood. I'm not a very good actress, you know."

Delores's uncanny ability for self-assessment always amazed Scarlett. She could tell the truth about herself without flinching.

"Besides," said Delores. "I'm getting a little long in the tooth."

Scarlett had never heard this expression. "What do you mean?"

"Old," said Delores.

"But you're only thirty-five!"

"That's almost over the hill for an actress. A woman isn't saleable after a certain age in Hollywood."

"But what about John Wayne? Anthony Quinn? Stewart Granger? There's a whole bunch of them. They're really old and they're still working."

"They're men," was Delores's terse reply.

Delores knew how the game worked in Hollywood. If you were a woman, you sold how you looked. Very few actresses made it on talent alone, and the ones who did paid a high price. She had come here in the fifties when Hollywood canonized female sexuality. Marilyn Monroe, Mamie Van Doren, Diana Dors and Jayne Mansfield were just a few of the actresses on an extensive list that, for the most part, was made up of buxom blondes. It was the look that sold. Delores understood it very well. Her career took off after she became a blonde.

A lifelong student of the mirror, Delores had learned its lessons well. The wrinkles were coming. The time was coming. She must soon step down from the screen. Aging actresses weren't welcome in Hollywood. Tinseltown wouldn't humiliate Delores, though; she would dump it before it dumped her. She had shrewdly planned her exit long in advance, investing in everything from several small apartment buildings and a motel chain to a fast-food franchise. Her stock in hamburgers and French fries alone was turning her into a millionaire. Delores was set for life and Scarlett knew it.

"Well, are you coming to live in L.A. or not?" asked Delores, putting the script back down.

Delores had offered to let Scarlett stay rent free in one of her apartment buildings so she could go to UCLA. That was the place to graduate from, Delores told her, not from some small school no one had ever heard of outside of Georgia.

"Yes," said Scarlett. "But it'll take a while before I can get in. It's already the fall semester."

"I've got a friend in admissions. I'm sure she can hurry your application along. For next spring, I mean."

Scarlett regarded Delores with renewed amazement. If she set her mind to it, she could move the mountain to Mohammed, or in this instance, to UCLA.

Chapter

89

Scarlett returned to Townsend for the fall semester and threw her-self into the study of classical Greek. She chose the rigors of this subject for three reasons. First, it was a challenge. Second, it was part of her self-created mythology. It would look good on the blurb of her future books and add to her stature as a scholar. Not many other writers could claim being able to read the works of Homer and Euripides in their original form. Third and last, it would help her not think so much about Gina and the widening hole in her heart.

Delores called Scarlett every day on the private phone she had installed in her room. Sally Trout, Scarlett's new roommate, was fascinated by all the attention.

"Telephone calls. Roses. Chocolates. That guy spends a fortune on you," observed Sally enviously. "How did you get so lucky?" She looked at the picture on Scarlett's desk and swooned again. "And handsome too. Where did you say you met him?"

"In Greece last summer," said Scarlett, picking up a picture of Jonathan Lucas taken in Vietnam. Several cameras dangling from his neck, he cut quite a figure in his military fatigues. Every girl in the dorm commented on his body and that handsome, unshaven face.

"When are you going to see him again?"

"When he gets back from the Congo."

"He sends you flowers and chocolates all the way from there?" Sally could hardly believe such a man walked the face of the earth.

"He's resourceful," replied Scarlett. "You have to be when you're dodging bullets." She stuck her face back in her book. "I have to study, Sally."

"Well, okay, Miss Uppity. Just because you have a boyfriend in the Congo."

Delores had sent Jonathan's photograph knowing Scarlett would need a "beard," someone to divert attention from the real source of all those calls and gifts. It took the heat off Scarlett, but mostly it protected Delores.

"Here's your mail," said Sally, barging back into the room. "Can't keep your mind on your studies, can you? I saw you staring at his picture again."

"May I have my mail?"

"Guess what?" teased Sally.

"What?" said Scarlett on the verge of exasperation.

"There's one here from Mr. Lucas." She handed Scarlett the letter. "He sure has feminine handwriting."

"He's sensitive," said Scarlett, looking at the letter from Delores. "That's what I like about him."

"Do you mind?" asked Scarlett as she began opening her mail.

"No," said Sally, finally walking away. "I've got a date."

"Good. Enjoy yourself."

Scarlett hoped Sally would hurry up and leave. She hated the way Sally hovered around her talking non-stop. She was attractive enough but only marginally intelligent. Her biggest negative, though, was her almost complete lack of self-esteem. People with weak egos made Scarlett nervous. They could sell you down the river and often did. Sally's opinion of herself rose and fell around the boys she dated. When she was seeing someone, she was on top of the world, thinking herself worthy of everything life had to offer. When she was breaking up, she was in the pits of hell, tormented by demons of her own self-hate.

"Did you get the letter I left on your desk yesterday? The one from Paris?"

"What?" said Scarlett. Her heart sank. "I didn't see it."

"Of course not," said Sally snidely. "Not under that mess. How can you study like that?"

Scarlett pushed aside her books and rifled through her notes and papers. At the bottom was a letter. She recognized the handwriting immediately. It had been sent to Dillinger and then forwarded on to her by her mother like all the others.

"You look like you just heard from a ghost. Another boyfriend?"

"Shut up, Sally," said Scarlett. Her hands trembled as she picked up the letter. She was glad Sally couldn't see them.

"You're so touchy sometimes," accused Sally. She picked up her purse and walked to the door. "I bet you've done it with both of them," announced Sally, sounding jealous.

Scarlett didn't answer. She waited for Sally to leave. When she heard the door close, she took a deep breath and opened the letter.

Dear Scarlett,
   Did you receive my other letters? Will this awful silence ever end? Love is grace, remember? Please don't throw ours away.

                                             I love you,
                                             Gina

There had been many letters over the past few months, but Scarlett had chosen not to read them. Unopened, she threw them away, pretending they never were. Why she decided to read this one was inexplicable because exactly what she feared happened. Gina's words made her feel. Scarlett opened the drawer of her desk and pulled out the simple gold band. She read its inscription, then slid the ring on her finger and wept. She still could not forgive.

Chapter

90

Poems for Lovers of a Different Kind was published just before Thanksgiving. The publishing house was delighted at the early sales. Its success was unexpected because there had been no publicity. Word of mouth in certain circles, especially lesbian ones, was turning the book into an overnight sensation. There was a fair share of readers from the other side of the street too. For them such books were a big curiosity. It allowed voyeurs a teasing glimpse into the forbidden, perhaps even a peek into the dark world of their own secret fantasies.

Scarlett was ecstatic. She was finally going to make some money off her writing, real money, royalty money. When her book was first published, she had initially regretted using a nom de plume. Anonymity wasn't that gratifying. She couldn't bask in it. The only people who knew she wrote the book were her closest friends, so for the moment Scarlett's secret was safe.

As the book's popularity grew, however, so did people's curiosity. Everyone wanted to know more about Georgia Hill, the woman from Savannah, who wrote such passionate poems about other women. What did Georgia Hill look like? How old was she? When would her next book be out? These were just a few of the things her fans wanted to know.

If there had been two reasons for choosing anonymity before, her mother and her own fear, now there was a third, Delores Sheridan. Scarlett knew Delores could not associate with an out-of-the-closet lesbian. Her career would never survive it. Delores was already suspect. Being seen in public with a known lesbian writer would confirm her sexuality in many people's minds.

Delores actually didn't give a shit whether or not people knew she was a dyke, but when there was money on the line, she played the game. That's why she had her own publicity firm. To make sure the truth didn't get out. Not yet anyway. Not until she stepped down from the screen.

It was strategy time for Scarlett. She realized she was going to have to play the game too, at least for a while. One book of poems was hardly going to make her rich. It might give her notoriety, but Scarlett wanted more than that. She wanted it all, and she knew Delores Sheridan could help her get it. Delores was her passport to the Big Three. Associating with someone as rich and famous as she already was could help a shrewd person like herself procure power, fame and money a lot faster than she could do it on her own.

"Using that nom de plume was smart. A book like this could limit your options," Delores told Scarlett on the phone after she read the book. "People aren't ready for openness—yours, theirs or anyone else's. The hypocritical assholes. Secret titillation is what they want. Their real desires scare them."

It sounded to Scarlett like Delores had been smoking. She could ramble on forever after that most favorite of cigarettes touched her lips.

"God forbid anyone finds out just how much Mrs. Smith would like to plant one on her next-door neighbor, the lovely Mrs. Jones."

Scarlett laughed. "Sometimes they do."

"Of course," said Delores. "And then spend the rest of their lives pretending it was that martini." She paused and took a hit off her joint. There was a brief silence as she held it in her lungs. "Or they begin fucking one guy after another trying to prove it's not women they really want. Like Celeste Morgan."

"Celeste Morgan!" Scarlett couldn't conceal her surprise.

"Yeah," said Delores. "She couldn't handle loving me."

Delores's admission was a stunner. Delores had never talked about the other women in her life before and certainly not about love. Celeste Morgan had been one of the biggest stars in Hollywood during the late forties and early fifties, a superstar. Scarlett remembered her mother taking her to see *Wild Abandon*.

In that movie Celeste Morgan had dyed her hair red and played a Mata Hari-type character. She was wonderful. Mysterious and sensual in her belly dancer costume, Celeste weaved her way across the screen like a beautiful, exotic snake. Just thinking about the picture sent chills up Scarlett's spine.

"I remember her," Scarlett finally said. "She got married a lot."

"Five times," said Delores. "She hated the fact she liked to fuck women so she kept running off with men." Delores took another breathy drag off her joint. "I'll see you next week," she said and hung up. Obviously, Delores didn't want to talk anymore. Not about Celeste anyway.

Chapter

91

"I'll be there for Christmas, Mother. I can't come home right now. I've got midterms and, besides, I have to give a speech the day after Thanksgiving."

Scarlett wasn't about to tell her mother she was spending Pilgrim's Day, as Ollie called it, with Delores Sheridan out in California. As far as Ollie was concerned, actresses were all floozies. No one else but an actress would bare their legs and body parts on that big wide screen for every man in the world to see.

"A speech on what?"

"Women's rights."

"What's that?" Ollie wanted to know.

Scarlett smiled. Her mother's question said it all.

"What rights are you talkin' about?" Ollie pressed on.

"Equal rights, Momma. You know, having the same rights as men."

"We get to vote, don't we? Just like them."

Scarlett smiled again and shook her head. Like so many other women, Ollie Mae didn't have the slightest notion what equal rights meant. She simply accepted that women were men's charges because men knew best. It was the natural order of things. God had made men smarter.

"Okay. This call must be costin' a fortune. You just make sure you're here for Christmas."

"I will, Momma."

"I almost forgot. Cecil's gettin' married on the 25th."

"Really?" Scarlett was surprised. "Why then? On Christmas Day, I mean?"

"Something about their vows being presents to each other. Now, ain't that just the sweetest?"

"Yes, Momma, the sweetest," echoed Scarlett, hoping Phyllis was truly the gift Cecil's life deserved. "Tell them I'll be there."

Ollie said good-bye and hung up. Scarlett felt a little guilty lying to her mother about giving a speech but that was what popped into her mind at the time. She had been writing a midterm paper on the subjugation of women.

Chapter

92

Scarlett pressed her face up against the window as the plane descended into L.A. A witch's brew of ozone, car exhaust, factory emissions and God knows what else clung tenaciously to the city. There was no escaping it. Smog was as much a part of Los Angeles as earthquakes and movie stars.

"Hey, Scarlett, over here," yelled a low, husky voice as she walked into the terminal.

Scarlett immediately recognized Jonathan Lucas's voice and wondered what he was doing at the airport. She swung around and spotted him coming toward her from across the terminal. Suntanned, wearing a tight pair of faded Levi's and a white tee shirt, he was more handsome than she remembered.

"Delores sent me to pick you up," he explained as he caught up with her. "She had to reshoot some last-minute scenes at the studio." He gave her a big hug. "Welcome to L.A."

Scarlett smiled. "What I can see of it."

"Don't worry. This stuff will blow off," announced Jonathan with the habitual optimism of a native Angeleno. "It's not as bad as it looks."

"That's encouraging."

"Any more luggage?" he asked, taking Scarlett's garment bag out of her hands.

"Nope. Just that."

"You look great," he said, taking her hand, guiding her through the crowd out of the terminal to a waiting convertible. "My girl-friend came along for the ride. We brought her car," chuckled Jonathan. "She hates my Jeep." He tossed Scarlett's bag in the backseat and opened the car door for her. "Karyn, this is Scarlett. Delores's friend."

Scarlett extended her hand to Karyn as Jonathan got into the passenger seat and closed the door. Scarlett had been so busy arranging her bag in the backseat, she hadn't noticed the panicked expression on the woman's face. Scarlett looked at her more closely and realized she had seen her before.

"Nice to meet you," said Karyn, adjusting her sunglasses, hoping no one had detected the uneasiness in her voice.

"Same here," smiled Scarlett, finally remembering where she last saw Karyn. It was in Paris at the Katmandu. Judging from the look on Karyn's face, Jonathan didn't have a clue about her sexual complexity.

Karyn was one of the two women who had caused such a stir the night she and Gina were at the club. In their mid-to late-twenties, Karyn and her lover had fabulous bodies and long hair, one fair and blond, the other dark and brunet. Everyone had talked about the couple, not just because of their uncommon height and beauty, but because of their visible passion. They had been running red-hot and seemed unaware of anyone else. They had fused together as they danced, every muscle and movement in their bodies speaking eloquently to the longing inside them. A lover's tango of rhythmic sensuality.

"Karyn has a dress shop in Beverly Hills, the Europa Boutique," Jonathan said, turning to Scarlett as his girlfriend pulled away from the curb. "She sells rags to the rich."

"Do you know Delores?" Scarlett asked Karyn, trying to figure out who knew what about whom, if anything at all.

"No," said Karyn with that edge still in her voice.

Scarlett wondered where her lover was now and what she was doing with Jonathan. Many women were double-gaited; perhaps Karyn was too.

"I hope you enjoy L.A.," Karyn told Scarlett as she sped down the freeway, looking back at her in the rearview mirror. "If you need anything Jonathan or Delores can't provide, maybe my father can help. He's the mayor of Beverly Hills."

Scarlett smiled to herself. She had just heard the age-old dyke plea for anonymity and with it, some of the reasons why—family and politics. "Thank you. That's very nice of you, Karyn."

Jonathan was surprised at Karyn's sudden openness and generosity. He turned around to Scarlett. "She usually doesn't let people know that. Much less offer his help."

"Maybe I feel like Scarlett and I already know each other," said Karyn, signaling her appreciation for Scarlett's complicity as she rounded the street corner to Delores Sheridan's house. "Well, here it is."

Scarlett stared in disbelief at the huge, green-shuttered mansion. It looked as if it had been plucked right out of the antebellum South and plopped on that knoll, white columns, weeping willows and all. It was imposing, lording over the rest of the block as it did.

"Another one of Dad's impoverished electorate," laughed Karyn.

Scarlett grinned. "Somehow I can't imagine his voters fretting too much."

They all laughed as Jonathan opened the car door and helped Scarlett out, retrieving her garment bag from the backseat. "Want to come in?" Jonathan asked Karyn. "Delores won't mind."

"Can't. I've got to get back to the store," she told Jonathan and then turned to Scarlett. "It was nice meeting you. Make sure you drop by my shop before you leave. I'm sure there's a dress there with your name on it." She paused and flashed her best Beverly Hills smile. "A sort of welcome-to-L.A. present."

As Scarlett thanked Karyn, Jonathan did another double take, again surprised at his girlfriend's generosity to a perfect stranger.

Karyn smiled at him. "Hurry, darling."

As Jonathan walked her to the house, Scarlett decided not to tell Delores about Karyn's offer. It would be her secret.

"Have a happy Thanksgiving," said Jonathan, opening the front door and giving Scarlett the keys.

"Thanks," she said. She looked back down at Karyn and waved. "You too, Jonathan."

Chapter 93

"Where the hell are you?" yelled Delores, barely through the front door of the house.

"In the den," Scarlett yelled back. "One of your old movies is on TV."

"Which one?" Delores put her script down and walked toward the den. She was happy. Scarlett was in L.A. and her latest film had finished shooting today.

"Some cowboy flick."

Delores recognized the music and a few bits of dialogue. It was *Drums Across the Rio Grande.* She didn't know which she had hated most, the script, the director, or the leading man.

"It's the one where you get Mickey Malone all hot and bothered," elaborated Scarlett as she emerged from the den. "You were just getting ready to fuck him."

When Scarlett saw Delores, she felt a sudden rush. She had forgotten how stunning Delores really was, how much she enjoyed looking at her, being with her, having sex with her. "You look beautiful," Scarlett told her.

"Thanks." Delores put her arms around her. "I don't think you've ever told me that before."

"Why should I? You hear it from everybody else."

"It's still nice to hear you say it. It means more."

Delores gave Scarlett a kiss, long and tender, loving. It was the first time Scarlett had ever felt any real emotion in one of Delores's kisses, apart from lust, that is. When Scarlett opened her eyes, she glimpsed a vulnerability in Delores's face she had never seen before. It was only there for an instant, but it had been there.

"I've told you not to swear," said Delores, quickly distancing herself from that momentary lapse in her defenses. "Fucking Mickey Malone, what kind of talk is that? A girl like you with a college education and all."

"You swear too."

"That's different," said Delores.

Scarlett was about to take her to task but changed her mind. After all, it was her house. "Okay," Scarlett finally said. "I'll mind my tongue."

"Good," answered Delores, and smiled. "It has better things to do."

She kissed Scarlett again. This time Scarlett felt the familiar lust, the hunger, and she instantly responded to the body pressing up against hers.

"I need to take a shower. Care to join me?" Delores asked. "A little wet sex before dinner might be fun."

Scarlett smiled. "Which bathroom?" There were seven in the house. She had already counted them.

"Upstairs," said Delores, taking Scarlett's hand.

"The one with the swimming pool?"

"Yes," laughed Delores. "That one."

Scarlett was referring to her oversized Jacuzzi done in expensive Italian marble.

"Its jets are an engineering marvel," said Delores. "One could get very lazy, if you know what I mean."

Chapter

94

Since Scarlett and Delores were in bed until midnight of the following day, they missed Thanksgiving altogether. Delores had planned a fabulous feast, the gourmet cook she was, then changed her mind. The best possible ravishment was already being shared, and she didn't even have to set the table.

Scarlett couldn't have agreed more. If the Pilgrims hadn't been so boringly Calvinistic, they too might have discovered the real meaning of that scriptural variant, "Woman does not live by food alone." Of course, champagne and sex, water crackers and caviar, can't hold any woman forever either, so Delores ordered out. She sent a taxi to pick up fettuccini alfredo and a tossed salad at a popular Italian restaurant on Santa Monica Boulevard where the stars and up-scale hookers all hung out.

"This is delicious," said Scarlett.

Delores smiled and ran her hand up Scarlett's thigh. "Good. I like to see you enjoy yourself." Her mouth curled up at the edges ever so slightly. "Can't have you bored."

Scarlett shoved playfully at Delores's arm and then moved to the other side of the bed. "You're so cocky."

"I don't know if I'd phrase it quite that way," said Delores. "Speaking of which, how's Jonathan?"

"He seems fine."

"How's his girlfriend?"

"Tall and pretty," informed Scarlett.

"Maybe I'll get to meet her when I'm not so busy," said Delores, and she took a final bite of her fettuccini. She washed it down with wine. "Is she smart?"

"Sounds like it."

"She must be," observed Delores. "I hear that store of hers makes a fortune." She paused and lit a joint. "I bet she's crazy about Jonathan. All the women are."

Scarlett's face must have betrayed something because Delores was suddenly curious about her expression. "Does that surprise you? Men and women do fuck, you know. Not everyone's queer."

For some reason Scarlett just couldn't imagine Karyn having the same passion for a man that she had for that woman at the Katmandu. Maybe it was some instinctual sense of Karyn's true feelings.

"I don't know," Scarlett finally said. "It's just hard to visualize those two together."

"What an odd thing to say," said Delores. She inhaled, holding the smoke in for a long time before she exhaled. "Believe me, they get together. Fucking is Jonathan's favorite sport, apart from taking pictures of war."

"Did you ever go to bed with him?"

"Jesus, Scarlett! I can't believe you're asking me that. I don't fuck men. I've always known what I liked." Delores paused and regarded Scarlett with sudden suspicion. "Don't you know yet?"

"Well, yes," said Scarlett. "I'm gay." Scarlett, however, was not altogether completely sure of anything at the moment. She remembered Michel and how much she had enjoyed him sexually. She hadn't faked it. "What difference does saying it make anyway? It's just a label."

"It's a little more than that," said Delores. "It organizes reality for me."

"Of course," nodded Scarlett.

She wondered if Delores was right. Were definitions necessary? Did they really organize reality? Did who you enjoy in bed determine your sexuality? Who made you come? Both men and women could make her do that. At least Michel could. So what did that make her? Gay? Bisexual? What?

It was a provocative puzzle, and Scarlett was plainly stumped. For the life of her she couldn't explain how she felt right now, and she wasn't about to discuss it with Delores. She wouldn't put up with any of it, not for a second. For Delores the world was divided into them and us. The assholes in between were simply fooling themselves—at least that's what she had told Scarlett in Mykonos. "Bisexuality is what you do until you have the courage to be who you are," was the way Scarlett remembered her putting it.

"Yep," Scarlett finally confirmed for Delores's ears. "I'm queer. Gay as a goose."

"Good," said Delores. "Because I don't like sharing who I fuck with men." And then she added, "Or other women. Got it?"

"Got it," responded Scarlett, thinking how territorial Delores just sounded.

But then, as Scarlett thought about it, she realized Delores's outburst probably had more to do with Celeste Morgan than anything she had said. Celeste's repeated betrayal and abandonment of Delores for men left a cruel and indelible mark. Delores Sheridan no longer trusted, no longer hoped, no longer believed in love. Celeste's need for convention had stolen her dreams.

"We better turn in," Delores said abruptly. "I've got a dubbing session tomorrow and you've got UCLA."

Chapter

95

The UCLA campus was as big as some cities. Located in Westwood, it sprawled over hundreds of acres of prime real estate. Parking, Scarlett would learn, was at a premium and even if you could get a permit, it cost a small fortune. No wonder everyone on campus looked healthy. At UCLA you walked and walked, sometimes miles a day.

Scarlett became frustrated looking for the administration building. She decided that one needed a contour map and compass just to get around this campus or they could end up in Pasadena. She consoled herself by admiring the beauty of the grounds and the co-eds. UCLA had acres and acres of attractive women.

Scarlett finally located the administration building and, as arranged, met with Sarah Denton, Delores's friend. Shortish and serious, Miss Denton made no concessions to style. Her dress looked like a potato sack. Her oversized glasses, however, might have hidden a certain appeal.

Scarlett was surprised Delores had such an unstylish-looking friend. She decided it must be history, an ancient gratitude of some sort, or present power. Sarah Denton sat on the University of California Board of Regents. Delores told Scarlett she could pull a lot of strings, and Delores was right. Scarlett was immediately accepted for the spring semester at UCLA.

"Give Vida my regards," Miss Denton told Scarlett at the end of their interview. Scarlett must have looked surprised because Miss Denton quickly amended the name. "Delores, I mean."

"Certainly," said Scarlett and smiled to herself. She would have never guessed that the Queen of B Movies once had a handle like that. Scarlett thanked Miss Denton for her time and asked directions to the student cafeteria. "I'm meeting an old friend," she volunteered and then walked out the door.

Scarlett's smile was as bright as the sunny California day beaming down on campus. Sarah Denton's relationship with Delores assured her a place at UCLA, and that made Scarlett very happy. The university boasted an academic world in which Scarlett hoped to lose herself. If not in it, then in Delores Sheridan. Either way, life in California promised to keep thoughts of Gina at bay.

"What's that smile for?" asked a familiar voice.

Scarlett looked over at a woman waiting in front of the student union and smiled again. "For you, Clotelle Carver. You look wonderful."

Clotelle stood up and hugged Scarlett. "I see California is agreeing with you as well."

"So far."

The two friends went inside the student union to the cafeteria, where they picked out some sandwiches and a couple of salads. "That looks like a good place over there," said Clotelle, organizing everything on a tray.

They walked over to a table in the corner. Once they sat down, Scarlett and Clotelle began reminiscing about their lives and their serendipitous meeting two years before on that bus to Socorro, New Mexico. Between bites of food, they almost managed to get caught up, cramming as much personal history as they could into a couple of hours.

"The top of your class, huh?" said Scarlett. "Well, that doesn't surprise me. What about boyfriends?"

"With my schedule, honey? I barely have time to romance my hand."

Scarlett laughed.

"Three years of law school in two and then I'll have to study for the bar." Clotelle stopped talking and took a sip of coffee. "What about you, Scarlett? What about Gina? You didn't say much in your letters."

"It didn't work out," replied Scarlett, avoiding her friend's eyes. "That's all. It just didn't work out."

Clotelle knew better than to push Scarlett, at least not at the moment, not when there was all that pain on her face. There would be plenty of time to pursue the question of Scarlett's heart when she moved to L.A.

"Okay," said Clotelle. "What's this actress thing you've gotten yourself into? Delores Sheridan of *Commanche Princess* notoriety, I believe?"

"You saw the film?"

"Yes," nodded Clotelle. "Every miserable frame of it after you wrote me about her. She looks about as Commanche as the Virgin Mary. Why didn't they use an Indian?"

"Hollywood," said Scarlett, defending Delores. "She doesn't have a lot of choice about scripts. Believe it or not, Clo, she said the same thing. That she shouldn't be playing an Indian."

Scarlett didn't tell Clotelle the real reason Delores hated that role. Nope. She didn't say a word about how that dark pancake makeup had trashed her face, screwed up her pores for weeks and how Miss Sheridan had bitched the whole time.

"It's good to know you're seeing a woman with some social and political awareness. We need all of those we can get."

"Absolutely."

"So she's not just another pretty face?"

"No. She's smart too." Scarlett took a sip of water and glanced out the window. "This one has it all."

Clotelle doubted that. She certainly didn't seem to have Scarlett's heart. "I'm glad you're coming to school here," Clotelle told her. "We can finally catch up."

"Yeah," said Scarlett. "We won't have to exchange letters anymore, which should give you lots of time for lawyering."

"And you time for writing."

"I hope so," said Scarlett.

"Anything in mind?"

"I'm making notes for a novel," said Scarlett. "A love story," she added, her voice cracking.

"You okay?"

"No," answered Scarlett, and her eyes dropped away as she struggled with herself. "Things aren't right in me."

"Soul chiggers?" inquired Clotelle gently.

A bruising look of recognition flashed across Scarlett's face as she remembered what Clotelle meant by the metaphor. That brand of chiggers rarely left her alone anymore. Only sex made them go away and then only briefly.

"You've got to talk about them, honey, or they'll take you straight to hell."

The color suddenly drained from Scarlett's cheeks. For a second, Clotelle thought she might faint. But she didn't. Then it looked as if she might say something. But she didn't do that either. Not a sigh left her lips. She just sat there, trapped in her own pain.

Chapter

96

"Terrific," said Delores. "I knew you could do it."

"I didn't do anything," said Scarlett. "I just signed a piece of paper and Miss Denton said she would see me at UCLA in January."

Delores smiled. "It's nice to have influential friends."

"Where did you meet her?"

"We grew up together back in South Dakota."

"Did you two ever do it?"

"Hell, Scarlett. Does Sarah Denton look like my type?" Delores took a sip of wine and then answered her own question. "No. Besides, she's straight as an arrow and a real tart. The boys back home used to call her 'Hot Socket.'" The memory made Delores chuckle. "And, apparently, the nickname still applies. Even Jonathan's done her."

"That's hard to believe."

"Well, he did and according to him you'd swear she's the eighth wonder of the world. Insatiable is the word I think he used."

"A nympho?"

"Could be," smiled Delores.

"Jeez," said Scarlett. "Who'd ever think a Tinker Bell like her could have such a gargantuan sexual appetite? She doesn't look the type."

"How's a cocksucker supposed to look?"

They both laughed. Scarlett reached over and took the joint out of Delores's hand, inhaled it into her lungs and gave it back. "You tell me, Vida."

"So Sarah slipped, huh? She knows I hate that name."

"What's the rest of it?"

"I'll tell you, Scarlett Turner, but only if you promise never to tell. Understand?"

"Understood."

"Duday."

Scarlett laughed so hard, she slid off the bed onto the floor. "How does anyone get the hots for someone called Vida Duday?"

"Easy when you have a body like Vida's," said Delores with a playful touch of arrogance in her voice. "You're lucky I'm stoned." Delores took a final toke. "You ever tell anyone and I'll have you bumped off."

Scarlett howled until tears welled up in her eyes.

Chapter

97

Delores still had some footage to dub so she called a taxi to take Scarlett to the airport. As it honked outside, she gave Scarlett a present. "It's for Christmas."

"Jeez, isn't this a little early? I haven't even bought yours yet."

"This is just one of them," smiled Delores. "You can open it on the plane if you want. Now give me a kiss and get out of here."

They embraced briefly and gave each other the shortest of kisses. They both hated good-byes and the gift helped decoy their feelings about separation, probably more so for Delores than Scarlett. Vida Duday had built herself a lonely existence up there on that knoll in Beverly Hills.

"I'll see you in January," said Scarlett.

"Your apartment will be ready." Delores opened the front door and waved out to the taxi driver. "Want a TV?"

"Yeah," answered Scarlett, secretly delighted. "That would be great."

Scarlett walked down the bricked path to the taxi. As the driver took her bag and opened the back door, Scarlett turned to wave good-bye, but Delores had already shut the door.

"L.A. International?" confirmed the driver.

"Yes," said Scarlett. "But I need to go to the Europa Boutique in Beverly Hills first. You know where it is?"

"Yeah. That fancy dress shop on Rodeo. Takes bucks to shop there."

Scarlett smiled to herself. So this guy thought she was rich. "I'm going to see a friend," said Scarlett proudly. "The owner."

"My, my. Don't we know the right people?" said the taxi driver, looking at Scarlett in the rearview mirror. "Who are you?"

"I guess I'm a friend of the right people," replied Scarlett, laughing.

The taxi driver laughed too and drove his fare to Rodeo. Before Scarlett knew it, he hopped out and opened the door for her. "Well, here we are."

"That was fast," said Scarlett, getting out of the taxi.

"Beverly Hills is not that big. Just rich."

Scarlett paid the fare and slid a nice tip into the man's hand. "Thank you," she said and then quickly disappeared into the Europa Boutique.

Chapter

98

"How nice of you to come," said Karyn, walking over to Scarlett, looking very sexy in a tight sweater and lavender suede mini-skirt.

Scarlett smiled, appreciating every inch of Karyn's statuesque body. "I couldn't leave L.A. without seeing your store," she said, glancing around. "It's beautiful."

"Thank you," said Karyn. She took Scarlett's hand and guided her to a rack of dresses. "See if you like any of these. I believe they're your size."

Scarlett quickly checked them out. "They're all beautiful. Maybe you can help me decide. My flight leaves at noon."

"Of course." Karyn selected several dresses and turned back to Scarlett. "You can use my office as a dressing room."

Scarlett followed her down a hall through a set of double doors. "You can change behind that partition over there. That's what it's for, for my most exclusive customers. Care for a glass of champagne?"

"No," said Scarlett, walking behind a Japanese-style partition. "I'm afraid I overdid that the last few days." Scarlett slipped out of her clothes and slid into a blue silk dress that hit her mid-thigh. Scarlett gasped when she saw the price tag. It was $550.

"Well, let's see," said Karyn.

Scarlett emerged from behind the partition, and Karyn made a few adjustments to the dress. "It looks wonderful on you, Scarlett. It shows off your body."

Scarlett decided that was quite a compliment coming from Karyn. "I like it too. A lot."

"It's yours," said Karyn, and she poured herself a glass of champagne. "I appreciate your discretion."

"Please. It's not necessary," replied Scarlett, dissimulating. She wanted the dress. "No thanks is necessary. I understand."

"I know you do, but I still want you to have the dress." Karyn's hand trembled slightly as she raised the glass of champagne to her lips.

"Thank you," offered Scarlett. "I really like it."

"Then it's settled." Karyn put down her glass and regarded Scarlett with a sudden curiosity.

"What happened to the woman you were with at the Katmandu?"

Scarlett was surprised. "You remember her?"

"Distinctly. Medium-length black hair and the bluest eyes. At least what I could see of them. There was something about her. Something I can't describe."

"I know," said Scarlett. Karyn's memory of Gina cut through her like a knife. "Everyone said that."

"Where is she?"

"In Paris. We broke up."

"I'm sorry," said Karyn. "It looked like you were in love."

"Sometimes you get fooled," said Scarlett, avoiding Karyn's eyes as she walked behind the partition. She didn't want to answer any more questions. "What happened to the woman you were with?"

"She got married."

"You're kidding? That's hard to believe."

"There was a lot of pressure from her family. Big Texas ranchers."

Karyn fell silent for a minute and Scarlett peeked around the divider at her, hoping she would continue.

"I didn't think she would cave in to them, but she did," Karyn finally added.

"Maybe she'll come to her senses," offered Scarlett, trying to sound encouraging. "You two looked like you belonged together. Everyone was talking about you that night, how much in love you both seemed."

"We were." Karyn took another sip of champagne. "I still am."

Scarlett pulled off the dress and put her other clothes back on. "Then what are you doing with Jonathan?"

"Trying to bury my feelings," Karyn answered matter-of-factly.

"With a man?" Scarlett hadn't meant to sound so abrupt, but the question just slipped out before she could stop it. When Karyn didn't respond, she pushed her welcome. "Do you enjoy him? Sexually, I mean?"

"I try."

"Can't he tell?" asked Scarlett, emerging from behind the partition.

"I guess not."

Scarlett walked over and handed the dress to Karyn. She looked depressed as she put the dress on a hanger and slid it into a garment bag.

"I'm sorry you hurt so much," said Scarlett.

Karyn burst into tears, and Scarlett gave her a hug, then a Kleenex.

"Why don't you go see her?"

"She won't see me."

"Maybe she will," said Scarlett. "There just might be a way."

Karyn looked over at Scarlett, a trace of hope on her face. "How?"

"Poetry," informed Scarlett. "Poetry."

Chapter
99

Sally Trout got kicked out of school the first week Scarlett was back from Thanksgiving vacation. It was a big scandal, maybe bigger even than the one Scarlett and Sissy had endured in Charleston. Scarlett found the rumors difficult to believe. No one seemed to know what had really happened, but everyone was blaming Sally.

If Scarlett didn't already have an accurate bead on just how different boys and girls, men and women, were treated by society, the Sally Trout incident made it clear. The female of the species got fucked over, literally and figuratively, then was blamed for the fucking.

It was "football politics" at its best. Not one guy from Murdock Boy's College got expelled for the incident. Who had snitched remained a mystery, but the details of the smutty episode didn't. It was all over both campuses the following day. Murdock's entire football team had gone "trout fishing" in the basement of their school church, and Sally was now in the infirmary recovering.

"Hi, Sally." Scarlett had no idea how to begin this conversation.

"Oh, Scarlett, thank you for coming," said Sally, grabbing her hand. "No one else has." She started crying and sputtering out the lurid details of the night before. "I was at the Hootnanny having a drink with Brad Stevens. Can you believe it, Scarlett? He finally asked me out."

Brad was Murdock's quarterback, a big football star, all-American second year in a row. Every girl at Townsend had a big crush on him.

"Did you get drunk?"

"No," said Sally and winced.

"You okay?"

"No. They gave me a shot for the pain. I had to have stitches."

What kind of animal/maniac fucks in packs? wondered Scarlett. Not even wolves did that. She gently brushed the hair back from Sally's face.

"I need to talk about it, Scarlett. I have to figure out what happened." Sally started crying again, sobbing. "I can't remember how I got in that basement. I only had one drink. Really, that's all I had."

Mr. all-American had apparently slipped something into Sally's drink. The girls at Townsend had been cautioned about such things, but no one believed they really happened, not in Savannah.

"What do you remember last?"

"Going for a ride in Brad's car and making out behind the church." Sally struggled, trying to recall more. "Several other cars drove up next to us because there were lots of headlights shining on the church. At least I think so. Then the next thing I remember is being in the church basement. I don't know anything for sure from that point on. But I have flashes of things, awful things. I was hoping it was a nightmare."

"It was," said Scarlett.

The shot was taking effect, and Sally began drifting off. "Don't go. Please don't go," she pleaded with Scarlett and closed her eyes. "Did I really let the whole football team fuck me?"

"No," said Scarlett. She didn't know how to soften the truth. "You were raped."

"Oh, my God!" exclaimed Sally, her eyes suddenly wide open in alarm. "Why would they do that to me, Scarlett? What did I do?"

"Nothing, Sally."

Mercifully, Sally shut her eyes again and began to drift off to sleep while Scarlett held her hand. Scarlett went to the police the following day and told them what Sally had told her. Between the averted eyes and sniggers, she realized Sally's violation would never be taken seriously. That even though her blood work only revealed a low alcohol level, there was no way she could explain the drugs in her body.

Thus, it was decided that Sally Trout was not a reliable witness to her own rape. She had been too stoned. Besides, Brad Stevens was an upstanding young man, an all-American who would never be involved in anything as sordid as what was rumored. Damage control began, and Murdock's football team was promptly exonerated. Sally Trout had fucked someone for sure. Maybe even been raped. Her vagina proved that. But it wasn't anyone from Murdock.

Even when several used rubbers were discovered in the church basement, the football team, and above all Brad Stevens, was isolated from the scandal. Sure, he and Sally were at the Hootnanny that night, but he had a Coke and left while she stayed and flirted with some guys he had never seen before. Guys from some other school.

Eventually bits and pieces of the truth did come out, but neither Brad nor a single member of the Murdock Trojans was ever implicated in what went on that night in the church basement. Not Mr. All-American. He had just thrown another touchdown pass and was now being considered by the pros.

What happened to Sally Trout after she left Townsend Scarlett never knew. It was as if she had disappeared off the face of the earth. Who knows? Maybe she did.

Chapter

100

"You sound depressed," said Delores.

"I keep thinking about Sally."

"There are lots of Sallys in the world."

"I know," said Scarlett with a rising frustration in her voice. "And it's got to change or they'll go on being victims."

"That's the way it is, Scarlett. The way the world is. The way it's always been."

"That's nice and negative."

"I understand power," said Delores matter-of-factly. "Most women don't have it, and without it they can't protect themselves. It's the simple, sad truth."

"It's going to change."

"Yeah?" said Delores. "How?"

"The Women's Movement."

"We've had those before. They always get stamped out."

"This time it's going to be different."

"I hope so," said Delores. "In the meantime, since we can't change the world tonight, how about a little diversion?"

"Okay," Scarlett finally answered, realizing a little phone sex might be exactly what she needed. It would make the world go away, for a while anyway.

"How are you dressed?" Delores suddenly wanted to know.

"A sweater and jeans. It's cold here."

"Why don't you take them off and get in bed."

"What are you wearing?"

"Nothing," said Delores in a low, sexy voice. "And I'm already in bed."

Chapter

101

It was a small wedding. A dozen or so of the bride's friends and relatives were there and so were a few of Cecil's. Just as they had wanted, the bride and groom were married on Christmas Day. It was a beautiful day too, with the sun shining and a light dusting of snow on the ground.

"She's very nice," said Scarlett, congratulating the groom.

Cecil glanced over at Phyllis, who was busy talking to Ollie Mae and the preacher. "I'm a lucky man," he said. "Life giving me a second chance like this."

"You deserve it. You were alone too long."

"Too long is right," said Cecil. "And missing out on love when it was there all the time."

"When did you meet her?"

"I met Phyllis years ago. Right after I got back from the Foreign Legion. She tried to get close to me then, but I wouldn't let her. I was too afraid of loving."

"It was understandable. Lorraine hurt you."

"Not as much as I hurt myself by throwing away all those years." Cecil looked across the room at Phyllis. "I'll be there in a minute, honey. Scarlett and I are having a little catch-up talk." He winked at his new bride. "About love." He looked back at Scarlett. "I used that hurt to close off my heart. Phyllis opened it again."

Scarlett regarded Phyllis with new interest, wondering what those hidden charms were. "How?"

"Teaching me that love casts out fear. She said it was in the Bible." Cecil paused and looked briefly over at the new Mrs. McMurty again, beaming. "You know I've never been much of one for religion, but that made a lot of sense, Scarlett. I'm here today, aren't I? A married man."

A wan smile came to Scarlett's mouth as she remembered hearing the same thing in different words not so long ago. "Love takes fear away," was how she remembered Gina saying it.

"Are you okay?" asked Cecil.

"Yes," lied Scarlett.

"Anyway," he went on, "this time I didn't run. I let Phyllis love me. What about you, Scarlett?"

Scarlett didn't hear Cecil. Her mind had drifted. He put his hand on her shoulder. "Scarlett?"

"Yes?" she said, slightly startled. "I'm sorry, Cecil. What did you say?"

"Are you letting someone love you?"

Scarlett felt a sick feeling in the pit of her stomach. "I need a drink," she said. "I mean, some punch. Do you want any more?"

"No, thank you," answered Cecil. "It's time Phyllis and I were leaving on our honeymoon."

"Where are you going?"

"To heaven," smiled Cecil.

"Yeah?" said Scarlett, and she smiled. "Have a wonderful trip."

Chapter

102

Between Christmas and New Year's, Scarlett composed a few more poems for Karyn to send to Veronica. By now that lost Texas sweetheart had received enough rhyme to woo the hardest of hearts. Scarlett wondered if it were working, if Veronica had broken the silence, or if she had decided to stay corralled in Texas until those memories of her inconvenient love turned to dust.

It never occurred to Scarlett that every poem she wrote to open Veronica's heart might also do the same to hers. Poetry worked liked that. It didn't observe boundaries. It went beyond even language and gave voice to the soul.

"How come you're lookin' so glum?" Ollie Mae wanted to know. "Someone ransack your heart?"

"No," answered Scarlett, secretly marveling at her mother's dead-on intuition. "I'm just thinking."

"Well, now there's the problem. You gotta do something 'steda that all the time."

"Like what?"

"Like loving somebody."

"Yeah," replied Scarlett unenthusiastically, sensing one of those big mother-and-daughter talks coming up.

"You gotta open up to some nice fella, Scarlett, or you're gonna turn into a pinched-up old maid with a noodle full of facts and an empty heart."

"What about you, Momma? What did filling your heart up with Joe Turner ever do for you?"

"It taught me about loving."

"Yeah?" Even now, after all these years, Scarlett could barely disguise the bitterness she felt for her father. "How?"

"It taught me that no one's perfect. You accept 'em warts and all, the whole package, and love 'em anyway."

"But he tried to shoot you, Momma. How can you love someone who did that?"

"I knew his brain had got addled by drink. That it made him mean. I also knew I hadda leave him if he didn't quit," said Ollie, and her voice softened. "And I woulda, believe me, 'cept then he had that stroke."

Scarlett was surprised at this revelation and the firmness in her mother's voice when she said she would have left Joe Turner.

"He was sick, honey. Sick from what he couldn't control and gettin' worse. I had the money put away. Ask Etta. I was gonna leave him."

Again, Scarlett was surprised. She had no idea her mother was made of such mettle. It was amazing Ollie had seen Joe Turner's problem clearly enough to devise an escape plan. It would not have been easy for a woman to leave her husband back in the early fifties, especially one without any education who had a small child.

"I had no idea, Momma."

"That's because by the time we coulda started talkin' about these things, really talkin', you went away to school."

Scarlett hugged her mother for a long time, realizing how much she must have underestimated her all these years. Someday, perhaps someday soon, she would find the courage to tell her mother the final secrets that divided them, her secrets.

"So what did you learn about loving?" Scarlett asked, hoping to discover a bit of wisdom for a broken heart.

"That it's made up of a whole buncha parts. Passion is one thing. Gets it started. But there's other stuff too. Like patience and understanding." Ollie paused and reflected awhile. She knew this talk was important. She had heard it in Scarlett's voice when she asked the question about loving. "Compassion too," Ollie finally added. "Yeah, that one there's real important. Helps you realize what it's like to be behind that other pair of eyes. Helps you learn how to forgive."

Scarlett's heart suddenly felt as if a silver bullet had pierced it. She remembered having no such compassion and forgiveness for Gina. She had withdrawn her love without ever looking behind "that other pair of eyes."

"What's the matter, honey?"

Scarlett was unable to stop the tears rolling down her cheeks. "Oh, Momma," she sobbed as she buried her face in her mother's breast. "I miss . . ." She stopped the name in time. "So much."

"Sounds like you got an achin' heart, Scarlett Faye."

Chapter

103

Scarlett never did come clean with Ollie Mae about her aching heart. She chickened out at the last minute and told her mother she was nervous about going so far away from her, all the way out to UCLA. That seemed to satisfy Ollie, for the time being anyway.

"Come on, Momma."

"Come on where?"

"Dress shopping."

"What with? My good looks?"

"That and some Christmas present money I received," Scarlett quickly explained. "One of the girls at Townsend. She wanted to give me money rather than shop for a gift."

Ollie raised her eyebrow.

"What was I supposed to do? Give it back?"

"How much?"

"A hundred dollars."

"She made a' money or somethin'?"

"Yes," said Scarlett.

Scarlett, of course, didn't dare tell her mother about the money's real source, Delores Sheridan, or how much she had actually received, a check for a thousand dollars. She had read Delores's handwritten Christmas card with her check on the flight back to Savannah. "Hoping this is just the beginning of many fun holidays to-gether," it said. At this rate Scarlett hoped it was too.

"Now get your coat. Etta's coming to pick us up," said Scarlett as she looked out the window. "That's her honking right now."

Ollie was surprised. She couldn't figure out what her daughter was up to now. Scarlett had insisted on buying her a pretty new dress and enlisted her best friend's help to do it. Ollie, of course, had no idea that Etta and her daughter were planning to spruce her up for a New Year's Eve party, a big one at Etta's house, where Abe Millet would be.

Abe had moved to Dillinger the year before and bought the local feed store. In his middle fifties, he was only ten years older than Ollie and nice-looking to boot. He had inquired about Ollie Mae from Etta, asking about the nice lady who always came into his store to buy birdseed. When Etta told Scarlett about his interest in her mother, Scarlett went down to the feed store to check him out.

"I'd like a five-pound bag of birdseed."

"Sure thing," said Abe gently. "But there aren't many birds out this time of year, young lady."

"I know. It's a Christmas present for my mother, Ollie Mae Turner. Just thought I'd surprise her with a little extra seed come spring. You know how she loves to feed those birds."

"Yes," smiled Abe Millet. "Sure loves those birds." He paused. "I do too." He handed Scarlett two five-pound bags of birdseed. "What's your name, young lady?"

"Scarlett," she answered. "But I only need one."

"The second bag is from me. I'd like to give it to your mother as a little holiday present." As Abe rang up the cash register, he quickly amended the nature of his offering. "Rather, Dillinger Feed and Tackle would like to give it to her for being such a good customer."

Scarlett smiled. Abe was smart. He knew how to get her mother to take the birdseed. Ollie Mae could understand being a good cus-tomer. She would never understand a gift from an almost perfect stranger, which at this moment Abe Millet still was. After Scarlett left the feed store, she rushed over to Etta Paine's house.

"I like him," she told Etta, showing her the bag of birdseed Abe had given Ollie. "Let's fix them up."

Etta grinned wider than a Cheshire cat as the matchmaking plan was hatched. Etta would have a New Year's Eve party and invite Abe Millet plus a couple of other friends. Not too many people, just enough for a cozy gathering. Scarlett gave her fifty dollars to do it up right.

Chapter

104

Etta Paine's New Year's Eve party came off without a hitch. Neither Ollie nor Abe suspected a thing. To move things along and loosen up the guests, Scarlett had made the recipe for Wilma Bell's punch, the wild kind. In a few hours everyone was feeling inordinately good.

Scarlett never remembered seeing her mother so happy. She was positively glowing, lit up like a lightning bug. Maybe she was signaling Abe with an unconscious mating ritual, not unlike that of those fireflies in France. With that thought came a rush of memories, and Scarlett found herself on the verge of tears. All of a sudden she wanted to reach out to Gina, write a letter, make a simple phone call, do something to end the silence. But she knew she couldn't. Fear held her hostage.

"You okay, honey?" asked Ollie, suddenly at Scarlett's side.

"Maybe a little nostalgic," answered Scarlett, still fighting the tears.

"Well, that's what this night's for," said Ollie, patting her daughter's hand. "Missin' and rememberin' and revisin' what ain't right."

"Yeah," agreed Scarlett, secretly wishing she could magically revise it all, especially the end of that summer with Gina.

"Honey, this here party punch of yours is somethin' outta this world. I ain't never tasted anything like it. What's the magic ingredi-ent?"

Scarlett smiled. "Sugar, Momma. Lots of sugar." It wasn't a com-plete lie. It was full of alcohol. "How about another cup?"

"Good girl. Tasty stuff."

Scarlett took her cup. "Here. I'll get it for you." She had just seen Abe Millet at the punch bowl ladling up another serving.

"Good evening, Mr. Millet."

"Why, Scarlett. How are you?"

"Fine. Getting ready to leave for school day after tomorrow," an-swered Scarlett, filling Ollie's cup.

"Where would that be?"

"Out in California. Los Angeles. UCLA."

"Lucky lady. Going to the land of sunshine to get smart," said Abe, and he looked over at Ollie. "Your momma looks mighty pretty tonight. That's some dress."

No doubt about it, Ollie Mae Turner could turn a head or two. After Scarlett and Etta got her to say yes to that red dress and a pair of shoes to match, they had taken her to the beauty parlor. A new hairdo was just the thing to make Ollie look her age and not ten years older like she usually did. The last thing Scarlett got her mother to do was leave her glasses at home. At first Ollie protested, saying she couldn't see a thing, but Scarlett prevailed.

Etta just shook her head. She knew how blind Ollie was. The "gift of the leprechauns" was at work again, as Etta Paine referred to Scarlett's uncanny ability to convince anyone of anything no matter how irrational or preposterous it was.

"Yep. She's a fine-looking woman," said Scarlett, and she quickly took advantage of the moment. "Mr. Millet, would you mind taking this cup of punch over to my mother? I seemed to have spilled something on my dress and I'd like to wash it off."

"Why, certainly," said Abe, seizing the opportunity.

Scarlett handed him the cup. "Besides, I know she would love to thank you for that bag of birdseed. She's just so shy."

Scarlett didn't bother mentioning that her mother probably hadn't even seen him yet and wouldn't until he was standing right in front of her face. Abe had no idea how much she needed those glasses. It was with absolute delight that Scarlett watched Abe walk over to Ollie, hand her the cup of punch, say something and sit down in the chair next to her. It wasn't long before they were both smiling.

Chapter
105

"Come on, Scarlett, or you'll miss your plane," said Etta. "We gotta drive two hours yet just to getcha to the airport."

"Okay, okay," yelled Scarlett, rushing down the stairs. "I'm ready."

"Abe's coming too," beamed Etta. "He said he just couldn't pass up a Sunday drive with three beautiful ladies."

"Yeah? I wonder who invited him along?"

"Cupid musta'."

Scarlett grinned. "Good move, Etta. Where's Momma?"

"Primping." Etta nodded toward the bathroom and raised her voice. "Ollie Mae, Abe's expectin' to see you, not some newfangled, Avon version of yourself." Etta winked at Scarlett and continued ribbing Ollie. "Go overdoin' that rouge and you'll end up lookin' like somebody sucked on your cheeks."

Ollie finally emerged from the bathroom straightening out her favorite dress, the yellow one with big clumps of bright purple grapes all over it. She smiled and walked straight into the side of the knick-knack hutch.

"Momma, maybe you should put your glasses on."

"Lordy me. How could I forget those?" she said, pulling them out of her pocket.

"Easy," said Etta. "Vanity vapors."

Ollie ignored Etta's teasing and adjusted her glasses. "Where's Abe?"

"In front of the feed store. Let's get down there and pick him up," said Etta. "Quick. Before he snaps out of his love trance."

Ollie giggled like a young girl and flew out the front door. A few minutes later Etta, Scarlett and Ollie pulled up in front of the feed store.

"Well, well, Mr. Millet," said Etta, rolling down the window. "Ain't you looking fit today."

Abe smiled from ear to ear. "Why, thank you, ma'am. Never felt better."

"Well, come on and get in then before you freeze your whiskers off standing there feeling so good," advised Etta.

Abe rushed down the steps and got in the backseat next to Ollie. "You're looking as lovely as can be, Ollie."

Ollie just blushed and murmured an almost inaudible "Thank you."

After a bit, the two began talking and then talked up a storm all the way to the airport. Etta and Scarlett said something to each other now and then, but mostly they looked at the scenery and eavesdropped on the conversation going on behind them.

Abe told Ollie about his dear late wife, Millie Millet, who had passed away in the mid-fifties from some unnamed illness. Their only child, Sam, was in Vietnam. A professional soldier, he had been there for three years and was a colonel now.

Ollie said she had lost her husband to a stroke many years before. As they exchanged life stories, Scarlett was glad her mother's good sense prevailed. She didn't mention Joe Turner's alcoholism or the deep-enders in the family (those with mental difficulties) or Aunt Fannie or the homosexuality. No, that last secret was the best kept one of all; not even Scarlett's own mother had a clue about that one yet.

Abe Millet's family had secrets too, similar secrets, shameful ones some would say. Take, for example, his son Sam. Who would have ever guessed the deep, dark truth about that hunk of manhood? That a Vietnam hero, twice purple-hearted, was a "fag?"

Abe had suspected there was something different about his son a long time ago. He loved hanging out with the guys in high school a lot more than he did with the girls. Of course, it was nicely hidden under the guise of sports. All that butt slapping on the football field kept a lot of secrets from seeing the light of day.

"What's your favorite thing to do, Ollie?"

"Sewing and feeding the birds."

"Ever gone bird watching?"

"I watch 'em when they eat."

"No, Ollie. I mean bird watching with binoculars and keeping a list of all the different ones you see."

Ollie looked fascinated. "I don't own no binoculars."

"I do," said Abe. "We gotta go watch them down by the river. There are more birds down there than God can count."

Scarlett smiled and remembered Delmos, the birdman of Dillinger. He had spent his life by the Monongahela watching birds when she was growing up. She guessed bird watching was as good a way as any to begin a courtship.

"I'll miss you," Ollie told Scarlett when they arrived at the airport.

"Me too," said Scarlett, getting out of the car as Abe retrieved her suitcase from the trunk. She smiled and took it out of his hand.

"Please, Scarlett. Let me carry it in for you."

"No, thank you, Abe. I would rather you keep my mother company. She hates good-byes."

Abe nodded. He understood and got back into the car. Ollie was already wiping her eyes.

"I'll be home before you know it, Momma," said Scarlett, peering in the car window.

Ollie mumbled something, but the roar of an overhead jet blocked out her tearful good-bye. Scarlett briefly grabbed her mother's hand and then disappeared into the terminal. Her flight to L.A. was ready to board.

On the plane Scarlett wrote a long-overdue letter to Twila letting her know she had been accepted at UCLA. She told her she would finish her last year and a half of college there. After that, Scarlett promised she would go back to New Mexico for a visit. She knew it had been too long. Where was Maggie, she wanted to know, still in Morocco?

Scarlett composed another letter to Sissy, acknowledging hers from several weeks before. She told Sissy she wished she could be in Zurich for her upcoming concert, but there was no way she could get away from school that week. She would be having midterms.

I'm glad Bertrand's going to be there, Scarlett ended her letter, *not only to hear your concert but to read the reviews as well. Both of which, I'm sure, will be superlative.* She smiled and sealed the envelope just as the stewardess arrived with lunch. As soon as she ate, she pushed her seat back and tried to sleep but couldn't.

Somewhere over the Arizona desert between Phoenix and infinity, Flight 222 began to experience turbulence. The seatbelt sign went on and Scarlett nervously fastened herself in. It was going to be a bumpy ride. But then, so was L.A.

Chapter

106

"So how do you like living in Los Angeles?" Karyn wiped her mouth with a napkin and picked up her wineglass. She had invited Scarlett to lunch in Beverly Hills while Delores was on location in Mexico.

"I don't know yet. The traffic. The smog. The attitude."

Karyn smiled. "But the sunshine, Scarlett. Don't you just love it?" She sounded like a true Angeleno. "L.A. has the best weather this side of Eden. You'll get used to the other things." Karyn took a sip of wine. "What have you been doing besides studying and . . ." She hesitated. "Seeing Delores Sheridan?"

"Writing," answered Scarlett, evading Karyn's curiosity about that relationship. She didn't want to talk about it. It left her feeling oddly hollow. "Here are some more poems for Veronica. Are they working yet?"

"Yes," said Karyn, smiling as she slid them into her purse. When her hand reappeared, it was holding a letter. "It's from Veronica." She lowered her voice and read it to Scarlett:

Dear Karyn,
I've tried to ignore your poems but they were too insistent. In spite of all my efforts, they got inside me and unlocked my heart, the heart I

tried to bury here in Texas. I'm scared, Karyn. I don't know what to do. I still love you.

Elton has to make a business trip to L.A. next month and insists I accompany him. I'll call you at the shop. Seeing you again is all I think about.

Love,
Veronica

"How wonderful," said Scarlett.

"Thanks to you." Karyn folded the letter and put it away. "Oh, Scarlett," she said, her eyes suddenly welling up with tears. "Your words did it."

Scarlett smiled. The pen was powerful. It opened hearts. Everyone's, it seemed, except hers. "You can use my apartment," she told Karyn.

Scarlett knew Karyn had nowhere else to go. Checking into a hotel would be too risky. Karyn might be recognized and besides, people would wonder why she was staying at a hotel in the first place. She still lived with her parents.

"Thank you. It'll still be difficult." A sudden anxiety clouded Karyn's face. "Her husband knows."

Scarlett's surprise was obvious. Karyn explained.

"Elton found out last time I was in Texas. He saw Veronica's car parked outside a motel and bribed the clerk into letting him have a key to the room. He thought she was in there with an old boyfriend. Imagine his surprise."

"That's not difficult. What'd he do?"

"He went crazy. He started yelling and screaming. I can't remember half of what he said, but I know it was awful. He pulled her out of bed and told me to get dressed, to get out of Houston. He didn't want any Beverly Hills pussy-licker running around Texas with his future wife. Then he slapped Veronica."

"God, I would have punched him in the chops."

"I did."

A sudden smile came to Scarlett's face. "You did?"

"Yep." Karyn didn't know whether to feel proud or chagrined. "In the eye actually, and hard. I guess it stunned him because he left and waited in the car."

"How could Veronica marry such a jerk?"

"Easy. He threatened her. He threatened us both. First he said he would make sure everyone from Beverly Hills to Dallas knew what we were doing in that motel room. Then he told us if we ever saw each other again, he'd kill us both."

"Jesus, what a psycho."

"Male ego," said Karyn despondently. "It's frightening."

"Yes," Scarlett agreed. "And frequently very dangerous."

Chapter

107

"How's Mexico?"

"Just awful. Hot and humid. Dusty. With mosquitoes the size of bats."

Delores's voice trailed off and Scarlett heard her tell someone to bring her a glass of water, that she was dehydrating just opening her mouth. She also wanted to know where her lunch was and not to bring her another damn taco. Scarlett could hear it. She was on a tear.

"I miss you. I want you to fly down this weekend."

"But I have midterms coming up."

"Bring your books. There's a ticket for you at the airport."

There was a brief silence.

"I need you down here, Scarlett."

There was an urgency in Delores's voice Scarlett recognized. The movie was running behind schedule. She hadn't had a drink or a cigarette or a snort in more than three weeks. She desperately needed a fix, one the camera couldn't see. Sex.

"Do you have money for a taxi?"

"Yes," replied Scarlett.

"Good. I'll replace it when you get down here. You'll enjoy yourself. Plus, there's a writer I want you to meet, darling. A film writer. It's a good connection."

Delores's enticement worked. "Okay," said Scarlett. "I'll see you in Puerto Vallarta."

"Scarlett?"

"Yes?"

"Bring my toys."

"Jesus, Delores. What if they look in my bags?"

"They won't."

"How can you be so sure?"

"Scarlett!" Delores was getting exasperated. "If they do, use your brain. Figure it out."

"Okay, Delores. Bye."

Scarlett was also getting irritated and figured she better hang up before they had words. Verbal duels were occurring with increasing frequency as Scarlett felt more and more controlled.

Chapter

108

"What is this, señorita?" asked a young Mexican woman staring into Scarlett's bag. She poked at a gift-wrapped box with a mangled ribbon.

"A birthday present for a friend I'm visiting down here." Scarlett smiled, trying to be casual.

"What is it?"

"A dictionary."

"It's much too big for a book."

"Not for the *Oxford Dictionary of the English Language.*"

The señorita poked at it again and then picked it up. "For such a big book it's not very . . . very *pesado.*" She couldn't remember the word for heavy. She shook the package. When it rattled, she eyed Scarlett suspiciously and told her, "Open it, *por favor.*"

A desperate paranoia seized Scarlett. She had heard they were pretty macho down here. They might take offense at her smuggling fake penises into Mexico and throw her into jail. Scarlett moved the ribbon aside and tore off the paper. Sure enough, printed there in big bold, letters on the very box it came in were the words, *Oxford Dictionary of the English Language.*

The señorita opened the box and her eyes widened in surprise. There was no dictionary inside. Whether she was perplexed or fascinated, or both, Scarlett couldn't tell. Obviously, she had never seen what she was seeing now, fake or otherwise. She stroked one of the dildos and gingerly squeezed it here and there.

"Be careful," cautioned Scarlett in a low voice, hoping the people in the line behind her hadn't seen anything.

The young woman looked up. "Why?"

"They're prosthetics."

Since the word was very close to what it was in Spanish, the young woman got it. She was instantly incredulous.

"War injury," said Scarlett with a doleful expression on her face. She was pushing her luck. "Lost it all."

The señorita now looked even more skeptical but seemed stumped as to what to do, if anything. This situation was not in the books, and the people in line were getting restless. If it were a medical item, it was allowable. If it weren't, it would have to be classified. But as what?

The señorita wondered *qué infiernos* (what the hell) this young Americana was doing with them anyway. She didn't have a wedding ring on her finger. Did that mean something immoral was going to go on in Mexico? Was the Americana going to do some sin with an *amigo?* It never occurred to Señorita Velasquez that it was an *amiga* with whom Scarlett would do the sinning.

"Okay, miss," she finally said, slamming Scarlett's suitcase shut and staring at her with a mixture of disbelief and edgy curiosity. "Welcome to Mexico."

"Gracias." Scarlett smiled. "Mucho gracias. That's how you say it, isn't it?"

No. It was *muchas gracias,* but Señorita Velasquez didn't bother to correct her. She just waved her on, on into the heat and ambiguities of macholand.

Chapter

109

The driver left the airport and drove, not toward, but away from Puerto Vallarta, out to where *The Night of the Iguana* had been filmed several years before. No wonder Delores was unhappy. The place was awful. Only the skeletal remains of the old set could be seen.

It was easy to understand the rumors. Rumors that Ava Gardner had swilled herself through countless bottles of bourbon to get through the picture. Bourbon Richard Burton had no doubt helped her finish off. How else could they have survived the forlornness of this place with its stifling heat and choking humidity?

Scarlett saw *The Night of the Iguana* with Sissy their first year at college. Already initiated into the delights of each other, they openly enjoyed Ava Gardner's role as the lusty proprietress of a run-down resort located on the edge of nowhere. Scarlett and Sissy liked one scene on the beach in particular. With the waves washing over her, Ava Gardner danced in the wet sand, her clothes clinging to her full, mature breasts. She enticed several beach boys to join her and then they all abandoned themselves to the night, the moment and the moon.

Though Ava was no longer considered box office material (the lines had come), she could still seduce you. She was total sensuality, the quintessential woman. As Scarlett thought about Ava, her reverie suddenly took a dangerous turn. She hadn't realized it before, but the cast of Gina's eyes was eerily similar to Ava Gardner's. It was haunting the way those eyes found you and held you in their gaze.

"*Bueno*, señorita. Here we are."

The driver's words brought Scarlett back to the present, to the set of Delores Sheridan's latest picture, *Lost in the Amazon*. Originally slated to film in the Brazilian jungle, budget considerations took the cast and crew to Mexico, to here, to where Delores's plane went down in the script, in the middle of nowhere.

As the driver pulled up, they were just finishing a scene. Scarlett watched Delores in her present incarnation as Amanda Houseman, one of four airplane crash survivors trying to hack their way out of the Amazon. Jeopardy for Miss Houseman came not only in the form of headhunters, snakes and barracudas, but from the other three survivors, all men, vying for her favors. Delores delivered her lines, as she always did, competently. Satisfied, the director yelled, "Cut!" and she walked off the set.

That Delores Sheridan was beautiful and smart no one could dispute. That her emotions might be buried at the core of the earth few realized, certainly not her fans. Scarlett remembered a line from a Baudelaire poem describing a lover's breast "wherein no heart had ever been confined." Such a description, of course, greatly exaggerated Delores's emotional deficits and projected many of Scarlett's own. Both women avoided their feelings the way claustrophobics run from caves. They wanted to play it safe, to skim the surfaces, to ignore the depths. It was too dangerous down there. Intimacy was required to survive the journey.

"Well, what are you waiting for?" yelled Delores with a broad grin as she walked toward Scarlett. "Welcome to hell."

Scarlett got out of the car. The humidity had to be a hundred percent. She wiped her forehead and asked, "Which circle?"

Delores laughed. Scarlett's allusion to the *Divine Comedy* amused her. This part of Mexico would no doubt fit quite neatly into one of hell's nine circles.

"Take your pick. They're all here. This is a movie set." Delores turned to the driver. "Juan, please bring Miss Turner's bags to my trailer."

"*Sí*, Señorita Miss Sheridan."

Juan grabbed the bags and followed Señorita Sheridan and Scarlett as they made their way through the set toward her trailer.

"How was your flight?"

"I had some time to study."

"Good."

Just as Delores was going to ask Scarlett about customs, a loud, crashing noise startled them. They both reeled around at the same time and saw the complete contents of the *Oxford Dictionary of the English Language* bounce and scatter about the set.

"Oh, God!" gasped Delores.

Juan had bumped one of Scarlett's bags into a klieg light, almost toppling it over and springing the suitcase open. Señorita Velasquez apparently hadn't snapped that particular one shut with as much vigor as she had snapped it open. The entire crew peered down at the contents of the dictionary, not saying a word, stupefied. It looked like Juan might pass out.

Even Delores was daunted by the sight of all that penile litter. "Well, what is everyone staring at?" she challenged the crew. "They don't have to be attached to work, you know."

The men shuffled around. Some averted their eyes. Others began walking off the set. No way did anyone want to take on Delores Sheridan's mouth. It had a reputation. Fast, abrasive, sarcastic, witty, challenging, vengeful, demeaning, it said what it took to master the moment.

"Besides," Delores went on. "The ones that are frequently don't work anyway."

With that remark the remaining men quickly disappeared. No telling what might come out of her mouth next. Just last week she had trashed a gaffer's reputation as a cocksman. Who knows, maybe he deserved it. That dyke joke he had told was pretty crude.

"Juan, please pick up what you dropped and burn it."

"*Sí*, Señorita Miss Sheridan. Right away."

"Damn it!" Delores turned to Scarlett. "All my toys!"

Scarlett knew Delores would never use them again, not after they had been dropped in the Mexican dirt. There was no sterilization process in the world that could cleanse the picture Scarlett knew was in Delores's head right now. The one of foreign grime and flies and that stray dog over there licking at one of them like it was a bone or something.

"Come on, Scarlett. Let's get out of the sun. Now!"

They quickly escaped into Delores's trailer. Primitive by state-side standards, its air conditioning barely worked. She used bags of ice to cool herself off. At the moment, however, cooling off was not on her mind. Delores pinned Scarlett to the wall and pressed her body up against hers. "I've missed you," she said, and then her mouth quickly found Scarlett's.

Scarlett didn't mind Delores's intensity right now. She needed the edge too. What Ava Gardner had made her remember, Delores Sheridan could help her forget.

Chapter
110

Delores showered and went back on the set to finish her work. She looked around, defying anyone to snicker or make any reference to what had happened earlier, no matter how indirect. No one did. Filming proceeded as if the incident had never happened, and Delores thrashed through the jungle desperately looking for a way back to civilization.

In the meantime Scarlett talked with Fannie Promesa, the screenwriter who had been brought down to Mexico to try and fix the script. Distinctly unattractive, she was a huge woman with short blond hair who looked and dressed the role she pursued in life, that of super-butch. She came on to anything that vaguely resembled a woman.

"You can't revise a mess like this when half the script's already been shot," said Fannie, leering at Scarlett. "I don't know what Vida . . . Delores, I mean, was thinking. I'm a writer, not a miracle worker."

Scarlett wondered how someone who looked like Fannie ever got a woman into bed. She couldn't find one attractive feature on her. Her teeth were small and the color of corn and her nose spread across her face like a rotting cauliflower, reddish rather than white. It was probably from rosacea, something a lot of boozers got, a condition best described as the W.C. Fields malady.

"I understand you want to write."

"I already do. I've got a book out," Scarlett said proudly.

"I don't mean poetry."

Scarlett was a bit taken aback. She wasn't sure whether or not Fannie had just demeaned her accomplishment. Fannie read the expression on Scarlett's face and quickly shifted gears.

"Your poems are wonderful. Delores read me a few. I was just talking about writing scripts. That's where the real money is, Scarlett."

"Maybe someday I'll learn how to do that."

"I can teach you," said Fannie, tossing out the bait.

"Why would you do that?"

"Because you're a friend of Delores's." Fannie paused to give Scarlett her most sincere smile. "And because I know talent when I see it." Fannie leaned back in her chair. "Call me at Promesa Productions when you get back to L.A."

"Thanks. I'll do that," said Scarlett, staring at a black cloud of rising smoke.

The burning rubber smelled just awful. Scarlett couldn't believe it. Juan was disposing of Delores's toys only a short distance from the set.

"What the hell!" yelled the director. "What's that jerk doing? Smoke is getting into the shot."

Chapter

111

"Scarlett?

"Yes?"

"It's Jonathan. Can I come over and talk to you?"

"Jeez. I don't know." Scarlett looked at the clock. "It's late. I have classes tomorrow."

"Please, Scarlett. It won't take long."

Jonathan's choice of Scarlett as a confidante made perfect sense. Delores was still in Mexico and he wanted to talk about Karyn. He knew she and Scarlett had become friends. Even if his mind had been inclined to suspicious thoughts about their friendship, he knew he didn't have to worry. Karyn was into men. He could testify to that. He had fucked her and fucked her a lot. No one could fake orgasms like those. Karyn loved men. He just wished she didn't drink so much.

As Scarlett hung up the phone with Jonathan, it rang again. This time it was Karyn. "Jonathan just called," Scarlett told her. "He wants to come over."

"And . . . ?"

"I said he could. He sounded bummed out."

"He is. I told him I couldn't see him anymore." Karyn paused and took a deep breath. "Veronica's coming in tomorrow."

Scarlett could feel the excitement flow right through the telephone line. Jonathan's feelings were probably the last thing on Karyn's mind. "Butterflies, huh?"

"Hordes, Scarlett. They're trampling me."

Scarlett laughed. There was a levity in Karyn's voice she had never heard.

"They won't go away. I hope I can survive the night."

"You will. Those flutters are just a preview. Enjoy them," said Scarlett and she took a sip of Coke. "What does Jonathan know?"

"Nothing. Maybe you'll think of something. Other than the truth, I mean."

Scarlett teased, "You want me to lie?"

"With all your heart."

Scarlett laughed.

"Please, Scarlett. Help me out. I'm afraid he might go see my parents to try and win me back," said Karyn and then added, "I've already called off more engagements than any girl in Beverly Hills."

"Tell your parents he's after your money."

"I can't. I've used that excuse before and, unfortunately, Daddy found out most of them were rich," explained Karyn with a nervous catch in her throat. She tried to clear it. "He's suspicious now. Why would his sweet little princess lie about her suitor's assets?"

"Then tell him how rich Veronica is. Lay it on. You know, all those cattle ranches and oil fields."

"Oh, Scarlett. You mustn't joke about this. In Beverly Hills if you're twenty-nine and unmarried, it's the stuff of scandal. My parents are already mortified."

Karyn's anxiety was almost on a par with her excitement. Time was running out. One way or another, with or without Veronica, life was getting complicated. Scarlett wondered how she would deal with her future. Would she, like so many other women, gay or not, end up marrying for convenience and bury herself in the glitz of Beverly Hills, pretending to a life she didn't feel? Would she too hide herself in a lot of cheek kissing while her real feelings, the deep, erotic ones, got sublimated in shopping sprees, beauty salons and bikini waxes?

Relationships between women were complicated. They had non-sexual affairs all the time. They did it with the looks, the touches, the words only women know how to share. Karyn had seen it a thousand times in her boutique.

"Oh, darling, you look absolutely fabulous today. Who did your color?"

"Abner. You know, the balding one with the long sideburns."

"Well, it's just wonderful," effused Mrs. Madelaine Neutra, kissing Vana on each cheek. "Where do you want to have lunch?"

Vana smiled. "Where we can be seen, of course."

God forbid Vana and Madelaine go where they might not be seen. No. They couldn't do that. Too much aloneness together might stir something up, like all those unused feelings locked away in their loveless marriages. Touching in public was safe. Vana could take Madelaine's hand and admire the high-lacquered sheen of her perfectly manicured nails while the subtle electricity of her touch communicated what would never be overtly expressed. It's not that these women were gay, although some of them certainly were. They were desperate for affection, needing to touch and be touched but never crossing the erotic line into each other's arms. Many of them were with men who were really no more than legal Johns who had taken them as trophies in a bargain called marriage. Karyn's mother was one of those women, and Karyn had sworn long ago never to repeat her unhappiness.

"Are you still there, Karyn?"

"Yes, I'm sorry, Scarlett. I spaced out for a minute."

"Don't worry about Jonathan," Scarlett assured Karyn. "I'll figure out something to tell him."

"Thank you."

"What time do you want my apartment?"

"Noon," answered Karyn and then she took a sip of something. "Oh, Scarlett, I'm so excited."

"Me too. In fact, I think I'm a little jealous."

"You don't have to be," said Karyn.

"What do you mean?"

Karyn finally dared ask the question that had always been at the back of her mind. "What about your Veronica?"

"She doesn't exist anymore."

"I'm sorry. I didn't mean to push, Scarlett, but I'm just so happy. I want everyone to feel good."

"I'm fine. I'm with Delores now." Scarlett felt her heart squeeze shut. "I'll leave the key under the mat." She paused. "Karyn?"

"Yes?"

"I'm happy for you. I really am."

Chapter

112

Scarlett answered the door. "Hello, stranger." She hadn't seen Jonathan in a long time. Not surprisingly, he looked upset.

"Coffee?"

"Yes. Black, please. I've had a little too much to drink."

Scarlett poured Jonathan a cup and another for herself. "Here," she said, handing him the coffee. "What's going on?"

"Mind if I smoke?"

"No. Go ahead."

Jonathan lit a joint and took several deep drags off it. He handed it to Scarlett.

"No. I've got classes tomorrow."

"Just try one hit," said Jonathan. "It's Colombian gold."

Scarlett had never heard of this kind of grass and had no idea how potent it was. "Okay," she said and took the joint. She inhaled deeply like Delores had taught her and held the smoke in as long as she could. By the time she exhaled it from her lungs, she felt the power of the gold flowing through her body, mellowing out her edges, delivering her into a delicious languor.

"Karyn said she won't see me. Just like that." Jonathan snapped his fingers and took another hit. He handed it back to Scarlett.

"She didn't give a reason?" asked Scarlett, and she took a second toke. It was great stuff. It even made Gina leave her head.

"No. I can't figure it out. Do you think there's someone else?"

"Oh, no," lied Scarlett. "She digs you."

"Then what the hell could it be?"

Scarlett took yet another drag. She was so stoned now even her storytelling muscles had relaxed.

"Maybe I should have a talk with her old man. He'd like to see us get married. My family has money, you know."

Scarlett didn't know and right now she didn't care. "No. Don't talk to him. It might upset Karyn." She took another toke. She had no idea what she was going to tell Jonathan.

"How about a little coke?"

"I can't. I have school tomorrow."

"It won't interfere. Trust me."

Jonathan pulled a small vial out of his shirt pocket. He snorted first and then handed it to Scarlett. She hesitated, fingering the magic in her hand, and decided she might as well. It might help her think of something. The rush was immediate. Scarlett suddenly found herself riding the edge of the most extraordinary high. She felt magical, on top of it, energetic and mellow all at the same time, consumed, consuming, brilliant.

Jonathan smiled. "It's a great combination, huh?"

"Yes," agreed Scarlett as her mind tripped off into another dimension.

"So, tell me. What do you think is going on with Karyn?"

Scarlett still hadn't figured out what she was going to say. All she knew for sure was that she didn't want to bum herself out with any heavy rap. She felt too good. As she looked back over at Jonathan, Scarlett's mind suddenly took a surprising turn and she found herself thinking how attractive he was.

"I told her I had a crush on you."

"What!" Jonathan was stunned.

"I told her I wanted to make it with you, to see if I could go straight. She finally agreed but said I would have to explain everything to you. That's why she bowed out. To give me time."

"I see," said Jonathan, brightening. "Wasn't she jealous?"

"No. She's cooler than you know."

Scarlett couldn't believe Jonathan was actually buying this pack of lies. One thing, however, she soon discovered was not a lie. She had gotten turned on when she noticed the stirring in Jonathan's faded blue jeans. Scarlett wondered if he could be as exciting as Michel.

"And she said yes?"

"Yes," said Scarlett, running her hand over Jonathan's pant leg. "Karyn's a good friend."

"What about Delores?"

"Who's going to tell?" answered Scarlett in a sexy whisper. She began unbuttoning his Levi's. "Not me."

Chapter

113

"You're incredible in bed," Jonathan told Scarlett the next morning. "You're not gay. No lesbian could get off the way you did last night."

Scarlett smiled inwardly and didn't say a word. She knew why she had been so hot. There were the drugs, of course, and then there was the fact she wasn't emotionally involved with Jonathan. Fucking a virtual stranger could be very exciting. It was easy in fact. Not a shred of intimacy was required.

"Come here," said Jonathan. "I want to taste you again."

Scarlett brought him a cup of coffee. "Taste this and get out of here. I don't want to be late for class."

"My, my. Do I hear a little coke bitch?" said Jonathan teasingly as he opened Scarlett's robe and ran his hand over her breasts. "I'd like to fuck you again right now."

Scarlett quickly pulled away and closed her robe. "I told you. I have class."

"Okay," said Jonathan. He took a sip of coffee and put the cup down. "I'll go but not willingly. You sexy, closet heterosexual."

"Jesus!" said Scarlett. He had just waved a red flag in front of her face. "You can't say anything about last night. Not to anyone, ever. Do you understand, Jonathan? And I'm not just talking about Delores."

He looked at her curiously and waited for her to explain.

"I plan to make lots of money writing lesbian novels someday. I don't think my audience would appreciate it if they found out I'm . . ." Scarlett had trouble finding the right words. "Uh . . . sexually complicated."

"Aren't you getting a little excited? No one knows who Georgia Hill is."

"They will soon enough. I'm not staying in the closet forever."

"I'd think about that," cautioned Jonathan. "A girl who looks like you. Why limit your options? Besides, you're not really gay."

Scarlett rubbed her head and tried to think but it was difficult. Her mind was still a mess from last night's drugs. She unexpectedly found herself questioning her sexuality. What was she anyway? Straight like Jonathan was suggesting? She doubted it. She enjoyed being with women too much. That mixture of cocaine and Colombian gold had stirred up a lot of troublesome introspection.

If you considered yourself heterosexual and suddenly found yourself in bed with someone of your own sex, did that make you gay? And vice-versa? Perhaps the words "homosexual" and "heterosexual" were descriptive only of an act rather than a state of being. After all, people were a collection of widely varying impulses and attractions. What they did today they might not want to do tomorrow. So what did that make anyone? Scarlett was confused.

Then there was the question of love. Just where did it fit within this need-to-label folly? If homosexuality was "the love that dare not speak its name," then was bisexuality the love that defied being named? A complexity too discomforting for most people to entertain? Were there really people in this world capable of loving one sex as much as the other, with the same physical passion and depth of emotional feeling? Or was it, as Delores said, a cop-out, a rationalization for cowardice, an excuse for not stepping up to the plate and declaring yourself?

Was it your heart that determined your sexuality or the gender of the person with whom you shared your bed? If your heart was the ultimate arbiter, then a lot of people were lying, decided Scarlett. Perhaps love was the equation after all.

"I don't care what I am," lied Scarlett. "I just don't want my sex life talked about. It could compromise me financially."

"Okay, Georgia Hill," said Jonathan teasingly. "You've made your point. No tales of your sexual prowess shall ever pass my lips."

"Don't call me Georgia Hill." Jonathan was starting to get on her nerves.

"Pseudonym forgotten." Jonathan put his hands up in mock surrender. "When can I see you again?"

"Call me." Scarlett thought about this and then changed her mind. "No. I'll call you."

Chapter
114

Scarlett's mind was still so dull from the night's drugs, she could barely concentrate on medieval history and Christendom's Second Crusade to Jerusalem. Thankfully, she had no exams today. However, she did have that meeting at two o'clock in Fannie Promesa's office and she wanted to be sharp. After class, she went to the student union cafeteria and fortified herself with more coffee, eggs and toast. She ruminated about Fannie Promesa's call earlier that week.

"I'm calling you from the Paramount lot in Hollywood. That's where my production office is, Scarlett. Remember?"

According to Delores, Fannie had cut herself quite a deal at Paramount and was receiving a handsome chunk of money to develop properties for them. If things went well, she might even get to produce a script or two.

"Go see her," said Delores, who was still in Mexico and getting more irritable by the day. She now had more mosquito bites than she could count and was having to wear bug repellent on her face so it wouldn't get "bumped up" and ruin her close-ups.

"But I don't know how to write scripts yet."

"So? No one else in Hollywood does either. The proof is this piece of shit I'm making down here in Mexico."

"Do you really think Fannie would give me a job? To write, I mean?" Scarlett suddenly sounded excited.

There was a long pause on the other end of the line.

"Look, Scarlett, I want you to know how it works up there. Fannie's coming on to you under the guise of offering you work. She's always trolling for girls using head writer, producer, whatever the credit of the moment is."

"But she knows I'm with you."

Delores chuckled. "That doesn't matter, Scarlett. There are no loyalties in Hollywood. Just games played by a circle of liars and fools."

"I've never heard you talk like this."

"There was no need to say it before. It's all so dreary."

Scarlett heard Delores sigh and take a sip of something. She finally went on.

"People in that town will cut your heart out for the price of a plastic necklace if they think it'll close a deal for them. It happens all the time. And the few powerful women there will do it just as fast as the men."

Scarlett was shocked. "You . . . You'd," she stammered. "You'd think women would be sensitive to other women because of what we've all gone through."

"I've dodged as many passes from dykes as I have from men."

"But you never sold out?" Scarlett paused. "Did you?"

"Not really," said Delores, her voice sinking. It wasn't an admission she liked making. "But there were times I wished I had done it differently. In the beginning especially, when I first got there."

Delores was barely eighteen when she arrived in Hollywood. She never talked about those beginning days and now Scarlett knew why. They had cost her. She was hearing the price in her voice right now.

"Jesus," said Scarlett. "I'm sorry you got hurt."

It was years before Scarlett appreciated the full significance of Delores's pain. Women who used and abused women were everywhere, not just in Hollywood. The reasons varied from perversity, *No one helped me so why should I help you;* to sadism, *Dangle out there, bitch, and pay your dues, I did;* to fear, *If I help you, you might be better at this than I am and steal my job.*

When Scarlett joined the Women's Movement some years later she often spoke, and not to everyone's delight, about a theory born out of her discussion with Delores that day. If the terms of power were not redefined, Scarlett would ask her sisters, wouldn't women have to play by the same rules as men? If so, would they behave any differently? Was power in either gender's hands really any kinder or any more benevolent? But that was later, when Scarlett was a bit more enlightened. Right now all she cared about was The Big Three.

"Go down to that big troll's office and finesse yourself a job," Delores ordered.

"How do I do that?"

"By playing the game."

"How?"

"You know how, Scarlett. Let instinct guide you."

"What if she tries to get friendly or something?"

"Smile, dodge and get a contract."

Scarlett smiled. Delores was on a tear again.

"One more thing."

"Yes?"

"Flatter her. A well-timed scrape and bow works wonders in Hollywood."

Chapter
115

"Show Miss Turner into my office," croaked Fannie Promesa. The shapely secretary, barely out of college, relayed the message to Scarlett. "Miss Promesa will see you now."

Scarlett picked up her books and purse and was led down a short hallway. Stenciled on a door in bold gold letters were the words, *Promise Productions*. The secretary opened the door and showed Scarlett into a plushly appointed office.

"Well, hello, young lady. How are you?" asked Fannie.

"Fine. Thank you."

"Good. Please sit down. You can put your books on my desk if you want."

"Thanks," said Scarlett and stacked several large volumes at its edge.

"How's school?"

"Straight A's," answered Scarlett, settling down into the chair. "Not much of a challenge so far."

Fannie smiled, showing her yellow corn teeth. "Maybe we can provide some challenge in another area."

"Yes?" said Scarlett, her face brightening. "How?"

As she crossed her legs, Scarlett's skirt hiked just far enough up her leg to make the view interesting. A view she hadn't intended but one Fannie Promesa took eager advantage of. One of Scarlett's history books also caught Fannie's eye.

"What do you know about the Kings and Queens of England?"

"Which house? Which King? Which Queen?"

Fannie was amused at the seeming knowingness of Scarlett's questions. She doubted, however, that this young upstart's knowledge matched her attitude. "The Angevins."

"Easy. Henry II and Eleanor of Aquitaine. A rather unhappy union that produced eight ill-behaved children, including Richard the Lion-hearted, one of England's first fairy princes, and his sibling, John, who signed the Magna Carta."

"I'm impressed," said Fannie, and she was.

"Don't be. I love history. It's a natural for me."

Scarlett settled back into her chair. When she did, her hair fell away from her blouse and her breasts became unintentionally, but abundantly, obvious. Fannie's eyes instantly seized on them. Scarlett leaned forward, her hair once again covering her breasts.

"Well, I'll get right to the point," said Fannie. "I'm looking for someone to do research for a picture we're developing." She paused and brushed her sparse, once blond, now whitening hair away from her forehead. "It's a film on the Angevins, of course."

"But hasn't that been done?" asked Scarlett with a half smile. "I can't see where *The Lion in Winter* leaves much room for improvement," she added, referring to an early 1960's picture with Katherine Hepburn and Peter O'Toole, a sort of medieval *Who's Afraid of Virginia Woolf?*

Scarlett's observation made Fannie bristle. No one, but no one, called her judgment into question. She was about to object when Scarlett turned on the charm.

"But that's why you're the producer. You know best about these things. Don't you?"

If Fannie Promesa weren't so persuaded by the numbers confirming her intellect, she might have thought she was being toyed with. But she knew better. She was the one who did the toying. It was never the other way around.

"I see you know your movies."

"I love them."

"Well, this one's going in a different direction. It's more about Eleanor." Fannie lit a cigarette and pushed away from her desk, lolling about in her high-backed leather chair as she smoked and leered at Scarlett. "Think you might be interested doing the research?"

"Actually, Fannie, I'd be more interested in doing the writing."

Fannie emitted a spastic gasping cough. Apparently, smoke got caught in the wrong place. "But you told me you didn't know how to write scripts," she said, coughing again.

"That was before," said Scarlett. "Before I read a couple of Delores's."

Scarlett's attitude verged on arrogance and she knew it. But if Fannie wanted to play this game, it was going to cost her. Scarlett was determined to be paid to play and to learn something while she was doing it.

"Of course, I would need help. One can always learn a few secrets of the trade from someone who's at the top of their profession," flattered Scarlett. "Delores says you're the best."

Fannie feigned modesty. "Well, that's a compliment coming from Delores. She doesn't pass a lot of those out. Did she say anything about *River to the Sky?* I'm trying to get her to commit to the project, as the lead, so we can get a deal."

"She likes the role," lied Scarlett. She had never heard Delores mention the script.

"Good," said Fannie, rubbing her hands together. "That's good. That means she's thinking about it." She took another drag off her cigarette. "Now back to you and your writing career. Where were we?"

"Getting to the part about the contracts."

Fannie seemed thrown.

"I would want one naturally. That's how it's done, isn't it?"

Fannie's mouth dropped open and her cigarette fell out.

Chapter
116

"A writing contract?" said Clotelle. "Of course I'll go over it for you."

"Thanks, Clo," said Scarlett, glancing out at the dance floor. "Ever been to a gay bar?"

"No," said Clotelle. "First time. Can't say much for the decor."

Scarlett agreed. The Jasmine Club looked as if it might have been decorated by a Tijuana drag queen. The red-flocked wallpaper and dark wood gave it the feel of a bordello, not a lesbian bar. A few neon beer signs, a jukebox, a pool table and a smattering of tables finished off the decor. In spite of its unseemliness, the Jasmine still drew a large crowd. There was no place else for women who liked women to go.

"So you're really going to slum it?" said Karyn, surprised when Scarlett told her where she was going that evening.

"Yeah. It should be interesting."

"Just be careful," she cautioned. "This isn't Paris."

There was no way Karyn would ever go to the Jasmine Club, even if Veronica weren't in town. It was too risky. She might be seen, or worse, she might be arrested. Women weren't supposed to touch each other in L.A., at least not if they were lesbians. Deviant behavior was monitored by the law and homosexuality was a jailable offense. Nonetheless, women showed up at the Jasmine Club, lots of them. The jeopardy only added to the excitement. Even straight women sometimes came out of curiosity. They wanted to know what attraction, what secret energy, drew their sex to each other.

The Jasmine's bartender was always on the lookout for cops. If she got the signal from the front door, she flipped a switch and a red light came on, a warning for the Jasmine's patrons to stop dancing, to stop touching each other.

"Well, what do you think?" asked Scarlett.

"Interesting," said Clotelle, glancing around the bar. "But something puzzles me."

"What's that?"

"Why do a lot of these women look like men?"

Scarlett laughed. "Some of them don't have a choice, Clo. A lot of them were born that way."

What Clotelle observed, however, went beyond a genetic roll of the dice. There were women in the Jasmine Club whose look was a studied choice. They had cultivated a walk, an attitude and a style that was distinctly unfeminine. How a woman looked identified her as aggressive or passive, butch or femme, and helped organize attractions. It was an artificial classification to be sure because there were feminine women who were with other feminine women and vice-versa. But many lesbians frowned on such pairings. For them, it only confused matters.

"Who's that?" asked Clotelle, pointing to someone across the room.

Scarlett looked over and recognized the woman immediately. She had heard a lot about her. Tall and reasonably attractive, the woman had the calculated demeanor of a professional poseur. Studied and smooth, every attitude she struck had been designed for one purpose, to draw attention to her. There wasn't a spontaneous gesture in her entire repertoire.

"That's Marcia Munkin, the local Queen of Hearts. A real player, or so they say," informed Scarlett, making a reference to the maniacal queen in *Alice in Wonderland*. "She supposedly goes through lovers faster than croquet balls."

"And that stout-looking thing over there?" asked Clotelle about a huge woman with gobs of dark, frizzy hair standing near the door.

"Matilda, the Hun," said Scarlett.

"Why do they call her that?"

"Because of her brawling talents," said Scarlett. "She's so good with her fists the Jasmine hired her to stand guard."

"Against what?" Clotelle wanted to know.

"Dyke bashers. Every so often," Scarlett explained, "a bunch of guys show up here and want to demonstrate how macho they are by beating up gay women."

"They really get that violent?" Clotelle was incredulous.

"Not anymore, not since Matilda showed up. See those women over at the pool table?" pointed out Scarlett. "They're friends of hers and they all swing a mean pool stick."

Scarlett's attention suddenly shifted to a blonde standing behind the bar. Though the woman's body was lean and defined, it was not muscular and it moved with an exciting, panther-like fluidity. A skin-tight tank top showed off every curve of her well-formed breasts. Androgynously attractive, the woman was deeply tanned with short hair and large, expressive eyes. She picked up a cigarette and smoked it like Greta Garbo.

Clotelle noticed Scarlett's lingering interest in the woman and shook her head. Scarlett had that willful look in her eye. "What about Delores?"

"She's still in Mexico," said Scarlett, standing up. "I'll be back in a jiffy." She smiled down at Clotelle and then started making her way through the crowd toward the bar.

"Hey, pretty thing. What about a dance when they fix the juke-box?"

"Sure," smiled Scarlett, her eyes firmly fixed on her destination.

"Where'd you get those legs, sweetheart?"

Scarlett ignored that and several more daring remarks about her other body parts. She had just about made it to the bar when a huge commotion broke out around her and women began exploding apart, backing away from each other as they fast as they could. One woman ended up in Scarlett's arms, blocking her view of the red light that had just gone on above the bar.

"Excuse me," Scarlett told her. "You're stepping on my feet."

When the woman didn't respond, Scarlett took her by the arms and gently began moving her aside. As she did, a hand came down hard on Scarlett's shoulder.

"You're under arrest, miss."

"What!" exclaimed Scarlett, whipping around to find herself face to face with a plainclothes police officer. "For what?"

"For lewd conduct. For touching that woman like that."

Chapter
117

Clotelle came down to the police station and posted bail. It didn't matter that the charges were trumped up, they still had to be fought and dismissed or Scarlett would have a record. Scarlett's arm touching had become "breast touching" in the indictment.

"Did you sleep?" asked Clotelle.

"No. Not a wink," said Scarlett sullenly, then paused. "You know what they did to me?"

"Yes."

That awful strip search was only part of what Scarlett had had to endure. She had to "bend over and spread 'em" while a police-woman invaded her body. After that, she was hosed down with DDT.

"I can still smell it on me," complained Scarlett.

"I'm sorry. I know it was awful." Clotelle put her arm around her. "How about some breakfast?"

"I guess."

Scarlett still seemed in shock.

"There's a Denny's down the street. Want to walk?"

"I guess."

Clotelle knew she needed to stretch her legs. After the strip search, Scarlett had been confined to a cramped jail cell all night with the nine other women the police arrested at the Jasmine. Clotelle was working pro bono for several of them, trying to get their charges

dropped too. Not even the broadest interpretation of the "lewd behavior" statute was applicable in any of their cases.

Bleary-eyed, Scarlett looked at the menu and tried to decide
what she wanted to eat. She wasn't hungry, but she knew she had to
get something in her stomach. She was feeling weak and irritable.
The shock was beginning to wear off.

"Hash browns and eggs, over medium."

"Toast?" the waitress asked Scarlett.

"Yes," she answered, looking up from the menu. "And please, I
don't like it burned."

"Then I'll make sure they don't use the open pit."

Scarlett was amused by the woman's reply. She noticed the name
embroidered above the pocket of her white, starched blouse. "Sorry
for being so crabby, Louise. But I just spent the night in jail."

Clotelle rolled her eyes.

"Yeah?" Louise smacked her gum. "For what?"

"You don't want to know."

The waitress peered down at the unlikely felon. "Probably not."
She turned to Clotelle. "What can I get for you, honey?"

"Waffles and a cup of coffee."

"Coming right up," said Louise as she left to put in the order.

"Thanks for getting me out, Clo."

"I'd rather spring you from jail than hell."

Scarlett looked puzzled. That was an odd thing to say.

"You were going for it last night. Weren't you? You liked that bartender."

"I wasn't going for anything."

"You're lying, Scarlett."

Scarlett's cheeks flushed.

"What's going on with you? When are you going to tell me what
really happened in Paris?"

"Why?" asked Scarlett. Her mouth suddenly felt dry.

"Because that's where you left your heart."

"Yeah?" said Scarlett defiantly.

"Yeah," said Clotelle. "And ever since, you've been running around like a chicken with its head cut off. Only in your case, it's the heart that's missing."

Scarlett scowled at Clotelle. "You certainly have an appalling way of putting it."

"Think you could hear it any other way?" said Clotelle pointedly. She took a sip of water. "Want to tell me about it?"

Clotelle knew what a night in jail did to one's emotions. If Scarlett were ever going to open up and talk about Paris, it was now. Her guess was right. Scarlett finally shared everything about that summer.

Chapter

118

When Louise brought the check, she noticed that Scarlett had barely touched her breakfast. "What's the matter with the food?"

"Nothing. I lost my appetite."

"Too bad, honey. I'd give you a doggy bag but fried eggs don't travel too well." Louise smacked her gum and chuckled. "Here's your check." She put it down and left.

"Tell me something."

"Yes," said Scarlett, glancing up at Clotelle, dreading yet another one of her questions.

"How was what you did with Sissy Langtree any different from what Gina did with that man?"

Scarlett seemed confused.

"Didn't you accept expensive gifts and money from her? Like that Rolex on your wrist?"

"Why not? Sissy's a friend. I liked her. Plus she's a woman."

"So?" challenged Clotelle. "Maybe that man was Gina's friend. Maybe she liked him too."

Scarlett sat there, mute as a stone, unable to counter Clotelle. Reality was coming home to roost.

"The only difference I see," observed Clotelle, "is the sex of the giver." She took a sip of coffee before going on. "Some might say that your behavior was no different than Gina's. That you used your charms to manipulate someone you didn't love," said Clotelle. She paused briefly. "Well, didn't you?"

Scarlett bit her lip and slid down in her seat. The truth had a nasty, loud ring to it. She glowered at Clotelle over the top of her sunglasses. It was true. She had lied to Sissy when she told her she loved her. If she hadn't, Sissy might have yanked that wonderful carpet ride through the world of affluence right out from under her feet. But love aside, no one could say Scarlett had not liked Sissy. She had liked her a lot and she had certainly enjoyed having sex with her. Together they had discovered the vast, erotic world of pleasure.

"And you're still doing it, Scarlett," Clotelle continued. "Manipulating. Only this time you're using Delores Sheridan to get what you want."

Scarlett sat up in her seat and objected. "She's using me too."

"That's not the point."

Scarlett got sassy. "Okay, Miss Lawyer. Rake your friend over the coals. How do you think I feel right now, an almost felon, being told she's also a whore?"

"I didn't say that, Scarlett. Don't put words in my mouth." Clotelle paused and regarded Scarlett with a long, level stare. "When are you going to start telling yourself the truth, Miss Turner? Especially about Gina?"

Scarlett felt a sudden flash of anger. Just because Clotelle had gotten her out of jail didn't give her the right to torture her like this, especially at a time when she was feeling so awful. She felt as if she had just been flayed from the inside out. Scarlett stabbed her egg and broke the yolk. She wanted to run away. Clotelle was worse than jail.

"Okay. I guess that's enough, huh?" said Clotelle, sensing Scarlett's limit.

Scarlett didn't answer.

"Ready to go home?"

"Yes," replied Scarlett crisply.

"Well, then, madame," said Clotelle with a French accent on the last word. "You'll be glad to know I brought the Rolls."

In spite of herself, a smile came to Scarlett's lips. "Oh, Clo. Why do you have to be so tough on me? I'm just a kid."

"The only kid in you," clarified Clotelle, "is in your kidding."

In the days to come Clotelle got all the charges against Scarlett dismissed. Her record was clean, at least as far as the police were concerned. Her heart, though, was another matter. Its purification wouldn't be so easy.

Chapter

119

"Scarlett! Are you in there?" An urgent knock came at her back door.

Scarlett rolled over and looked at the clock. It was ten-thirty in the morning. She cursed herself for missing class. Now she regretted the wine and spending the night with Jonathan again. Her head hurt. Her body hurt. Her soul hurt. When the knocking became louder and more insistent, Scarlett finally threw off the covers and stumbled out bed. She wondered who it could be as she made her way through the living room and kitchen to the back door.

"Okay, okay. Hold your horses. I'm coming."

"Oh, Scarlett! Thank God you're here."

Karyn's voice sounded desperate. Scarlett slid back the bolt and opened the door. Karyn didn't wait to be invited in; she whisked passed Scarlett with Veronica following right behind her. Scarlett shut the door.

"I'm sorry for barging in like this," apologized Karyn. "But there's not much time."

Karyn and Veronica were so filled with apprehension that Scarlett swore she could smell it. The reason wasn't hard to guess. Not with those fresh cuts on Veronica's face and that chain of black-and-blue marks around her neck.

"Hello, Scarlett," said Veronica with a nervous catch in her voice.

Not even her Texas accent could hide the fear she was carrying that morning. "Sorry we have to meet like this."

Scarlett took Veronica's hand and, as she shook it, met her eyes. They were dark and luminous, beautiful and oddly determined in their vulnerability. She was a stunner with long, chestnut hair and a bone structure nothing short of perfection. Scarlett was about to say something when Karyn interrupted.

"Veronica's husband's had her followed yesterday. We were spotted at a restaurant in Malibu."

Scarlett glanced at Veronica's face again, recalling the threats her husband had made to Karyn and her back in Texas. "What are you going to do?"

"Leave," said Karyn.

Scarlett couldn't scan her thoughts. Too much was happening too fast. There were so many questions.

"To go where?"

"Paris."

Karyn glanced over at Veronica, and the look that passed between them said it all.

"To do what we should have done a long time ago." Karyn took in a deep breath and smiled. "Be together. Our plane leaves in two hours."

Karyn deposited three letters into Scarlett's hands. One was for Karyn's parents, another for Jonathan, and a third for Mr. and Mrs. Matthew Haroldson III in Dallas, Texas, Veronica's parents. With the stamps already on the envelopes, Scarlett's mission was self-explanatory.

"Mail them tomorrow."

"What about your families? They're going to be worried sick."

"The letters will explain everything. In the meantime they think I'm in Palm Springs," said Karyn, and then she dropped a bomb. "I came out to my parents in the letter, Scarlett. Veronica did the same with hers."

"Oh, my God!" was all Scarlett could say. Their courage shocked her. Everything she thought she wanted from life, Karyn and Veronica had just put at risk to be together. They might be disowned or, worse yet by Scarlett's lights, disinherited.

Scandal, however, would be averted at all costs. Being the political animal he was, the Mayor of Beverly Hills would tell everyone Karyn went to Paris to set up a Europa Boutique there. Ruth, his other daughter, would now run the one here on Rodeo. In order that no rumor of lesbianism ever touched his office, Mr. Mayor would give Karyn free access to her trust fund with the condition that she live abroad.

Veronica's parents, however, were not to be so obliging. They would immediately disown and disinherit her, incredulous that their genes had bred a lesbian, and end up sympathizing with their son-in-law, Elton Masters, never believing he was the wife beater Veronica said he was. In time they would even encourage a second wedding to Janine, their other daughter. No way did they want all that Masters money to take a hike down the road. Together the two families formed the most powerful oil and cattle ranching alliance in Texas history.

"Jesus," said Scarlett as she looked down at the letters in her hands. She took a deep breath. They would change lives forever.

"My parents were always afraid I might get involved with a married man or a gentile," said Karyn with a soft laugh, perhaps trying to lighten the mood. "Think they'll see the humor in this?"

"I doubt it," said Scarlett.

"Me either." Karyn managed a tight smile, then informed Scarlett, "We'll be at the Georges V Hotel. That is, until we find a place to live."

"I'm so happy for you," said Scarlett, and she hugged them both.

Actually, Scarlett didn't feel much of anything at the present moment except maybe a little dazed. Lives and plans were changing too fast to make sense.

"Thanks again for the poetry," said Karyn, a faint smile coming to her lips as she noticed Scarlett's eyes dart in Veronica's direction. "It's okay, Scarlett. She knows. I had to tell her or she'd expect a poem from me every day for the rest of our lives."

"I want to thank you too," said Veronica warmly. "For the courage."

Scarlett was bewildered. Veronica quickly explained.

"I don't remember how you said it, not exactly anyway. But it was something about dreams and how many of them are lost because we don't have the courage to make them real."

"I said that?"

"Yes." Veronica nodded her head. "And partly because of those words," she said, taking Karyn's hand, "we found the courage."

Chapter
120

It was difficult to know what to say to Jonathan. He just kept reading bits and pieces of Karyn's letter over and over again, incredulous, stunned, his anger growing. "I can't believe it," he said accusingly to Scarlett. "Why didn't you tell me?"

"That was for her to do."

"Why did she fuck me?" he suddenly yelled out in frustration. "Why did she say she wanted to get married?"

"Because part of her wanted to."

Jonathan searched Scarlett's eyes for an explanation.

"I'm sure Karyn would have preferred being straight. After all, it's a lot easier in today's world, isn't it?" said Scarlett almost bitterly. "More convenient and socially acceptable."

"It's not something I've thought about," he said, anger creeping back into his voice.

"You're lucky, Jonathan. You found out in time. Do you have any idea how many women throw their hearts away in marriages that are lies? Why do you think Karyn drank so much? When she was touching you, she was wishing it was Veronica."

It was a bitter pill but one Jonathan had to swallow if he were to let go of his fantasy about Karyn.

"Jesus, didn't she care about me at all?"

"Yes," replied Scarlett. "She did. But you're not a woman. And only a woman who desires nothing else but to hold another woman in her arms can understand that."

"Were you lying too, Scarlett?"

"About what?"

"When you fucked me? Did you enjoy it or were you faking it too?"

"No, Jonathan. I enjoyed it."

"Then what about you, Scarlett? What does that make you?"

"Chicken shit, Jonathan. Chicken shit. But that's about to change."

Chapter
121

Scarlett called her publisher and told them to set up an interview with *The Village Crier* in June, after the school year was over. Georgia Hill was coming out of the closet. Once Scarlett made the call, she felt a sudden weakening of resolve. The interview would change her life. Once given, there would be no taking it back, no retreating from its consequences. Regardless of how empowered Scarlett originally felt by Karyn and Veronica's courage, she still had to find her own, and that was proving difficult indeed. While her life might have been lived boldly, it had never been lived courageously.

"I'm nervous, Clo," said Scarlett as she cleared the table. She had invited Clotelle over for salad and spaghetti. "I don't know how my mother will react. Look what happened to Karyn and Veronica."

"You want a stranger to tell her?" said Clotelle, raising her voice as Scarlett disappeared into the kitchen. "Or for someone to send her one of your poems?"

Scarlett's stomach knotted up. "How about another cup of coffee?"

"No, thanks. I've still got some."

"I don't want my mother to pay for my choices," explained Scarlett, returning and sitting down at the table. "She's had enough pain already."

"For heaven sakes, you're not trying to kill her," said Clotelle pointedly, referring to the time Scarlett's father tried to shoot her mother. "You're just telling her who you are."

Scarlett's face filled with doubt and pain.

"Still mulling over the direction of your proclivities?"

"Yes," was Scarlett's sinking response.

"I see," said Clotelle. "Perhaps we should try and find a little perspective."

"I've tried."

"Then let's try again," said Clotelle gently. "If today were your last day on earth, who would you spend it with?"

"Someone I liked," answered Scarlett.

"Someone you liked!" challenged Clotelle. "Get real, girl."

"Someone I loved," Scarlett finally replied and turned her eyes away.

"Then the rest of this riddle should be easy," continued Clotelle. "In whose arms would you want to draw your last breath?"

Scarlett bit her lip. "A woman's," she finally answered. "Gina's."

Scarlett looked out the window, far away into the unseen distance, into another time and place, one filled with sunflowers, funny cars and red farmhouses. Clotelle didn't speak for a while. She could feel the weight of the moment. Scarlett's heart had just won and was no doubt savoring one of its few victories.

"Thanks for not giving up on me," Scarlett finally said, turning back to the table. "And for badgering me back into reality."

Clotelle smiled. "I love you, Scarlett."

Scarlett got up and draped her arms around Clotelle's neck. "Me too," she said, giving her a big hug. "How about an ice cream cone? My treat."

"I can't," said Clotelle, checking her watch. "Date time."

"Again?" asked Scarlett. "That's three nights in a row. This must be serious."

"I'd say it has potential," mused Clotelle. "Lots of potential." Then she added with a twinkle in her eye, "I'm not romancing my hand anymore."

Chapter
122

"Well, well," said Fannie Promesa, rubbing her hands together at Scarlett's surprise visit to her office. "Aren't we the eager beaver? I wasn't expecting you until next week."

"I thought I'd come a little early," said Scarlett and handed Fannie the contract.

Fannie gave it a cursory look and then turned to the back page. "Tsk. Tsk. You forgot to sign it, Scarlett."

"No, I didn't. I've decided I don't want the job."

Fannie was flabbergasted. She looked at Scarlett incredulously. "Are you okay?"

"Yes."

"Do you know what kind of opportunity you're throwing away?"

"Perfectly. If that's what you call it."

Fannie lit a cigarette and leaned back in her chair, scrutinizing Scarlett. "Care to explain?"

"This contract is bullshit. You can cut me loose anytime you want. And you would, wouldn't you, unless I played the game?"

"Game?" said Fannie archly.

"The one called Please the Producer."

"I'm afraid you've lost me," said Fannie, one corner of her mouth curling up into a sneer.

Scarlett went on. "This contract doesn't even give me the right to complete a first draft if you decide you don't like it somewhere along the way. This deal isn't about a writing opportunity for me, it's about a poaching opportunity for you. If I let you poach, you let me write."

"Scarlett dear, I believe you have a rather vaunted notion of my interest in you."

"Yeah? Then why is it every time I see you, you're drooling?"

That was it. The color in Fannie's cheeks went from rose to crimson in a flash, and her eyes narrowed into tiny slots. "That's enough, Miss Turner. Please leave my office right now."

Scarlett stood up. "I would like to thank you for one thing, however."

Fannie raised an eyebrow. "Yes? Not that I care to hear it."

"Thanks for helping me realize some prices are just too high to pay."

Chapter
123

The visit to Fannie Promesa's office and Scarlett's grueling Comparative Literature final had drained her. She got a bottle of Coca-Cola out of the refrigerator and sat down on the couch. She glanced at several unopened letters on the coffee table. There was one from her mother, another from Karyn, and the last was from Sissy. Scarlett would have given anything if just one of them had been from Gina. Even though she had never answered a single one of her letters, Scarlett missed them when they stopped coming. Apparently, Gina had gotten tired of writing to a ghost.

Scarlett ripped open Sissy's letter and a smile came to her face as she read it. Sissy told Scarlett a wedding invitation would soon arrive in the mail. Michel and she had set the date. Their nuptials would take place at Notre Dame Cathedral on June the 10th. Sissy said she wouldn't take no for an answer. Enclosed was a round-trip ticket for her to Paris. Sissy went on to apologize for not asking Scarlett to be the bridesmaid. She hoped she would understand, which, of course, Scarlett did. Sissy's parents would rather have their daughter institutionalized than see her anywhere near a lesbo again.

Isn't it wonderful, Scarlett? Sissy ended the letter. *I'm going to be married in the most romantic city in the world. But then, you know that too. Don't you?*

Scarlett leaned back on the couch and shut her eyes, wondering why Sissy had made that particular assumption. Then suddenly her decision to come out of the closet was back on her mind again and with it, just how she was going to tell Delores and her mother. Neither one of them would want to hear it. Scarlett wondered if she were not making a dreadful mistake. She would find out soon enough. Delores was arriving back from Mexico the following day.

Chapter

124

"You must be self-destructing!" Delores was incredulous. "Throwing away an opportunity like that. I can't believe it."

"The writing assignment wasn't real and you know it."

"It could have been."

"Yeah. If I played the game and let her paw me."

"I'd have stepped in long before it got that far and believe me, she would have behaved. Fannie wants me for that picture, *River to the Desert*, or whatever the shit it's called."

"*River to the Sky*," Scarlett corrected her. "It wasn't honest, Delores."

Delores was surprised. Scarlett never talked like this. "Who gave you sodium pentothal?"

"I don't know. My conscience maybe."

"I see," remarked Delores. "Dangerous territory." She looked down at Scarlett's naked body and craved it all over again. She needed its opiate-like lift to help her forget, to block out all this crazy talk. "Anyway, we'll discuss it later," said Delores as she rolled over on Scarlett.

She kissed her hungrily, long, passionate kisses, kisses intended to awaken the deepest cravings. To light the fire and let it burn, to feel its heat as long as possible. That was what Delores wanted, what she wanted for both of them.

"What the hell's the matter with you?" exclaimed Delores, leaning back in bed, completely frustrated when nothing happened. She lit a joint.

"I'm not sure," said Scarlett, surprised as well. "Maybe I'm tired."

"What else is going on?" insisted Delores as she anxiously snorted some coke. The grass had dulled her mind, and right now she needed to think. "If you come out of the closet, do you know what that means?"

"Yes," said Scarlett, slowly nodding her head. "That you can't be seen with me."

"For God's sake, at least wait until you get back from the wedding. I'm sure things will look different then."

"I'm sorry but I can't. I've got to do this now or I may never do it."

The color began to drain from Delores's face. "I don't want to lose you," she said, her voice trembling slightly.

The emotion surprised Scarlett. In Delores it was rare.

"We're not good for each other," Scarlett said with difficulty.

"What the shit does that mean?" The edge was back in Delores's voice. "We're great in bed. The best."

"Because it's all about fucking."

"So? What's wrong with that?"

"Never feeling."

A knowing look passed over Delores's face. "Wasn't that what we both wanted?"

Scarlett didn't answer and Delores decided not to pursue it, at least not for the time being. She was positive Scarlett would change her mind.

"Don't make any decisions right now," Delores urged her again. "Think about it over the summer." She stroked Scarlett's hair. "In the meantime let's get dressed and get out of here. I'll make reservations at Chasen's."

It was Scarlett's favorite restaurant, one of the most expensive in town.

Chapter

125

Scarlett flew into Albuquerque around noon and rented a car. She wanted to spare Twila and her old green-paneled station wagon the long trip up from Socorro. Besides, thanks to Delores, she now had her driver's license and she needed time on the road by herself to think. In the last month her life had turned upside down.

Scarlett tossed her luggage in the trunk of a new 1967 Chevrolet Bel Air convertible and headed south out of Albuquerque on Highway 25. Even though it was hot, she put the top down. She wanted to feel the wind in her hair and the sun on her face, to breathe again. She was again questioning every decision she had made over the past month, especially her pending interview with *The Village Crier*. Perhaps she was mad. After all, who but an insane human being would willingly come out of the closet in 1967? Now, even if she wanted to, there was probably no turning back. The publisher had already given *The Village Crier* her real name.

The question, "Who is Georgia Hill, the name without a face?" would at last be answered and what an answering that would be. Scarlett's use of a pseudonym had stirred up more interest in her real identity than anyone could have imagined. Incredibly, her very anonymity had set the stage for a "succès de scandale." *Poems for Lovers of a Different Kind* would soon be hyped into a bestseller.

As Scarlett drove down Highway 25 that hot Saturday afternoon, she could not imagine success being hers anytime soon. How could she possibly think otherwise? She had just thrown away two opportunities for it in the space of a week. She had given Fannie Promesa back her writing contract and she had told Delores Sheridan goodbye.

Leaving Delores had been much harder than Scarlett anticipated and not only because of the money and the exciting lifestyle. There was that other thing, that powerful thing between them, which turned her mind off and her body on like nothing else on earth. Because of Delores, Scarlett now knew what junkies felt like when they couldn't get a fix. Miss Sheridan had become an addiction, a sexual opiate of the most exquisite sort. Forgetfulness in a touch. Heaven and hell in a kiss.

Scarlett ached for Delores right now, and the withdrawal symptoms were proving intolerable. Instead of feeling nothing, she was feeling everything. Without Delores to numb her emotions, Scarlett was finding herself strangely vulnerable. She chewed at one corner of her lip until it bled. Yes, physical pain she could endure.

Scarlett had given Delores back the keys to her apartment and even refused her generous gift, a beautiful 1956 T-Bird in perfect condition. The temptation was considerable, and the bribe almost worked. In fact, Scarlett was not sure what she would do until that last, painful conversation with Delores. For a few brief moments, Delores let it all hang out. She had been openly vulnerable.

"Maybe we can learn how to feel again," she entreated Scarlett.

"Not from each other." Scarlett's voice was so muted, Delores barely heard her.

"If we're willing, why not?"

"Because we're both wounded in the same way. We need someone who already knows how to feel," said Scarlett. "How can you help anyone else out of hell if you're already there?"

It was an agonizing good-bye. They held each other and wept. The truth of their relationship had finally been admitted.

"Well, I'll be damned," muttered Scarlett. Traffic on Highway 25 had suddenly slowed to a crawl. She craned her head over the side of the car and burst out in laughter when she saw why. A door on a poultry transport truck had sprung open and hundreds of chickens were on the loose, maybe thousands, running all over the highway and off into the desert.

Scarlett settled back in her seat and grabbed a can of Coca-Cola. She pulled the tab off the can and took several long gulps as the chickens continued to scatter. Several desperate men chased after them but only managed to catch one or two of them. By the looks of things, New Mexico would soon be adding a band of renegade chickens to its wildlife register.

Scarlett was grateful when the traffic started moving again because the day was quickly going from hot to hotter. She stripped down to her tank top and let the wind evaporate the perspiration beading her skin as she turned up the radio volume. She sang along with Dusty Springfield for a while and then was soon deep back in thought. Fifty-five miles later, she pulled off the highway and stopped at the Hot-Stop, a precursor of all the 7-11's and Circle K's that would soon dot the American landscape.

"Where's your cold Coca-Cola?" asked Scarlett.

"In that case on the right over there," answered a man with a gut the size of a watermelon hanging over the top of his pants.

Scarlett pulled out a six-pack of Coke and another of Pabst, Twila's favorite. "Where are your Peanut Pattis?" she asked, looking around. She couldn't get those in Los Angeles.

"Where the rest of the candy is. In the middle of the store."

Scarlett grabbed a handful of Pattis and several Big Hunks and went up to the cash register to check out. "A carton of Camels, please. Filterless."

The man looked Scarlett over and then picked a carton off the shelf. "These must be for somebody else," he said, leering at her breasts. "You don't look like the unfiltered type."

"What type is that?"

"Don't you know?" said the man, still leering at her breasts as he rang up the sale.

"No."

"The tough, cowgirl type," he explained contemptuously. "You know, those women that think they're smarter than a man, who try and be just like one." He switched his toothpick to the other side of his mouth. "That'll be $5.56 with tax."

Scarlett put a five-dollar bill and the exact change down on the counter as the man bagged her purchase. He was still staring at her breasts.

"Don't let these fool you," said Scarlett, putting her hands on her breasts, cradling them, then shoving them straight up, practically out of her tank top. "I chain-smoke Camels."

The man's jaw dropped.

"And I don't want to be like a man. Why the hell would I? I enjoy these too much." She playfully pushed at her breasts again and smiled mischievously. "And not just mine."

Chapter
126

"How could you do this to yourself?" said Twila as she slathered Noxema on Scarlett's shoulders and arms. "You look like a giant fire ant."

"Ouch!" said Scarlett.

Her back was particularly tender. The sun had burned right through her tank top.

"Here," said Twila, handing Scarlett the jar. "Take off that bra and finish the job."

Scarlett removed her brassiere, thankful she had worn one since it had protected her most sensitive skin. She glazed the top of her breasts with Noxema and then spread a thick layer of it over her stomach. When she tried to put her blouse back on, she winced.

"Do you mind?" asked Scarlett. "Clothes hurt right now. I'd rather not wear anything on the top."

"Suit yourself," said Twila, lighting up a fresh new Camel. "Don't want you being any more miserable than you already are."

The double entendre wasn't lost on Scarlett. It certainly wasn't one of Twila's more subtle ones.

"Do I seem that down?"

"At odds is how I'd put it." Twila took a long drag off her cigarette. "At extreme odds."

It was true. Scarlett's emotions were all over the place, disjointed, like a Cubist painting. Her heart was shattered.

"How about a beer?" said Twila. "Helps soften the fright off some of these feeling sieges."

"A beer?" said Scarlett, almost as if she hadn't understood the offer. "That'd be great."

When Twila left the room, Scarlett ran her hand over her sunburn and felt the heat and pain rising up out of it. Maybe that was why she had burned herself, as a way of escape. The hurting outside provided a distracting relief from the agony inside. Maybe it was also to help her forget Clotelle's scolding back in L.A. Clotelle had lowered the boom when Scarlett said she was having second thoughts about that interview with *The Village Crier.*

"What's so awful about lying is its cowardice," she told Scarlett.

At first Clotelle's rebuke had been indirect, but it became direct very rapidly when she got to Scarlett's sexuality and her ongoing, tiresome ambiguity about it. "You could sleep with a hundred men, Scarlett. It wouldn't matter and you know it. It won't change who you love."

Scarlett tried to object, but Clotelle wouldn't hear it. She hadn't made her point yet.

"What you really fear about coming out of the closet, Scarlett, is not admitting your sexuality but embracing it, allowing yourself to love." Clotelle paused and rested her case. "Who you really love, women." Once again, Clotelle had exposed the raw truth.

"Hope I'm not interrupting too much good thinking," said Twila, finally returning with a couple of chilled beers. She handed one to Scarlett. "Sorry for taking so long but Luis wanted a snack and you know how spoiled that macho king of the desert is."

Scarlett laughed. "Where's Geronino and Midnight?"

"Lizard hunting."

Just then Luis strolled in and stretched out on the Indian rug at Twila's feet. "Think Luis would join them? Nope. No way. He wants his treats out of a bag. Don't you, señor?"

''He's sure gotten handsome.''

"Yes." Twila smiled, gently nudging him with her foot. "And he knows it."

Scarlett rolled the chilled bottle along her cheek, absorbing its coolness.

"So you're going back to Paris?"

"Yes. For Sissy's wedding, remember?"

"I remember," said Twila. "But what about you-know-who? The one you haven't talked about yet."

"I . . ." Scarlett's voice faltered. "I don't know."

Twila took a long drag off her Camel. "Want to tell me about it?"

"Yes." Scarlett nodded. "More than anything." She looked down and picked at the label on her bottle. "Twila, I'm scared."

Chapter
127

What if I've lost her? was the question burning itself into Scarlett's heart. For three days she had searched the desert for an answer and found none.

"Come on and watch the sunset with me," yelled Twila. "It's our last one together."

Scarlett was just returning from a late-afternoon walk. Her cotton tee shirt was soaked, and she looked exhausted. Her face was transparent with doubt and confusion. She was feeling some of her real feelings for the first time in her life and Twila knew it.

"Still trying to sweat that orneriness out of you?" Twila joked as Scarlett walked through the front gate. "Here," she said and handed Scarlett a tall glass of lemonade.

"Yeah. Think I'll succeed?"

"I'm betting on it."

Scarlett smiled and took a long drink. "Fresh squeezed, huh?"

"Just like I used to make for you and Billy Ray."

"I remember," said Scarlett, a shadow of sadness quickly passing over her face.

"Well, come on and sit down. The show's about to start."

The moment of magenta soon began and swept across the Magdalenas like a giant, translucent curtain, signaling dusk, transition, night.

"Look at that moon," insisted Twila. "It's round and plump as a pumpkin."

It was huge as it rose over the Magdalenas. A magnificent sphere of glowing light, softening the hard edges of the mountains.

"Wonder if Maggie's looking up right now?"

"Probably," answered Twila. "She loves the night."

"What's the name of that place where she is in Morocco? I can never remember."

"Tenerhir. In the High Atlas Mountains. Imagine how the moon must look peeking over those big old hills tonight?"

Both women fell silent and watched the night sky unfold. Unlike L.A., you could see the stars here, uncountable numbers of them, stretching on forever across an endless universe.

"Why did she go there?"

"To paint and sculpt and do whatever Maggie does." Twila finished her lemonade. "Winston Churchill used to go there too."

"Why?"

"To do his watercolors."

"But didn't you say Tine . . . Taner . . ."

"Tenerhir."

"Didn't you say it was at the edge of nowhere?"

"Geographically, I guess. But its distance from somewhere is apparently not its measure." Twila struck a wooden match on a rock and lit herself a Camel. "Maggie and Winston seem to have found what they wanted there."

"Didn't Maggie send you any pictures?"

"No," said Twila, exhaling. "Never did."

Scarlett leaned back in her chair and looked at the Milky Way arching across the sky. As a little girl, Scarlett had told her mother she wanted to sleep in that luminous band of light. It looked so peaceful, so safe, so far away from Joe Turner.

"Changing is lonely, Twila."

"I know, honey. It kinda feels like dying. Doesn't it?"

Chapter
128

The plane would set down in thirty minutes. Two hours after that Scarlett would be in Dillinger, and another moment of reckoning would be at hand, the one with her mother. As it approached, the more apprehensive Scarlett became. Twila was right. Fear had been a thief in her life. It had numbed her heart, and it had led her into lies both in and out of bed.

"How do I get rid of the fear?" Scarlett had asked her.

"You kill it."

"How?"

"With love."

Scarlett knew the answer before she ever asked the question. Clotelle had told her as much and so had all her other friends, each in their own way. Now their words resounded in her ears like a Greek chorus: *Love overcomes fear. Love casts out fear. Love drives fear away.* It all seemed so ironic, so oddly reversed. To overcome fear she must first love and become vulnerable to a world she had never trusted.

As the seat belt sign went on, a stewardess picked up a *Vogue* magazine on the empty seat across the aisle from Scarlett. "Do you mind if I look at that?"

"Go right ahead," said the hostess, handing it to Scarlett. "I was just going to put it away."

Scarlett leafed through the magazine until she came upon a page that almost made her heart stop. There, in full color, was Gina Jamison. Two other women were also in the picture. One was much older than Gina and the other looked to be in her thirties, an attractive blonde. The caption read: "World famous couturier, Madame LeRouge, plans her next line with protegée, Gina Jamison and associate Margot Duval."

Chapter

129

"Oh, Momma. I can't believe you're getting married after all these years. How wonderful."

"Then you approve?"

"I think it's wonderful." Scarlett paused to take a sip of tea. "Abe is such a nice man."

"Oh, good, honey. I just wanted your blessing. Now, why don't you tell me about you? Who's this mystery man of yours?" giggled Ollie. "Maybe we can have a double wedding?"

Scarlett smiled and her mouth twitched. "Somehow I don't think so, Momma."

"Well, come on then. Spill the beans."

Scarlett took a deep breath, then another one. She was either going to screw up the courage to tell her mother or pass out. Thankfully, a knock at the door saved her from having to do either.

"That must be Etta," said Ollie. "She couldn't wait to hear the good news. Now you can tell us both, sweetheart." Ollie raised her voice. "Well, come on in. You know the door ain't locked."

Etta walked into the living room with a chocolate layer cake, Scarlett's favorite. "Hi, Scarlett. Thought I'd bring a little celebration treat."

"Hurry and sit yourself down, Etta. Scarlett's ready to make the big announcement."

Etta put the cake down and scurried over to the couch next to Ollie. They both looked expectantly across the coffee table at Scarlett. Etta couldn't contain herself another second. "Well, what's the lucky fella's name?"

Scarlett didn't know what to do now. She hadn't planned on Etta being there, but she decided to go ahead anyway. Besides, Etta would find out soon enough. Friends since childhood, Ollie and Etta were as close as two peas in a pod. They couldn't keep anything from each other even if they tried.

"Scarlett?" nudged Ollie Mae gently. "Don't you go teasin' us with a buncha silence and mystery. Etta and I just gotta know who's gone and caught my little girl's eye. Now come on, honey. Tell us. What's his name?"

Scarlett braced herself, and the word dropped out of her mouth like a big marble. "Gina," she said.

Ollie Mae and Etta both had a delayed reaction to the name. When it finally sank in, they looked at each other as if they'd just been time-warped into another galaxy.

"I musta heard ya wrong, honey," said Ollie Mae. "I coulda sworn you said Gina and not Gene."

"Me too," giggled Etta.

"You both heard right then," said Scarlett, "because I said Gina."

Ollie's face flushed, and Etta turned as white as a sheet.

"You talkin' about that uppity Mary Queen of Scots person?" asked Ollie. She couldn't say girl or woman.

"Herself."

"Oh, Lordy. Tell me my ears is trickin' me."

Etta began fanning Ollie's face and telling her to calm down, that she was the color of Rudolph's nose.

"They're not tricking you, Momma. Gina is the one I love."

To Ollie's ever-lasting credit, she didn't shame Scarlett or herself by saying something like, "How could you do this to me?" or, "What did I do?" or, "Didn't I raise you right?" No, Ollie Mae just sat there stunned for a quite a piece and let Etta try and fan her disbelief away.

Scarlett sat in silence too. It wasn't easy telling her mother she loved a woman. It never was. Not for any woman. But if it were the truth, it was the only way to honor that love and let it know the light of day. The light it deserved.

"You sure about this?"

"Yes, Momma. Sure as the sun."

"Well, I don't know what to say then. It ain't my business to go buttin' in where I don't understand. And I don't, honey, I don't understand this kind of love. But then," she said, looking over at her lifelong friend. "Etta never understood mine neither for Joe Turner. Did ya, Etta?"

Etta shook her head and managed to push a very small "No" out of her mouth. She still wasn't back from the other side of the universe.

"If this is what's in your heart, Scarlett, who am I to say it oughta not be there?" said Ollie Mae. "I'd be more than mighty foolish if I was to let what makes you happy go makin' me miserable."

"That's right," agreed Etta, closer to home now, somewhere between earth and the moon.

Chapter
130

Scarlett missed her plane out of New York. At the last minute the publisher wanted additional information to run with her picture on the book's cover. The truth about Scarlett Faye Turner, it seems, was proving far more titillating than any fiction created about Georgia Hill, the anonymous author of *Poems for Lovers of a Different Kind*. It was a publicity bonanza, and the publisher was going to play it for all it was worth. Georgia Hill's readers were about to be treated to the writer's real identity and have a face to go with it, a beautiful one.

If traffic to Kennedy Airport hadn't been so snarled, Scarlett might have made her flight to Paris in spite of the delay. Now the next plane she could catch left in six hours. She was lucky to get booked on it. Everyone, it seemed, was going to Paris. Scarlett took a deep breath and looked at her watch. If everything went well, she would have enough time after she landed in Paris to get over to Karyn and Veronica's apartment, change her clothes and make it to the wedding.

Scarlett took another deep breath. By now her anxiety was coming in bucketfuls. She went over to a vending machine and impulsively slid forty cents into the slot. The first cigarette she lit made her dizzy and gave her a coughing fit. By the time she was trying to smoke the third one, she actually seemed to be calming down.

Scarlett's anxiety was not just about her missed plane. She was obsessing about the interview she had given *The Village Crier* earlier in the day. The questions had been bold and surprising, but then, so were her answers.

"When did you first realize you liked girls?"

"Women," Scarlett corrected Mr. Vincent Mathers, the interviewer. "As long as I can remember. I even had crushes on some of my mother's friends when I was little," said Scarlett, remembering Wanda, wonderful Wanda. "Of course, I didn't know what it was then."

"How old were you when you first slept with a woman?"

"Eighteen."

"Have you ever slept with a man?"

Scarlett hesitated. She thought it was a very strange question for her coming-out interview.

"Yes," she finally said. "Several."

"I must admit I'm surprised," said Mr. Mathers.

"Why?"

"Dykes don't like men."

"Who told you that?"

Mr. Mathers suddenly looked cornered and got defensive. "Everyone knows that."

"Where'd they get their information?" said Scarlett, beginning to feel combative. The guy was an asshole. However, she knew she had to keep her cool. He could cremate her in print.

"It's known," was Mr. Vincent Mathers's authoritative reply.

"Well, you know how those things go, Mr. Mathers," said Scarlett softly, ratcheting down her emotions a few notches. "It's like that very bright man said centuries ago, 'The exact contrary of what is generally believed is often the truth.' "

Mathers bristled and shifted uncomfortably in his chair. Scarlett had used the words of some "very bright man," some irritating gainsayer of "centuries ago," to put him in his place, and in front of other people. He hoped they hadn't noticed. He had a reputation to protect. He changed his tack.

"You mean we're dealing with stereotypes?"

"Well, of course," answered Scarlett, letting Mr. Mathers save himself. "After all, what about me is stereotypical?"

"Maybe we should explore that."

By the middle of the afternoon, Mr. Mathers had explored it all and seemed pleased with the interview. Following George Bernard Shaw's advice on skeletons, Scarlett finally decided to stop hiding hers and make them dance instead. Years later, Scarlett joked that she came out of the closet so fast that day that she left skid marks in the doorway.

"Are you in love with anyone?" asked Vincent Mathers. It was his last question. She had finally charmed and won him over.

"Yes," said Scarlett.

"With a woman?"

At that point Mathers was still obviously confused about Scarlett's sexuality. He couldn't get over the fact that she had slept with men.

"Of course. That's what makes me gay, Mr. Mathers." Scarlett paused and took a sip of her Coke. "Anyone can sleep with anyone and enjoy it. But that's not the decider. Who you love is."

As the interview receded from Scarlett's mind, she lit another cigarette and got up from the table to make a phone call.

"Are you okay?" Scarlett asked her mother while she waited for her flight.

"Yes, honey. Why?"

"I was just wondering," said Scarlett and then she told her, "I gave that interview to *The Village Crier*." She paused for a second. "And I told the truth about everything."

It was a while before Ollie broke the silence. "It's okay, Scarlett. We agreed. No more fibbing."

Scarlett breathed a sigh of relief. "Did I ever tell you how sorry I am for underestimating you sometimes?"

"No."

"Then I'll say so now. I'm sorry, Momma."

"Thanks, honey. That's very nice to hear."

Scarlett took a puff off her cigarette. "I'm worried about how Abe will handle all this."

"Just fine is how he'll handle it."

"How do you know?"

"Because his son is a lot like you. Abe told me so last night. Likes stayin' on his own side of the fence."

Scarlett smiled at the sweet irony of the coincidence and plunged her cigarette into the white, speckled sand of a nearby ashtray.

"Of course, Sam ain't gonna make no announcements, being in the military and all," added Ollie.

"Not if he wants to make general."

"What was that, honey?"

"Nothing, Momma. I love you. I'll write you from Paris."

Scarlett hung up the phone and tossed the remaining cigarettes in the trash. It was a dreadful habit. She was grateful hers had lasted only a few hours.

Chapter

131

The plane landed at Orly Airport at nine A.M. The wedding was at eleven. Scarlett knew it would be a miracle if she got there on time. She signaled a taxi.

"We have to hurry," she told the driver. She showed Karyn's address scribbled on a piece of paper. *"Vite, vite. Tout suite."* When none of Scarlett's rushing instructions impressed the driver, she remembered the word for bride. *"Mariée,"* she told him. *"Aujourd'hui: A onze heures.* Today at 11 o'clock."

"Est-vous la jeune mariée?" he wanted to know. "Are you the bride?"

"Non. C'est une amie," Scarlett told the driver in her rather limited but intelligible French. "A friend."

"Bon," he said, giving the car a little gas, telling Scarlett something to the effect that if she were the bride he would go faster. But since she wasn't, he didn't want to risk an accident in his new taxi.

The fabled French anything-for-love spirit was nowhere in sight so Scarlett waved a green bill from the backseat. *"Dix dollares.* Ten bucks. But you have to step on it, buster."

A translation wasn't necessary. The cab driver got the message. He smiled and suddenly floorboarded it, swerving around traffic, hugging the guard rail, laying on his horn. It was Toad's Wild Ride all over again. Only this time a frog was driving.

Scarlett fished her compact out of her purse and snapped it open. She hadn't slept much on the plane and the proof was in the mirror. But there was something else too. The certainty was gone from her face and in its place was a vulnerability she had never seen before. She sank back in the seat and watched the city blur past.

"Mademoiselle," said the cab driver at last in a loud voice. *"Vous est arrivé.* We're here."

Chapter

132

"This place looks like a miniature Versailles," observed Scarlett as she glanced around at Karyn and Veronica's apartment. It was large by Paris apartment standards and filled with well-chosen antiques. "Everything is so beautiful."

"Thanks," said Karyn. "Need any help?"

"Not unless you can take a shower for me."

Karyn laughed. "Come on. I'll show you where it is."

Scarlett followed her down a long hall filled with artwork. Some of the paintings looked to be originals. At least one of the Picassos did. Apparently, their business was going well. Stateside dealers were gobbling up the art and antiques they bought either in small shops or the French countryside. Karyn opened a door off the hall.

"This is your room. It has its own private bath," she informed Scarlett cheerfully. "Make yourself at home."

The bedroom had high ceilings and tall windows. Its walls were paneled with a delicate wood *boiserie* painted a pale gray. A floral-carved oak armoire sat in one corner and a bombe commode, richly appointed with gold ormolu in another. A canopy bed with a silk brocade coverlet was at its center.

"Is there anything from this century?"

"The bathroom," said Karyn.

"Thank God," laughed Scarlett as she glanced at a bronze table clock sitting on the commode. "Jesus. I have forty minutes to pull off a miracle.

"Here," said Veronica, unzipping Scarlett's dress. "Let's get you started because it'll take fifteen minutes to drive you to Notre Dame."

"I guess the pressure's on," said Karyn.

"No way," kidded Scarlett. "You can tell?"

Veronica took Karyn's hand. "Come on, honey. Let's get dressed too so we can go to lunch after we drop Scarlett off."

Scarlett noticed the matching rings on Karyn and Veronica's left hands. There were those who knew how to commit. In their case, it was to be for life.

"Come on. It's a beautiful day," insisted Veronica.

"For heaven's sake," scolded Scarlett. "Take the woman to lunch. Can't you tell? She wants to flirt with you in public."

Karyn smiled and capitulated. "Okay. Okay. See you at the front door, Scarlett."

Chapter

133

Karyn stopped the car in front of Notre Dame to drop Scarlett off. "Happy wedding."

"Yes," echoed Veronica. "But don't catch the bouquet. It's bad luck."

"Only in Texas." Karyn winked at Scarlett. "You look terrific."

"Beautiful," said Veronica.

"Thanks," smiled Scarlett. "See you two later."

As the Fiat pulled away from the curb, Scarlett waved good-bye, then hurried across the courtyard toward the church. The Mitterands had insisted on a Catholic wedding. Religious or not, the appearance of propriety was a social exigency Michel's family would not forego. Façade was everything in Europe, often as important as the truth itself and sometimes even more so.

The Langtrees hated Catholics, being the proper Episcopalians they were. But in the case of the Mitterands, they made an exception. They weren't going to let a few extra sacraments come between them and all that Old World money and a name the caliber of Mitterand. They were direct descendants of Charlemagne. Of course, so was practically everyone else in France, but that never occurred to the Langtrees.

Scarlett stepped inside the church and was instantly swallowed up in the immensity of Notre Dame. The "intimate ceremony" included about 300 people, already seated, waiting for the bride to walk down the aisle. As the organ began playing, Scarlett rushed to take a seat. She slid into a pew and looked over at the person next to her. It was none other than the maestro himself.

"Hello, Mr. Neeps."

Scarlett's sudden presence startled Bertrand. He managed to squeeze out a thin smile. "Hello, Miss Turner."

Scarlett was actually surprised he recognized her, what with her hair up in a French twist and the big dark sunglasses. It had to be her voice he placed because nothing else was the same. She was wearing makeup and her hair was lighter by several shades. Plus he had never seen her in a dress, certainly not one with a mid-thigh hemline.

"You can relax, Mr. Neeps. I'm just here for the wedding." Scarlett noticed the muscles on the back of his neck spasm. "Really. There won't be any trouble. I promise."

Bertrand rubbed his neck as they both looked up at the front of the church where Michel stood waiting for his bride. He was far more handsome than Scarlett remembered. At the first notes of "Here Comes the Bride," everyone turned to watch Sissy. She was radiant, beautiful, liquid hauteur gliding down the aisle. Her lace-brocade wedding dress fit her torso like a glove and from there fell into graceful folds to the floor. Her bridal train streamed twenty feet behind her with enough material in it for several more gowns.

Though solemn and formal, the ceremony didn't last long. Before Scarlett knew it, Sissy and Michel were sliding rings on each other's fingers and sealing their vows with a kiss. Scarlett handed Bertrand a Kleenex. The maestro was weeping.

"Want to come to the reception with me?" asked Scarlett. "We can take a taxi together."

Bertrand cautiously nodded his assent. "Yes," he said. "If I have your word you'll behave like a lady."

"You have it," promised Scarlett. "Don't I look like one?"

Bertrand made no reply.

"Let's go," said Scarlett, offering the maestro her hand. "I'm famished."

The reception was being held at one of the most expensive hotels in all Europe. The huge banquet room was filled with rows of tables piled high with shellfish and sauces, canapés, fresh fruit, tartes and pastries. At the center of one of the tables was a twelve-tiered wedding cake. Nearby a chamber orchestra played. The bride and groom walked onto the floor and began to dance. Other guests eventually joined them, and the floor was soon filled with the rich and titled from all over France and Europe.

"Scarlett!" said Sissy excitedly, spotting her friend. She rushed over and hugged her. "Thank God you came. When you sent back the ticket, I thought you might not."

"I wouldn't have missed your wedding for anything, Sissy. And there was no way I was going to let you pay my way, Mrs. Mitterand."

"Oh, Scarlett. You're always full of surprises. I just love you to pieces."

"I love you too," Scarlett said, and she meant it, but not in the way she had lied about it before. No. What she was feeling now was genuine, heart-centered love with no physical desire attached.

"I guess you're going to see Gina while you're here."

Scarlett was taken completely aback. "I hope so." She searched Sissy's eyes. "How did you know?"

"From the postcards. After you left Lausanne to come here to Paris two years ago, you never sounded the same."

Sissy smiled. "And I knew who was here."

"Well, well. My two favorite ladies." Michel leaned over and kissed Scarlett on both cheeks. "Could I possibly interest you in concubinage?"

Scarlett laughed. "I don't think so. A dance maybe?"

"Go ahead, Scarlett," said Sissy. She kissed Michel briefly and tenderly on the mouth. "Enjoy my husband."

"I like the way that sounds," said Michel.

"Good. Because I don't intend to stop saying it," warned Sissy. "Remember? This is a forever duet."

Michel led Scarlett out onto the floor, and as they danced, Scarlett spotted Mrs. Langtree staring at her in horror, her jaw on the floor. Scarlett waved, then smiled at her and winked.

Chapter

134

As Scarlett rode the elevator up to Karyn and Veronica's apartment, she leaned against the wall and closed her eyes. The past few weeks had taken their toll. She was exhausted and desperately needed sleep, but she couldn't stop thinking about Gina. What if Gina didn't want to see her? It was certainly a possibility. In all this time Scarlett had never written her a single letter.

The elevator suddenly bumped to a stop on the fifth floor and Scarlett got off. She made her way down the dim hallway to Karyn and Veronica's apartment. The instant she rang the bell, she knew something was terribly wrong by the look on Veronica's face.

"What's the matter?" asked Scarlett anxiously.

"There's been an accident."

Scarlett panicked. "Is it my mother?" Her heart was suddenly up in her throat.

"No," said Karyn, and she took a deep breath. "It's Gina."

Veronica put her arm around Scarlett. "Please come and sit down."

"No," she said, pushing away. "Tell me now."

"It was on the news," said Karyn. "It must have just happened."

"What!" cried Scarlett. "What just happened?"

"A plane crash in Morocco."

The world suddenly went out of focus, and Scarlett collapsed onto the sofa. Veronica patted her face with a damp cloth, but Scarlett barely responded.

"She was with the dress designer, Madame LeRouge, and two other people in a small plane. They were sightseeing over the Atlas Mountains," informed Karyn. "Tomorrow morning they're sending out a search party to look for . . ." The sentence got caught in her throat. "To look for survivors. Near a village called Tenerhir."

"Where?" asked Scarlett incredulously. She had heard the name before. It was where Maggie lived.

"Near a place they think the plane went down."

"Oh, God! Don't let it be true," pleaded Scarlett. "Make the Source take it back, Maggie."

Karyn and Veronica looked at each other in alarm, wondering what Scarlett was talking about and whose name she had just invoked as passionately as a prayer.

"I'm getting you a strong shot of whiskey," Karyn told Scarlett. "And you're going to drink it."

There was nothing Karyn or Veronica could do to change Scarlett's mind. After several shots of whiskey, she was determined to take the next plane to Rabat, the capital of Morocco. From there, she would get a connecting flight to Marrakech, then take a bus, a car, whatever, for the trip to Tenerhir. With great misgivings, Karyn and Veronica drove Scarlett to Orly and the unknown that waited only a few hours away.

"I'll be in touch," Scarlett told them and then she quickly disappeared into the terminal.

Chapter

135

Three hours after leaving Paris, Scarlett arrived in another world. As she waited for her flight to Marrakech, she heard a muezzin's call to prayer, the last one of the day. It sounded lonely, as if his were the only voice in the universe.

Scarlett could smell the rain in the wind as she boarded the DC-7 for Marrakech. With all those dark clouds gathering in the distance, it was probably going to be a bumpy ride, but she didn't care. Nothing mattered right now except the slender possibility of a miracle. And in the hope God might grant one, Scarlett prayed. So did everyone else aboard. The storm pitched the plane about furiously and lightning ripped open the blackness where heaven was supposed to be. If fear has a smell, it was on that plane to Marrakech.

Those who saw Scarlett's lips move no doubt thought she was praying for her own safety. A natural enough assumption; everyone else was praying for theirs. Only Allah could deliver them from this terrible storm. But Scarlett's prayers had a different goal. They were all for Gina and the three other people on that plane. Scarlett now knew who else had flown on that fateful flight. Other than the young Moroccan pilot and Madame LeRouge, there was a woman named Margot Duval. Scarlett remembered Margot's face from the picture in *Vogue* magazine. She was young and very pretty.

Sometime around midnight the DC-7 finally landed in Marrakech. The rain had stopped. In fact, the tarmac was dryer than a bone. God's fury had died over the desert. Scarlett claimed her luggage and managed to find a man who spoke some English. "How much to Tenerhir?"

The man protested, saying such a trip was impossible in the dark. The roads were terrible. A landslide or an accident was possible around every bend and turn in the road. The High Atlas were treacherous mountains. Didn't she know?

"One hundred dollars," said Scarlett.

When the man saw her wave the money in front of his face, any thoughts of danger quickly evaporared. "Okay. We go."

Scarlett told the man he would get a bonus if they got to Tenerhir by daybreak and waved another twenty-five at him.

"We go," he said again.

Hamid opened the door of his old Peugeot and Scarlett got in. As he drove the narrow streets out of the city, Scarlett felt Marrakech's energy. In the late sixties it had become a magnet for the soulless and dispossessed, Mecca with an earthly solution. Name your drug and Marrakech could produce it or invent it. In was the antidote for a whole generation's anomie.

The city was full of expatriates, rich and poor alike. John Paul Getty Jr. found his way here, as did Halston, designer extraordinaire. Halston, in fact, loved Marrakech so much he now lived here part of the time. "H," as his friends called him, found a whole new world of design possibilities in Marrakech. Having earned his reputation back in the States with Jackie's pillbox hat, "H" was now looking for something else, something he intuited in the fabrics and deep, rich dyes of Morocco. Here he could play with the visual aspects of fabric like no place on earth because the sun in Marrakech was the sun of a different light. It shimmered.

Apparently, what Halston had discovered was not lost on Madame LeRouge. Gina's trip to Morocco several years earlier convinced her of that. Its fabrics and dyes had yielded their secrets up to her as well, and now she wanted to beat all other designers to the punch. That was why she had come. Maybe she would introduce her new line in Marrakech, in this glorious, magnificent light.

As Hamid and Scarlett left the outskirts of the city, Scarlett looked out the window at the endless stream of stars above, at the immense, borderless universe.

Chapter
136

The old Peugeot tracked the road like a mountain goat and it was a good thing it did. The road was very narrow and dropped steeply off to the valley floor below. Thousands of feet it fell in some places and in others more than a mile. Scarlett took a deep breath and looked down. No darkness could hide that abyss. Hamid's tires rode the edge of nothingness. Eternity was inches away.

If two cars met, one would have to back up or down until it found a niche in the mountain and waited for the other to pass. Hamid assured his passenger everything would be fine, she didn't have to worry. He said he was a very good driver and besides, it was late; he would be surprised if they met a single car.

"I'm not worried," said Scarlett and then, exhaustion finally claiming her, she gave in to sleep. Dreams came quickly and she found herself back in Paris, in Gina's bed.

"I swear," said Gina, their bodies slowly pulling apart. "This time I swallowed part of your soul."

"Don't forget to give it back," pleaded Scarlett teasingly.

"I can't," said Gina, her eyes gazing intently at Scarlett's. "You're in me forever now."

Hamid glanced back at his passenger and wondered what had made her so sad. She'd mentioned something about a plane crash, but he hadn't heard anything. It couldn't have been a big one. A hole in the road suddenly bounced the car to one side and jarred his passenger awake. Startled, Scarlett looked up at the rearview mirror into Hamid's eyes.

"Not worry, miss. Bad road."

Scarlett twisted the simple gold band on her finger and wondered if she would ever feel Gina next to her again. Was love's grace enough for a miracle? The car hit another hole. Scarlett couldn't understand how the old Peugeot had any axles left. It sure didn't have any shocks.

"You okay, girlie?"

"Yes," said Scarlett, again closing her eyes. She was suddenly back in Paris standing on a street she didn't recognize. Gina was there too, dressed all in black, wearing large, dark shades. As Scarlett walked toward her, Gina quickly receded into the distance, always moving farther and farther away the closer Scarlett got. "Wait for me!" Scarlett yelled out to her.

"What?" asked Hamid.

"How much farther to Tenerhir?"

Chapter

137

When day broke, Scarlett saw a small village in a valley cradled by the Atlas Mountains. The emerging sun somehow felt reassuring.

"Tenerhir?" she asked the driver.

"Yes," nodded Hamid.

"It looks like a mirage."

A village oasis nurtured by the waters of the Oued Todra, Tenerhir was surrounded by emerald fields and towering palms. Crenellated earthen buildings rose proudly out of the ground, their notched towers the only reminder of fierce tribal wars that once swept across Morocco. These ancient battlements now housed a peaceful mountain village and a redhead called Maggie Donovan.

"I need to find someone."

"Yes?" replied Hamid.

"A redhead."

Hamid looked confused. He didn't understand the word.

"A woman with red hair," explained Scarlett. "You know, henna," she went on, touching her hair. "The color."

"Oh! *Ahmar*," said Hamid, finally understanding and pointing to a Berber girl with reddish hair.

"Yes. But American."

Hamid stopped and asked several early morning vendors where

such a person might be found. After several inquiries, he turned to Scarlett and pointed east. "By the river."

"Let's go," said Scarlett. "Quickly, please."

As Hamid drove the distance, a fever of swirling thoughts and vague terrors seized Scarlett. She felt nauseated, defeated by doubt and fear. Right now she needed Maggie, perhaps more than any human being on earth.

Hamid finally pulled up in front of a two-story adobe building with a big blue door. "Here," he said, turning to Scarlett. "Here is the redhead."

Scarlett handed him a hundred dollars for the fare, twenty-five for a bonus and another twenty-five. When Hamid asked why he was being paid so much, Scarlett told him it was for his courage, "for the guts."

Hamid obviously didn't understand. He just sat there smiling and said, "I wait."

Scarlett got out and knocked on the door. She took a deep breath. Three years was a long time. How would her old friend be? When the door opened, she saw the answer in Maggie's face. In it time had stood still; not a day had passed.

"I guess maybe I was expecting you," said Maggie and put her arm around Scarlett. "Please come in."

Hamid waved at them and then drove away, wondering what had brought two American women together in Tenerhir.

Chapter

138

The breakfast was Berber. Thick chunks of bread, goat cheese, honey and figs accompanied by strong black coffee. Scarlett did her best to get some food down.

"I can't eat any more."

Maggie didn't insist. "Do you want me to go with you?"

"No," said Scarlett, shaking her head. "Just tell me where."

Maggie directed her to the southern edge of the village where a Berber tribe had formed a search party the night before and gone up into the mountains. It was the same place a helicopter landed at morning's first light. Despite the odds, the French Embassy insisted a search be mounted for possible survivors, and the Moroccan government responded. People wanted answers. Madame LeRouge was an international celebrity, one of the world's top couturiers.

"Here," said Maggie. "Why don't you put this on? It'll be hot today."

Scarlett took off her clothes and put on the long cotton pullover. Then, as if in a trance, she walked out the front door into the streets of Tenehir. The High Atlas Mountains towered over the village like a giant fortress, its highest peaks still covered with winter snow. That such beauty might contain tragedy was unthinkable, utterly incomprehensible to Scarlett. Not today anyway. Today was too beautiful.

Scarlett walked the dusty streets in the direction Maggie had sent her, mouthing a silent prayer. Without realizing it, she stopped and leaned up against an ancient stone wall, tears flowing down her cheeks. A young Berber woman watched her for a while across the street and then walked over to where she stood. She touched Scarlett's cheeks with her shawl, wiping away the tears. The gesture brought Scarlett back to the present moment and the loving smile on a stranger's face.

"Thank you," said Scarlett. She touched the woman on the arm and then continued walking.

A helicopter suddenly rose straight up and flew toward the mountains, its reverberations pounding the valley floor as Scarlett neared the southern edge of the village. There several groups of Berbers watched the chopper disappear and then resumed loading their pack animals. With effort Scarlett found a man who spoke a few words of English. She explained that one of the people he would be looking for was very important to her, to please bring her back alive. The man told Scarlett he would, if that were God's will.

After all the search teams had left, Scarlett wandered the village until dusk. A wet, heavy wind kicked up, the kind that announces a storm. Scarlett touched the ring on her finger and felt her heart sink.

Chapter
139

"How about some tea?"

"Yes. Please, Maggie. I'd like that."

Scarlett sat at the table and watched Maggie quietly prepare the bitter green tea she would sweeten with honey. As before, she felt an enormous comfort in her presence, a great wordless compassion.

"Aren't you ever afraid, Maggie?"

"No," was Maggie's simple reply.

"What took it away? The fear, I mean?"

Maggie put two small glasses of hot Moroccan tea on the table and sat down. "Love," was her simple reply.

Tears suddenly came to Scarlett's eyes. There was that answer again. Love, it seemed, had helped everyone but her. "How?" asked Scarlett, nervously twisting the ring on her finger. "How could love do that?"

"By surrendering to it and letting it heal me."

"Then I'm in big trouble."

Maggie took a sip of her tea and waited for Scarlett to explain.

"Because I've mocked love," said Scarlett, anguish filling her voice. "And now it's mocking me." She buried her face in her hands and whispered, "What if she's dead?"

Maggie put her hand on Scarlett's, tracing her finger over the ring she wore. What she was about to say wouldn't be easy to hear. "Healing can go on even after death."

"How do you know?" challenged Scarlett.

Maggie sat silently, not reacting to the defiance in Scarlett's voice, understanding the crippling grief. "Because love is that powerful."

A wild desperation filled Scarlett. In her experience with death, and there had been a lot of it in her young life, nothing could reach across that abyss that separated life and death. Nothing.

"It was our honeymoon," said Maggie. "We were mountain climbing in Nepal when it happened."

Until now, Scarlett had known almost nothing of Maggie's past. She never talked about herself. She had only listened. Scarlett searched Maggie's face for some pain or sorrow, some remorse, some ghost or suffering that still owned her, and found none.

"Even after the rope was proven defective, I still blamed myself. I thought I should have tied a better knot. I watched my husband fall, Scarlett, fall into eternity." Maggie paused and briefly looked out at the mountains. "We never found his body."

Scarlett felt herself shiver. She couldn't imagine the horror of witnessing an accident like that and then enduring the impossible grief of such a loss.

"Is that why you hide out in deserts? To bury your pain?"

"No," Maggie replied with a soft smile on her face. "That's all gone. And so is the guilt."

"You've got to tell me how you did it," pleaded Scarlett.

"I didn't," Maggie answered her. "Love did."

Scarlett was now more anguished than ever. Nothing seemed to ease her despair. She wondered if that Greek tragedy was right when it warned, *There shall be no solace for those careless with the human heart.*

"This ring?"

"Yes," said Scarlett, wondering why Maggie had focused on it again.

"Its love is powerful. If you let it, it can transform your pain and even change you."

Scarlett was stunned. The ring's inscription was unknown to Maggie but she had just divined its meaning more clearly than Scarlett ever had.

"Real love isn't bound by a single lifetime, Scarlett. It connects us forever, like an eternal bridge. To have it is true grace."

Chapter
140

The threatened storm never came. What Scarlett thought was thunder was the distant sound of an allun, a Berber hand drum, beating its rhythms into the night. Perhaps God had listened. The weather had suddenly changed.

"It's the biggest moon I've ever seen," observed Scarlett, checking out its appearance over the High Atlas.

"Full moons are like that in Tenerhir," assured Maggie. "Bold. Insisting on notice."

They were sitting in a couple of chairs on top of Maggie's roof. Part of the old fort structure that once dominated Tenehir, flat rooftops were a favorite part of most people's homes. They were used for everything from drying clothes to entertaining, praying and watching the stars. Scarlett looked over at Maggie, who looked so young in the moonlight, so completely at peace.

"Have you ever seen the rabbit in the moon?"

"Every time it's full. Handsome, isn't he?" Maggie got up and walked over to the edge of the roof.

The rabbit was handsome tonight, and huge. Scarlett prayed Gina was seeing him too.

"How's our friend Twila?" asked Maggie after a long silence.

"Still sliding through the raindrops chasing lightning."

Maggie laughed. "The same."

Other Berber drums now joined the first one. The night didn't sound so lonely anymore.

"Who do you love, Maggie?"

"The Beloved," was her unhesitating reply.

"You mean God?"

Before Maggie could respond again, there was a sudden commotion in the street below and a loud knock at the door. "I'll see what's going on," she told Scarlett.

Scarlett took a deep breath and tried to relax but couldn't. The nauseating anxiety had returned and with it, thoughts that cut like glass.

"Scarlett. Can you come here?"

As she frantically made her way downstairs, Scarlett heard Maggie talking with a man in a language she didn't understand. She wondered if he belonged to the mountain Berbers who had formed the rescue party.

"They found the plane," said Maggie, turning around to Scarlett.

Scarlett's heart raced and she suddenly felt like she might pass out. The room spun and the floor came up at her. She put her hand on a chair to steady herself. The man speaking to Maggie had a soothing, familiar voice. When she looked up again, Scarlett recognized him and moved toward the door. He was the man she had asked to bring Gina back alive.

"There's one survivor," said Maggie, hesitating briefly. "And she's young. They're putting her on the helicopter to Marrakech right now." She put her hand on Scarlett's shoulder and stepped away from the door. "Go."

Scarlett slid past Maggie and the man and ran down the street as fast as she could, choking on the dust and her own tears, hardly able to breathe. Which young woman had come down off the mountain alive tonight, Margot Duval or Gina Jamison? Others in the village must have heard the news as well because a large crowd had already gathered when Scarlett finally reached the makeshift heliport.

"Please," pleaded Scarlett. "Please let me through."

When she caught a glimpse of a woman on a stretcher being lifted aboard the helicopter, Scarlett panicked. There was no way to see who it was in the dark. She fought her way through the crowd and even managed to get past several soldiers.

"Halt!" ordered a man in uniform. "You're not allowed any closer."

"I've got to," cried Scarlett. "Please. I've got to see."

All of a sudden Scarlett heard Maggie's voice behind her. She turned and saw her speaking to a soldier. He finally nodded, then ordered the man detaining Scarlett to step back and let her pass. When he did, Scarlett ran over to the chopper and climbed aboard. Inside were several people with their backs to her, busy treating the survivor.

"Gina?" said Scarlett. "Please. Is it you?"

"Yes," came the barely audible but instant reply.

The medical rescue team looked at each other, then at Scarlett, then back at their patient. She was unconscious again, having briefly broken through her coma to answer to her name. Scarlett was immediately tossed off the helicopter. The survivor had to be stabilized.

"It's Gina!" she screamed at Maggie. "They've got to let me back on."

Maggie did her best to comfort Scarlett and then spoke with another soldier, one with lots of ribbons and medals pinned to the front of his uniform. He finally nodded his head and looked back over at Scarlett.

"Go ahead, Scarlett. The general is going to let you ride back to Marrakech with Gina."

Scarlett climbed aboard the chopper again and looked back out the door at Maggie. "How did you do it?"

"Knowing the Moqqadem helps," Maggie replied. "The village chief. The Moroccan government likes to keep him happy." She waved good-bye and backed away from the helicopter. "They're ready," she yelled to Scarlett. "Embrace the journey."

When the whirling dust kicked up by the chopper blotted out Maggie and all the lights of Tenehir, Scarlett sat down. The chopper hovered briefly and then climbed straight up, flying away with those whom the Berbers had found, one living and three dead. Scarlett kept her eyes on Gina all the way to Marrakech.

Chapter

141

Gina remained unconscious. As she lay in the hospital hovering in that shadowy, twilight world where life and death come and go, Scarlett told Gina how sorry she was, how much she loved her, to please forgive her—that she would never betray love's gift again.

Scarlett held Gina's hand and rubbed her wrist. It was awful, all those needles and tubes, bruises and wounds, and whimpers of pain. The doctors had told Scarlett that the cuts on Gina's face and arms were relatively minor and would probably leave no scars. Her inability to regain consciousness, however, was of great concern as was a lacerated kidney. If the kidney shut down, she would have to have emergency surgery.

When Scarlett wasn't praying, she spoke to Gina in a language they had once invented. The made-up gestures had silent, tactile meaning. A caress from the fingertips down to the wrist and then back up again, followed by a slight squeeze of the other's hand came to express "I love you" as eloquently as words. Scarlett repeated the gestures a thousand times hoping for some response from the twilight journeyer.

"How is she?"

Startled, Scarlett turned to the stranger at the door and answered, "Still unconscious."

The woman hesitated a moment and then walked into the room. "I'm Catherine Duval."

Scarlett felt her heart contract when she heard the woman's last name and the pain in her voice. "I'm sorry about your sister," she said, standing up. "I'm Scarlett Turner, a friend of Gina's."

As the two women took each other's hand, the full weight and sadness of the Atlas Mountains suddenly descended into the room. Scarlett gestured to a chair and Catherine sat down. Their silence soon became as uncomfortable as their grief.

"Were Gina and your sister good friends?" asked Scarlett, needing to break the silence.

"They were lovers."

Scarlett felt as if all the oxygen had been sucked out of the room. There was a spasm, a hollow ache in her stomach, and she had to fight off a sudden dizziness.

"Are you all right?" asked Catherine.

"Yes," Scarlett finally said. "This is all so difficult."

"Yes," agreed Catherine, wiping away the tears. "It is. They were so happy together."

Catherine's disclosure devastated Scarlett. A part of her had always assumed Gina would wait, but love's grace, it seemed, had found another heart. The two women fell silent again for what seemed like hours.

"Take good care of Gina," Catherine finally said, getting up to leave. "My sister really loved her."

"I'm sure she did," replied Scarlett, managing a soft but very difficult smile. "And I will."

When Catherine left, Scarlett removed the ring from her left hand and put it in her pocket. Wearing it wouldn't be appropriate right now, and there was a possibility it might not ever be again. She looked over at Gina and told herself that had to be okay. All her prayers must be for this woman's life, nothing more.

On the third day of Scarlett's vigil, Gina finally opened her eyes.

"Scar . . . Scarlett?" she stammered, disbelieving. "What are you doing here?"

"Trying to help."

Bewilderment filled Gina's face as she looked around. "Is this a hospital?"

"Yes."

Tears began to trickle down Gina's cheeks. "It was awful."

Scarlett silently agreed. Three lives had been swept into the void.

"It was awful," Gina repeated again. "Why me?" she asked, expressing the guilt and confusion of all survivors. "What about Madame LeRouge and the pilot?"

When Scarlett shook her head, Gina turned and stared out the window at the mountains. She didn't have to ask about Margot. She already knew. She reached for Scarlett's hand and wept.

"She died in my arms," said Gina, and then her anguished voice suddenly became a whisper. "I heard my name in her last breath."

Chapter

142

A month later Gina was released from the Royal Hospital in Marrakech. She was told she would have to wear the back corset for a couple of months. It took fractured ribs a long time to heal. The cuts on her face were much less noticeable now so there probably wouldn't be any scars. Scarlett was grateful for that; Gina wouldn't have to remember every time she looked in the mirror. She would remember enough as it was.

As soon as they boarded the plane for Paris, Scarlett ordered a Coke for herself and a tonic water to go with the small bottle of vodka in her purse. Gina was understandably nervous about flying and the drink would help. Scarlett held her hand on take-off and talked about Los Angeles, hoping it might distract her.

Gina smiled. "Remember, Scarlett. I was born there."

Scarlett laughed. She always thought of Gina as more European than American. Having traveled and lived everywhere as an Army brat, she had a distinct cosmopolitan flair and even a different accent, sort of mid-Atlantic, neither here nor there. A woman of the world, Gina now lived in it without Margot, or even her own family. All ties had been severed the year before when they found out she was gay. If Gina's family had learned about the crash, they made no effort to get in touch with her.

"How do you feel?" asked Scarlett as the plane leveled off.

"Nervous about going back to Paris."

Scarlett understood. The city would be a lot lonelier now and her professional challenges even more enormous. Madame LeRouge's son would see to that. He was now in charge of his mother's fashion dynasty.

Somewhere over Spain, Gina asked Scarlett when she was returning to the States. Scarlett was completely caught off guard by the question. She hadn't thought about her own future since the accident. Even when she telephoned Karyn from Marrakech and was told about the excitement and the scandal her book was causing back in the States, Scarlett had felt oddly apart from it all, as if she were being told about someone else.

"You're becoming famous, Scarlett. You're even in the papers over here," Karyn told her on the phone.

The Herald Tribune, a Paris-based, English-language newspaper, reprinted a review from *The Village Crier* praising Scarlett's book and calling it one of the most daring of the decade. It predicted a bestseller and sudden fame for its talented writer. In the context of the past few months, and especially this last one, all that now seemed somehow flat, empty. Even Scarlett's coveted trilogy of power, fame and money was no longer important in the way it had once been.

In fact, she didn't feel the same about a lot of things anymore. Perhaps she had finally begun the journey into change. The old fears and hurts were no longer there. As Scarlett speculated about their disappearance, she remembered what Maggie had once said: "If one really wants to, Scarlett, they can reach across the universe and change in an instant. Surrender travels at the speed of light."

"Scarlett?" said Gina tentatively. "Did you hear me? When are you going back to the States?"

"Next year."

Gina was surprised and actually, so was Scarlett. Staying in Paris beyond the summer had never occurred to her until this very moment. "Maybe I'll take a few classes at the Sorbonne," she told Gina. "I don't have to graduate right away." Then she paused, suddenly unsure if Gina would want her around while she grieved for Margot. "I would like to stay and help if I can. If you want me to."

"Yes," said Gina. "I would."

"Good," smiled Scarlett. "You know, I have some good friends living in Paris now. I think you'll enjoy meeting them."

Chapter
143

Maggie was right about love. There are those for whom it seasons in the soul and becomes stronger, inviolate, arching across time, eternal. She was right about grace, too, and for some, as Scarlett had intuited one day in Paris and inscribed inside a simple, gold ring, it is forever. A match of souls as old as the Atlas Mountains.